Last Song
Before Home

Dr Indira Das was born in Kolkata, where she was raised amidst literature, classical music and dance. A practising gynaecologist based in Delhi, she earned her medical degree from Calcutta Medical College and completed post-graduate training at PGIMER, Chandigarh. Despite a demanding medical career, her passion for writing and music flourished.

Indira has published several acclaimed poetry collections, short story anthologies and novels in both Bengali and English. Her English debut, *The Last Dance and Other Stories*, offers poignant glimpses into urban Indian life. Her works have appeared in national journals and international anthologies, reflecting a distinctive voice that explores human complexity with empathy and grace.

A trained singer in Rabindrasangeet and Nazrulgeeti, she has also composed music for her own verses.

Dr Bina Biswas is an academician, translator, poet, critic and editor. She previously taught at a college affiliated to Jawaharlal Nehru Technological University, Hyderabad. An alumna of the University of Delhi, she holds a PhD in English Literature from Andhra University and is widely recognized as a Tagore scholar.

Dr Biswas has authored nine books and led four major translation projects. Her bilingual English translation of *Meghnaadbadh Kabya* was launched by former President Pranab Mukherjee, and her study 'Tagore's Heroines: Portraits of Gender Orientation' has received critical acclaim. Her translation of Masum Reza's *Araj Charitamrita* was published in the UK by Methuen Drama, an imprint of Bloomsbury Publishing Plc.

She currently serves as the Chief Executive Officer of Rubric Publishing, New Delhi.

Last Song
Before Home

Indira Das

Translated by

Bina Biswas

RUPA

Published by
Rupa Publications India Pvt. Ltd 2025
161-B/4, Gulmohar House,
Yusuf Sarai Community Centre,
New Delhi 110049

Sales centres:
Bengaluru Chennai
Hyderabad Kolkata Mumbai

Originally written and published in Bengali in 2022

P-ISBN: 978-93-7003-588-1
E-ISBN: 978-93-7003-688-8

First impression 2025

10 9 8 7 6 5 4 3 2 1

Printed in India

To those who have experienced darkness and struggle,
yet strived to live, to rise and to inspire hundreds
through their unwavering effort—
You are proof that light will always prevail.

Author's Note

My mother was, and will forever remain, a guiding force in my life—a remarkable woman whose influence shaped the very core of who I am. She nurtured my sibling and me with a rare and delicate balance of affection, discipline, and unyielding principles. Her quiet dignity, innate sense of fairness, and unwavering moral compass defined not just her role as a parent but also her larger identity as a teacher and mentor.

In the classroom, she commanded respect without ever raising her voice. As a principal, she led with wisdom, grace, and deep compassion, becoming both guide and guardian to generations of students. The values she instilled left an indelible mark on countless young minds, and even years after her retirement, heartfelt letters and nostalgic anecdotes from former students would reach us—each one painting a portrait of an educator who had been far more than just a teacher.

Yet there was another side to her—quieter, almost hidden—that few outside the family knew. A passionate botanist and an ardent lover of nature, she found joy in the smallest wonders: a dew-soaked leaf, the hush of the morning breeze, or the delicate blooming of a forgotten flower by the garden wall. She was also a gifted storyteller, her words spinning worlds that lingered long after the story ended. These facets of her personality deepened further in her later years, especially after the devastating loss of her life partner, my beloved father—a loss she bore with the same stoic grace that had defined her life.

In grappling with the void left by his absence, she turned

inward, reflecting on her life, her journey, and the world she had watched transform over the decades. Looking back, I now realize that her quiet introspection was her way of navigating the depths of her grief—a courageous attempt to find solace and meaning amidst an irreparable loss.

When she came to live with me, our home became enriched by her presence and her stories. Her vivid recollections of childhood, youth, and the myriad experiences that had shaped her life would often enthral my children, who gathered around her with wide-eyed curiosity. What struck me most was her extraordinary ability to recall not only events but also the emotions and life lessons woven into them.

Sensing the importance of preserving these memories, I encouraged her to put them down in writing—a diary she had always kept over the years. As she began filling its pages once again, I discovered a treasure trove of insights: stories of struggle and triumph, evocative descriptions of a bygone era, and her deeply personal reflections on life and loss.

Much of her writing, I noticed, was addressed to her elder sister—Di-bhai—the sibling with whom she had shared an unbreakable bond. Though her sister had long passed away, my mother found comfort in these one-sided conversations, as though speaking through the pages kept their connection alive, transcending time and absence.

It was during this time that the first signs of dementia began to emerge. At first, they were subtle—a misplaced memory, a fleeting confusion, an occasional lapse in conversation. But over time, these moments grew more frequent, and her mind began drifting between the clarity of the present and the vivid landscapes of her past. There were occasions when she would ask me to connect her to her sister by phone, only to pause moments later, realizing—with a small, embarrassed smile—that such a call was no longer possible. Yet, despite these lapses, her journal remained her sanctuary—a private space where she could escape, relive cherished memories, and sustain her bond with her beloved Di-bhai.

As her daily routines slipped quietly into the background, her recollections of earlier decades grew sharper, more vivid, and often more poignant. Together, we began the delicate task of preserving these reflections. In her final months, as her physical strength waned, I took up the mantle of documenting her memories—a responsibility that felt as much a privilege as it did a duty. These writings became more than just a personal chronicle; they grew into a living legacy—a window into the heart and mind of a woman whose life had spanned nearly a century of history, upheaval, and quiet resilience.

This book is the culmination of that journey. It stands as a tribute to an extraordinary woman whose life was defined by courage, grace, and unwavering love. But it is also something more: a chronicle of socio-political, cultural, and economic transformations that shaped not only her life but the life of our nation across a hundred years. It captures the spirit of a bygone era, the challenges of a lifetime, and the enduring strength of a soul who touched countless lives, both within and beyond our family.

Through these pages, I hope to preserve and share her story. I hope to immortalize a woman of rare tenacity and compassion whose journey left indelible footprints on my heart. In doing so, I also hope these memories will offer solace, inspiration, and reflection to others—ensuring that her luminous presence continues to shine for generations to come.

Translator's Note

Translating this book has been a profoundly moving and enriching journey—one that offered unexpected insights and gently compelled me to revisit themes I had long taken for granted. At its core, the narrative unfolds as a poignant dialogue between the protagonist and her elder sister, Di-Bhai. Their relationship transcends time, and Di-Bhai's presence becomes more than familial; she emerges as a constant, anchoring the protagonist in memory, love, and emotional continuity.

This story resonated with me on a deeply personal level. My own mother belonged to the generation that bore witness to the wrenching displacement during the Partition of India in 1947. The trauma of uprooting, the rupture from ancestral soil, and the painstaking process of rebuilding a life amidst the debris of loss—these were not just historical abstractions for me. Many of the memories woven into this novel echo the stories I heard growing up, passed down in fragments and silences. With each line I translated, I felt as if I were paying homage to the unspoken truths of a generation that endured so much, yet often remained unheard.

At the heart of this narrative lies the protagonist's struggle against the creeping fog of memory loss. Her thoughts, suspended between clarity and confusion, reality and hallucination, form a mosaic of recollection and yearning. Her urgency to articulate, to preserve, and to connect is both tender and urgent. In this delicate act of remembering, her elder daughter Tilottoma—Titai—becomes a quiet observer and recorder, capturing her mother's fading recollections in an attempt to preserve her essence before it slips away.

The story is, above all, a celebration of resilience—a portrait of a woman who, despite the relentless trials of personal, political, and emotional upheavals, remains steadfast in her pursuit of selfhood. It is a testimony to the strength of the human spirit, the quiet endurance of grief, and the redemptive force of memory.

This book is not simply a narrative—it is a mosaic of survival, and the search for belonging. As John Berger once wrote, 'Never again will a single story be told as though it is the only one.' The protagonist's journey is part of a greater collective—a shared history of migration, exile, and emotional displacement. Her voice rises in a chorus of the grieving—each thread woven with shared loss and a fierce resolve to cling to identity.

She is a figure many will recognize: a woman who, though exiled by circumstance, carries the remnants of home in every gesture and memory. Her story becomes a vessel for inherited struggle, for resilience passed from one generation to the next. As Milan Kundera so memorably stated, 'The struggle of man against power is the struggle of memory against forgetting.' This translation, then, is not merely an act of language, but of remembrance.

In walking through these layered memories, I came to appreciate the power of remembering—not only for those who lived through the anguish but for those who inherit its aftershocks. This translation is a tribute: to the displaced, to the survivors, to the storytellers. May it honour the unwavering strength of those who endure in silence, and the stories that echo across borders, languages and time—reminding us of who we are and what we carry within.

Prologue

The doctors name it vascular dementia. Memory thinning like old silk, they say, after two brain-strokes. Their remedies feel like spells spoken in a tongue I no longer know, yet I abide by their orders because that makes my dear daughter happy.

I realize it is daytime by the light streaming in. Though I cannot open the window, I still long to put the water on boil for tea. I must prepare breakfast and cook lunch before hurrying off to school. Are my classroom, my laboratory and my students still waiting for me? How beautiful those days were, filled with so much activity, respect and love. Were those bygone days truly mine? If so, why did they not remain that way?

Sometimes mornings wrap me in soft silences. I sit beside the window, sketching your face upon the sky, Di-bhai. You were the sister among so many of us siblings, who was dearest, closest to me. As throughout the day, off and on, memories visit me—pictures of different times of life tumble free, vivid as a painted dream.

If you can be here with me, I wonder—can we still play our favourite games of childhood? Let us try, if only in thought. And if not, let us weave our old stories again—right from the younger days through youth and maturity.

Like moving pictures, images appear in front of my eyes—our growing up in a land with paddy fields and rivers, my struggles and my career, the socio-political turmoil of the world around me, the little family in the small Moulali house, the birth of my two daughters, the years of their blossoming and our professional lives. I remember their father passing away suddenly. Then came the chapter of my life in the affectionate care of my elder child, my loving girl, companionship of my grandchildren. Time to time I can even recall my younger one's visits with her husband and their adorable little daughter.

The world outside the window remains a mystery to me now. Is the sun shining, or have the clouds returned? Is it summer or monsoon? Or perhaps autumn has already arrived? In the winters, not much sunlight entered our rented flat in Moulali; I remember Titai's father buying an all-day tram ticket and setting off, taking his daughter's hand in his so she could enjoy basking in the winter sun. I can almost visualize them both.

He carries an old penknife and a bit of newspaper with him. I have packed some guavas, apples and oranges for them. I see my daughter waving goodbye, skipping joyfully on her little feet as she walks away with her father. I can envision all this now when I close my eyes. However, I cannot recall how long it has been.

Rain on the other side blurs the trees in veils,
Here, a hundred rubies sparkle, amidst clouds' fiery trails.
A poetry from childhood days still stirs our souls,
Pitter-patter raindrops, the river overflows.*

I cannot quite recall whether I first heard this from my mother or someone else. Nonetheless, I had made it a ritual to recite the verse to my daughters whenever there was a heavy shower. In this eternal leisure that I lie in, the lines still come back to me with so much of joy.

---

*Poem from *Shishu* by Rabindranath Tagore

One

Winter was on its way, though it had yet to gain its full potential. Titai, ever the vigilant one, however, was not ready to wait. With brisk efficiency, she pulled out a light shawl and a pair of socks, her voice animated as she painted a vivid picture of the days ahead.

'This season in Delhi,' she said to Sukhalata, my caretaker, 'is the most deceptive of all. Don't try to brave it like a soldier—it might feel mild now, but the chorus of coughs and sneezes is just around the corner. How many times must I remind you that the shawl must be wrapped around Ma's neck both in the morning and the evening.'

She handed over the socks with a firm look. 'Make sure she wears these. Her feet were freezing yesterday—I felt it myself when I touched them in *pronam* just before leaving for the clinic. It's already getting dark after six. As soon as she finishes her evening tea, slip them on, will you?'

Di-bhai, you know Titai has always been like this—much like her father. He too had a similar disposition, didn't he? She is a doctor now, so she tends to worry more. Observing her stirs memories of her dad, a man I haven't seen in ages. I remember knitting those half-sleeved sweaters, then carefully placing them on the middle shelf of his wardrobe. Will he take them out and wear them? Perhaps he won't wear them at all. Who knows?

Though Titai's fussing nearly sends me into a fit of laughter, I hold it back. She is my eldest daughter, yet over the years, our roles seem to have quietly reversed. In a strange turn of fate, it is I who now feel like her youngest child.

Truth be told, right around the time her daughter was nearing the end of her college curriculum, Titai's son ventured off to pursue engineering in Rajasthan. Titai needed something to occupy her time, so she transformed me into her child. However, I cannot deny quite enjoying this arrangement.

However Di-bhai, today I am in a mood to reminisce about our childhood with you. As you remember, after Baba passed away, you and Ma returned to her paternal home in Barisal, along with our other siblings. It was Kaka and Kaki who wanted me to stay back with them in Calcutta (now Kolkata) as they were childless. Kaka had impeccable taste. He would bring me frocks trimmed with delicate white lace and the most delicious chocolates from Hogg Market. Back in Barisal, you enjoyed ripe mangoes and jackfruits, but I know you could not help feeling a twinge of envy when you heard about my little treasures—could you?

Though I never felt deprived of affection, Di-bhai, but I rarely had occasions to be close to our biological mother. The profound void of never being able to utter the word 'Ma' has lingered throughout my life.

Baba died when we were young. Now, it is at this age that I realize what a shoreless sea it must have been for our recently widowed mother to be in, with six young daughters and a son. While crossing the Padma River at the Goalunda Ghat, I suppose our mother didn't turn back more than once to look at little me waving from Kaki's arms. Wasn't it so, Di-bhai?

Our maternal grandfather—Dadu—often recounted the inception of the Eastern Bengal Railway back in 1871. Trains would chug along the tracks, carrying passengers from Calcutta to Goalunda Ghat. From there, travellers would embark on a journey across the Padma River aboard a steamer to reach

Narayanganj. Even the letters dispatched from Calcutta arrived at the Ghat by the night mail, patiently awaiting the break of dawn. At the confluence of the Padma and Brahmaputra rivers, mighty steamers ferried passengers not only to Narayanganj or Chandpur but also to far-off places like Madaripur, Barisal, Sylhet and Cachar, now in Assam. Sailing on the Brahmaputra, people could even reach Dibrugarh. Dadu shared tales of our relatives working in Assam who occasionally embarked on such river journeys.

Kaki and I once travelled to Barisal for Mama's wedding. I must have been about five then, and Dadu was still alive. When we arrived at Dadu's mansion, I stood in silent awe of the grand house—its vastness overwhelming, especially as I climbed the sweeping central staircase. Enchanted by the scale and stillness, I wandered down the long veranda, where I came upon a strikingly fair woman. She looked as though she had just bathed; her damp hair was wrapped in a *gamchha*, but glistening water droplets were dripping from the curls framing her pretty forehead. With a gentle smile, she held out a bunch of keys and said, 'Go, child. Take these to your Kaki downstairs.'

I longed to inhale more of the delicate fragrance that lingered around her. I wished that a few droplets from her damp hair might fall upon me like gentle rain. But a quiet shyness held me back. Like a dutiful child, I simply took the keys and descended the grand staircase to look for Kaki.

'A lady in a white sari asked me to give this to you, Kaki,' I said, holding out the keys.

My innocent words made her laugh, as she unlocked the great almirah in the spacious room we had been given. 'What are you saying, child? That is your mother!' she corrected me with a smile. Then, as she returned to her work, I darted off to the garden, drawn by a flash of turquoise in the trees—a Neelkanth had landed among the branches, and I stood watching it, wide-eyed and silent.

I had almost forgotten who my mother was—what she looked like, how she spoke, what made her smile. At that age, I lacked even a basic understanding of what it meant to have a mother. A child only begins to recognize his or her mother when given the chance to be near her, to share her warmth, listen to her voice, be in her presence. It was only much later that I came to realize that the words I had spoken so innocently had brought tears to Ma's eyes. Alas, at the time, I could not fully comprehend the depth of her pain.

It so happened, that noon, when Dadu was having lunch, Ma approached him, tears streaming down her cheeks. 'I did not bring this little girl with me when I returned to Barisal. Now, she doesn't recognize me! I won't let her go back to Calcutta this time, Baba.'

Dadu finished his meal in silence, sipped his milk from the bowl, and gently wiped his moustache. His handsome face looked a little grave, and without a word, he rose and walked away. Kaki's face held a trace of worry, her anxious expression lingering before slowly easing back into calm.

As for me—with all the understanding a five-year-old could muster—I could only watch, puzzled, as I looked from my mother to my 'motherly' Kaki. I did not fully grasp what had just passed between them. But in the end, it was Dadu who made the decision: I would return to Calcutta from Barisal, in Kaki's care.

While growing up under the affectionate care of my paternal uncle and aunt, away from my other siblings, Kaki—slender yet resilient—impressed me with her strength of character and discipline. The lessons and values Kaka instilled in me were priceless too. I received an abundance of love from them but never made any undue demands.

After all these years, do I still yearn to see Ma's face again? Di-bhai, these days, the faint outlines of her face in my memory have slowly been replaced—by Titai's. Who could have imagined that my firstborn, the very first fruit of my body, would one day become a mother to me, while I slip into the role of her child?

And yet, as I reflect, I remind myself—my mother is here. She is the one now watching over me, seeing to my meals, clothes, and medicines, sometimes gently scolding, sometimes patiently explaining, always with affection. Day after day, she tends to me without a trace of complaint—tirelessly, lovingly, as if it were the most natural thing in the world.

Dadu—my maternal grandfather—belonged to a large and well-known household, widely referred to as Pal Bari. In those years, he, Dinesh Pal, lived in Manikganj, in East Bengal. Having lost his father at a young age, the burden of caring for three younger brothers fell squarely on his shoulders. Determined and enterprising, he secured employment and eventually found his way to the Cooch Behar estate.

Work led him from place to place, and it was during one such journey that he arrived in Barisal—a land brimming with rivers, lakes, and ponds. The groves here were dense with fruit-laden trees; coconut palms shed their bounty freely into the courtyards. And in the swelling rivers, the silvery hilsa darted in abundance. So plentiful were they that the villagers could hardly consume them all. I had heard stories of how people's hands carried the scent of hilsa long after their meals—whether the fish steamed with mustard paste, the fish's head cooked with lentils or pieces served as a tangy curry. Hilsa was a way of life in Barisal, but beyond this fish, the people also needed essentials—rice, lentils, vegetables—often brought in from elsewhere.

Across the Padma, in western Bengal, the people of Calcutta

regarded hilsa from these waters as a delicacy, craving it with deep longing. Dadu, ever astute, saw a rare opportunity. He knew that hilsa, once caught in the net, could not be left to last long. And so, by the river's edge, he established an ice factory to preserve the daily catch. In time, the demand soared, and two more factories followed.

Thus, it was not on lotus petals or golden chariots, but on blocks of ice and crates of hilsa, that Lakshmi—the goddess of wealth—entered the Pal household with quiet grandeur.

Dadu decided to stay on in Barisal. He brought over his younger brothers and mother there too. The goddess of wealth had already graced him, but his industrious hands continued to draw in more and more prosperity. As his earnings steadily grew, Dadu began purchasing land in various places around Barisal.

By then, the Burmese pirates had lost their sting and relocated from Rangoon to Kalatoli, south of the Ganges-Brahmaputra delta. Dadu, ever resourceful, negotiated with them, enlisting their assistance to cultivate the lands he had acquired.

In Dadu's expansive two-storeyed house, his mother, a petite woman of quiet strength, was revered by all. The home had grown to accommodate his three brothers, their wives, and their children. As the family expanded, so did the house: new wings were added, and each brother was given a section of his own. One joined Dadu in business; the other two pursued independent careers.

I have often heard of a great brass bell that hung in the central courtyard. The task of ringing it at mealtimes fell to Umesh—an ex-dacoit and a Mog, they said. Mogs were once feared pirates of the Arakanese coast who raided Bengal's riverine settlements. The era of the 'Mog' bandits had come to an end. Umesh, one from the same community, had abandoned his past. Under Dadu's firm but compassionate influence, drawn into a world ruled by order and affection, Umesh transformed into Dadu's most trusted aide—a man-Friday in every sense.

I had heard tales—how during mealtimes, the younger ones, after rinsing their hands, would sit on *piri,* large wooden planks on the long, stretched veranda, and be served food on brass plates that shone like gold. The rice, white as jasmine blooms, and *shona moong,* golden yellow split lentils were served followed by other delicacies. Once the children had been fed by their *dhai-mas*, the men of the household arrived for luncheon, flaunting their pleated dhotis.

Boro Dida, Dinesh Pal's mother, our great grandmother, never missed a thing. Seated on the veranda as she chewed on *chhecha paan* in her toothless mouth—she would call out instructions to her daughters-in-law, saying: 'Give the middle son the fish head, Boro Bou—he likes it a lot! And why don't you give Chhoto some more jackfruit curry? You are the daughter of a noble man. Serve your brothers-in-law and your husband with elaborate care and devotion.'

By then, the eldest daughter-in-law had assumed charge of the household and was familiar with its nuances. Chhoto, the brother-in-law in question, was years younger than her. 'Of course. Please relax and see for yourself, Ma. Do you really think I would ever neglect your children? Look, I've got a bowl of fried hilsa oil for Chhorda, along with a green chilli—just the way he likes it, I know he'll devour a plate of rice with his favourite fiery combo. Sure, he was born of your womb, but he is almost like my child too,' she said, grinning slyly at her youngest sister-in-law.

With her motherly instincts, she knew that the young woman's stomach must be growling with hunger. It was only natural—she was carrying her second child. The noon hour had already passed, and the baby in her womb was likely kicking up a fuss. Soon, a new member would be welcomed into the household.

The family tree had begun to branch out, as more children were born into the household. Beyond tending to their health, well-being, and upbringing, Dadu remained deeply attentive to their education. Two college students lived in the outhouse of the mansion. The Pals provided for all their needs—meals, college fees, and other essentials. In return, the young scholars regularly tutored the children of the family.

Over time, little girls of the family blossomed into young women. There were occasions when two brides were married at once—both to grooms of high social standing—at a single grand venue. Amidst the celebratory clamour, at a corner where delicacies were being prepared, one could hear the booming voice of the head cook, Ramesh, issuing orders with practised authority:

'Oi, while you're cutting the fish, make sure each slice is bigger than Pal-babu's mighty palm! And that spice paste—grind it till it's smoother than butter! You there—the Brahmin's son—don't hold back now, empty that whole pot of sugar into the syrup for soaking the piping hot *rosogollas*! These people are used to fine food, my brother.'

And that was how my father came to marry my mother, Birajbala—the youngest daughter of Dinesh Pal. It was a twin wedding, where two sisters were wedded to two grooms beneath the same sprawling canopy. A multitude of relatives and in-laws had gathered to make it a grand and memorable affair—so Dadu would fondly recall.

Boro Mashi—my mother's elder sister—was married to Meshomoshai, a doctor posted in Assam at the time. Shortly after their wedding, the couple moved there and made it their home. Our mother, by contrast, was married to Dr Angshu Mohan Bose, a physician at the Calcutta School of Tropical Medicine.

Our Dadu was blessed with three sons. The eldest, Boro Mama, was married to the sister of Sudhir Bose, the renowned lawyer from Dhaka. His wife, Boro Mami, endured the pains of childbirth to bring two sons and a daughter into the world, but she was not inclined to live under her mother-in-law's authority in her husband's home. She chose instead to remain in her parental house, and Boro Mama had no objection—he was free to visit her whenever he pleased.

On the rare occasions when Boro Mami came to visit her in-laws, the household would stir with excitement. Vast nets would be cast into the pond to catch the finest fish, and the air would hum with preparations for a grand feast.

Di-bhai, do you remember Debu Da—Debabrata Pal—one of Boro Mama's sons? He was a brilliant footballer! Later, he moved to Calcutta for his studies, became an engineer, and eventually settled in Switzerland after marrying a Swiss woman. He never returned to this land.

And what about our other maternal cousin, Shubho-da? We saw him now and then, did we not? We also had a cousin sister, though by the time we were grown-up, she was already married.

Only Dadu's youngest son, Chhoto Mama, inherited his business acumen. As for Dadu's middle son, Shona Mama, his love for East Bengal remained unwavering. Unlike the others, he chose to stay in Barisal forever.

Di-bhai, remember that after marrying off his children, Dadu didn't confine himself to Barisal. He bought two houses in Calcutta—one in Park Street and another in Park Circus. He took up residence at the Park Circus house, accompanied by his Mejo Bhai, while the third and fourth brothers were allotted the Park Street house as their inheritance. I recall you mentioning that the proceeds from the ice-factory were regularly shared among all the brothers. The younger ones respected the elders unconditionally and the elders, in turn, showered them with love and affection.

It was a time marked by trust and faith, Di-bhai—a golden era. The family's eldest son displayed remarkable foresight and an unparalleled sense of responsibility. It is truly astonishing how far ahead Dadu planned everything. That's precisely how they secured their place and settled safely in the two Calcutta houses after the Partition of India.

Do you remember the colossal three-storeyed Park Circus house, where the eleven of us spent our childhood days, Di-bhai? We six siblings were friendly with our cousins—Chhoto Mama's five daughters—and formed a merry gang! Chhoto Mama also had two sons, and then there was Dada, our only brother. All of us grew up together in that enormous house! I, of course, lived with Kaka and Kaki but frequently visited Park Circus. However, lest the constant commotion in the huge household disrupted my studies, Kaka and Kaki never permitted me to stay there for extended periods.

Dadu indeed lived a long and fulfilling life. He passed away at the venerable age of ninety-six, the very year I was preparing for my BSc examinations. On the thirteenth day of mourning, the traditional rituals were performed to release his soul. Invitations were sent far and wide to relatives for the *shraddho*—the funeral ceremony—and the arrangements were nothing short of grand. Our patriarch was given a regal farewell, a tribute worthy of his life and legacy.

After Dadu's passing, it was Choto Mama who took up the mantle of overseeing the family's business and household affairs. As he stepped into this role, his own family—comprising five daughters and two sons—took possession of the Park Circus house, marking the beginning of a new chapter in the family's journey.

Di-bhai, do you remember how frail you had become after

repeated bouts of malaria in Barisal? That was precisely why Dadu decided to bring you back with him to Calcutta—to help you recover. During that time, you and I spent a few wonderful years together at Kaka and Kaki's house. Otherwise, we mostly met in Barisal.

In our family, younger siblings were generally addressed by name, while elder sisters were known as Bordi or Mejdi. But you and I, separated by just two years, shared something different—something closer. We could never keep secrets from each other for long, and that's why I called you 'Di-bhai'—with all the affection I could hold. You, my Shejo Didi, were unlike anyone else. Our bond was something I did not share with our other siblings. Without doubt, you were my favourite—and I knew the feeling was reciprocated.

We attended the municipal school together for about a year. Kaki showered us with love but also scolded us just as fiercely when we were mischievous. But back then, a telling-off from the elders did little to dampen our spirits. Since Ma had entrusted me to her brother-in-law and his wife, they took on the full responsibility of raising me—with authority as well as affection.

Those were joyful days! I remember how you grew fond of the toys and clothes Kaka brought for me—so he simply began buying everything in twos. I was always the one with the heartier appetite. I still recall how, at school, I would polish off my lunch and then proceed to finish yours as well. And those moments—do you remember—when I would lose a game, pull at your fishtail plaits in frustration, and let out a wild scream?

Do you recollect those days, Di-bhai? Or have they slipped quietly into that grey space between remembering and forgetting?

Why did you leave without so much as a whisper of goodbye?

Two

I often think that these numerous pages I keep writing will eventually be sent to you as letters. The only challenge is that I do not have anyone around me right now who can provide your correct address. Perhaps one day I'll remember it and then you'll receive a bundle of letters, Di-bhai.

You and I were born just two years apart, and because of the love between us, Dadu named us Atasi and Aparajita—both names of flowers. I was affectionately called 'Apu'. Bordi and Mejdi were named after flowers too—Bakul and Togor. Our younger sisters were named Malati and Dolonchampa. Do you think Dadu loved flowers a lot, Di-bhai? Before Bordi was born, we had an elder brother who lived for only a month. Though Dadu didn't get a chance to name him, he, however, did name our only surviving brother Parijat, after the celestial flower.

It seemed that our mother consistently favoured her only son throughout life. Perhaps, after giving birth to Bordi and then Dada, she had hoped for more sons—but instead, five daughters followed, including me. From the very beginning, she made it abundantly clear that Dada was the apple of her eye, beyond any reprimand. Consequently, despite his many gifts, Dada did not learn to set goals for himself or shoulder any responsibility.

Be that as it may, Di-bhai, today I feel like sharing old memories of the other household. The grandeur of our Mamabari, the illustrious Pal family have been reflected upon. Now, I feel inclined to talk about our father and our paternal uncles—the Boses. Our paternal grandfather, Lalit Mohan Bose, had two brothers, and their hometown was Bikrampur—a place surrounded by the Padma on the west, the Dhaleshwari on the northeast and the Meghna on the south. At that time, Bikrampur was an upcoming area, full of opportunities.

Thakurda had married a woman from Shyamsiddhi village in Bikrampur's Srinagar sub-division. I do not remember our paternal grandmother at all as I did not get to see her much. Di-bhai, did you? I've heard she passed away a few years after our father got married.

Thakurda had moved to Jorhat as a young man to work as a postmaster, and had made a name for himself there. His elder brother, Nabin Mohan Bose, worked as an ordinary salaried employee and his only son, Jatin Mohan Bose, was an outstanding student. Jatin Mohan Bose eventually became a high court judge, earning respect and fame. Our judge-uncle married the daughter of a famous Indian Civil Service officer. I have heard that his bias for agreeing too often with his wife and in-laws in most contentious matters strained his relationship with his own parents. As for Thakurda's younger brother, he had passed away in his teens—a rather unfortunate incident.

Not only our uncle—Jatin Bose—fathered seven sons, he was also blessed with two lovely daughters. Truly, the boundless grace of Shashthi, the goddess of fertility and protector of children, was showered upon him—what say, Di-bhai?

Sadly, two of his sons passed away in childhood. In those days, there were few medicines available for illnesses like malaria and typhoid. People often had many children, perhaps fearing that not all would survive into adulthood. The mortality rate in the birthing rooms was not low either.

I always found Jatin Jyatha's elder daughter utterly enchanting. Not only was she beautiful, but she was also remarkably gifted. She played the sitar with such finesse! I had the privilege of hearing her perform a couple of times during my childhood visits to their home. She and her younger sister both completed their graduation before they were married—a rare and admirable thing in those times.

Yet, during that period, it felt as if the Bose family had fallen under some silent curse. Jatin Bose was a respected man, socially established and well-off. His eldest son was an exceptional student—brilliant in every way. But for all his intellect, he carried a strange, whimsical restlessness. In the midst of his BA examinations, he abruptly left the examination hall in a deeply disturbed state. Despite his immense knowledge and potential, he never sat for another examination again.

I remember seeing him during those troubled years. Even now, in my later life, I look back and wonder—how could someone so intelligent, so gentle, so full of promise, lose his mental balance at such a decisive moment in his life?

It still leaves me with a quiet ache, Di-bhai—one of those silent sadnesses that never fully fades.

Jatin Jyatha's other two sons returned from England after earning their engineering degrees. Unfortunately, history repeated itself. Just as their father had once distanced himself from his own parents in his youth, the sons too distanced themselves from the family after their marriages and subsequently displayed little interest in keeping in touch with other relatives.

You had once mentioned, Di-bhai, that one of the brothers—the younger one—fell victim to tuberculosis. Despite extensive treatment, he could not be saved. Before his illness, when he had come to Calcutta for some work, he purchased a piece of land in Dumdum, on the outskirts of the city. A small house was later built there.

Jatin jyatha spent his final days in that modest home belonging to the lesser-known and somewhat less accomplished son—our Toy Dada. You must remember Kaka's younger son too, the strikingly handsome Tota Dada, Di-bhai. Each time we met him, he would regale us with stories so vivid and enchanting, they lingered long after he had left. And thus unfolds the chapter of our grandfather's brother, Nabin Mohan Bose, and Judge Jatin Bose's family—woven into the quiet tapestry of our shared past.

Returning to our grandfather, Lalit Mohan Bose had two sons and a daughter. Our father, Angshu Mohan Bose, was always an exceptional student and had joined the Calcutta School of Tropical Medicine after his studies. I can vividly recall Baba, Di-bhai—tall, imposing figure with a serious demeanour. You must remember him even better, right?

In comparison, Kaka, Himanshu Mohan Bose, had more a bohemian spirit. He remained steadfast in his principles, which were often contested by his father, our Thakurda. When Baba commenced his medical studies, the First World War was already underway. Kaka, despite objections from the family, enlisted in the 49th Bengalee Regiment during those tumultuous times in 1917.

Kaka often spoke about the most terrifying war in history. In 1914, in Sarajevo, Bosnia, the young Archduke Franz Ferdinand of Austria was assassinated by a Serb's bullet. Austria-Hungary held Serbia responsible and declared war at the end of June that year. Old conflicts had already been simmering among the neighbouring states, and before long, not only did their allies become involved, but eventually, all the economically strong nations joined this war.

Kaka would emphasize that the conflict had not been sparked solely by the assassination of the Austrian Archduke. There was, in fact, a growing rivalry among nations to establish colonies and secure markets for the surplus goods produced by the nineteenth-century industrial revolution. It's astonishing to think, Di-bhai, how human competition and self-interest could lead to such an unimaginable calamity!

That dreadful war claimed millions of lives—both of soldiers and innocent civilians. Just imagine the scale of that tragedy! I remember, as a child, whenever Kaka began speaking about it, he would become deeply moved. His voice would turn sombre, and I would sit there, trembling as I listened. Kaki would quietly bring him his favourite large mug of tea and settle beside me, silently absorbing every word.

Kaka explained that international relations in those times were veiled in secrecy and fraught with complexity. Initially, because of France's long-standing enmity with Germany, Britain had maintained cordial ties with the Germans. But once Germany began to rival Britain in naval strength and technology, that friendship swiftly gave way to competition.

Meanwhile, Russia and France swiftly entered the war, and Germany soon found itself locked in a formidable struggle on multiple fronts. However, in Britain's eyes, Germany was emerging as a potent new empire—more threatening, perhaps, than either Russia or France. To preserve its own position of power, Britain declared war on Germany. The entry of such a dominant force signalled impending disaster for the German campaign.

The immense loss of military resources, combined with the rising tide of communist propaganda, eventually led to the downfall of the Russian emperor and the country's defeat. Over the course of three gruelling years, the German army also suffered heavy casualties while attempting to penetrate the vast, frozen interior of Russia during the unforgiving winter.

And yet, Germany made a grave miscalculation by launching attacks on American ships—an act that roused the sleeping giant. With Germany's defeat becoming increasingly inevitable, the

United States abandoned its long-held policy of non-intervention and entered the war at the eleventh hour. Its arrival shifted the balance entirely.

Under the leadership of President Woodrow Wilson, a new form of international politics was introduced to the world stage—one that would reshape the global order in the years to come.

Indeed, the world was bathed in blood. The German, Austro-Hungarian, Russian, and Ottoman empires all met with catastrophic defeat. Perhaps every inhumane and destructive act is eventually followed by a stern reckoning—retribution delivered by Mother Earth herself. After the war, as if to deepen the wound, millions perished in the influenza pandemic that swept across the globe.

Kaka would say that just when the world had begun to hope such a man-made catastrophe would never recur, the victors and the vanquished alike had already begun their covert manoeuvring—quietly laying the groundwork for what would become another devastating conflict in history: the Second World War. But I shall speak of that another time.

The British Raj, ever opportunistic, seized its own moment during this global crisis. In 1916, it formed the 'Bengali Double Company' under the leadership of Lieutenant General Taylor. The educated youth of our country—spirited, brave, and full of nationalist pride—stood by the British, convinced they were serving a greater good.

During this worldwide power struggle, the Bengali Double Company too demonstrated its loyalty to the Raj. By 1917, the unit was renamed the 49th Bengalee Regiment. Many of Bengal's educated sons, especially from modestly well-off families, risked their lives travelling to distant places like Punjab and Karachi to enlist.

The Bengali Regiment served in various capacities: as infantrymen, in the signal corps, and in ambulance services, caring for wounded soldiers and helping to revive the dying. And yet, Di-bhai, it is painful to reflect that what the Indians received in return for their service—rendered at such great personal cost—was only further exploitation.

Our own Kaka was sent to Karachi as part of this very effort.

Towards the end of 1917, Kazi Nazrul Islam too joined the ranks of the 49th Bengalee Regiment. He began his training at Fort William in Calcutta and was later posted to Naushera in the Frontier Province. After completing his training, he served within the confines of the Karachi military base. Starting as a corporal, Nazrul gradually rose to the rank of Quarter Master Havildar. It is often said that even in the harshest of conditions, true talent finds a way to flourish. While stationed in Karachi, he learned Persian from the regiment's Punjabi Maulavi and continued to write prolifically.

In September 1918, the British Raj established the 'Dhaka Depot' by assembling Bengali soldiers from East Bengal. Sadly, sixty-three of them lost their lives during this period.

Meanwhile, on another front, the British faced a significant setback at the hands of the Ottoman Turks in Iraq—then known as Mesopotamia. The young recruits of the 49th Bengalee Regiment were deployed to Baghdad, where they were assigned the task of safeguarding military forts. However, even before they saw combat, many among them succumbed to the region's unforgiving climate and harsh living conditions. In the sweltering heat of March, the regiment was moved from Baghdad to Al Aziziyah, then on to Al-Kut, and finally to Tanuma near Basra by October, each relocation further straining the health conditions of the young soldiers. In 1919, a contingent of infantrymen from the regiment was dispatched to Kurdistan to help suppress a local uprising.

Di-bhai, did you know that in College Square, Kolkata, there's a plaque commemorating the forgotten soldiers of the 49th Regiment? Titai saw it during her time at the Medical College, Calcutta. I, too, had the chance to see it. The plaque bears the names of the fallen—young men from Kolkata, Bardhhaman, Murshidabad, Medinipur, Nadia, Mymensingh, Pabna, Jessore, Barisal, Chittagong, and Faridpur. Their regiment numbers, ranks, dates of death, and birthplaces are etched into stone—a quiet, enduring tribute to their sacrifice.

When the war finally came to an end, the disarrayed men of the regiment somehow managed to return home. However, many a mothers' loving bosom was left empty, their sons lost forever.

Listening to Kaka's tales of those immensely courageous young men, I used to get gooseflesh. I could not help but feel grateful to God that our Kaka had returned to the country unharmed. But I could not help but think about those souls who never came back. Did they ever receive enough recognition for their supreme sacrifice? Who cared for their families after their departure?

It makes me ponder, Di-bhai, how their presence could have been invaluable in India's struggle for independence.

Three

Let me return to our family once more. Lalit Mohan Bose, our Thakurda, arranged for his daughter's—our pishima's—marriage while he was residing in Jorhat, Assam. After his retirement, he moved to Calcutta. His wife, our grandmother, was still alive at the time. He then set his sights on arranging the marriage of his elder son.

Meanwhile, the Pals—our mother's maternal family—were in search of a suitable groom for their daughter. Shejo Dadu, who lived in Calcutta, somehow managed to find a handsome doctor employed at the Calcutta Medical College's Tropical Medicine department. The Pals seemed quite eager to establish a marital alliance with the Bose family. That is how the daughter of Pal bari of Manikganj was united in matrimony to the son of the Boses' from Bikrampur, of East Bengal.

Di-bhai, did you ever manage to learn the exact date of our parents' wedding? Anyway, after marriage, our beloved mother arrived in Calcutta to take charge of the household of Angshu Mohan Bose, her husband.

By then, the First World War was already over. The Boses lived in Doctors' Lane in Taltala in Devendra Mansion, occupying the ground and first floors, as well as the terrace. Wasn't Devendra Mansion located in an affluent area of the city back then, Di-bhai? I have heard Fazlul Haque was one of our neighbours, and that Baba was friendly with him.

Mr Haque was the son of a renowned and formidable lawyer from the Bakarganj district of East Bengal. He completed his education at Barisal District School before pursuing higher studies at Presidency College (now Presidency University), where he earned honours in three subjects during his graduation. Fazlul Haque then went on to complete his legal studies at Calcutta Law College and began practising law under the mentorship of Sir Ashutosh Mukherjee during what is often referred to as Bengal's golden age.

In that era, luminaries like Ashwini Kumar Dutta and Prafulla Chandra Ray held great admiration for Mr Haque for his intellectual prowess and amiable personality. In those times, a student's capabilities were assessed solely based on their intellect—caste or religion played no role in such evaluations.

Following his father's demise, Mr Haque returned to his hometown and practised at the Barisal court for some time. Eventually, he was appointed as Deputy Magistrate by the government. However, on the advice of Sir Ashutosh Mukherjee, who is often referred to as the 'Bengal Tiger', Fazlul Haque returned to Calcutta and resumed practising in the Calcutta High Court. Despite his growing stature, he remained committed to staying in touch with the rural people of East Bengal.

In 1934, Mohammad Ali Jinnah was re-elected as the president of the All-India Muslim League. During that time, Haque had differences of opinion with Jinnah's as the former was dedicated to the emancipation of farmers from the grip of landowners and middlemen. His words of hope encouraged many.

In 1935, Fazlul Haque was elected Mayor of Calcutta. The following year, his newly founded Krishak Praja Party contested the 1936 elections and secured a notable share of the vote, emerging as the third-largest party. Though they attempted to form a coalition with the Congress, their proposal was turned down. Eventually, Haque entered into an alliance with the Muslim League—a development that Jinnah had reportedly foreseen, given the political climate of the time. Thus, the Haque–League coalition came into being.

Fazlul Haque served as the Chief Minister of undivided Bengal from 1937 to 1943. Notably, in 1942, he publicly opposed the Muslim League's 'two-nation theory'. I later learnt from Kaka and Kaki that even during the riots of 1946, he took sincere steps to ensure the safety of his Hindu neighbours. After independence, he served as the Home Minister of Pakistan and later as the Governor of East Pakistan.

Four

Di-bhai, do you remember how Kaki became part of our family? She came from a family of the Maheshwardi Pargana of East Bengal. By the time Kaka and Kaki got married, our mother had already given birth to many of our siblings, and the marriage provided Ma with some relief from household duties. Kaka and Kaki held our parents in such high regard that they consistently endeavoured to offer support and assistance in any way they could, trying to alleviate any burden or inconvenience. The younger members of a family learn much by observing the behaviour and values of their elders.

I've heard that Baba followed a ritual of never leaving the house without touching his mother's feet, as a sign of respect. One particular incident illustrates this well, which you must have already heard from others. Thakurma, our grandmother, was taking her bath one morning. She was quite frail by then, and hence, considerably slow. Father was about to leave for work but could not do so without first touching her feet. Growing impatient, he began pacing outside the bathroom door, continually checking his watch. His car was ready, but he could not bring himself to rush his mother even though he was getting late.

As soon as our fair as a nymph Thakurma emerged from the bathroom, Baba quickly approached her, prostrated on the ground to touch her feet and took his mother's blessings. Then the illustrious Dr Bose rose, adjusted his tie and hurried off to his hospital duties. I can visualize the toothless smile on our grandmother's pretty face as she proudly told her daughters-in-law, 'See? What a son I've raised! Isn't he the best?'

Sadly, Thakurma didn't live much longer.

I was quite young at the time, Di-bhai, but I heard that our doctor father was unhappy about his daughters, especially Bordi, walking to school. Soon after, he purchased another car solely for our school transportation.

Kaka often mentioned that Baba enjoyed not only driving his car but also servicing its parts himself. I've been told that Dada, who was a bright but mischievous boy, was always eager to imitate our father, especially when it came to handling machinery.

Kaki often recounted a story about Dada. With so many children born in quick succession, our mother had her hands full. Dada, born after Bordi, was followed by five sisters—mother must have had a very challenging time looking after all of us when we were young!

Keeping a track of our feeding times was becoming a task for Ma, so Baba bought her a large table clock to monitor the time. One day, Dada, eight-years-old at the time, skipped school and remained at home. He was prancing around when he noticed the large table clock. Curious about what was inside, he decided to disassemble it. Unnoticed by anyone, he managed to open the clock bit by bit and then submerged the parts in kerosene before stashing the tub under the large four-poster bed.

When Baba came home from work and couldn't find the clock after an extensive search, it was Ma who bore the brunt of his scolding. By the time the clock was finally discovered from underneath the bed, Baba was furious. After a stern interrogation, Dada had only one thing to say: 'I always see you cleaning car parts with oil and a cloth, Baba. I wanted to do the same with the clock, just like you! If you had let me continue, I would have become an expert in cleaning car machinery too. But you stopped me!'

'You wanted to clean the clock, did you, boy?! I'll throw you out of this house today, you little rascal!' Baba thundered with rage. At that time, I would probably be asleep downstairs in the lap of our nanny, but later I would hear the terrifying story from Kaki.

Baba had seized our eight-year-old brother by the collar and dragged him towards the terrace. Ma's tearful pleas to stop him fell on deaf ears. As the scene unfolded, Kaki, shaken by what she saw, ran to summon Kaka.

In a moment of uncontrollable fury, Baba had resolved to punish his son by throwing him off the terrace. Just imagine the tension, Di-bhai! At that critical juncture, our courageous and deeply compassionate Kaka arrived just in time. Without a word, he climbed onto the projecting cornice of the terrace himself and shouted: 'Borda, if you throw the child, you will lose this brother of yours as well. You'll never see me alive again! The child may have misbehaved, but this punishment—this is beyond cruelty. I would rather die than stand by and witness such a sin committed before my eyes!'

Those words, spoken in raw defiance and love, stunned Baba for the time being. In that moment of madness, it was Kaka's unwavering stance that pulled him back from the edge.

'Himanshu, I say, get down from there right now! That part of the terrace is old and in need of repairs. But tell me—how did this boy gather so much courage? How could he dare to tamper with my belongings, my valuable possessions, without my permission? Are you telling me to endorse this demonic behaviour? Shouldn't I discipline him?' Baba attempted to justify his actions.

'Even I cannot tolerate injustice, Borda—you know that well. That's why our father scolds me so often when I challenge him on certain matters. But tell me—does a little child deserve a punishment as grave as death for something like this? He needs to be guided, taught the difference between right and wrong. Only then will he grow into someone who can judge wisely and become a sensible human being.'

Defeated by Kaka's words, Baba quietly placed Dada in charge of Ma and stormed away from the scene.

In time, Dada—Parijat Bose—became a skilled hand, technically adept with machines. He never had much of a flair for academics, and Ma's indulgent affection allowed him to carry on as he pleased. As an adult, he took up various jobs, though his whims and frequent disagreements often led him to leave them midway. Still, whenever anything needed repair—radios, fans, lamps, even electric irons—Dada was everyone's first port of call. Neighbours, relatives, and even shopkeepers would summon him for repairs, and he never disappointed anyone.

With his Albert-style hairdo and a poised manner that almost resembled an Englishman, Junior Bose wandered from house to house in the neighbourhood, in exchange, sampling *luchi*, *payesh*, and all manner of delicacies, before returning home like a triumphant hero. I imagine Ma must have taken quiet delight in watching him—her beloved son—completely unaware of the love-struck glances sent his way by the young girls of the neighbourhood. Wouldn't you agree, Di-bhai?

Even now, I cannot help but smile when I think back to those days.

'Dear boy! Look how sweaty you are! What are your sisters even doing? Girls, bring him some *sherbet*, will you? Fan him now!' I can vividly picture of Ma's gleaming face as she fussed over her darling son as he returned home.

Brash as he was, Dada was also incredibly kind-hearted. He never accepted a single rupee from any neighbour or relative for his assistance in repairing things. If anyone tried to pay him, he would immediately say, 'In that case, I propose not to visit you ever again.'

The Junior Bose truly had a heart of gold. He may have switched jobs often, but he never learnt to put himself first—because he felt happy helping those in need. Isn't that right, Di-bhai?

Do you remember our Pishima's frequent visits to Calcutta after her marriage? Baba and his sister were kindred souls—both endowed with hefty statures and a profound love for food. Kaki used to say that whenever Pishima visited, Ma barely had a moment's rest, continuously planning and preparing different delicious dishes with painstaking effort. After every meal, Kaki would stand by with a paan in her hand for Pishima, who would have it immediately after rinsing her mouth.

Baba had a deep fondness for both of his younger siblings. However, he showed a touch of favouritism towards our aunt, perhaps because she lived far away in Assam. Evening drives in Baba's car were a luxury she particularly enjoyed. I've been told that, before starting the engine, Baba would look over his shoulder, count the passengers, and teasingly say to his sister,

'Oi Tuni, make sure you're sitting diagonally behind me in the back—otherwise the car won't start! You and I are the only ones blessed with good health, you see. The rest are just extra baggage!'

Baba, despite his deeply affectionate nature, harboured a dangerously volatile temper beneath the surface. Mischief or any act of defiance could ignite his fury in an instant. As Kaki later recalled, one such episode unfolded on a Sunday morning.

Baba was beneath his car that day, lying flat on a plastic sheet, servicing it with his usual precision. Judge Jatin Uncle and his family were visiting us at the time. His wife, adorned in jewellery, was bustling about in the upper floors, while the Judge himself relaxed upstairs in one of the rooms. Lavish preparations were underway for lunch.

Although Baba approved of the arrangements and the cheerful atmosphere, he did not particularly enjoy noise or disorder. He believed in quiet decorum—amongst women, children even servants of the house.

That morning, however, the neighbourhood milkman arrived to collect his monthly dues. Receiving no response after calling out from the ground floor, he perhaps glanced upward towards the upper levels and raised his voice further—entirely unaware that Baba was lying beneath the car, in the portico, just out of sight. But Baba, of course, did not miss a thing. To him, this was not mere impatience—it was outright insubordination.

His temper ignited.

Silently, he slid out from under the car, unnoticed, and ascended the stairs to his room. There, he reached for a *Shakosh machher lej*—a hard, dried tail of a large shark once brought from Bikrampur. Wrapping it around his wrist with the clear intention of disciplining the intruder he descended down the stairs.

By the time he returned to the courtyard, the poor milkman had already sensed something was amiss. Trembling with fear, he began pleading for forgiveness.

Judge Jatin Uncle, observing the unfolding drama from the upper floor, called down calmly, offering his seasoned legal advice:

'Angshu, give him a thrashing if you must—but make sure there's absolutely no bloodshed!'

On that occasion too, Kaka rushed to the scene and intervened, saving the milkman. Kaki told me that Kaka paid the man double his dues and implored him to scurry back to his home as fast as possible.

Even with so many children, Baba was particular about each

child's diet. Di-bhai, I was once told that I was always hungrier than the rest. As soon as I emptied my milk bottle, I would start crying.

One day, when Baba returned from the hospital and witnessed the situation, he asked Ma to bring more milk in the feeding cup. I was a plump little thing with a hearty appetite. I quickly finished the extra milk, perked up in no time, and began playing cheerfully.

That day, Baba gently explained to Ma, 'This chubby little doll of ours needs a bit more nutrition, in proportion to her weight. Keep that in mind and make sure she's properly nourished.'

Kaki would always laugh heartily while recounting this story.

However, our blissful days were not to last. One day, while at work in the hospital, Father began experiencing excruciating abdominal pain. Dr Euthin, his senior colleague, suspected gallstones and prescribed medication to ease the discomfort. With reassurance in his voice, he promised, 'Doctor Bose, I'm due to sail for England soon—but I'll perform your gallbladder operation before I leave.'

But fate had other plans.

Just after the blood reports came in, and before a date could be finalized for the surgery, Baba's pain intensified. He was rushed to the emergency unit. As soon as morphine was administered in preparation for the operation, Dr Angshu Mohan Bose departed this world—suddenly, silently—into the eternal unknown.

It was 1937. We—six sisters and our brother—were left shattered by the loss of our beloved father. The family was plunged into grief.

Di-bhai, you must remember how Kaka had always given himself, heart and soul, to the Congress party—placing politics above personal and family matters. And yet, that very man eventually set aside his ideals and took up a job, a position at the Commercial Museum, quietly accepting the demands of circumstance.

At one time, he had been a close associate of Dr Bidhan Chandra Roy—the radiant star of Bengal in that era. Dr Roy's brilliance, progressive outlook, and unwavering commitment to the welfare of Bengal's people earned him deep admiration and affection across the land.

I have heard that Dr Roy, after completing his medical studies at Calcutta Medical College, went on to pursue further education in England, where he earned his F.R.C.S. Upon returning to India, he began practising medicine and also took up a teaching position at Calcutta's Campbell Medical School—now known as Nilratan Sircar Medical College.

Dr Bidhan Roy later entered politics under the influence of Deshbandhu Chittaranjan Das. In time, he became the General Secretary of the Indian National Congress and was elected Mayor of the Calcutta Corporation. In 1931, he was even imprisoned for his involvement in the Non-Cooperation Movement led by Mahatma Gandhi.

Kaka once told me about an incident from 1933, when Gandhiji was fasting in Poona. Hearing that Bapu was unwell, Dr Bidhan Roy rushed there to attend to him. Upon seeing him, Gandhiji asked with gentle reproach:

'Why did you leave your duties and come here, Bidhan? Am I to receive your treatment without paying a fee? Why should I take your medicines free of cost either? Can you afford to run around the country treating all thirty-three crore Indians without charge?'

Do you know, Di-bhai, what Dr Roy—wise and composed as ever—replied?

'No, Gandhiji, it is not that. I do not treat the entire country, nor do I offer free treatment to all. But the responsibility of caring for the representative of these thirty-three crore Indians has been entrusted to me by the people. I cannot return without fulfilling that duty.'

His voice, Kaka said, was calm, respectful, and resolute. Gandhiji, in time, recovered from his illness.

It was a remarkable time, was it not? These towering figures—each a master in their own field—served the nation with rare dedication, honesty, intellect, and love. There may have been differences among them, but their mutual respect never wavered.

Dr Bidhan Roy assumed the role of Chief Minister of West Bengal in 1948. At the time, millions of men, women, and children were pouring into the state—desperate to save their lives after being violently uprooted from what had just become East Pakistan. They were forced to abandon the land their families had inhabited for generations.

Yes, Di-bhai, I am speaking of those turbulent times during the Partition.

Kaka would often say that it was Dr Roy who offered these shattered lives shelter—and, more importantly, a glimmer of hope for the future.

The arrival of refugees led to a terrible food and shelter crisis in the state. Businesses suffered as the supply of raw jute from East Pakistan stopped. Dr Roy tried to rejuvenate the damaged lands and introduced jute cultivation. With raw jute once again available, thousands of jute mill workers, who had faced possible loss of livelihood, found relief.

He also set up the Haringhata Dairy Project to ensure a steady milk supply and employed educated young women in dairy supply. This helped increase the income of many refugee families as well. As Chief Minister, he established the State Transport Corporation, which offered employment to a vast number of educated but unemployed youth.

During his fourteen-year tenure as Chief Minister, Dr Bidhan

Chandra Roy spearheaded a remarkable wave of development across West Bengal. Among his visionary initiatives were the establishment of Durgapur Steel City and Chittaranjan Locomotive Works—cornerstones of his meticulous plan to industrialize the state.

West Bengal will forever remain indebted to Dr Roy for his far-reaching contributions, which laid the foundation for its modern industrial landscape.

Five

Di-bhai, I was around five or six years old at the time, while you had just turned seven or eight. The tumultuous events unfolding around the world between 1939 and 1945, you might remember better than I do.

The Second World War raged for those six years. It began as a competition of economic, commercial and technological prowess but soon spiralled into the mindless mass murder of civilians, the Holocaust, ending with America dropping atomic bombs on Hiroshima and Nagasaki. This war was perhaps the most cruel and devastating conflict in history.

Japan attacked China in 1937, aiming to establish monopoly over East Asia. Later, in September 1939, Germany attacked Poland, prompting France and the UK to declare war on Germany. I think the second incident may be regarded as the beginning of the Second World War.

In June 1941, the European Axis powers invaded the Soviet Union, leading to the largest fiasco of combat and armed conflict in the world. In December of the same year, the US joined the Allied Forces. The Axis powers, Germany and Japan, almost forced the US into the war by attacking it. On the other hand, Japan held old grudges against China, as the Second Sino-Japanese war had been ongoing since the mid-1930s. As a result, China joined the Allied Forces as well. With the unconditional surrender of both Germany and Japan in 1945, the Second World War finally came to an end.

In 1941, Rangoon was still part of the British Indian Empire, even as the Second World War gradually edged closer to Asia. Many of its residents had deep roots in India—their parents, grandparents, and even great-grandparents had been born there.

But during the war, Japan launched an aggressive campaign of a very different kind. Following the attack on Pearl Harbour in the United States, Japanese forces rapidly seized Malaysia and soon turned their sights on Rangoon. Aerial bombings rained terror on the city, plunging its people into fear and confusion. They did not know where to seek shelter, or whether they would be allowed into the underground bunkers constructed by the British.

A growing dread took hold: many feared that the British might abandon them—or worse, hand them over to the advancing Japanese.

The Indian community in Rangoon, which played a vital role in the city's industry, commerce and agriculture, was also gripped with fear and started congregating in the northern part of the province. Within days, the roads were blocked. It seemed as if a human tsunami had descended upon the streets! To avoid traffic congestion, the escape route was split into two directions. One group fled eastward towards Chittagong, traversing the perilous Arakan hills. Though short, it was a journey fraught with danger that claimed many lives. The other group took the Chindwin River route along the Irrawaddy River towards the north, patiently covering the longer distance across the mountains, hoping to somehow reach Manipur. By that time, the Japanese, intoxicated by power and success, were already celebrating their victory in Malaysia.

Di-bhai, as I write this, I am reminded of a friend with whom I studied during my ISc (Intermediate with Science course). Her name was Devika. She had the appearance of a quintessential Bengali but her complexion was slightly fairer. She was very taciturn. It was from her that I heard a strange story of survival.

Devika's mother, Pemala, was Burmese. She had fallen in love with Devraj, an Indian engineer working in Rangoon, and they were soon married. Devraj held a position with the Burmese Railway. Initially, there had been some resentment within Pemala's family over her choice of an Indian husband. Nevertheless, following the birth of their daughter Devika, the little girl gradually won the hearts of her grandparents, bringing harmony back to the household. She enjoyed a happy childhood with her affectionate parents. Pemala's brothers however remained distant towards Devraj.

Devika was just seven years old when the Japanese bombs began devastating Burma, plunging countless lives into turmoil.

Japan's behaviour was growing increasingly hostile and oppressive. It was during this troubling time that Devraj realized something unsettling: his Burmese brothers-in-law were determined to deny him any legal rights to the family property in Burma. They even forbade their parents from leaving him any inheritance.

Meanwhile, Pemala had become pregnant again but sadly suffered a miscarriage, which left her severely weakened from persistent bleeding. Devraj took her to several doctors at various hospitals in Burma, but the chaos of wartime had thrown the healthcare system into disarray, and his efforts yielded no relief. Around the same time, Pemala's elderly parents passed away within six months of each other, and her brothers flatly refused to offer any further support to their sister and her family.

Desperate, Devraj now yearned to return to India with his wife and daughter, convinced that the well-equipped hospitals there would offer Pemala a better chance at recovery. Despite fully understanding the grave risks the journey would pose to her fragile health, Pemala bravely decided to undertake the perilous journey to India.

Though Devraj managed to secure expensive steamer tickets that would get them from Rangoon to Madras, all the seats were taken up in advance by the British and Anglo-Indians. Their lives were regarded as more important than those of the native Indians. Though disheartened, Devraj did not give up. He made enquiries in the railways and somehow boarded a goods train with his family. Carrying only a few essentials—some medicine and food—they began their long and arduous journey.

At a place called Memo, on the banks of the Chindwin River in northern Burma, they found temporary shelter in a Buddhist temple. But that was only the beginning of the most arduous leg of their journey. A long stretch still lay ahead—part by boat, and the rest on foot. They had to reach the Naga Hills; without making it that far, survival seemed almost impossible.

They joined hundreds of others fleeing Burma, a desperate mass of lives in motion. After seven punishing days and nights of travel, Pemala's condition worsened severely. She began vomiting repeatedly, her body too frail to endure the strain.

Devika's father, frantic to ease his wife's suffering, arranged for Pemala and their daughter to ride in a bullock cart while he continued on foot. They moved on towards the foothills of the Naga mountains. The unspoken question hung in the air like a shadow: how much farther to India?

But fate, like a silent predator, was never far behind. One morning, as dawn broke over the mist-covered trail, Pemala did not open her eyes again.

Devika stood frozen, her eyes wide with shock, as her mother's final rites were performed by the roadside, with the help of a few kind-hearted Sikhs and members of the Indian Marwari Society. The onerous journey of the father-daughter duo had to continue. Her father, Devraj, pressed on with quiet determination, carrying Devika on his shoulders whenever her little feet gave way to exhaustion.

At night, beneath the vast, star-lit sky, Devika would gaze

upwards, believing that her mother was now one of the countless twinkling stars above. From time to time, she would ask her father, 'Which one is my mom?'

Devraj would gently point to the brightest star in the sky and whisper, 'Look, darling—that one. She's smiling at us. She's letting us know that we're on the right path.'

After crossing the hills, they made their way to Imphal and then to Dimapur. From there, they squeezed into a packed compartment of a train bound for Sealdah. Quite a few weeks passed before they finally found refuge in an ashram in Calcutta.

During their stay at the ashram, Devraj managed to secure a new job. It wasn't until a year later, after much upheaval and adjustment, that little Devika was finally able to begin school.

Di-bhai, Devika was just a year older than me, but I can never forget the melancholy and maturity in her eyes. Over time, I began to understand why she spoke so little, why she struggled to concentrate on her studies, as our camaraderie improved. I shared my tiffin with her every day, and little by little, she opened up to me.

'Apu, while we were floating down the river for days, some kind strangers on the banks waved to us, signalling us to stop. They cooked rice, dal and vegetables over wood fire in the forests by the river. After eating, we embraced and thanked them before resuming our journey. Apu, I shall never meet those people again. I do not know if they too have become stars like my mother. But the memory of the love they showered on us will always remain with me.'

Di-bhai, I'm old now—but why do the words spoken by that frightened, trembling young girl still echo in my ears? These days, I often find myself forgetting things. Sometimes I call my grandson and ask, 'Which month is it now, my dear? What's the date today?' He smiles gently and brings the calendar to me.

And yet, deep beneath the layers of time, the memory of Devika remains—unfaded. That child, so traumatized by the loss of her mother at such a tender age, still lives somewhere within me.

I lost all contact with Devika after completing my ISc And though the world gradually returned to a semblance of normalcy after the Second World War, Di-bhai, for people like us—ordinary people—there was no real reparation. What was lost could never truly be restored.

Six

The unjust demands and daily oppression of the British were steadily intensifying. Patience and levels of tolerance of people of India had reached a breaking point. In August 1942, during the Bombay (now Mumbai) session of the All-India Congress Committee, Mohandas Karamchand Gandhi raised the slogan, 'Quit India.' The very next day, Gandhi, Jawaharlal Nehru, and other Congress leaders were arrested by the British government.

With the message of 'Do or Die,' Gandhi made it clear that those who witness oppression must no longer remain silent. Across the country, people mourned the arrests, expressing spontaneous grief. Gandhi firmly declared that Indians must no longer cooperate with the British. In other words, it was unacceptable to continue living under the rule of oppressors! The British had to be driven out, and Indians were called upon to assert their identity with resolve and courage.

We were 'uncivilized natives' after all as addressed by the proud British Empire! All over the country, waves of protests, assemblies, and marches began.

By mid-1942, Japanese forces were closing in on India's borders. The US and China were eager to learn what the future held for India once the war concluded. In response, an Englishman named Stafford Cripps came from England with a letter. The British government had shown 'mercy' and agreed to grant India dominion status, but only after the war ended. However, the Congress rejected this 'generous' offer. Viewing it as an opportunity to corner the British, Mahatma Gandhi demanded their complete withdrawal from India. In line with Gandhiji's principles, it was decided that all protests would be conducted through non-violent means. The British government, in a shrewd move, declared all forms of mass movements illegal. As a result, more arrests followed, with individuals being randomly detained for no reason.

Oder bnadhon jotoi shokto hobey, totoi bnadhon tutbe,
moder totoi bnadhon tutbe
Oder jotoi ankhi rokto hobey moder ankhi phutbe

As they tighten their grip, our bondage will shatter, we shall break free,
As their eyes glow red with rage, our eyes shall gleam, the light we'll see.

Written during the Bengal partition movement of 1905 by Rabindranath Tagore, these lines became even more relevant at the time.

In 1905 itself, on the 16th of October, to commemorate the sacred-thread-of brotherhood ceremony or Rakhi festival, to protest the partition movement, also to unite the Hindu and the Muslim community, the great patriot, the respected bearded bard also wrote:

Banglar mati, Banglar jol,
Banglar bayu, Banglar phol
Punyo houk hey bhogobaan.

The soil of Bengal, the water of Bengal,
The air of Bengal, the fruits of Bengal
May they all be blessed, oh Lord.

The words carried profound emotional weight and value and resonated with great patriotic significance.

The movement, accompanied by the arrests of over a hundred thousand innocents, relentless torture and insults of Indians—especially the imprisonment of Gandhiji—awakened all Indians with a jolt. This time, the people of the nation stood side by side and cried out in unison, 'Quit India'.

Upon his release from prison, Gandhiji embarked on a 21-day fasting odyssey. Meanwhile, the Second World War ended, Japan withdrew, and a seismic shift dramatically rattled the foundation of the British Empire. The clamour for Indian independence resounded across the globe, a force that could no longer be ignored.

The danger facing Bengal, however, came from an entirely different direction. In August 1942, a devastating tornado struck the Midnapore district, leaving a trail of destruction in its wake. At the same time, a severe shortage of rice began to take root across rural Bengal—a crisis that had been forewarned by A.K. Fazlul Huq. Yet, despite these warnings, the British colonial administration failed to act, neglecting to ensure food security for the very people whose land and labour they had long exploited.

Water levels fell to historic lows, and to compound matters, a fungal blight known as 'brown spot disease' afflicted the winter paddy crop, further decimating rice yields. The result was a famine of horrifying proportions. Death and suffering spread across the villages and suburbs, eventually drawing the concern of even British military officers and Viceroy Linlithgow, who appealed for food imports to replenish Bengal's empty granaries. Their pleas, however, were ignored.

The famine of 1943—often referred to as the Famine of Fifty, after the Bengali calendar year 1350—would later be recognized globally as a man-made catastrophe, entirely preventable had timely measures been taken.

After the arrival of Bengal's new governor, Sir Thomas Rutherford, Lord Wavell succeeded Linlithgow as Viceroy of India. He travelled extensively across Bengal and swiftly submitted a report calling for the urgent dispatch of 1.5 million tonnes of rice. His warning was sent to London. But Prime Minister Winston Churchill, unmoved by the scale of human suffering, dismissed the crisis with a cruel remark to Secretary of State for India, Leo Amery: 'I hate Indians. They are a beastly people with a beastly religion... All they can do is breed like rabbits.'

Moreover, during the war, numerous warehouse owners concealed their rice stocks in secret reserves, giving rise to hoarding and black marketing. The rice hoarders became rich overnight, while impoverished villagers were forced to part with their possessions. Women sold their jewellery, men their livestock and land, just for a meagre two fistful of rice. Many rural residents left their families—wives, old parents and children—and flocked to the cities in search of any employment to fight their hunger. Hunger is a dreadful affliction, Di-bhai.

Among these scrawny villagers, some managed to survive, while others succumbed to illness. Many more helpless souls perished, their final moments filled with curses for their Maker, gazing into the sky with vacant eyes and hunger-filled bellies. Corpses lay beside rivers, desolate rice fields and even along railway tracks. Meanwhile, abundant food remained stocked within military barracks and in the possession of the wealthy and capitalist businessmen.

Fearing Japanese bombings, Burmese Indians had by then, begun adding to Bengal's already struggling population, but rice imports from Burma dwindled. At the same time, the British Raj wasted no time converting fields into military camps. Matters took a turn for the worse when the British Government imposed restrictions on grain transportation by boat.

Limited consignments of wheat trickled in from Punjab. Though Bengalis were unaccustomed to eating rotis, they were compelled to rely on them for survival. Even that scant aid soon came to a halt. Inflation soared, financial distress deepened, and hunger became a constant, unforgiving presence.

Vultures and jackals began feeding on corpses left scattered across the fields, gradually contaminating rivers, streams, and drinking water. Hospitals overflowed with the sick, while the bodies piled along the roads became indistinguishable—anonymous in death.

I heard about those horrific days from Kaka—he would shudder as he spoke of them. History tells us that nearly 3.5 million lives were lost in that famine.

Finally, in October 1943, Viscount Wavell initiated a relief operation using military resources, which helped ease the food shortage to some extent. But by then, unspeakable damage had already been done. Under government orders, the military had even stripped the impoverished of their meagre clothing to manufacture parachutes, blankets, and uniforms. Bengal's cotton had been exported to Britain, creating an acute shortage of fabric.

The following year thus brought yet another crisis—the cloth famine, a tragic scarcity of clothing. Women, half-naked, wandered the streets carrying emaciated, naked children in their arms—walking skeletons. Their desperate cries echoed in every alley: 'Ma, give me some rice-gruel...just a little gruel, please!'

Kaki would often wipe away tears as she recalled those heart-wrenching days—her voice faltering with sorrow, even after all those years.

Desperation knew no bounds. People stole clothes from dead bodies—even digging up graves—or snatched garments from pedestrians. Women flocked to the city, resorting to prostitution and begging in exchange for a little food. Some men, once farmers or labourers, turned to pimping as their main source of income. In their desperate struggle for survival, people abandoned all vestiges of morality and shame.

Private organizations made significant efforts to save as many lives as possible. Even in the following year, despite sufficient rainfall, the scarcity persisted. Gradually, farm loans were provided, along with rice seeds and livestock for the farmers. Projects were initiated to construct reservoirs for water storage and create stone wells. Daily wagers were employed for in these efforts.

By that time, Ma wished to return to Barisal, to her father's home, and she wanted all of us to go with her. It was clear to everyone that Kaka and Kaki's greatest affection was reserved for me. The childless couple longed to keep me with them, and given the circumstances, Ma had no choice but to agree. Di-bhai, you and the rest of our siblings left for East Bengal with Ma, leaving me behind. Unfortunately, for a long time, you and I were separated.

Di-bhai, if you remember, after our father's demise, we moved from Devendra Mansion to a modest two-storeyed house on Shambhu Babu Lane. Our new neighbours were not people of high social standing but belonged to the city's working class. Among them were several Bihari milkmen. Some could be seen early in the morning, milking cows with a few of their customers standing by, waiting to carry home the fresh milk. Others would arrive on bicycles, clad in vests and dhotis, metal milk cans jangling by their sides, delivering milk across the neighbourhood.

These men had left behind their wives and children in distant villages—what they fondly called their 'homelands'—to seek a living in the city. On winter evenings, they would gather and entertain themselves by singing in chorus. One of their favourite songs was 'Jug Jug Jiye Lalawa, Bhagvaan Ke Bhaag Jaagal Ho', a devotional tune believed to have been sung by Mother Kausalya while bathing her infant son, Shri Ram, as described in the Ramayana.

They sang with heartfelt devotion, their simple voices joined by rising rhythms and the spirited beats of *dholak*s and *khartal*s. Though we Bengali neighbours barely understood their language, we never complained about the lively noise. Instead, we accepted it as an enjoyable torture—cheerfully endured, night after night. I too often found myself swaying to their rustic rhythm, smiling at the unpolished but joyful cacophony that filled our narrow lane.

Fate had brought these people into our lives as we rode the rollercoaster of life.

At first, Kaki was hesitant to let any Ram Da, Kyabla Da or Kanai Da from our locality to carry me in their arms, but it was an era of trust, and no one would betray that faith reposed in them.

I was growing up amidst limited means. Even so, my uncle would bring me a variety of books, including those well beyond my school curriculum. He would read aloud stories from across the world, filling my young mind with wonder. We continued our subscription to *The Statesman*, the daily newspaper. And despite his own personal challenges, Kaka would never forget my birthday—each year, he would buy me a cake from Hogg Market. But true to his values, he made sure I shared the cake with all our neighbours after I had cut it.

During those formative years, a few scenes I witnessed left an indelible impression on my young mind. I soon began to cherish the idea of accompanying Kaka on his morning walks. At dawn, I would often see a man walking down the road, a leather bag slung over his shoulder, from which water steadily dripped. As he walked, the water cleansed the dusty path. Kaka told me the man was called a *bhistiwallah*.

Di-bhai, speaking of water, I'm reminded of certain strange places along the roads—contraptions where water used to flow with a gentle gurgling sound beneath thick iron meshes! Everyone referred to them as hydrants. As a child, I could not fathom where the water came from or disappeared; it all appeared very mysterious to me.

Nearby, in Entally, a grand annual fair—the Rath er Mela—was held every year in the month of Ashadh, right in the middle of the monsoon season.

Do you remember, Di-bhai, the day we got lost at the fair?

We were little girls then, visiting the bustling fair with Kaki in charge. While gazing at colourful birds in tiny cages, munching delicious papads and blowing on the *bhepu* to make funny noises, we must have become unmindful. Excited with the fanfare, we did not notice when we separated from Kaki. Hand in hand, we had walked in the opposite direction, leading towards the exit.

It wasn't until we reached the main road that we realized perhaps we had lost our way. Strangely, at that moment, I did not feel like crying; instead, I felt quite happy. For right here, near the footpath on the main road, stood a large hydrant! I could hear water gurgling inside it. And beside it was a small, square reservoir. Some of the water from the hydrant splashed upwards like a fountain, which I found amusing to look at.

Remember, Di-bhai, how I let go of your hand and gleefully jumped into the puddle, shoes and all? For a moment, it seemed like you had also forgotten your responsibility as the elder sister and considered joining me in the fun. Alas, before you could, Kaki arrived—panting and puffing, questioning every passer-by. 'Have you seen my twin daughters? They're wearing similar clothes!'

As it happened, Kaka got us matching clothes most of the time, and that day, it made Kaki's search for us a little easier. Before long, she spotted us.

Poor you! Your participation in the game remained incomplete that day. If I could be born again, I'd happily be your younger sister once more, Di-bhai. Then we'd play in that muddy fountain puddle—over and over again.

That day, after receiving a rebuke from Kaki, we returned home, pouting in disappointment. But later, when Kaka came back from the office, he scolded Kaki gently—reminding her that it was she who had become engrossed in buying a Chinese vase at the fair. Seizing this perfect moment, I slipped beside him and asked about the magical source of that gurgling water in the middle of the road.

Kaka chuckled softly. Then, with gentle patience, he explained that the water came directly from the river Ganges. Whenever a fire broke out somewhere in the city, the red fire brigade trucks would quickly draw water from these hydrants through thick pipes to extinguish it. Those small square reservoirs next to the hydrants served another purpose: they stored drinking water for the horses pulling the phaeton carriages that frequently trotted through Calcutta's streets.

From that day onward, whenever I spotted a fire engine or two on the road, rushing by with bells clanging, I would stand by and watch intently. A courageous fireman always stood on the footboard, while his companions atop the truck, prepared pipes and ladders. Sometimes, one of them would catch sight of my curious little eyes, smile kindly, and wave to me. It always brought back memories of the enchanting water sources that fascinated me.

I haven't seen those hydrants for a long time now, Di-bhai—not in my previous neighbourhood, nor in the one I now call home.

Though I left my childhood behind long ago, some memories return to me again and again. On *Chaitra Sankranti*, I would rise at dawn and head to the Ganges ghats with Kaka and Kaki, travelling by tram carriage. Any trace of sleepiness would vanish the moment we arrived.

What a grand sight it was! Near the water's edge, towering men clad only in loincloths would be engrossed in their morning exercises. With great effort, they swung enormous dumbbells and grappled with one another, straining to throw each other to the ground—seizing each other's necks with fierce determination, though seemingly without any particular provocation. It was, I was told, their way of building strength and resilience.

I would often find myself torn—unsure whether to watch the wrestlers or the flower-sellers. The women sat with neat heaps of roses and marigolds piled around them, their bright blooms a feast for the eyes. Kaki would wade into the river, holding garlands of flowers and raw mangoes in her hands—her offerings to Mother Ganges. Emerging from the water, shivering in her wet clothes, she would suddenly disappear from sight, only to reappear minutes later, swiftly changed into dry clothes.

Much later, after my marriage, I too visited the sacred Ganges many times with my husband to offer Chaitra Sankranti prayers. On those mornings, our elder daughter, Titai, stayed at home, sleeping beside Kaki. When my Titai awoke to find the rose bouquets, we had brought back for her, she would jump with delight.

Those were the days of simple pleasures—when being happy was easy.

Di-bhai, you must remember how all the elders of the neighbourhood looked after us youngsters like conscientious guardians! One day, you and I took some money from Kaki and went to buy Lily biscuits from the shop around the corner. Oh, how we loved those biscuits! I wanted all the elephant- and horse-shaped ones, while you wanted the tiger- and bear-shaped ones. To settle our little dispute, the kind shopkeeper-uncle gave us a few extra biscuits of our choice to make peace.

And then, something astonishing happened. A man, balancing a large ladder on his shoulders, was running about, lighting up the gas lamps on the lampposts one by one. It was truly amazing! I had never once considered how the streets magically lit up after dark!

We stood there in awe until a harsh voice jolted us back to our sense. 'What are you two doing out so late? Why are you on the streets? Go home, freshen up and start studying!' It was Thakur Moshai—the tall, lanky priest who chanted difficult-to-pronounce Sanskrit mantras during Saraswati Puja. Of course, on Lakshmi Puja, he also praised the childish *alpona* designs I made on the floor of our house. He would exclaim, 'Mother Lakshmi will reside in this girl's home.'

Kaki would smile and touch his feet, wrapping her *anchal* around her neck. 'Bless us, Thakur Moshai,' she would say. 'It is the little one who has drawn this. However, she is very naughty too.'

Before us stood the same stately man with his fair complexion and a sharp aquiline nose, his voice brimming with a Brahmin's virtue as he acted as our guardian and ordered us to return home.

We immediately started running, our little legs moving as fast as they could. It was only when we reached home that we realized your packet of Lily biscuits had slipped from your grasp somewhere along the way.

I wiped away your tears with my palm and shared my elephant- and horse-shaped biscuits with you. Didn't I, Di-bhai?

But now, you no longer come to share your life with me. I miss chatting with you so much! Without you, my reminiscences of our childhood remain incomplete.

As we grew older and you returned to Barisal, I was admitted to Entally Hindu Balika Vidya Mandir—a slight improvement over Kailash Chandra Hindu Girls' High School. With Kaka absorbed in his office work, it was Kaki who took full responsibility for my studies. Even as she moved briskly about the house, completing her endless chores, she would pause to correct my mistakes as I sat reciting my multiplication tables. She taught me grammar and painstakingly worked on improving my poetry recitation. Even now, I can almost hear her voice, guiding me through the cadence and emotion of Kazi Nazrul Islam's 'Durgam Giri Kantar Moru'.

Di-bhai, our Kaki was truly a well-educated woman. In her school days, she had passed her *Britti* or scholarship examination with honours—an achievement she carried with quiet pride.

More often than not, I would sit studying just beyond the kitchen threshold, my books spread before me, while Kaki coached me through my lessons as she stirred pots and cooked in that cramped little kitchen. Thanks to her unflagging support and dedication, I completed my schooling at the Entally Hindu Balika Vidya Mandir with flying colours.

Seven

Di-bhai, last night I dreamt of our childhood and remembered a particular song. During the Second World War, though we were very young, perhaps we all had sung this one:

Sa re ga ma pa dha ni,
Bom phelechhe Japani
Bomer modhye keute saanp,
British bole baap-re-baap!

Do re mi fa so la ti,
The Japs are bombing a plenty,
Bombs are laden with cobras—why?
'Hail Mary!' the British cry!

Di-bhai, I still remember the tune!

While it is true that the Second World War began around 1939, Bengalis started to feel its impact only when the Japanese attacked and conquered Burma. In fact, the thought that the Japanese might invade and drive away the British perhaps brought joy to some of the Indians. Everyone also hoped that Netaji Subhas Chandra Bose, having successfully escaped from his house-arrest, would join the Japanese and bring about independence.

At the time, Netaji was a hero to many. He had served as President of the Indian National Congress for two consecutive terms. However, due to political differences with Gandhiji and his criticism of both the Congress's foreign and domestic policies, he was compelled to step down.

Subhas Chandra Bose firmly believed that Gandhiji's policy of non-violence alone would not be sufficient to secure India's independence. He openly advocated for armed rebellion as the only effective path towards freedom. With unwavering determination, he established the Forward Bloc, persistently demanding complete and immediate independence from British rule.

Despite being imprisoned by the British authorities on eleven occasions, his voice could not be silenced. His resounding call to his countrymen rang out across the nation: 'Give me blood, and I'll give you freedom.'

His ideals did not change even after the declaration of the Second World War. On the contrary, Subhas Chandra saw the war as an opportunity to exploit British weakness. At the onset of the war, he secretly left India and travelled to the Soviet Union, Germany and Japan, seeking assistance in attacking the British in India. With Japanese support, he established the Azaad Hind Fauj. The soldiers of this army were primarily Indian prisoners of war and workers from British Malaya, Singapore and other parts of Southeast Asia.

While some historians and politicians criticize Subhas Chandra for aligning with the Nazis and other war-mongering nations to fight the British, many others view his actions as a manifestation of realpolitik rather than ethical or idealistic principles. The latter still sympathize with his political ideology.

When, for a brief period, the Congress committee favoured Dominion status for India, Subhas Chandra Bose was the first to support the call for complete independence. Young leaders of the Congress and even Jawahar Lal Nehru aligned with him. Eventually, the Congress had to accept the idea of complete independence in its historic Lahore session.

The execution of Bhagat Singh—and the Congress leadership's inability to save him—left Subhas Chandra Bose deeply disillusioned and furious. In protest, he openly opposed the Gandhi-Irwin Pact. The British authorities retaliated by imprisoning him and later exiling him from India.

Defying the ban, Bose returned home, only to be arrested once again.

Indian leaders like Aurobindo Ghosh, Surya Sen and Bhagat Singh, and poets like Rabindranath Tagore and Kazi Nazrul Islam were inspired by the ideals of Netaji. In 1934, Subhas fell seriously ill while in captivity in Burma's Mandalay prison. The British government agreed to release him on the condition that he would leave for a foreign country without setting foot on Indian soil. Subhas Chandra decided to go to Europe and reached Vienna. During the two years he was under treatment, he wrote two books—his autobiography, *Indian Pilgrim*, and *India's Struggle for Freedom*.

Official reports claimed that he died in a plane crash on 18 August 1945 in Taiwan. Yet, to this day, doubts linger. Numerous accounts and pieces of evidence have emerged over the years, casting shadows over the so-called accident and raising unanswered questions about whether he truly perished that day.

On a rainy day in 1941, Rabindranath Tagore left this world. I was about eight years old then, but I still remember Kaki's reaction as if it were yesterday. The moment she heard the news, she broke down in tears. The whole neighbourhood seemed plunged into sorrow. An uncle, anxiously pacing his veranda, declared with sudden resolve, 'Even if I do not get a bus or a tram, I have my legs—I'm going to Jorasanko!'

His wife, equally insistent, decided she too would accompany him to the Nobel laureate's home.

In the midst of her sobbing, Kaki turned to them, her voice trembling,

'Please take me with you! Let me see him one last time.'

For the first time in my childhood, she left me alone at home, hurriedly setting out after thrusting my books into my hands. I watched from the doorway as she joined our neighbours—her sari dishevelled, her hair uncombed, and her eyes red and brimming with tears.

Di-bhai, I cannot put into words how much it pained me to see Kaki like that.

'We reached Dwarkanath Tagore Lane, but he was no longer there. Where could we find him? College Street? Muktaram Babu Street?' Kaki narrated once she had returned. 'All the offices and businesses had shut down. College students, shopkeepers, unemployed youth—each one of them yearned to catch a final glimpse of him. Upon reaching Chowringhee, we saw lawyers in black robes, office babus, the Chinese, the British, Madrasis—all wandering aimlessly through Dharmatala, Curzon Park and Corporation Street. It was hardly surprising; after all, he was everyone's beloved Rabi Thakur.

'We boarded a bus but even before we reached Harrison Road, it was packed with grieving people. You know, Apu, a young girl sat next to me, a newspaper spread on her lap. Tears streamed down her face, wetting the daily!

'When we finally reached Jorasanko, we learnt that the funeral procession had already departed. No one seemed to notice that dark clouds had started gathering in the sky. Then, in Central Avenue, we heard a commotion—'There he is! They're coming!'

'Apu, his body was covered in flowers. I could not touch him, but the procession passed close to me—I saw him one last time. Do you remember the song you used to sing, Apu? "Prano bhoriye trisha horiye, more aaro aaro daao praan"—Fill my heart, quench my thirst, grant me more and more of life.'

Kaki could not complete her words, Di-bhai. Her voice

quivered and her breathe grew heavy as fought back her tears.

I closed my eyes and began to sing—

Aaro aalo aaro aalo
Ei nayone, probhu, dhaalo.
Sure sure bnaashi pure
Tumi aaro aaro daao taan.

More radiant beams, O Lord, into these eyes do pour,
Filling the flute with notes, grace us with melodies, evermore.

Di-bhai, it was the first time I saw Kaki break down like that. She had always been a very strong lady!

In 1942, an Air Raid Precaution office was set up in our house. Rumours spread that Calcutta could be bombed. Trenches were dug deep into the ground. At the sound of the siren, everyone had to drop whatever they were doing and rush underground.

That year, Kaka sent me to Bikrampur in East Bengal. Our homecoming to our village proved to be a blessing in disguise, for the next year saw the start of the Great Bengal Famine.

At our ancestral house, I sat with the elders, listening to their stories. The men smoked tobacco and spoke about the terrible Famine of '76—the famine of 1770, which according to the Bengali calendar year was 1176.

The drought of 1769 had ruined both harvests that year, leading to mass starvation in Champaran, Bettia, Birbhum, Murshidabad and Orissa. It was only the beginning. Soon after, smallpox swept through Murshidabad, claiming countless lives. Back then, people died of smallpox as there was no cure available. Even royalty was not spared; Nawab Nazim Najabat Ali Khan and his brother also perished in its grip.

And yet, despite such calamity, the British East India Company increased taxes for their gain. The situation had become severe due to the combined impact of coercion, the forced cultivation of indigo and opium, and the seizure of farmers' lands—drastically reducing their ability to grow rice.

Why is it that foreign powers, time and again, have trampled upon the lives of our people—people of a land rich in rivers, rain, forests, and the warmth of good hearts? What was it they sought to conquer in a country already so complete in its grace?

Eight

During that period, Jatin Jyatha and Toy Dada came to Bikrampur for a few days. Di-bhai, do you remember the temple at the entrance to our village? Oh, how many times we went there in our childhood! Madanmohan, or Lord Krishna, our family deity, was worshipped there. The *bhog* was always prepared in our house. Every evening, children from both Hindu and Muslim families would gather to receive *prasad*—sugar candies distributed as 'Harir loot'.

Oh, how beautiful was the idol of Madanmohan! How magical was his smile! He wore a gold necklace, which had a pendant of a single, sparking blue stone. We never knew which of our ancestors had placed this ornament on the idol, but we knew it symbolized good fortune.

Though the temple has not survived over time, the blue stone pendant was somehow saved by Kaka and he gave it to Kaki during his last moments. Much later, Kaki passed it on to me. Do you know that stone is still kept in my almirah? Did I ever show it to you, Di-bhai? Perhaps I forgot! Forgive me! If we ever meet again, we will definitely look at it together.

It is said that humans should not wear jewellery from figurines of Gods, so the stone will never be used to decorate any ornament again. But maybe, by looking together through the beautiful, transparent ancient jewel, we will be able to see the echoes of our childhood.

Di-bhai, I can still see us running through the mango groves and along the furrows of the rice fields that entire year. Do you remember how we would sit side by side, listening wide-eyed to Toy-da's thrilling horror-tales? By then, you had become an expert swimmer, diving fearlessly into the village ponds. In those days, village children had no choice but to learn how to swim.

During the monsoon, when the ponds overflowed, Koi fish would sometimes wriggle right onto our porch! All one had to do was scoop them up with a gamchha.

On the other hand, I was a city-bred child and had no opportunity to learn swimming. It was only when I visited Bikrampur that our male elder cousins gave me swimming lessons. One of them would carry me on their shoulders to the riverside, while you followed on foot. After the lessons, we would return home, all red-eyed and wet.

Di-bhai, do you remember how Kaki would drag me into her room and scold me for staying in the water all morning? She would quickly change my clothes, dry my hair and try to make me look neat and tidy again. She considered me even more precious than her own blood and care for me so much. She hoped that before I returned to Calcutta, her 'city girl' would regain her fair complexion!

That year, a distant cousin of our father came to stay with us, and her daughter, Basona, soon became a close friend of mine. We were just six and seven years old. One quiet afternoon, while the women of the house rested in their siesta, Basona and I wandered down to the riverside and noticed a boat moored in front of a house.

In East Bengal, during the monsoons, it was customary for every household to keep a boat tied near the porch—often the only way to reach nearby places when the land lay submerged.

Impulsively, Basona and I climbed into the boat. I untied the rope and Basona propelled it forward using the oar. The boat sailed away, carrying us along with it. It was just after the monsoons and the paddy fields near the riverbanks were filled with stagnant water. As the boat rushed towards the water-logged fields, our courage quickly began to fade. We floated a little further and then the boat suddenly stopped; we only saw dense shrubs around us. We tried to get the boat moving again but could not. I was afraid and started crying. 'Take me to Kaki; I want to go to my Kaki,' I pleaded.

Basona too, losing confidence, started pouting and looked ready to cry. Just then, we heard a splashing sound in the distance. Peering through the rice plants, we spotted one of our relatives swimming towards us.

'Oh, Dada, save us! Please take us home! We're very hungry! We have done nothing wrong!' Thanks to God, our combined cries reached him through the stillness of the banks. Maran-da reached us and, somehow, with his robust and well exercised body, managed to drag the boat out of the dense growth of plants and allowed it to float back to solid ground. He then carried us—one on his back and the other on his shoulders—to our house.

'Oh, Maran, what would I have done if you were not there today?' Kaki cried out when she saw us. Seething with anger, she dealt me a few blows on my back, for the first time in my life. Basona stood there, scared to death, as her mother looked on with wide eyes.

Maran-da flexed his muscles and proudly said, 'Kakima, my grandma named me Maran because five brothers died in the birthing room before me. Then I was born and survived. Since that time, nothing has harmed me; no snakes bite me and I never drown. However, these two girls—I almost went deaf from their shrieking!'

Di-bhai, after receiving my first-ever thrashing from Kaki, I was furious. My pride had taken a beating in front of all our cousins. But what could I do? I stayed quiet.

Time passed, and early summer arrived, bringing with it the mango season. Di-bhai, I'm not sure if you recall the large mango tree on the porch of our ancestral house. Whenever mangoes fell, someone would surely hear it, and whoever reached first to pick them up got to eat them. One evening, a storm sent mangoes tumbling down in quick succession; even Kaki joined the others and ran to gather a few. But as luck would have it, a huge mango fell right on her head and she started bleeding.

Our neighbour, Dr Paresh, was summoned immediately. He bandaged her wound tightly and left after prescribing some medicines. Di-bhai, I felt deeply ashamed that day. Ever since Kaki had thrashed me in front of everyone, I had secretly wished that God would punish her in the same way. I thought I would feel happy then! Di-bhai, how could my tiny brain understand that God himself would climb the mango tree and, in the form of a mango, crack her head open! That night, I punished myself by skipping dinner.

'No, no, Kaki, I'm not feeling well. Please allow me skip my meal,' I said and lay down on the cane mat, resting my head on her lap. I felt something hard under my head. Though Kaki had suffered an injury, the mango that had struck never reached the ground. She had tied it securely in her anchal, saving it just for me. Though I did not eat dinner that night, I did devour the divine fruit and then fell asleep, snuggling close to my Kaki—who was nothing short of a mother to me. At that moment, I felt like the most treasured being in the world.

Di-bhai, even after all these years, I cannot comprehend whether a relationship which grows over nine long months between a mother and her child, culminates into a final episode of severe agony of birthing, surely is the only basis of a lifetime bonding!

Or is it, in fact, the unwavering passion, the deep sense of belonging and the boundless affection that bears more significance—even when there is no profound connection of blood.

In our maternal house, there was a tradition of music being taught to the children along with their school curriculum. Every day, two teachers would arrive—one to help the children with their studies and the other to teach music. Mejdi, our elder sister—second in order after Bordi—was the best singer. Even you sang quite well, Di-bhai.

We inherited our mother's melodious genes. Do you remember, Di-bhai, how you and I would sit in the Puja room in the evenings, listening to our dear Mother sing a devotional song?

Premer purnimar chand, phire aay phire aay
Andhokarer Nadiay
Sedin jemoni Nadiar kole khelechile brojo khela
Ke sudhalo haye kandiya janoni, gothe jete holo bela?
Sajaye de ma, gothe jete holo bela, rakhaliya saaje sajaye de ma
E kulete kande Shochi 'Nimai, Nimai re'
O kul kandiye kahe nai, nai, nai re
Phire aaye, phire aaye, Nadiyar chand ore, phire aay
Nimai amar, phire aaye, andhokarer Nadiay.

Return, O full moon of love,
To the dark Nadia.
There were days when you played around in Braja—a delightful sight!
You remembered too, you had to tend your beloved cows.
Your young voice called out to me, and you would say:

'Dress me as a shepherd, Mother, I must go to my herds now!'
Time passes on, and Sachi misses you still.
Here she weeps, 'O Nimai, my dearest, come back home, it is dark.'
From the other shore, the echo sighs, 'He is gone, never to return…oh hark.'
Return, return, O Nadia's brilliant moon, to end our sorrowful plight.
My Nimai, come back to Nadia's dark and endless night.

I didn't quite understand who this shepherd-king was, but I used to be cross with him. Why would he abandon his poor mother and make her cry so? Meanwhile you would silently point towards our Ma. Tears streamed down her cheeks as she continued singing—

Keshav karo koruna dine, kunjo kanonchari
Madhav manomohan, mohan muralidhari.

O Keshav, bestow thy grace on the poor, O Lord of the gardens and greens,
Madhav, you enchant all of us, play your flute through life's thick and thin.

I still faintly remember those songs, but you seem to have forgotten all about them, Di-bhai. You don't even come to visit me anymore. I can no longer sing them with you.

Titai has picked up a few of those melodies from me and sings them in her sweet voice. But in my mind, I still see it all—a dimly-lit Puja room, the brass lamp flickering, the Krishna idol posing beautifully, and the rapt face of a beautiful woman lost in her prayers. As endless tears flow from her closed eyes, I watch her, mesmerized by her devotion.

Nine

The next year, when I returned to Calcutta from Bikrampur, I once again enrolled in a school after clearing their admission test. I received a double promotion that year, which allowed me to skip a class to be promoted to the upper standard. It felt good to be studying in Calcutta once more. I also performed well in my examinations!

I must tell you about an incident from that period, Di-bhai.

I was about twelve when Tota Dada came to Calcutta for a few days to make inquiries about his college classes. Kaka and Kaki would not hear of him staying anywhere else. In those days, there was no hesitation or awkwardness about visiting relatives and staying with them for a while—nor would they let them leave too soon.

Though I was much younger than Tota Dada, back then cousins were each other's closest friends.

You may remember, Di-bhai, Kaka, Kaki and I used to live on Shambhu Babu Lane near Entally. That house had a large terrace—my favourite place in the whole world.

Calcutta was still reeling from the horrors of the famine. Amal Home, the publisher of the *Calcutta Municipal Gazette*, had just then printed an insightful article on food grain distribution, methods for improving crop yields, careful rationing, fair price distribution, and even the importance of a balanced diet and eating without waste.

While discussing all this with Tota Dada, our conversation would inevitably veer towards delicious treats, much to Kaki's amusement. She would laugh heartily at us.

Tota Dada loved reading newspapers and would keep us informed about events unfolding across the country and the world.

It was 15 August, and the sky was overcast. Durga Puja was about a month away, and my spirits were high.

Tota Dada planned to go to College Street to buy some books and then meet his bosom friend Bipin at his Upper Circular Road residence. Bipin Dada, who lived with his elder brother, had a knack for magic. He performed tricks with matchsticks and coins, making them vanish and reappear under a handkerchief at his will! I was a great fan of his. That day I clung to Tota Dada, pleading with him to take me along. Though unwilling, he could not refuse his younger cousin.

Once outside, we noticed an unusual silence in the streets. Further ahead, some people had stacked broken furniture and other discarded things at the crossing. Tota Dada held my hand as we passed that stretch, muttering something under his breath. No rickshaws were available near our lane. To hell with it! We decided to walk down to Moulali, chatting all the way.

After a long wait, only one bus came by. We boarded and found it almost empty. Two men seated at the back were engaged in a low, hurried conversation. We caught the phrase 'direct action' mentioned more than once. They spoke mostly in Bengali, occasionally slipping into Hindi.

Whatever it was about, our plans for College Street had to be cancelled—Tota Dada had forgotten to bring his list of books.

For some reason, all the schools were closed that day. Many shops, too, had their shutters down as we passed through Sealdah and neared Rajabazar. Still, we faced no great difficulty reaching Upper Circular Road.

Before going into Bipin Dada's house, I tugged at Tota Dada's arm, begging for some sweets. He walked towards a small shop nearby, but as we approached, we saw the shopkeeper hastily pulling down the shutters.

Quick on his feet, Tota Dada managed to scoop out a few sweets from a glass jar and dropped some coins on the counter.

'Why are you closing the shop at eleven in the morning? Planning to snore away the rest of the day?' he joked.

The shopkeeper shot him a nervous glance and snapped,

'People are saying something bad is going to happen today. Am I supposed to risk my life just to sell you candies?'

Without waiting for a reply, he continued yanking the shutters down and vanished inside.

Tota Dada and I looked at each other but decided to focus on our handful of sweets as we walked away.

On reaching Bipin Dada's house, we learnt that his elder brother was in Noakhali, overseeing repairs to their country house. His Boudi made omelettes for us, while I enjoyed a few magic tricks performed by Bipin Dada. The two friends chatted, and soon it was time to leave.

'I will see you out, Tota! I'll come along with you,' said Bipin Dada as he put on his slippers, ready to escort us out.

By then, it was one o'clock; we were expected back home for lunch. However, just as we reached the ground floor, three shabbily dressed men approached us, speaking all at once and gesticulating frantically. On being asked to speak one at a time, one of them said, 'Do not go out sir! There are men moving around Rajabazar, wielding long knives. The girl is young, please stay indoors.'

Hearing this, we froze, uncertain of what to do next. As we stood there, looking somewhat puzzled, a group of men rushed past, shouting the word 'Esplanade' over and over again.

Anxiety gripped us at the thought of Kaki's impending scolding as we retreated into the safety of Bipinda's house. Boudi served me lunch and later took me to her room for a siesta. By evening, we were trying to figure out a way to return home. Meanwhile, Kaka arrived in his friend's car. We got ready in no time and left the house with him. On the way, we saw small groups of people gathered in some places, while most areas appeared desolate. After covering some distance, the car screeched to a halt. The driver swiftly turned the steering wheel to swerve into a side lane and sped ahead. 'The ruffians have poured liquid tar on the road, sir!' the driver exclaimed.

Di-bhai, I was too scared to ask what was happening in the city or why. The moment we reached home, Kaki dragged me right inside the house, muttering something under her breath.

'People have died in Rajabazar, Borda. Stay alert tonight,' Lattu Mama, our neighbour, warned Kaka before vanishing.

As I listened to the elders talk that night, I began to understand that something terrible was unfolding around us. Though the windows were shut, I peered through the slits to see some people setting fire to the stacked furniture we had spotted in the morning. People gathered around the now ablaze heap shouted, 'We'll fight to the last breath to snatch away Hindustan; yes, we'll fight and snatch Hindustan!'

The next morning, everyone stayed indoors as Kaka had issued strict orders to that effect. The elders of the neighbourhood gathered in our front courtyard, but the main door remained firmly shut. I heard someone say, 'The Kamalalaya stores has been looted. Be careful, everyone. If they come to deal one blow, we will retaliate with two. We will not be subdued.'

Shambhu-da, Goran-da, Piplu Kaka and other young men listened intently.

Di-bhai, there was a large pile of bricks neatly stacked in a corner on our terrace. It appeared that the washermen from the enclave behind our house had also, surprisingly, joined in. They carried bricks on their heads and marched up to the roof for some reason.

Throughout the day, a sense of desolation lingered around us. After a quick meal of *khichuri*, I went to sleep, Kaki lying beside me. Just as I thought Tota Dada and Kaka had also retired for the night, I heard a commotion outside. It appeared that people were rushing to the terrace.

Kaki's sleep was legendary. She never napped during the day, but once all the household chores were done, she would sleep deeply—and snore just as loud! Taking full advantage, I quietly slipped out from under the mosquito net and tiptoed upstairs to the terrace.

Though it was late at night, a strange light flickered in the distance, making it seem as though dawn had already broken. As my eyes adjusted to the glow, I realized with a jolt—it was not the sun.

It was fire!

Yes—small fires were burning at scattered intervals, each one like a glowing wound on the night. Barely a furlong away, I saw a mob dragging people out of their homes. The air was thick with wails and screams. Somewhere nearby, a woman cried out in agony, and by then, even the slum behind our house had caught fire. Shadows chased other shadows—figures running, pursuing, stumbling and falling down.

Suddenly, I heard a child—a small, terrified child—shriek with a sound that tore through the night!

Dear God, what was happening around us?

On a terrace just two houses away, I saw something I will never forget. A bearded man snatched a baby girl from her mother's arms—and with one swift, horrifying motion, hurled her into the flames below.

Di-bhai, I could not remain silent. A scream burst from my throat—raw, uncontrollable.

That was the moment Kaka turned and saw me—standing there, frozen, witnessing everything with wide-eyed horror. It was the first time in my life he struck me. The blow was sudden and fierce. I fell to the ground from the force of it.

'What are you doing here, Apu? What do you think you're doing?'

The slap caused more anguish to my sentiments than my face. Me! How could he hit me, the jewel of his eyes! But obviously, for him, that was not the time to pacify or pamper anyone. He grabbed me by my arms and dragged me downstairs.

By then, more young men from the neighbourhood had gathered on the terrace. Hands moved quickly, relaying bricks, which were hurled down with force, targeting specific individuals. From the other side, fierce cries rang out, '*Nara-e-Takbir…Allahu Akbar!* Call to Takbir…God is great!'

'Why on earth did you let her out of the room? If Apu steps out again, I will never see your face, Nibharani!' Kaka warned sternly, his admonishment waking Kaki up.

Then, he did something strange. The brave soldier of the 49th Regiment knelt down on the ground, took my trembling little feet in his hands after I sat down on the bed and he said, 'I lost my mother at an early age, and then my Dada, too! Can't you see? You've become my dearest and most precious possession now. If anything happens to you, how will I face my Dada in heaven, Apu?'

Speechless, I could only shake my head slowly and whisper, 'I'll do everything as you say, Kaka. I know there are demons outside.'

Without another word, Kaka rushed out. I heard the door being bolted shut from outside.

Kaki was also trembling with fear. 'Do not go to the toilet tonight, Apu. Stay here, beside me. If needed, I'll make some arrangements,' she whispered.

Ten

It was the month of Ramzan. In the days leading up to Eid, many of our Muslim classmates at school—including Shakila and Afrin—observed a month-long fast, known as Roza. From dawn to dusk, they refrained from eating and drinking, following their faith with quiet discipline.

They told me they had their only meal for the day just before dawn, sitting with their families in the early morning darkness. After that, not even a sip of water would pass their lips until sunset. They offered Namaz five times a day, each time performing *wuju*—the ritual washing—before their prayers.

Watching Afrin struggle through the long, hot afternoons, I once said to her with all the frankness of childhood, 'Why does your God punish you like this, Afru? Will your suffering make Him happy? What kind of ritual is this? You'd better sneak a little food from my tiffin—just do not let anyone see!'

Di-bhai, I still remember the petrified look in her beautiful eyes. She immediately covered her face with her scarf, shook her head violently and held her ears. She whispered in my ears, 'Sister, do not even mention this to anyone else! If my father hears this, he will either kill me or get me married.' Then she ran off.

After that year, Afrin did not come back to school. Was she really married off? How would I ever know, Di-bhai? She never took me to her home. I could never find out what happened to her.

Even at this old age, I still remember how Afrin would bring thick, delicious *sewai payesh* in her tiffin, garnished with cashew and raisins. One day, in secret, she let me have two spoonfuls and said, 'If Allah wills it, I'll get more for you next time.' But I didn't know then that her Allah would never let her meet me again. I missed her terribly, especially while solving arithmetic problems in class. The poor girl found the concepts of multiplication tables and equations difficult, but with me beside her, she found them a little easier.

The political turmoil continued. The demons came the next day too but left after shouting a few slogans. Below, on the streets, a British officer and two watchmen patrolled with an armoured tank. Kaka and the others repeatedly requested them for something. The officers patrolled the area about four times, but that was only till the evening. The nights were far more dreadful. The fires raged continuously until the 17th; we heard chants of 'Jai Hind' and 'Vande Mataram'. It was still the holy month of Ramzan, yet we saw bearded men in lungis, long swords in their hands, running down the road. I never understood who their targets were.

On the 18th of August, a relief vehicle finally arrived in our neighbourhood carrying provisions like rice, pulses, milk powder and oil. People crowded around it, collecting whatever little they could. Clutching the supplies in the folds of their clothes as if they were precious as gold, they hurried back to the safety of their homes. The women and girls from the washermen's slum were packed into buses and sent to Ballygunge in south Calcutta. Apparently, the Hindus were safer there.

Eleven

We received the daily edition of *The Statesman* four days after the riots had ceased. As he read through the report, Tota-dada cried out, 'Nearly 500 Oriya labourers have been killed in Metiaburz—their throats slashed. Corpses are piled up in Rajabazar. Pyres are burning in several parts of the city. Bloated bodies have been spotted floating in the Ganges.'

Kaki shot a quick sidelong glance at me before saying, 'Dear Apu, go and study in your room.'

But I did not budge.

Kaka clenched his jaws, finished his steaming tea in one gulp, got up and left the room without saying a word. I could sense an atmosphere of hatred had been manufactured between Hindus and Muslims.

Di-bhai, I read the entire article titled 'The Great Calcutta Killing' pausing often to absorb the chilling weight of the scenes described in the report. In the published photographs, I saw men—who looked more like butchers than anything else—brandishing daggers and posing beside mutilated corpses with their innards spilling out grotesquely.

Trucks loaded with turbaned Sikh men from South Calcutta were reportedly stationed in Rajabazar, guarding the area to protect Hindu lives, even as another group hurled stones at them from across the road.

The headlines screamed in bold letters: FIGHTS IN FRONT OF PURABI CINEMA BETWEEN MIRZAPUR AND HARRISON ROADS, CLASHES AT HINDU HOSTEL.

Di-bhai, history records that in the 1940s, two major political parties dominated India—the Muslim League and the Indian National Congress. In 1946, the British Cabinet Mission plan proposed handing over governance of British India to Indian leaders. A subsequent proposal suggested creating two separate dominions—a Hindu-majority India and a Muslim-majority Pakistan. The Congress outright rejected this idea. In response, the Muslim League called for a hartal on 16 August 1946, demanding a separate Muslim nation.

This led to the horrific communal violence in Calcutta. In just 72 hours, over 4,000 lives were lost, and more than a lakh were rendered homeless. On 16 August, thousands had gathered at the base of the Ochterlony Monument (now Shaheed Minar) at the behest of the Muslim League, led by Mr Suhrawardy. Many among them may not have even known that a separate Muslim nation was being demanded; they had simply gone there out of curiosity. However, as rumours spread that Hindu-owned shops would be forcibly shut down that morning, minor skirmishes erupted across the city. Then, a chilling slogan rang out, 'Kill the Kafirs!'

Who could have imagined that everyday squabbles among common folk—milkmen, rickshaw pullers, washermen—would escalate into full-fledged riots! In the newspapers, they called it 'the week of long knives', claiming at least 10,000 people had been killed, and many more maimed, in just those few days.

Di-bhai, during this time, I learnt that Mr Suhrawardy came from a distinguished family in Midnapore. His father, Sir Zahid Suhrawardy, was a respected judge of the Calcutta High Court. After completing his Bachelor of Science with Honours from St Xavier's College, Calcutta, he pursued further studies at St Catherine's College, Oxford, where he earned a Bachelor of Civil Law degree. He was subsequently called to the Bar at

Gray's Inn in London in 1918 and began his legal practice upon returning to India.

He initially joined the Swaraj Party, led by Chittaranjan Das, which functioned within the Indian National Congress. In 1924, he was elected Deputy Mayor of the Calcutta Corporation. After the death of C.R. Das, Suhrawardy gradually distanced himself from the Swaraj Party and, by 1936, aligned himself with the Bengal Provincial Muslim League, which was gaining momentum at the time.

In 1946, as Chief Minister of Bengal, Suhrawardy emerged as a strong supporter of the Pakistan movement. Muhammad Ali Jinnah opposed the Cabinet Mission Plan and declared 16 August 1946 as Direct Action Day. The Suhrawardy-led government in Bengal declared a public holiday on that day, enabling his supporters to join the protest. In the aftermath, Suhrawardy repeatedly blamed the negligence of the British authorities for the horrific communal violence that followed.

Kaka often spoke of how tense the city had been in those days. Trains did not run until the 20th of August. The slums of Nakashipara and Sahibganj had been reduced to ashes. The Tala and Belgachia bridges were barricaded—Hindus had blocked them to stop Muslims from crossing over. On Vivekananda Road, nearly fifty Bihari rickshaw-pullers were hacked to pieces. Those poor men, who had come from Bihar and Orissa hoping to earn a living through odd jobs, had not been spared. In retaliation, thirty Muslims were killed near a temple on Central Avenue. The police opened fire on Harrison Road and used tear gas in Bowbazar. The whole city, it seemed, had turned against itself.

Tota-dada, ever meticulous with the newspaper, would often remark how Hindus were pouncing on any lone *mullah* they came across. Once the horrific news spread—that children were being thrown into fires—no lane or alley from Sealdah to Shyambazar remained untouched by violence. On the 21st of August, the Bengal Government was dismissed, and the Viceroy's rule was imposed. To contain the looting and killings, the British Raj issued a shoot-at-sight order.

People stayed indoors for safety. Street after street, neighbourhoods began to be cleared. We heard that in Beleghata, Chitpur, Maniktala, Benepukur, and other sensitive areas, soldiers patrolled through the nights—for a month.

Twelve

Though Tota Dada managed to return home after about fifteen days, his friend Bijonda's elder brother, Sujanda, could not make it back to Calcutta from Noakhali. Months passed. When he finally returned, nearly four months later, one of his hands was gone. Hidden beneath the sleeve of his panjabi, there was nothing. The violence that had begun in Calcutta had not ended there. It had crossed the Padma. What Sujanda brought back in silence told us everything.

A few days later, Kaka and Kakima went to see him. I went along. He spoke in a low voice, in that familiar 'opar Bangla' accent, and what he told us left the three of us numb. We sat frozen as he described the fire that had swept through East Bengal.

Bijonda's elder brother recounted the horrors of those days. 'It was 29 August 1946—Eid-ul-Fitr—the holiest festival for Muslims. That very day, a rumour was deliberately spread that Hindus and Sikhs in Noakhali were stockpiling weapons. The next morning, a clash broke out between some Hindu fishermen and Muslims in the Feni River. That was all it took. People began to grow anxious. And slowly, the quiet fabric of trust among neighbours began to fray.

'Soon, in the villages of Chattogram and Noakhali, agitated Muslims began composing rhymes, ballads, and plays—spreading hatred against Hindus. Bamboo theatres echoed with jeers. In markets and *haats*, venomous rumours ran unchecked. Mosques broadcasted racially charged sermons and verses. Pamphlets, leaflets, and street plays calling for boycott and retaliation were circulated widely. Even in gatherings and meetings, hatred was whipped up in the name of religion and revenge.

'Noakhali is a land of countless rivers and canals. In the remote areas, Muslim boatmen stopped ferrying Hindu passengers across. Bridges made of bamboo were broken, roads dug up—all part of a planned strategy to isolate the Hindu population.

'Then came Kojagari Lakshmi Puja. It was 10 October 1946. Hindu families in Noakhali were busy with preparations for the puja at home. At the same time, leaders and workers of the Muslim League began spreading a rumour that a group of Sikhs had attacked Diara Sharif—a sacred shrine for Muslims. Fueled by this claim, Muslim villagers from surrounding areas assembled at the shrine in anger.

'One leader, Kasem, marched into Sahapur Market with a group of armed men. That was the beginning. What followed was no ordinary riot. It was a planned onslaught.'

'In Raipur, the Muslim mob stormed through temples, smashed idols of deities, and left shrines in ruins. Hindu homes and shops were looted. After that, the mob marched to the local police station. The officer-in-charge, himself a Muslim, refused to listen to the desperate complaints of Hindu men. He drove them away from the premises.

The moment they stepped out, the crowd waiting outside set upon them. They were beaten and dragged to the nearby mosque. There, many were forced to convert to Islam—and to prove their conversion, they were made to eat beef.

Bijonda's brother also said that in some places, those forcibly converted were made to sign papers declaring that they had embraced Islam of their own free will.'

At that time, Hindus had to pay tax to the Muslim League, called Jizya, to ensure their survival. Di-bhai, during the medieval era of Islamic rule too, the Hindus of India had to pay Jizya to

Muslim rulers for their security. To date, I have not forgotten the terror in Sujon-da's eyes as he continued narrating his experience.

'On 11 October, Gholam Sarwar Husseini's Miyar Fauz attacked the home of Rajendra Lal Roychowdhury, the district head of the Hindu Mahasabha and president of the Noakhali Bar Association. At the time, Swami Tryambakananda of Bharat Sevashram Sangha was staying there. Rajendra Lal defended his house all day, firing his rifle from the terrace. As night fell and the rioters left, Rajendra Lal arranged for Swami Tryambakananda and some of his family to escape to safety. Alas, he was unaware of the fate awaiting him.' He stopped for a moment and gulped down a glass of water in one go.

'The next day, the Muslim rioters attacked Rajendralal's house again—this time setting it ablaze,' Sujon-da continued, his voice shaking. 'They killed Rajendralal, his two brothers, and about twenty or twenty-two other members of the family. But even that was not the end of it. They beheaded Rajendralal and, as I heard, sent his severed head on a platter to Gholam Sarwar Husseini.'

His eyes filled with terror once more Sujon-da added, 'And... they carried away Rajendralal's two daughters from the house.'

The man paused, falling silent as the weight of his words hung in the air.

'Our house—a small one—is in Raipur, Noakhali,' he began, his voice ragged, each word dragged from somewhere deep inside. 'I was desperately trying to leave behind the half-finished ongoing repairs and find a way to escape with my life.

Then, one night, they came. A mob descended on our area and dragged some of us Hindus out of our homes. Amidst the shouting and blows, I felt a sudden, searing pain—followed by a strange numbness spreading through my left side.'

He paused, struggling for breath.

'The man who struck me... I knew him. I'd seen him

countless times at the Raipur market. Whenever we spoke, he would smile—casual, almost friendly. But that night, with a long knife in his hand, the same man cut off my left arm.'

A shudder ran through him.

'He left me there, bleeding and half-dead, and moved on to claim more victims. I collapsed into a roadside ditch, unconscious...perhaps it was God's will that I survived the night.

'The next morning, with whatever strength I had left, I tore my shirt and tied it around the stump of my arm. I cannot describe how I dragged myself—crawling, stumbling—until I finally reached the relief camp.'

His eyes bulged, wide with the memory of terror. A vein throbbed violently at his temple, ready to burst. In a hoarse, broken whisper, he said,

'Kaka...somehow, I've made it back alive...but my severed limb...it still lies there...abandoned in that ditch.'

I was shocked to my bones, hearing this tale of carnage. How could—neighbours, friends—injure and kill each other so mercilessly, Di-bhai? I would not have believed such cruelty had I not seen and heard Sujon-da myself.

While Hindus were looted and burned alive, they in turn retaliated by setting fire to the paddy stock of Muslim farmers. Hindu women were forced to break their bangles and remove their sindoor, while men were forced to recite the *Kalma* for conversion to Islam. However, even in that situation, some Muslims laid down their lives trying to protect their Hindu neighbours.

The Noakhali riots raged for four long weeks. The unfortunate who survived were given shelter at temporary relief camps in Comilla, Chandpur, Agartala and other places. Having lost their self-confidence, these people could never go back to their previous homes in East Bengal or live normal lives.

Di-bhai, Mahatma Gandhi arrived in Noakhali and made

earnest efforts to restore communal harmony by visiting the town and its surrounding villages. He undertook an exceptional and deeply personal mission—walking from village to village, trying to rebuild trust and peace in the riot-affected areas.

Along with his volunteers, he surveyed places that had witnessed unspeakable violence and mass killings. Despite his tireless dedication and moral appeal, his efforts to restore lasting peace remained, for the most part, unsuccessful.

The presence of Gandhiji irked the Muslims, and their frustration grew over time. By the end of February 1947, the behaviour of some members of the community became increasingly vulgar. Sludge and rubbish were stacked on the roads wherever Gandhiji visited. The miscreants started boycotting his meetings. Agreeing to the requests of the leaders of the Bengal Muslim League, Gandhiji left for Bihar at the beginning of March, leaving his 'mission' in Noakhali incomplete.

Trust was broken; faith was shattered. A mass exodus took place. Majority of the surviving Hindus left their homes forever, migrating to West Bengal, Tripura and Assam.

Thirteen

The British Raj had finally realized that its hold over India was coming to an end. It was time to pack up and leave. After the violence of the 1946 riots subsided, Prime Minister Clement Attlee made a formal announcement:

'The British will leave India certainly by June 1948, but in the coming months, the Congress and the Muslim League must resolve their differences and decide how they will share power.'

He further declared that Admiral Lord Mountbatten would serve as the twentieth—and the last—Viceroy of India.

Di-bhai, between March and April 1947, Lord Mountbatten held several meetings with both Gandhiji and Jinnah. Yet Mohammad Ali Jinnah remained unyielding in his commitment to the Two-Nation Theory. By then, he was visibly eager for the prospect of leading a newly created country.

Since the rise of the Muslim League, Gandhiji had made sincere efforts to prevent the partition of India along religious lines—even offering Jinnah the post of Prime Minister in a united India. But most Congress leaders stood firmly against this. Jawaharlal Nehru and Vallabhbhai Patel, though keen on achieving independence, were perhaps also driven by political ambition. Faced with mounting tensions, they preferred to divide the country rather than hand over power to Jinnah.

Gandhiji, meanwhile, found himself increasingly isolated within the Congress, especially after the horrors of the Calcutta and Noakhali riots. As early as 1940, during a Congress committee meeting, Bapu had expressed his anguish over the looming prospect of Partition. With deep sorrow, he had asked:

'Has Islam taught only divisiveness to Muslims? In a land where Hindus and Muslims have grown up together, living in neighbouring houses, can they truly find happiness after being uprooted from their homeland? I ask my Muslim brothers—if India is not your motherland, then where will you be at peace?'

C. Rajagopalachari, popularly known as Rajaji, a Congressman had immediately replied, 'I too do not believe in Pakistan. But if the Muslims are not satisfied with anything else, why hesitate to let them go? Will we never ask for our own independence?'

Cornered and deeply disheartened, Gandhiji finally said at a meeting: 'I had once said that if there is any attempt to divide India, those close to me should know—they would not just be dividing the country, but my very body. But today, it seems those whom I considered my own, no longer consider me theirs. In any case, it is perhaps no longer in my hands to block the path to independence by imposing my will.

'Just as, when a joint family is divided, the brothers do not become enemies, I would expect the same spirit to prevail in a divided India. Hindus and Muslims must continue to treat each other with kindness—both in Bengal and in Punjab. Our first priority must be to drive the British out. Gaining independence should make us stronger—not weaker.'

A British lawyer named Sir Cyril Radcliffe—who had never set foot in India before—was hastily commissioned in mid-June 1947 to chair the two boundary commissions and redraw the map of South Asia. The British declared 15th August 1947 as the final deadline for India's independence—barely two months away.

With red ink on paper, Sir Radcliffe began slicing through centuries of shared history. He drew lines without knowing—or perhaps without caring—where the boundary would be, or what it would sever. His pen did not care for rivers, nor for rice fields, schools, colleges, temples, or mosques.

The barbed line slashed across courtyards, splitting homes in two and placing their halves in different countries. The local pond—where Shyam and Shafiqul had once learnt to swim together—was cut straight through the middle. Yet no ink or border could stop the Shefali tree in Arati's courtyard from shedding its delicate white flowers across Amina's porch next door.

Yet Di-bhai, could a barbed fence stop the wind blowing from the Padma in East Pakistan towards Hasnabad in India? Could it stop memories from crossing?

The poor Muslims, burdened with fear and heartbreak, packed their meagre belongings and left India—casting long, sorrowful glances at their Hindu neighbours, brothers they had laughed and lived with for generations. How heavy their hearts must have been, Di-bhai, as they walked towards an unknown future in an unfamiliar land!

And the Hindus—our forefathers among them—who had toiled for years to harvest golden crops on land they believed was theirs by birthright, found themselves foreigners in their own homes overnight. Teachers, doctors, small businessmen—those who had studied and worked hard to build lives in their homeland—became refugees, pushed to and forced to exist thereafter in a strange place where they have never been.

Wherever they arrived, they carried not just their belongings but also the heavy burden of enforced displacement. They endured years of insult and humiliation from local residents—mocked for their accents, their food habits, their clothes, and their grief that no one could see.

Kaka remained unwavering in his faith in the Congress party. It was only Thakurda who dared speak out against him.

'What did the Congress achieve by dividing the country like this, Himangshu? Why are you still supporting this party? I've been telling you for so long, that the smart and daring Subhas Bose not only had brains but also the courage to go around the world asking for help from foreigners. What has that old Gujarati gentleman got us by fasting at the drop of a hat? It's only women who fast when they sulk! I am telling you, Gandhi's fasting has had no effect and will never have any on those red-faced monkeys (the British) or these Muslims,' the old man would say, coughing a little.

Observing this schism in the house, Kaki would quickly get Thakurda a glass of water, while Kaka retorted, 'Baba, you exaggerate. Netaji didn't even tell us where he went. And when these white rogues want to leave the country, shall we keep quiet and do nothing? It is going to be difficult, but at least the country is ours finally, eh?'

Di-bhai, Kaka's colleague from the Commercial Museum, Prafulla Kaka, had similar beliefs. On one side, the Bengalis wanted the Hindu-majority area of Khulna to stay within India, but they were also unwilling to give away Murshidabad with its heritage, old palaces and mango groves. When Congress leaders pushed Khulna into East Pakistan to maintain control over the Hooghly's waters, Kaki wept profusely for days. Some of her maternal relatives lived in Khulna and she feared she would never meet them ever again.

On 14 August, Prafulla Kaka stayed back at our house and we kept the radio on throughout the night. At midnight, Nehru's optimistic speech was broadcast. His resonated with a tone of joyful confidence: 'At the dawn of history India started on her unending quest, and trackless centuries are filled with her striving and the grandeur of her success and her failures. Through good and ill fortune alike she has never lost sight of that quest or forgotten the ideals which gave her strength. We end today a period of ill fortune and India discovers herself again.'

Di-bhai, on the morning of 15 August 1947, the Indian tricolour was hoisted atop the Red Fort in Delhi to celebrate the auspicious and glorious day of the country's independence. Throughout the day, Prafulla Kaka, along with a group of young lads, was in high spirits; they left our house on a truck and decorated various spot and roads of Calcutta with flowers and flags. But Kaka, dampened by the sight of his heartbroken old father and sorrowful wife, did not join them.

Later in the afternoon, Prafulla Kaka returned to our home, wiping his sweat with a handkerchief. He embraced our Kaka and said, 'My dear Himu, what an amazing thing has happened today! I'm now a citizen of a free country. From today, the British won't be able to kick us on any pretext. It is a day to celebrate!'

Though Kaka willingly embraced his friend, he cast a quick glance at our grandfather.

'Prafulla, you know, one of my acquaintances is a schoolmaster who lives in Satkhira, now in East Pakistan. Earlier, the children of our household used to take lessons from him. I have heard that he was probably fleeing Satkhira by train with whatever belongings he could carry. But by then the mullahs of Pakistan had already taken over his house and slaughtered his cattle! And here you are, celebrating to the fullest. What are you exactly celebrating, Prafulla?'

Grandfather's words, though harsh and bitter, were absolutely true, Di-bhai.

The argument between the elders was unsettling for me. Still, I loved Kaka a lot. Perhaps more than I loved Kaki. So, I accompanied Kaka to Beleghata that evening; Gandhiji was fasting there. Di-bhai, I did not understand the lack of enthusiasm in Gandhiji's eyes or the tone of his speech, until much later.

As per the declaration of the British government, on the 15 August 1947, India gained independence, and the new state of

Pakistan was born. However, 14 August 1947 was the 27th day of the auspicious month of Ramzan. Therefore, from the next year, Pakistan would celebrate its formation day on the 14th. Di-bhai, does Pakistan use the term 'Independence Day'? Was Pakistan ever ruled by the British Empire? Didn't India's independence lead to the creation of Pakistan?

In any case, Bapu began an indefinite hunger strike on 1 September 1947. This time, his fast had the desired effect. By 4 September, both Hindus and Muslims laid down their weapons.

Mr Jinnah had finally realized his long-cherished dream—ascending to the throne of power. Now that Pakistan was born, he no longer concerned himself with the opinions of Muslim League members. He would not listen to anyone—not friends, not colleagues. In his radio broadcasts, he began speaking of unity—preaching that Sikhs, Hindus, and Muslims were brothers. The staunch pre-Partition devotee of Allah was no longer the enemy of Hindus. His pride in Pakistan knew no bounds.

Yet, behind the speeches and the grand vision, another truth lay buried.

It is said that despite Jinnah's best efforts to keep his illness a closely guarded secret, a Hindu doctor had already diagnosed him—not with throat cancer, as rumoured—but with advanced tuberculosis. Jinnah, desperate to hide this truth, struggled to make his way from Quetta to Karachi in search of better medical care. By then, he was already moribund. Years of secrecy, denial, and his relentless pursuit of power had taken their toll. Medicines, when finally administered, were far too late to be of help.

Within a year—yes, Di-bhai, barely a year after the birth of Pakistan—Jinnah's hold over his beloved seat of power came to an end.

He passed away.

Fourteen

A week after Independence, a man arrived at our doorstep. He had come from our father's ancestral village—now part of East Pakistan, and was thus allowed in. Dressed in tattered clothes, as he walked in without a word, he sank to the floor. For what felt like an eternity, he sat there motionless, his hands clutching his head as though trying to hold himself together.

Then, almost in a daze, he began muttering to no one in particular, 'I do not know what to say...what not to say... I have not stopped running since I left Dinajpur...'

Lifting his eyes towards Grandfather, he finally spoke with more coherence, his voice cracked and hollow, 'We had almost become used to the midnight cries of "Allah-hu-Akbar"...every night, louder...closer...

'Then, someone spread a rumour that a Hindu had set fire to a Maulvi's field in Mamudpur. That night...they came. Torches in hand... shouting... charging into our village like a wave of fire. My wife—carrying our two-month-old son—ran with me, along with a few other families from nearby.

'We jumped over bushes...stumbled through fields... and bolted towards the forest behind our houses. Barefoot... breathless...terrified of making the slightest sound, we ran for our lives in the pitch dark.

'We ran and ran... I do not know for how long...

'Suddenly, my wife pulled at my arm...begged me to stop... In her trembling hands, she held only the old cloth that had wrapped our baby. Somewhere along the way...in the blind panic...

our child had slipped from her grip... And in that stampede...in that madness...he must have been trampled...crushed under their feet...' His voice broke. The words dissolved into a raw, animal-like wail—grief tearing its way out of him.

Nagen Raha—or Naga-da, as he was being affectionately called—the same man who had once been one of the home tutors of mathematics, sat there, gasping for air between sobs.

Grandfather dabbed at his eyes with the corner of his dhoti, trying in vain to hide his own tears. Kaka lowered his head, bowed in silent grief—unable to speak.

'Somehow, we managed to reach Bhairav Bridge,' Naga-da continued, his voice quivering. 'Inside the train coaches, the walls were splattered with ghastly bloodstains. Looking out the window, it seemed even the mighty Meghna River below had turned red. Kaka, I remember breaking my wife's tell-tale red-and-white wedding bangles with my own hands, hoping against hope that she wouldn't be identified as a Hindu married woman. It was useless; they showed no mercy. The end of her sari caught the in the train's door… Suroma jumped into the river from the moving train. And I, her husband, stood there and watched helplessly; I could do nothing to save her.

'I alighted from the train at the next stop, changed my route and reached free India via Benapole-Petrapole. There, I saw a familiar face—the Maulvi from our old village madrasa. He had come to India about a month ago to find a suitable groom for his daughter. She was burnt alive in the Calcutta riots. The Indian soldiers at the border searched him thoroughly and took all his money and then they asked him to run away to Pakistan.

'What kind of independence is this, Kaka? Tell me, please, what does this freedom mean?'

Di-bhai, I had been hiding behind the curtains in the adjacent room, listening to every word. Nobody could answer his questions. The air in the room hung heavy as his words echoed,

'What kind of independence is this, Kaka? Tell me!'

Naga-da did not stay with us for long. One day, Kaki—perhaps lost in her own thoughts—left the front door ajar. Slipping out quietly, probably in his torn slippers, muttering indistinctly to himself, he disappeared.

And never returned.

Di-bhai, the dawn of freedom had indeed arrived. But no one could deny it—the light of that dawn was stained, deeply and irrevocably, with the blood of countless innocents.

Fifteen

After independence, Calcutta slowly returned to normalcy. Schools and colleges opened. I resumed my studies as a student of free India.

It was a Sunday morning. My Class Nine annual examinations were over, and we were all at home. Every day after breakfast, it was time for Kaka to shave. He always preferred lukewarm water for his lather, so I kept a bowl in front of him. I found his shaving routine hilarious. He twisted his eyes and mouth at odd angles, alternately contracted and relaxed his facials muscles to get a closer shave, resulting in funny facial expressions. Seated behind him, I would mimic him by twisting my own face. Kaki used to laugh seeing this. 'Apu won't grow up,' she would say tenderly. 'She's as childish as ever.'

Kaka would stop shaving and glance at me, saying, 'I see her antics in the mirror and quietly enjoy the entertainment. Hope she remains young like this for long. When it is time, life will automatically teach her what it means to grow up.'

Di-bhai, I learnt much later how true his words were.

Anyway, that day, Kaka could not finish his shave. A man had entered the house through the main entrance downstairs and was making his way up the staircase. He coughed lightly before calling out, 'Himangshu, are you home?'

Kaka listened intently to the voice and then, after hesitating for a moment, got up from his seat—razor in his hands and foam on his cheeks. By then, the visitor had reached the first floor and entered the room. He was tall, at least six feet, with a complexion that must have once been fair but had darkened to bronze, probably due to neglect. Though he was very slim, there was no sign of fatigue in his demeanour. What struck me most were his eyes—large and with a magical brightness in them! At the same time, they were as restless as an Oriental Magpie Robin yet also watchful! Where had I seen such eyes? Where?

By then, Kaka had set down his razor and stepped forward. What unfolded next was something I had never seen before. Without hesitation, Kaka wrapped both arms around the tall man in a heartfelt embrace. The man, in turn, held him just as tightly—an unspoken flood of emotion passing between them.

Meanwhile, Kaki, her *ghomta* carefully draped over her head, entered the room. But her hands trembled with excitement, and the cup and saucer she was carrying clattered noisily in her grasp.

'When did you return, Santosh? Why didn't you inform me?' Kaka asked, still holding the man close.

'First release me and let me breathe. Boumoni, you better hand me that tea,' replied Santosh.

Kaki stepped forward and then bent down to touch his feet.

'Why on earth are you touching my feet? I may have aged in prison, but I still remember our family connections!' he exclaimed. 'The Pal family may not be as educated and learned as the Boses, but we were no fools either. I am Santosh, the son of Dinesh Pal's nephew. By our family hierarchy, I belong to a younger generation than you. How could I ever forget that! What is your opinion, Himangshu?' He let out a hearty, breezy laugh. As I stood there, I could not help but wonder where I had heard it before.

I was trying to hide behind Kaki and then decided to emerge and stepped forward.

'Hey! The last time I saw you, you were this small!' Santosh-da exclaimed, gesturing with his hands. 'Look at you now—all grown up! Although I am much older, I am actually your cousin. Do you remember me at all?' he asked with a broad grin.

I noticed the sparkle in his eyes, the booming voice, and the innocence in his laughter—pure as gold. Yes, he was my cousin—a distant relative! Kaka had often spoken of him with great respect, mentioning their acquaintance through political circles in East Bengal.

Gently nudged by Kaki, I moved closer. As I bent down to touch his feet, I suddenly recoiled in horror.

'What happened, little sister? Are you frightened seeing my feet?' he asked with a smile, reading my reaction at once. 'It is natural to feel upset seeing the state of my toes. But one day... I will tell you the stories behind these wounds. Then, instead of fear or sadness, you will feel proud.'

Saying this, he took my hands in his own—hands rough from hardship, yet surprisingly gentle—and made me sit beside him.

His hands were like his feet—bare of all nails. His toes looked battered, as though they had endured unspeakable trampling. As he laughed again, I could not help but notice that apart from four or five teeth, his mouth was nearly empty.

A shiver ran down my spine. How had this happened? Who could have subjected him to such cruelty?

'My dear, those British jailers were rascals who could only rip out the nails from our fingers and toes! But could they suppress the indomitable spirit and courage within us, those who were imprisoned in the Cellular Jail in the Andaman Islands? When an inmate cried out, 'Vande Mataram' while being lashed with a whip at midnight, all of us in the neighbouring cells would rise from our floor mats and rush to the bars of our prison cubicles to cry out in unison, 'Vande…e…e…e… Mataram, Vande…e… e..e... Mataram, Vande...e...e…e…Mataram!'

'When the general-in-charge left after beating some innocent prisoner, leaving him half dead, others would start singing in chorus—

Shubhra-jyotsna-pulakita-yaminim
Phulla-kusumita-drumadala-shobhinim
Suhasinim su-madhura-bhashinim
Sukhadam varadam mataram.

O Mother, bright as the moonlit night,
Thrilled with joyful radiance,
Adorned with blossoming trees and flowers,
Smiling, sweetly speaking,
Giver of happiness, bestower of blessings—Mother!

As Santosh-da sang a few lines, his voice strangely touching, Kaka and Kaki also joined him. Listening to Bankim Chandra's song, I suddenly remembered where I had seen eyes like Santosh-da's before. I ran inside and, opening the drawer of my study table, took out a picture of Khudiram Bose. There he was—with Bhagat Singh, Binoy-Badal-Dinesh, Bina Das and Matangini Hazra! There, there was the similarity! I saw it in their eyes, too, the same passion for independence, the same bright gleam of self-sacrifice! Was he then, one of them too?

That evening, I listened to Santosh-da speak of the heroic acts of Khudiram Bose, Prafulla Chaki, Master-da and Pritilata Waddedar. He told us about his participation in the freedom movement—how he had learnt to fire a gun, how he had once faced a British lieutenant and cried out, 'Jay Bharatbarsha, Jay Matribhumi, Victory to India, Victory to the Motherland!'

Santosh-da had been imprisoned in Kala Pani (the Cellular Jail in the Andamans) for some years. It wasn't until approximately two months after India gained independence that he finally returned home. His crime? Well, he and his associates had set two buses ablaze, overcome with patriotic fervour after attending a gathering that vehemently opposed British rule. As punishment, the 25-year-old was exiled 400 miles away, across the vast, endless ocean, to a prison surrounded by water and water only. Attempting to swim to freedom was akin to courting death, and stepping out of the prison door to stand beneath the open sky was an impossible dream.

Like Santosh-da, Sushanta Basak too had tasted prison life early—as a devoted follower of Master-da. Premen Guha, a member of the Jugantar party, found himself dragged into that same dark cell after a bundle of letters—laced with secret codes—was discovered hidden beneath his pillow.

Even Ramesh Dasgupta, a brilliant student from Presidency College, was not spared. Betrayed by one of his own college mates, he was handed over to the British police. When they searched his bag, they found no weapons—only two addresses of gun sellers and a notebook filled with songs from the age of rebellion. The gun sellers vanished just in time, but Ramesh had no such luck. Without trial, without mercy, he was deported to the Andamans—sentenced to Kala Pani.

There, his life became a living nightmare.

Ramesh was thrown into relentless labour—stripped of dignity, humanity, and rest. From dawn till nightfall, he was forced to remove the husk of mountains of coconuts—using only his bare, bleeding hands. His palms split open. His fingers cracked. The skin tore away, but still, the overseers would not let him pause for breath.

And even that was not the end.

Once the outer shells were removed, the coconuts were tossed into the oil mill. Ramesh, along with others, was yoked like an animal to the mill's giant wooden press—forced to walk in endless circles, grinding the kernels into oil. Whenever he staggered, half-conscious from exhaustion, a kick to the ribs or a whip across the back would force him upright again.

'We didn't even have time to go to the toilet, sister!' Santosh-da said, his voice tight with the memory. 'We had to hold everything in...keep walking...keep working...in silence...until the overseers were satisfied we had earned that one bowl of watery khichuri in the afternoon.'

I shuddered as his words hung in the air, heavy and bitter like the taste of iron.

It was a calculated British strategy—to transport these courageous, patriotic young men across the Bay of Bengal and lock them away on a distant island. The colonial government knew well that isolating the nation's educated and spirited youth, cutting them off from the masses, would make it easier to break the spine of India's growing independence movement.

But what they failed to understand was this: no matter how many bodies they ravaged, no matter how many prisoners they tortured inside those dark, pigeon hole-like, iron-barred cells of that dreaded three-storeyed jail, they could not destroy the one thing that lived unbroken inside each man—the dream of a free motherland.

They whipped them. Starved them. Humiliated them. But the fire burned on.

Among them was Ramkamal Bandopadhyay. One day, in a moment of quiet, human desperation, he had merely requested that the latrine in his cell be cleaned. The water in his mug, kept too close to the filth, had become undrinkable.

For that simple plea, he was dragged out, limbs bound and beaten on the floor—publicly and relentlessly. The kicks rained down on him all night, as a warning to others, this is the price of asking for dignity.

By dawn, his spirit broken but not his will, Ramkamal made his final act of defiance. He tore the only dhoti he wore and hanged himself from the iron ring fixed high in his cell wall.

And as his body swung lifeless, just a short distance away on Ross Island, laughter rang out at the British officers' clubhouse. After their morning tennis, the officers cheered each other with coffee cups in their hands as though nothing had happened.

In 1933, another wave of defiance swept through the prison. A group of inmates began a hunger strike—a final, desperate protest. The jailors responded with unspeakable cruelty.

After four or five days without food, the strikers were tied to wooden planks. A British doctor stood ready with rubber tubes and a liquid mixture of milk, eggs, and sugar. Force-feeding began—but the process was brutal and blind.

Mahavir Singh. Mohan Kishore Namadas. Mohit Mitra.

Three names. Three bodies. Three martyrs.

All of them suffocated to death, choked by the very tubes forced down their throats. Their lifeless forms were stuffed unceremoniously into jute sacks and thrown into the Bay of Bengal—like discarded waste.

Who knows if their shattered souls ever found their way home across the waves…back to the soil they had once called their own.

Later, as if to deepen the insult, the remaining prisoners were served rice laced with gravel—each grain of hope crushed beneath the colonial boot.

'Since childhood, I had always loved to sing,' Santosh-da continued. 'Even in jail, I often sang patriotic songs. Once, to frustrate the British jailers, I started singing a particular set of songs night after night, for almost a week straight. I sang:

Maayer dewa mota kapor mathay tule ne re bhai
Din dukhini ma je moder, taar beshi taar sadhyo nai.

O brother, take upon your head the coarse cloth gifted
by our mother, so poor

> She is sorrowful and so grieved—this is all she can offer, nothing more.

'I sang one song after another—"Bolo bolo bolo shobe, shoto bina benu rabe" (Say it aloud, all of you, like the sound of a hundred veenas and flutes), "Chal re chal shobe Bharat santan" (March on, march forward, o children of India!) and many more like these.

'A few days later, while I was carrying stones at work, an Englishman kicked me from behind. He accused me of being sluggish during the day because I stayed awake throughout the night, singing. When I protested, I faced a barrage of expletives. Still, I did not stop.

'That night, they took me to a special torture cell. It was there that the butchers uprooted the nails from my toes and fingers one by one. I cried in pain but kept on singing: "Utho go Bharato lokkhi, utha adi jagato jana pujya!" (Arise, O India, our Goddess Lakshmi! Arise, you who are worthy of worship by the whole world!)

'When they saw that my spirit was still unbroken, a giant arrived brandishing iron pincers. He forced my jaws open and pulled out quite a few of my teeth! But when I got an opportunity, I bit the rascal's hand. "Bloody black man, take this!" he yelled, pulling his finger out of my mouth. Then he spat in my face. And thus, the rest of my teeth were spared.'

As he paused to catch his breath, Santosh-da gave a wide, gummy smile—revealing the few teeth that had survived.

You know, Di-bhai, it is quite striking how, in today's age, contentment often remains elusive. One cannot help but wonder why people accumulate vast wealth, much like the Tata-Birla-Ambanis, and still find themselves searching for more to add to their possessions. But back in those days, just the joy of retaining a few teeth was enough to fill a man like Santosh-da with the courage to endure those years of terrible torture.

It never ceases to amaze me what the bodies, minds and souls of those freedom-fighters were made of. I think I have found the answer, though. It was unwavering dedication, solitary devotion and an unstoppable desire to witness their motherland become free of foreign rule. Their eyes gleamed with that very dream!

Gandhiji fasted seventeen times in protest against the deaths of inmates at the Cellular Jail, the endless periods of incarceration, and the unspeakable tortures inflicted at Kalapani. At one point, both he and Rabindranath Tagore raised their voices together against this barbarism, denouncing the inhumanity with all the moral force they could summon.

Negotiations with Viceroy Lord Linlithgow continued over the years, drawing national attention to the horrors within those prison walls. Finally, in 1938, this infamous jail system was officially abolished.

By 1939, the British administration was compelled to empty the Cellular Jail, releasing the surviving prisoners whose bodies bore testimony to years of torment.

Two years later, during the Second World War, the Japanese seized control of the Andaman Islands. Ironically, the same Cellular Jail, once a nightmare for Indian freedom fighters, was converted into a prisoner-of-war camp—this time to hold British soldiers.

In 1945, in a brief yet historic moment, the Andamans became the first piece of Indian territory to be declared independent—hoisted under the flag of the Indian National Army.

Di-bhai, it was difficult to keep track of the many people who came to visit Santosh-da during those few days he stayed at our home! A week later, our maternal uncles took him to their house in Park Circus. But Santosh-da did not live much longer after that. While he was still alive, I would rush to meet him whenever possible, drawn by some irresistible force. He would share stories—tales of indomitable courage in the face of oppression—and often sing: 'Yeh waqt ka awaz haye milke chalo, yeh zindagi ka raaz hai milke chalo (It is the call of the times—walk together; it is the secret of life—walk together).'

His voice still echoes in my ears. It was he who taught me to sing 'Muktiro mandiro sopan toley'—beneath the steps of the temple of liberation.

Santosh-da is no more, but his memory lives on—etched in the rusted, bloodstained shackles of that prison, in the untold stories of those who never returned, and deep within my heart, filled with gratitude.

Inspired by him, I have passed this song on to both my children—Titai and Bukai—so that they too may remember the sacrifices that gave us our freedom.

Speaking of the song reminds me, Di-bhai—do you remember that summer holiday when you stayed with us in Calcutta? I think it was the year 1942. We two sisters were then aged eight and ten. Our neighbour, Amiya-da, had the most melodious voice in the locality. During community events, he would often gather the local children to form a choir. On one such occasion, around Janmashtami, it was decided that a group would sing at a temple function, and was chosen to organize it.

'Hey, Amu-da! This is Atasi, my elder sister,' I said, vouching for you. 'She sings even better than I do. She is here on holiday and will stay for some time. Please let her sing along with us!'

'Okay, okay, now all of you sit down around the harmonium. Let's begin! Hey, boy! You play the tabla—dha-dhi-na, na-ti-na—play!' Amu-da had let us join the group.

The event was a success. But quite often, Amu-da would take us to a rundown house nearby for rehearsals. Upon entering, a bright light would glare into our eyes!

'Tell me your name, soldier! Where are you from? Answer me, or I won't spare you! Ha-ha-ha'—followed by a monstrous laughter from the man with a thick, twirled moustache!

Later, we learnt it had been a theatre group! They were rehearsing for *Chhatrapati Shivaji*. At the time, Binoy Roy of the Bengal Cultural Squad was leading young people in street performances, staging plays that spoke of the people's suffering—especially those based on the British-engineered famine of 1943.

Now, with the clarity of hindsight, I realize that the seeds of resistance against tyranny were being sown in every corner of India—through poems, plays, and songs. Even the renowned scientist Homi Bhabha named a theatre group 'People's Theatre', inspired by the playwright Romain Rolland.

And what splendid actors they were! Bijan Bhattacharya, Ritwik Ghatak, Utpal Dutt, Salil Chowdhury, Sudhin Dasgupta—giants in their craft. Di-bhai, you and I—both of us—watched many of these stalwarts perform, didn't we?

Back then, alongside the Quit India Movement, waves of communist ideology were sweeping through Bengal. We became involved with the All-India People's Theatre Association (IPTA), and it was there that we began learning theatre songs—songs that spoke of struggle, hope and justice.

Though the Indian National Congress did not want the group to continue after 1947, artists like Ahindra Chowdhury, Tripti Mitra, Shambhu Mitra, and Utpal Dutt carried the torch forward, producing unforgettable plays like *Bahurupi* and *Raktakarabi*.

'O Alor Potho Jatri', 'Kono Ek Ganyer Bodhur Kotha Tomay Shonai Shono', and the mournful 'Ranar' (Runner)—Di-bhai, do you remember how we learned those spirited songs together?

In later years, Mejdi's husband—our Mejo Jamaibabu—and even my sister-in-law's husband would sit for hours, singing these very songs, accompanied by a harmonium. Dressed in dhotis and rolled-up-sleeve shirts, in the style made famous by Hemanta Mukhopadhyay, they filled the air with songs like: 'Gouri Shringo Tuleche Shir', 'Dheu Uthche Kara Tutche', 'Bicharpoti Tomar Bichar Korbe Kara', and 'Hey Shamalo Dhaan Ho, Kasteta Dao Shaan Ho'.

Even now, in my advancing age, when I often forget what I had for dinner yesterday—or even lunch the day before—my heart stirs, and my blood warms whenever I remember those songs.

Sixteen

A strange news came on 20 January 1948. I was about 14 or 15 years old then. Gandhiji was delivering a speech in front of the Birla House in Delhi when suddenly someone threw a bomb in the crowd. It was a crude, home-made device. When it exploded with a deafening noise, the crowd scattered in panic and the meeting was disrupted. What no one realized was that another bomb had been intended for Bapu. But the man assigned with the task lacked courage and fled along with the others. A Punjabi partition refugee named Madan Lal Pahwa was arrested.

Just ten days later, on 30 January 1948, an unspeakable tragedy unfolded.

That afternoon, after his bath and simple meal, Bapu gently scolded Manu-ben (Manu Gandhi, the daughter of his beloved nephew) for neglecting her diet and not taking proper care of her health. He urged her to eat better, reminding her that a twenty-year-old girl should have a strong and healthy body.

Afterwards, Gandhiji went to meet Sardar Patel—a meeting that delayed him by nearly ten minutes. By around five in the evening, looking a little weary, he set out for the prayer ground at the rear of Birla House, accompanied by Manu-ben and Abha-ben (Abha Chatterjee, his foster daughter who would later marry his grandnephew).

Upon arrival, he climbed a few steps to an elevated platform. The prayer dais lay just a little ahead.

What followed next, Manu-ben would later recount in heartbreaking detail.

A tall, heavily built man in khaki suddenly emerged from the gathering crowd. He moved with his head bowed, almost crouching, hands joined together as though in a respectful gesture—seemingly approaching Bapu for a blessing.

'What are you doing? Get aside! Bapu is already late for prayers. Make way for him!' Manu-ben said in haste, trying to clear the path.

But the man shoved her roughly. She stumbled and fell, scattering her prayer beads, the holy book, and Gandhiji's spittoon onto the ground. As she bent to gather them, three deafening gunshots tore through the air.

The blood-soaked body of the Father of the Nation fell down where he stood—collapsing into Abha-ben's lap. His hands were still folded in prayer, his eyes nearly closed. From his parched lips came only two final words: 'Hey Ram.'

Through the haze of smoke and rising panic, Manu-ben could just make out a few men rushing towards them. Her trembling hands fumbled for her pocket watch: it read 5:17 p.m.

It took nearly ten agonizing minutes to carry Gandhiji back to his room and lay him down on the cotton bedspread on the floor. Despite frantic efforts, no doctor could reach him in time. The blood from the bullet wounds—piercing his chest and stomach—continued to flow.

As life ebbed away, Gandhiji breathed his last while listening to verses from the *Gita*, softly recited by Manu-ben and Abha-ben at his side.

Later, we learnt that the assassin, Nathuram Godse, hailed from the Deccan—along with his associate, Narayan Apte, and others from their circle. In 1949, following a high-profile trial, both Godse and Apte were sentenced to death and executed.

After the 1946 Noakhali riots, Gandhiji had been deeply heartbroken, yet he remained largely silent—for the sake of India's fragile independence. In late 1947, the newly independent nation found itself caught in escalating tensions with Pakistan over the princely state of Kashmir. Adding to the strain, the Indian government had begun delaying the payment of funds owed to Pakistan as part of the Partition settlement.

Gandhiji, unable to bear this injustice, began yet another fast—insisting that, despite strained relations, Pakistan's rightful dues must be cleared. Under mounting public and moral pressure, the Congress government eventually relented and released the funds.

But this gesture became the final trigger for Godse, Apte, and their associates. To them, it was an unforgivable betrayal—a sign, they believed, that Gandhiji harboured secret sympathies towards Pakistan.

These were the same men who had failed in their earlier assassination attempt on 20 January 1948. But by the 30th, they had regrouped—this time, with chilling precision—and succeeded in their fatal mission.

Whenever news of Gandhiji's assassination was broadcast on the radio, it was accompanied by a pointed clarification, 'Gandhiji's death was caused by a Hindu's bullet—not a Muslim's.'

The horrific memories of the communal riots of 1946 were still raw in Calcutta and across Bengal. This repeated announcement was a desperate attempt to prevent another wave of bloodshed.

The next day, we children from the neighbourhood made a small tribute. We cut out a picture of Bapu from the newspaper and pasted it on to a piece of cardboard. Kaki prepared some home-made glue by mixing flour with water and heating it over the clay oven. We then made our way downstairs, where Kaka and his friends were waiting with Rajanigandha flowers. Kaka, who never allowed anyone to see him shed tears, stood with his eyes fixed on the ground as he garlanded the picture.

The adults paid homage with flowers and sang 'Patita Paawan Sita Ram...Raghupati Raghav Raja Ram...'

We walked down Shambhu Babu Lane with our heads bowed in a silent procession of mourning.

Thus, we bade farewell to the Father of the Nation, the saint of Sabarmati Ashram.

Seventeen

I was growing up and was doing well as a student in senior school. Kaka and Kaki were happy with my academic performance. Sometimes, Pishima would arrive to visit Thakurda, her six sons and two daughters in tow. The old man would sleep on his bed in one room, while the rest of us slept side by side on makeshift beds spread across the floor of another room. Even then, I never felt the need for solitude or privacy. I just kept in mind that life was all about moving forward while adjusting and cooperating with everyone.

Around 1950, my ISc examinations were approaching, so I could often be found studying late into the nights. If Thakurda needed to use the bathroom at night, it was I who assisted him. Thakurda did not suffer for long; however, after he passed away, Kaka felt even lonelier.

Approximately a year later, on a rainy evening, Kaka returned home from his office looking unusually fatigued. He rested but soon began experiencing breathing difficulties. We summoned the local doctor, who advised, 'He must be hospitalized without delay and given oxygen.'

Shocked, we rushed Kaka to the Medical College in a taxi. The following day, when I arrived at the hospital, the doctors were administering intravenous saline to him as he lay with his eyes closed, silent. At that age and in that situation, I wasn't sure what to do, but I realized it was not a moment to succumb to despair. It was a time to gather strength and become self-reliant.

By then, I had just completed my ISc Kaka had always hoped

I would follow in the footsteps of his late elder brother—our Baba—and become a doctor. It was a dream we all cherished. But the harsh realities of daily life—food, clothing, and the most basic needs—could not be ignored. Pursuing a medical education was simply beyond our means.

Fortunately, Kaki was acquainted with the headmistress of Sarojini School, conveniently located near our home. She approached her with a request for a teaching position for me. As luck would have it, there was a vacancy in the primary section. I seized the opportunity—ready and determined to shoulder my share of the family's responsibilities.

Though my studies were cut short, I did not lose heart. Handing over my monthly salary of forty-five rupees—along with the additional earnings from two private tuitions, bringing the total to sixty rupees—to Kaki gave me a quiet sense of satisfaction.

We were transitioning from a life of comfort and luxury to one of struggle and modest means. Yet, it did not fill our hearts with anguish, fear, shame, or disappointment. Instead, we accepted the change with quiet strength and dignity.

During that period, I never once thought of seeking assistance from Barisal property—my mother or my maternal family. I had rather made it my life's mission to repay the debt I owed to Kaka and Kaki, who had nurtured me as their own child.

After a few days in hospital, Kaka regained consciousness. But the doctors delivered heartbreaking news to Kaki. Kaka's lungs had been ravaged by cancer, and the disease had already spread to other parts of his body. There was no cure.

One day, Kaki asked me to accompany her to the hospital. Kaka had specifically asked to see me. As his trembling hands rested gently on my head, I felt him pouring out all his love and blessings—silently, but deeply.

A few days later, my pillar of strength, my precious source of affection, hope, and love—my dearest Kaka, Himangshu Mohan Bose—passed away.

In his final days, Kaka often said to me, 'Apu dear, you cannot measure a person's success by his wealth. True success belongs to the one who lives with equanimity, holds fast to his morals, and preserves his self-respect.'

As I stood beside his pyre, recalling those words, it felt as though, in that single moment, I had grown older—suddenly and irreversibly.

Di-bhai, by the time I had nearly completed my ISc course—I learnt from one of your letters that discontent over the choice of official language was beginning to surface in East Pakistan.

At the time of the Partition in 1947, more than 40 million Bengali-speaking people became part of the dominion of Pakistan. However, the Pakistani government, its administration and its military were predominantly made up of individuals from the western part of the country. At a national educational conference in Karachi, a proposal was made to adopt only Urdu as the national language in schools and the media. You had written that protests erupted immediately in East Pakistan.

When I read your letter, I was reminded of Yasmin-bua, the sister of Salam Chacha, our neighbour in Barisal. She had endured a difficult life. Widowed young, she lived with her brother and ensured her son, Rafique, received a formal education. Rafique-bhai was intelligent. Do you remember, Di-bhai, how our grandfather had gifted him a silver coin for scoring the highest marks in science in the district?

He knew that we would place our books at the feet of Ma Saraswati every year on the day of Saraswati Puja to receive the Goddess's blessings. Rafique-bhai would bring his books too.

'O Khuro, there's no puja in our house; please put these

books of mine at the feet of Ma Saraswati. Perhaps I'll get some more marks in the examinations then. I do not have a father—it is just me who is left to wipe away my mother's tears in times of her distress, isn't it?

'I haven't brought many books! Just mathematics, science, English, history, geography… Please keep the algebra book on top; I am a bit scared of that subject!'

The old priest would fume at the pile Rafique brought with him while chanting the prayers: *'Saraswati Maha-bhaage, Vidye Kamala-lochane'* (O Devi Saraswati, the most auspicious Goddess of Knowledge with lotus-like eyes).

How strange it was that the boy who could barely pronounce one line of the Sanskrit *shlokas* would stand reverently outside the door, his head bowed, until the puja and all rituals were complete.

When he returned the next morning to collect his books, our grandfather would place a marigold flower in his hands and say, 'Keep this inside your book, my boy. You will succeed in your examinations for sure.'

Rafique would nod and walk away, chewing the Kul that was given as prasad with joy. And not only would he pass, he would also top the exams. Yasmin-bua would make *firni* in small clay bowls and send some for us.

Di-bhai, whenever I recall the earthen scent of that firni, I find myself on the verge of tears. Is it because I have lost all connection to that soil? Or because we have lost brother Rafique forever?

The federal government of Pakistan's sweeping decision to declare Urdu as the sole national language enraged the Bengali-speaking population. A growing number of students began demanding that Bengali too be recognized as a state language.

On 21 February 1952, Bengali students rose in defiance, protesting against the government's decision. They openly violated

Section 144, which had been imposed to prevent public gatherings, and assembled within the Dhaka University campus. One group surged towards Dhaka Medical College, while others rallied inside the campus grounds—already encircled by armed police.

The students, determined and fearless, pushed against the barricades, crowding the gates in protest. We later learnt that Rafique bhai had been a third-year student there at the time.

The University's Vice-Chancellor, incensed by the unfolding violence, urgently called for the police to cease firing. He pleaded with the students to disperse. The students agreed. But as they began leaving, the police suddenly arrested several of them for violating the curfew.

When word of the arrests spread, the other students turned back, attempting to re-enter the campus to demand their release.

The police responded with brutal force.

Without warning, they opened fire again—indiscriminately and mercilessly. Students fell—shot, wounded, dying on the very grounds where they had once gathered for lectures and debates.

As the news spread like wildfire, Dhaka erupted. Shops shut down, offices closed, public transport halted. A general strike paralysed the city.

Undeterred by fear of arrests or torture, thousands of ordinary citizens joined the students. They gathered in and around the Dhaka Medical College hostel, where the injured were brought and the dead were mourned. The following day, a massive crowd assembled for the Gayebana Janaza—a symbolic funeral for the martyrs—held in the Medical College compound.

Di-bhai, my heart broke when I read in your letter about Yasmin-bua's heart-wrenching cries during Rafique's funeral procession. How she stumbled, collapsed again and again, trying to keep pace with her only son's coffin...until she finally lost consciousness.

Two days after bidding farewell to her son, Yasmin-bua too embarked on her own final journey—to the land of no return.

One family was completely shattered.

Yet, the sacrifice of Rafique and his fellow martyrs did not go in vain. Their blood-soaked legacy fuelled a movement that could no longer be silenced. On 7 May 1954, following the United Front's sweeping victory in the regional elections, Bengali was formally recognized as one of Pakistan's state languages. The constitution was amended in 1956 to reflect this hard-won truth.

Sometimes...sometimes...even after such darkness...good things do happen.

Much later, Di-bhai, around 1998, I saw on television that two residents of Vancouver, Canada—Rafiquul Islam and Abdus Salam—had appealed to the UN Secretary-General Kofi Annan to declare 21 February as International Mother Language Day. On 17 November 1999, at the UNESCO conference in Paris, the proposal was accepted. Since 21 February 2000, the day has been observed with reverence in all UN-affiliated countries.

Let me remind you, Di-bhai, that on this side of the border with Pakistan—the year before Titai was born—the same issue sparked unrest in the Barak Valley of Assam.

In April 1960, during a session of the Assam Pradesh Congress Committee, a proposal was tabled to declare Assamese as the sole official language of the state. The decision ignited immediate unrest. In their fervour, certain Assamese groups turned violent, targeting Bengali immigrants in the Brahmaputra Valley.

By September that year, fear and insecurity forced thousands of Bengali Hindus to flee the valley, seeking refuge in West Bengal. Many others migrated to different parts of the Northeast where Bengali-speaking communities formed the majority.

On 10 October 1960, the then Chief Minister of Assam

formally introduced the bill proposing Assamese as the only official language of the state. The bill was swiftly passed on 24 October.

In response, widespread anger simmered across the Barak Valley. The Cachar Gana Sangram Parishad emerged as the leading voice of protest. In April 1961, they observed Sankalpa Divas in Silchar, Karimganj, and Hailakandi—publicly opposing the linguistic imposition.

Determined and resolute, the Parishad announced plans for mass rallies and statewide strikes to raise awareness and resist the enforcement of Assamese on the Bengali-speaking population of Barak Valley.

On 19 May 1961, a general strike was observed across Silchar, Karimganj and Hailakandi. In Karimganj, activists picketed outside government offices, railway stations, courts, etc. In Silchar, the protesters staged a satyagraha inside the railway station from dawn. No train tickets were sold since morning.

In the afternoon, a truck carrying nine satyagrahis who had been arrested from Katigorah was passing through Tarapur station (present-day Silchar station). As the picketers protested when they saw the men being taken away, the Assam Rifles, already present and fully armed, began to beat them with rifles and batons.

Within just seven minutes, seventeen rounds of bullets were fired at the unarmed protesters. Twelve were shot. Nine died that very day. Two more succumbed to their injuries later.

Sri Krishna Kant Biswas clung to life for another twenty-four agonizing hours, a bullet lodged deep in his lungs, before finally breathing his last.

In the wake of this brutal massacre, the Assam government had no choice but to relent. Bengali was finally declared an official language in the Barak Valley.

The language in which I first learnt to call out to my

mother—a language without which expressions of joy, sorrow, fear, hope, or heartbreak seem incomplete—how unbearable it is to imagine living without the right to speak it freely!

Di-bhai, was this not the belief that bound you and me—indeed, all of it's—throughout our lives?

I have carefully preserved your letter about the Bhasha Andolan, tucked safely within the pages of my *Bhagavad Gita*. And there it shall remain—always treasured.

Eighteen

These days, I find myself reminiscing about my childhood even more, especially whenever the sky is overcast. Do you know why, Di-bhai? When you stayed with me at Kaka's house, we had memorized a poem by reading it together, swaying in harmony as we recited.

Today, the sky is once again cloudy; daylight is fading quickly and it seems rain is imminent. It has been a long time since we met, Di-bhai, and even longer since we recited that favourite poem together. So here I am, all by myself, recalling it once more:

Diner alo nibe elo, shujyi dobe-dobe.
Akash ghire megh juteche, chnader lobhe lobhe.
Megher upor megh koreche—ronger upor rong,
Mondirete knashor ghonta bajlo thong thong.

The daylight is almost gone, the sun will set soon;
Clouds gather in the sky, greedy for the moon.
Clouds hover over clouds, shades with hues they belong;
The bells are ringing in temple, ding dong and ding dong.

Di-bhai, is it that we yearn more for the daylight as darkness creeps closer? Do we think more often of our childhood when we reach the autumn of our years? Perhaps that is simply the rhythm of life—its inevitable.

In these moments of gentle recollection, I find joy in remembering our visits to East Bengal. Once, we travelled to

Sujatpur in Maheswari district, to the ancestral home of our uncle—the lawyer husband of our paternal aunt. He was a BA, LLB—a man of standing.

They also owned a sprawling house in Narayanganj. Sometimes, they would take Kaki and me along on their trips there. Large orchards dotted with many jackfruit trees were amongst their huge expanse of assets and landed property—an expanse of green that seemed to go on forever.

Uncle had been the only child of his parents. After his father's passing, the entire responsibility of the estate had fallen on his shoulders.

His younger daughter, Hena, was around my age. I still remember our very first meeting—she arrived carrying a large cardboard box. Curious, I peeked inside and found it brimming with little dolls. Captivated by her collection, I sat down on the floor of the long veranda, eager to see each one.

Very soon, little girls from the neighbouring houses arrived, each carrying their own dolls and tiny sets of doll clothes. Together, we played for hours, breaking down every barrier of unfamiliarity, difference in status. In those moments, none of that mattered.

Every afternoon, after lunch, we would quietly slip away to the attic. A sturdy branch of a mango tree bent low over the kitchen roof, heavy with tangy-sweet fruit. The fruits were handy from our position in the attic.

Throughout the lazy noon hours, we played and feasted on young mangoes, made even more delicious with a sprinkling of salt. By late afternoon, our lips would turn pale from all the salt and sourness, but our laughter never faded. With each passing day, our bond deepened—unbothered by the world and its worries.

But once the holidays ended and I returned to Calcutta, I

never saw Hena again. Perhaps the mango tree bore its tangy-sweet fruit again the following year. But Hena...a month before the same season returned, she had lost her battle with typhoid.

Di-bhai, Hena's death overwhelmed me. I sank into a melancholy I could not shake. She had promised we would meet again...but I knew now why she never could.

Back in Calcutta, I struggled to concentrate on my studies.

Time, as it always does, dulled the sharpest edges of grief. The wound slowly healed. Yet even now, as I speak to you about her, her memory returns—bringing with it echoes of carefree afternoons, dolls lined up on verandas, and the tang of salted mangoes in the air.

Around the same time, our Dadu—Ma's father—also passed away. By then, two of our maternal uncles were already living in Calcutta. Only Shona Mama had remained in East Bengal.

Chhoto Mama's two sons—our cousin brothers—were loved by all. Though it was long ago, I still recall how, whenever Ma came to Calcutta, the brothers would be treated to a grand lunch during *Bhaiphonta*. Arrangements were made for nearly thirty people to have a meal together—such festive gatherings they were.

Di-bhai, as you know, Dadu left a portion of the Park Circus house to our mother. He also left her a beautiful farmhouse in Bakarganj—a property that had once won first prize in the district. Shona Mama took care of that estate with great dedication. He had a generous heart—during the famine of 1943, he gave shelter to several Muslim families there, offering them refuge when they had nowhere else to turn. Later, they worked on the farm and came to care for him deeply.

Eventually, the farm was taken over by the government.

I heard that a local Muslim doctor, who regarded Shona Mama as an elder brother, looked after him well after the Partition in 1947.

As for what became of mother's share of the property—or any financial matters tied to it—we never really came to know.

We lost our mother in 1957. I cried my heart out when she died. Whenever I thought of her, only one image came to mind—a beautiful woman draped in a white sari, freshly bathed, water droplets dripping from her wet hair; yet I never was able to immerse myself in her affections to my heart's content.

For reasons known only to herself, our Bordi had taken the bold decision to remain single and never marry. Whenever we enquired about it, she remained stern and tight-lipped, refusing to discuss the matter. She was well-educated and able to earn her livelihood as a schoolteacher—a profession she dedicated herself to for the rest of her life.

However, much later, when Titai was studying medicine, Bordi finally opened her heart to her beloved niece. She confided that during her adolescence, she had suffered a severe accident—a fall that caused critical injuries to her uterus and ovaries. An emergency operation had been performed to save her life, but the doctor had delivered the harsh truth: she would never be able to conceive or give birth.

Bordi, with her deep sense of self-respect, took a decision then. She would not become a life-partner to any man, only to face pity or ridicule from in-laws for her infertility.

And so, she remained a lifelong spinster—but her maternal affection never diminished. She stood like a pillar of love and support during each of her sisters' weddings, showering them with the care and joy she had reserved in her heart.

Our mother had been present for Mejdi's wedding, but after that, she could not witness any more of her children's marriages—not ours, nor our brother's.

In her absence, it was Bordi who took her place.

Meanwhile, after the deaths of our Baba and Kaka, life became a daily struggle for both Kaki and me. I had begun working at Sarojini School, it was a little convenient as it was located near our home. However, although I started earning at the age of seventeen, I still nurtured the hope of pursuing higher studies.

Kaki, ever strong-willed, would often remind me of Kaka's dream—to see me well-educated. Her words became my constant source of motivation, pushing me to complete my formal education.

By then, I had changed jobs and joined Entally Hindu Balika Vidyamandir as a primary teacher. My classes were in the morning shift, giving me the freedom to attend my ISc lectures at St Paul's College, Calcutta later in the day.

When I passed my ISc course, the headmistress of my school promoted me to teach higher classes in the secondary section. My salary increased slightly—enough to encourage me to aim even higher.

Next, I enrolled in a BSc course with Physiology Honours at City College. But soon reality set in. I realized I could not manage both. The timings of my school and the honours classes at Science College (the Science Department of Calcutta University)—located at quite a distance—clashed frequently.

The situation worsened when I started noticing frequent absences marked against my name in the school register. The job, however, was more essential than the degree at that point.

Ensuring that Kaki and I had a roof over us and food on the table became my priority. With a heavy heart, I left my BSc studies midway but continued teaching at the Entally Hindu Balika Vidyamandir—clinging to whatever stability life could offer us then.

Later, I discovered that Bangabasi College offered BSc courses in the evening section. The Principal, Sri Prashanta Bose, happened to be the President of the Managing Committee of our school.

Finding no other solution, I nervously approached him one day. After listening to my circumstances and recognizing my unwavering desire to pursue higher studies, he introduced me to Professor Sukhen Roy.

Di-bhai, during those difficult days, the tall and lean Sukhen Roy—whom I later came to affectionately call 'Dadu'—was nothing short of God-sent. He became my shield against many of life's challenges.

I cannot describe how much support he gave me once he understood my situation and the exhausting hard work, I was putting in at such a young age. Dadu seemed to have taken it upon himself to ensure that I completed my education. In truth, he stood by me in ways even our closest relatives had not.

However, Bangabasi College did not offer Honours classes in the evening section. I had no choice but to enrol in the pass course. To add to my disappointment, the pass course did not include my preferred subject, Physiology.

But here, too, fortune favoured me. Principal Prashanta Bose, who himself had once been a student of Professor Sukhen Roy, stepped in to help. On Professor Roy's suggestion, the college introduced Anthropology as a new subject in the evening section—just so that I could continue to stay within the realm of biological studies.

And thus, I found a way to continue my academic journey. I, however, constantly found myself torn between the responsibility of earning a living and the dream of building an academic career—without draining Kaki's limited savings.

Meanwhile, Kaki, ever resilient, did not sit idle at home. Using her old certificate from her school scholarship days, she secured a job as a teacher in the primary section of a private school. Though the salary was meagre, to us it felt like a treasure—something earned with dignity.

We were not a mother-daughter pair by birth, and with Kaka—our only connecting link—no longer alive. But instead, the two of us stood firmly by each other, bound by love and shared struggle. Together, we carved out our own path—one defined by resilience, self-respect, and quiet determination.

One day, Professor Roy expressed a wish to visit our home. When he met Kaki, learnt about our family and saw pictures of our father and Kaka, he reassured her, 'Madam, please do not lose hope. Never let the girl give up. I will personally ensure that Aparajita completes her studies fully.'

Indeed, on many evenings while I was immersed in practical classes at Bangabasi College, I would notice someone standing quietly outside the laboratory, watching me. It was Professor Roy, having climbed up the stairs leading to the laboratory just to check whether I was focused on work or chatting away with classmates. He would often ask my professors, 'How is my granddaughter Aparajita doing? Please be honest about her progress.'

By then, in my desperation, I caste aside all boundaries of unfamiliarity and shame and shared every detail of our financial struggles with Dadu. Di-bhai, I was in dire need of support; I longed for a father-figure to guide me through the complexities of life and help me distinguish right from wrong. On some Sundays, Dadu would invite me to lunch with his family at his home near Ballygunge station. He often visited us too, checking in to see how Kaki and I were faring. We began saving a little when we decided to sublet a part of our house to a young couple.

My only study time was between ten at night and two in the morning. Each day, I reported to school sharp at ten-thirty in the forenoon to teach my classes. After finishing my lessons, I squeezed in a quick tiffin break. Before heading to evening college, I spent the afternoon giving private tuition to two students. By nine o'clock at night, I would return home, have dinner, and then sit down with my books once again.

Whenever confusion clouded my mind or any crisis arose, Dadu was my one and only advisor. His guidance kept me steady.

Finally, in 1955, I passed my BSc examinations.

Almost immediately afterwards, the school where I worked sponsored me for the Bachelor in Teaching (BT) course. I was sent on deputation to formally learn the art and science of effective teaching.

Di-bhai, do you remember accompanying me to many of the BT classes held at Hastings House? There were rumours the building was haunted, though we never encountered any ghosts. My classmates there became your friends too, and even they started calling you 'Di-bhai'! We were close sisters, and no matter how far away we stayed, we never grew apart. There was always a natural connection between us.

Today, I recalled a funny incident from that period. One of Dadu's students had gifted him four entry passes to the Dover Lane Music Conference, a time-old-reputed classical music program to be held in Calcutta. On his instructions, that particular evening you and I, along with Kaki, reached his house. We all left together for the recital in Dadu's car. Until then, my only exposure to cultural performances was one of attending a dance recital by Pandit Birju Maharaj at the Academy of Fine Arts. So, I was looking forward to experiencing something new.

Nikhil Banerjee enthralled the audience with his mesmerizing sitar recital, and we enjoyed it thoroughly. Then, a commotion erupted on stage. Two young men with huge *tanpura*s busied themselves with tuning the instruments, producing strange sounds over the microphone! A slim man appeared on stage with a pair of tablas, sat down, and began tuning his percussion with a small hammer, all the while chewing paan! Finally, a tall, imposing man took centre stage. Before I could learn who he was, I was captivated by his commanding voice. It was not just me, the entire audience was enchanted, listened with undivided attention to his powerful rendition of khayal.

Suddenly, the great singer paused. He spat into a spittoon, twirled his moustache and said something to the tabla player. Then, a transformation took place. He closed his eyes, and the most eloquent melody emerged. The words seemed to echo from the depths of his substantial frame: 'Yaad piya ki aaye, yeh dukh saha na jaye, haye Ram (I yearn for my beloved, this sorrow is intolerable, alas Ram!)'

The words, the music, the atmosphere—they seemed heavy, laden with longing! It felt as if the giant of a man was melting away, his frame crumbling with each note, embodying the sorrow of separation described in the lyrics. I cannot express the depth of pathos in his repeated cry of 'Haye Ram'. Yet, the *thumri* was presented with exquisite melody and refined musicality.

After the performance ended, the audience sat in silence for a moment, overwhelmed by the lingering emotion. Then, applause erupted. Claps and cheers echoed as the maestro acknowledged the ovation before leaving the stage.

In the midst of all this, I suddenly became aware of a slight pressure on my shoulder. Turning to my side, I found Kaki fast asleep, her head resting against me.

Amused, I gave her a gentle nudge. She stirred awake, blinked twice, and with half-lidded eyes said, 'Apu...what an amazing performance! Was it not?'

Dadu, standing nearby, gave me a playful signal not to laugh. We quietly gathered our things, and he dropped us home in his car.

Later, I learnt that the artist who had cast such a spell on us was none other than Ustad Bade Ghulam Ali Khan, the same maestro who had recorded two beautiful songs for the film *Mughal-e-Azam*.

Let me return to the story of my struggles now, Di-bhai. After completing the BT course in a year, I returned to work at the school in 1957. A few days later, Dadu asked me to enrol in a one-year special honours course in Botany. And so, I found myself studying once again. Whenever I broke down from exhaustion, it was Dadu who took care of me. He would take me to a sweet shop on my way back from college. Sometimes, he bought me cakes, candies or oranges, always encouraging me to keep going. Though unrelated to me by blood, he became my friend, philosopher and guide.

Throughout this time, I was fortunate to study either for free or by paying only half of the usual tuition fees. Without Dadu's support and guardianship, I do not think I could have survived those dark days.

Di-bhai, you know it was Kaka's wish that I study medicine and become a doctor like his elder brother. Keeping that in mind, Kaki once took me to meet Dr Sudhir Bose, the principal of Calcutta Medical College. He had known our father very well and had previously assured us of his guidance once I completed my ISc course. He even had a few of our father's books, which he said he would hand them over to me.

But Di-bhai, after Kaka's passing, our financial situation became such that pursuing an expensive medical education was no longer within reach. Still, as you know, my determination to understand the human body never wavered.

Though I could not study about diseases and their treatments, I chose to devote my life to the study and teaching of the life sciences.

With the blessings of our physician father, our beloved Kaka, and Professor Sukhen Roy—my 'Dadu'—I was able to accomplish that.

Yet, Di-bhai, as you know, good times never last long. When I was studying at St Paul's College, which admitted both male and female students, some of our relatives complained about it to Kaki, suggesting I might go astray in male company. They even proposed that I should be married off to a suitable groom without delay. Strangely, these people never offered us help or sympathy during the tough times we faced after Kaka's passing!

Kaka, while he was alive, had seen through their mentality. He would often say sternly, 'My daughter has not been born only to live as someone's wife. She will earn her own living and stand on her own feet. At the right time, she will bring someone to me and tell me, 'Look Kaka, I have chosen him to be my life partner. Do you like him?"

Di-bhai, it was impossible for me to forget those words. My courageous Kaki reminded me of them.

Meanwhile, the wedding of Dadu's eldest daughter, Khukudi, was finalized. I still remember how much fun we had at the celebrations. You were in Calcutta at the time, and Dadu had affectionately invited you too. Why would he not? By then, he had become your Dadu as well! How could anyone resist responding to such bonds of affection?

One day, shortly after Khukudi's wedding, Dadu came to our home and had a long conversation with Kaki. Let me confess something, Di-bhai—I had overheard their discussion while hiding behind the door.

I heard him say, 'Apu is grown up now. She is self-reliant. There's just one task left for me—to see her married.'

To be honest, I was not overjoyed. If anything, I felt nervous. What did we have? No money, no resources, no real support.

Who would arrange the venue? Who would bear the costs of the ceremony? At an age when most girls begin to dream of a happy family life, I found myself staring into the dark abyss of financial uncertainty.

Yes, I had learnt how to earn a living, but I had also learnt how painfully difficult it was to arrange for even modest funds. Kaka had been a man of refined tastes, but he had not managed to save much. And as for seeking help? I could not even imagine crying out for mercy or assistance from our relatives. We were poor, yes—but Kaki had raised me with ideals and with self-respect.

I remember telling her one day, 'To me, people who ask for dowry are like beggars. Do not even consider any marriage proposal from such people. I could never respect them.'

Di-bhai, you will also remember that by then we had lost our mother. Diagnosed with throat cancer, she had passed away after suffering for only a month.

Perhaps a year or two had passed since her death when a distant relative of Kaki's brought a marriage proposal for me. The groom was a government officer with an MA degree. Both Dadu and Kaki seemed interested. Dadu promptly contacted them as soon as he found their address.

Nineteen

The members of the prospective groom's family visited Dadu at his college office. There, they learnt how, after successively losing my father and uncle, I had struggled for years to pursue my studies while working to earn and survive at the same time. When Dadu spoke against dowry, they agreed and declared, 'This wedding will go ahead if you gift only *shakha* and sindoor to the bride as the traditional symbols of marital status and nothing else.'

Dadu was relieved to hear this. He appreciated the like-mindedness and happily gave his assent for the marriage. He took Kaki with him to visit the groom's family, who lived in Baranagar at the time. Later, the groom himself came to our home one evening, accompanied by his sister-in-law and uncle. I was a little irritated, anticipating the usual barrage of questions. That was the standard social practice. But oddly enough, the groom's uncle only asked my name, and none of the other visitors had any queries!

The groom's family belonged to the Kayastha Das community from the Mymensingh district in East Bengal. He was in a similar situation to mine—both his parents had passed away when he was young, and he had been raised by his uncle. This gentleman wanted his nephew to marry an educated girl. Though they had once owned a large house and other properties in Tangail, Mymensingh, the family had been uprooted during the Partition and had since resettled in Calcutta with modest means.

Still, the groom's younger brother and the sister were both

graduates, and he himself held a postgraduate degree. His elder brother was a medical officer in Arunachal Pradesh, then known as NEFA (Northeast Frontier Agency). Even his sister-in-law was a graduate—a rarity in those days. Clearly, this was a family that valued education and intellect.

However, I was not confident I would like the man I was going to marry. You were in East Pakistan at the time Di-bhai, and in your letters, you kept asking me for my opinion about the groom and the marriage. I found it difficult to reach a decision promptly. However, when he visited us to finalize the wedding date, Kaki asked him, 'We are unable to gift you anything special, still, kindly tell us which brand of wristwatch will you prefer as a wedding gift? Also, you hold a good position in the central government; I would like to gift you an expensive pen as a token, my son!'

Di-bhai, that day, the man who would be my husband replied very calmly, 'A watch? Why should you gift me a new watch? I am already wearing one on my wrist! And a pen? I already have one in my pocket, Kaki.'

My decision was made. I immediately felt a deep sense of respect and liking for the man who was to be my life partner.

Some of his relatives, who were visiting them from East Pakistan, urgently needed to return. Hence, they wished for the wedding to be arranged within the same month. According to the almanac, there were no suitable dates for marriage in that month. Dadu summoned the Brahmins from Bhatpara, who were experts in interpreting Vedic traditions. They opined that a girl who had lost both her parents—thus considered *arakkhaniya*, or an orphan—could marry during the month of *Ashwin,* which was otherwise inauspicious for weddings. They suggested that the fortnight of *Devipaksha,* which started after *Mahalaya*, could be considered an auspicious time for the ceremony to be held.

However, the question bothering Kaki and me was: how would we organize a wedding in the one-and-a-half-roomed house we lived in?

Di-bhai, Dadu turned out to be nothing short of a magician—someone who could make the impossible, possible. To me, he truly appeared that way!

He consulted with the Principal of my college, Professor Prashanta Bose, and together they made an extraordinary decision: the Puja vacation for our college would begin two days earlier than scheduled.

Dadu then coordinated with the groom's family and finalized the wedding date—17th Ashwin of that year.

Thus, the entire Bangabasi College building stood vacant during the holidays, providing ample space for both the wedding ceremony and the celebrations.

The housekeeping staff of the college came forward willingly, offering their services for the event. After enjoying the wedding feast to their hearts' content, they blessed the bride and the groom—referred to by many that day as the 'granddaughter of Professor Sukhen Roy and her husband'.

I still remember that it had rained in the afternoon. All the teachers from Entally Hindu Balika Vidyamandir arrived for the ceremony, beautifully dressed but carrying their shoes in their hands to avoid spoiling them in the muddy streets! Fortunately, the rain stopped just before the ceremony began.

Our paternal aunt, along with all of you—my siblings and cousins—joined hands with Kaki, helping her with the preparations. Relatives pitched in as well, ensuring that everything went smoothly without a single hitch. Dadu remained present throughout, supervising every detail with care.

And thus, Di-bhai, a new chapter unfolded in my life.

Twenty

The night of 4 October 1959, Di-bhai, Parag—your brother-in-law—and I, spent our time mostly discussing our uprooted refugee families, struggles, personal outlooks and likes and dislikes, gradually getting to know each other. Like the departing night, the darkness of unfamiliarity between us began to fade as dawn approached.

Parag was honest and open about his origins and childhood. Betka, in Tangail, where the Das family lived, was a large village bustling with life. Parag's grandfather, Rukminikanta Das, had been an affluent and highly educated man. He was a pioneer in advancing education in the district, and a primary school was established in his name in the village, where the children received their early education.

Rukminikanta and his wife Swarnamayee had four sons—Jogendranath, Birendranath, Saratchandra and Vijaychandra—as well as a daughter, who was married into a certain Guha family. Sadly, Saratchandra and Vijaychandra died in infancy from what was then known as Malta fever—an infectious disease transmitted through milk or milk products, which claimed many lives.

The eldest son, Jogendranath, was married to an exquisitely beautiful woman named Charubala. Though they shared a happy married life, they remained childless for many years. On the advice of the family priest, various rituals were performed, including many fasts at the Jagannath Temple in Puri—not only by the couple but also by Swarnamayee herself. Perhaps Lord Jagannath was eventually appeased, for their first son was born in 1927, named Nilmani by his grandmother.

More children followed: two more brothers, Parag and Pramatha, followed by two sisters—Anjali and Aruna. Tragically, Anjali died young due to illness. However, when Nilmani was seven and Aruna just six months old, Jogendranath left this world from colon cancer. Charubala was utterly devastated. How could she manage the estate, the school and the upbringing of her young children alone?

Jogendranath's brother, Birendranath, held his sister-in-law in the highest regard—almost treating her like his own mother. After the tragedy of Jogendranath's death, Birendranath took over the reins of the family's affairs. Not only that, like the legendary Bhishma from the Mahabharata, he made a solemn vow to remain unmarried so that he could dedicate himself entirely to the care and upbringing of his late brother's children.

The enormous mansion belonging to the Das family was not just a residence for the family members. It also provided space for the children's tutors, cooks, servants, nannies, and even a resident wrestler, whose task was to train the boys in wrestling and physical fitness. In the expansive courtyard of the house, idols of various Gods and Goddesses were crafted, decorated, and consecrated before the start of the pujas. Both Basanti Puja during the month of Chaitra and Durga Puja in the month of Ashwin were celebrated with great devotion.

It was a family tradition to host a grand feast after the immersion of the idol on Vijayadashami, inviting not only relatives and neighbours but also the less fortunate from the entire village.

It is said that during Rukminikanta's lifetime, Kali Puja was also celebrated at the mansion. The rituals included the practice of animal sacrifice. However, during one such occasion, after all the arrangements for the puja had been completed, a strange and unsettling incident occurred. As the neck of the sacrificial goat was severed, the butcher's sharp weapon accidentally slipped from his grasp and struck Rukminikanta on the forehead. Though the injury was not serious, it left a lifelong scar.

That very night, Rukminikanta had a vivid dream. In it, the Goddess appeared before him and instructed that from then on, she wished only to be worshipped as Goddess Durga, not as Kali, and that all forms of animal sacrifice were to be abolished.

My father-in-law, Jogendranath Das, had refined tastes. His true passion lay in sailing while listening to music. He would order large pleasure boats from Dhamrail and loved boat rides on the Burai River. The boatmen and attendants were informed in advance to ensure the gramophone on board was ready. Once the vessel reached mid-river, classical and devotional music would be played. Jogendranath Babu thus enjoyed his river cruises in full measure.

Though Betka had large plantations of mango and jackfruit, the Das family also owned more land and estates about a day's journey from Tangail, which included paddy fields and orchards. Fruits, coconuts and other produces would arrive at the house from these estates before Durga Puja.

Parag and his siblings attended the primary school in Betka before moving on to Shibnath High School in Tangail. Later, they also attended Bindu Basini High School there. Their sister pursued higher studies at Kumudini College. Eventually, the boys ventured to Calcutta for their advanced education.

Parag's mother Charubala loved to read Bengali literature. While cooking, she would read out from the *Mahabharata*, *Krittivasi Ramayan* and *Meghnadbadh Kavya* to Nilmani, Parag and Pramatha, as they sat on low wooden stools in their large kitchen.

A private tutor, Shri Khitish Biswas, taught the boys Mathematics and English. He encouraged Parag and his brothers to read widely beyond their school curriculum to build their general knowledge. The boys would often borrow books from a community library located somewhere between their school and home. Through countless Bengali and English storybooks, along with works on philosophy, history and other subjects, they developed a keen curiosity and a broad understanding of the world around them.

After losing her husband, Charubala raised her children with a delicate balance of affection and strict discipline. Her youngest son, Pramatha, was especially mischievous.

I remember hearing a story from Parag, Di-bhai. One summer, their mother gave Pramatha some money to buy a simple hand-fan made of *tal-pata*. The ten-year-old bought the fan as instructed but spent the remaining money on sweets for himself and a few school friends before returning home. True to her stern nature, Charubala broke the handle of the new fan on her son's back as punishment.

In those days, on the night of Nashtachandra, it was customary for boys from the neighbourhood to steal cucumbers, lemons and other fruits or vegetables from each other's gardens as part of a *broto*—a religious observance in Hindu culture. Inspired by his friends, Parag too joined in the mischief and returned home proudly showing off a few stolen lemons.

But alas! Charubala was far from pleased. A woman of unwavering principle, she immediately sent him back to the neighbour's house with the stolen fruits, instructing him to apologize and return them without delay. Parag obeyed her without question—another lesson in honesty, firmly delivered and never forgotten.

Charubala ensured that her children, who had lost their father young, grew up under strict discipline. She had a strong personality, spoke little and refrained from giving her children excessive comforts. Though she did not show affection without reason, she was not unkind; she rewarded them when deserved. Once, the librarian affectionately gave five guavas to Nilmoni. Although terribly hungry, he did not eat any on his way home and carried the fruits to his mother. He answered all his mother's questions regarding who gave them, where and why, despite being very tired. After verifying the story, Charubala kissed him on both cheeks. Perhaps that was the only time he received such overt affection from her. My eldest brother-in-law happily recounted this tale many times.

Di-bhai, it was an era when fear of dacoits was real. When my father-in-law Jogendranath Das was unwell, there were rumours that a robbery might occur. Charubala had hidden all the jewellery in kerosene cans under her bed. The burglars did enter the house, but never suspected that such mundane containers could conceal treasure. Charubala maintained her composure throughout, and the jewellery was saved.

Charubala, however, did not live very long after her husband's death. She handed over the estate to her brother-in-law Birendranath and passed away six or seven years later. Their uncle then took up the reins of the family, and raising the children with utmost devotion.

Parag's uncle, Birendranath, remained unmarried for many years, dedicating himself wholeheartedly to the care and upbringing of the children as though they were his own. However, over time, he increasingly felt the absence of a lady in the household—especially when it came to looking after the girl child in the family.

Under gentle but persistent pressure from relatives, Birendranath finally agreed to marry. Despite the considerable age gap between them, the new bride—now the children's aunt—took charge of household affairs with grace and efficiency.

Birendranath remained uncompromising when it came to the children's education, and his dedication bore fruit. My older brother-in-law, Borda, excelled in science during his final school examinations, while Parag earned the top rank in the entire Mymensingh district, setting academic records in history and economics. Borda went on to pursue medical studies in Cooch Behar, later becoming a medical officer in NEFA.

Following Partition, Parag shifted to Calcutta for his graduation, staying in a hostel while studying at City College. After completing his MA at Calcutta University, he secured a position in central government service. Meanwhile, my younger brother-in-law obtained degrees in BA and BT, eventually becoming a schoolteacher.

A few years later, their sister also graduated and joined government service. She married Amiya-da, a Baranagar resident, who was not only a government official but also a highly skilled singer.

Ranar choleche bujhi bhor hoy hoy
Aro jore aro jore he ranar durbar durjoy
Tar jiboner swapner moto piche sore jaye bon
Aro poth aro poth bujhi hoy laal purbo kon.[*]

Onward, the runner, as dawn draws near,
Swift and invincible, conquering fear.
Dreams trail behind, forests left in wake,
The eastern horizon, a reddening lake.

Di-bhai, I can never forget the way my sister-in-law's husband used to sing this song. I do not mean to say that today's singers lack talent or passion. Yet, with their exaggerated mannerisms, the cacophony of too many accompanying instruments, the dazzling

---

[*]Poem by Sukanta Bhattacharya and tune set by Hemanta Mukherjee

lights on TV screens and the overly animated hosts, I feel that the essence of music is often lost. I have heard my granddaughter while she was in school, singing in her sweet voice while playing around in my room: 'Aaloker ei jharnadharaye dhuiye dao' (Bathe me in this fountain of light). What a feeling that was, as the winter sun spilled through the window, lighting up the entire room and lifting my spirits. We are a generation that does not appreciate showbiz but love simplicity and melody; is it not so, Di-bhai?

Twenty-one

After my marriage, it became impractical for me to commute to school from my in-laws' residence in Baranagar, which was too far from my workplace. After much discussion with everyone in the family, we decided to move to a house on Linton Street in Calcutta.

There was no room for misunderstanding in our conjugal life. Both of us had grown up amidst abundance, yet, we had also experienced hardships at different stages of our lives. That was the time when we were trying to build a strong foundation for our future, entirely on our own. With mutual support, we gradually learnt to respect, trust and love one another. Our first child was born in 1962, in the month of Ashwin.

Di-bhai, do you remember how you used to touch my belly during my pregnancy and say, 'Somehow, this feels different'?

While seeking advice from Dr J.K. Chatterjee at Calcutta Medical College, it was discovered that the baby was in a breech position, that is the child was upside down. Dr Chatterjee advised that a caesarean section would be the only safe way to deliver. Interestingly, once upon a time the great doctor had been a student in Dadu's physiology class. Dadu, at our request, visited the hospital to meet the doctor. When Dr Chatterjee saw his former teacher, he immediately bent down to touch his feet. It was a powerful reminder that, regardless of the accolades and stature one achieves in life, genuine education instills gratitude and humility.

Indeed, that was a different time! Most births were still

natural then. My elder sister-in-law, who had already delivered three children naturally, was very curious about the surgical procedure. Though he tried to appear strong, the thought of my operation left your Parag-babu visibly restless and fraught with tension. Kaki did not want to come to the hospital but repeatedly reminded you, 'Atasi, make sure to check if the baby's fingers and toes are all intact. They will be taking it out after cutting open the mother's belly!'

My elder daughter, Titai, was born on the day of *Shashthi* of Durga Puja.

On that day, Parag came early to the hospital, wearing clean and neatly ironed clothes. The surgery went well, and after a few hours we, mother and child, were moved to the ward. After seeing the newborn, Parag could not take his eyes off her face, no matter how much you all teased him.

'See, Apu! Now that he's got his daughter, Parag has forgotten all about you!' you had joked.

I smiled a little, even though I was still under the influence of morphine. That day, Parag held my hands and, in front of you all and his sister-in-law, said candidly, 'No, Sejdi; a new arrival has graced us, and I am just inspecting to see if she possesses the same beauty as Apu. I am afraid once I take mother and daughter home, I may just forget about my work and spend all my time with them.'

Everyone burst into laughter, and even the nurse smiled. There were quite a few visitors who had come to congratulate us. Eventually, the nurse said, 'Please go home now, all of you. Let the patient rest a bit. It is hard to tell whether this is a hospital ward or a wedding feast.'

I spent the entire Durga Puja recuperating on a hospital bed in the Mary Herbert Ward at Eden Hospital, Medical College. The nurses had promised that they would show me the idols on

Vijayadashami, and true to their word, they did. They placed me in a wheelchair and took me to the ward balcony overlooking Central Avenue. From there, I watched truck after truck pass by, each carrying beautifully decorated idols on their way to immersion.

Cradling my newborn daughter in my arms, I gazed at the Goddess's image and prayed with all my heart. I wished for my little girl to grow up as powerful and courageous as Goddess Durga herself. And, thanks to the blessings of you all, Di-bhai, my Titai has indeed been blessed with a dauntless and upright spirit.

Even though I, her mother, could not fulfil the dream of becoming a doctor like her grandfather, she has done it—perhaps sensing, in some quiet way, the struggles I had endured all along the way. She, as the senior house surgeon working under reputed gynaecology professors in Medical College, had later herself successfully assisted and operated on patients admitted in the same Mary Herbert Ward. Her experiences about patients she handled and surgical operation she managed and the descriptions of her activities used to bring tears of joy to my eyes. That is why all of you have loved her so dearly and blessed her with such pride and affection, Di-bhai.

Kaki was an excellent seamstress. The 'mother'—who never heard me call her that—cut up her old saris and, with her own hands, embroidered them beautifully to make soft bedding for little Titai. In fact, Kaki had prepared the child's bedding even before I returned home from the hospital.

Despite our modest financial situation, Parag somehow managed to arrange for two helpers to assist me at home during the first two weeks. At that time, I was on maternity leave from my school, and Parag's salary was not substantial either. But who could restrain the proud father of his first-born daughter?

His joy knew no bounds. At times, he would gleefully read Tagore's poems aloud to our tiny two-month-old or even try to sing Tagore's songs to her in his somewhat off-key voice:

Ki paaini taari hishab milaate mon more nohe raaji.

Today is not the day when my mind would brood on
enumerating the losses that I have suffered.

Di-bhai, I did not know whether to laugh or cry.

'Do you get it, Apu?' he would say. 'Tilottoma—Titai—is our princess. I do not know what you had wished for, but for the past nine months, I have prayed for a little fairy. My prayers have been answered. I will not spare anything for her well-being—and yours. And don't you worry about money. While I am working, everything can be managed. The Almighty has given us this little bundle of joy—He will also shower luck upon us and gradually remove all obstacles.'

Kaki stayed home with me, but she had never had a child of her own. When Titai cried, she could not fathom what to do immediately. I recalled that the wife of Ananda Babu, Parag's colleague, had given birth six months earlier. They had recent experience with a newborn, and upon our request, arranged for a very efficient maid to help us. Nagen's mother, as she was called, joined us promptly and took care of Titai with great affection.

When Titai turned three months old, I resumed my duties at the school. I did not want to depend solely on Parag's salary to run the household. Even Kaki did not want to leave that small job of hers in that situation. Besides, both of us were full of dreams back then—dreams of raising Titai in the best possible way, leaving no wants unfulfilled. Now I know, our happiness provided us with indomitable energy and limitless enthusiasm.

Twenty-two

Even though India had attained independence from British rule by, the new republic was taking its time to set up its administration, border security and other essential services. In 1954, during a visit to Beijing, India's first prime minister, Pandit Jawaharlal Nehru, signed the Panchsheel Agreement, with the Chinese government. At the time, the agreement, emphasizing mutual honesty, respect and peaceful coexistence between the two countries, seemed promising. Pandit Nehru returned in high spirits, and people in India too embraced the slogan 'Hindi-Chini bhai-bhai' (Indians and Chinese are brothers).

However, bi-lateral relations started to shift after Nehru's subsequent meeting with Chairman Mao. China, by then, was brimming with confidence after taking a stand against the United States during the Korean War.

Di-bhai, do you recall when you and I watched the film *Neel Akasher Neechey* at Chobighor cinema hall? I woke up this morning remembering that movie!

It told the story of an innocent Chinese trader who had ventured far from his homeland to Calcutta during the early 1940s to sell China silk. There, he found sisterly affection in a young girl, Basanti, who belonged to an affluent family. Unbeknownst to her family, Basanti was involved with a nationalist political group. Wang Lu while refusing to get involved in the illegal opium trade run by his fellow countrymen, was inspired by Basanti's patriotic ideals. He eventually returned to China to protect his motherland from the Japanese aggression. Kali

Banerjee's portrayal of Wang Lu dumbfounded us, and we wept bitterly when the film ended with Wang Lu unable to reunite with Basanti.

Surely, you remember the songs, 'O nodi re ekti katha sudhai shudu tomare' and 'Neel akasher nichey'? Sung by Hemanta Babu, they were on everyone's lips in those days—their lyrics so heartfelt and their tunes so catchy and melodious!

After the film that day, we had Magnolia ice-cream to console ourselves. Though you wanted *ghoti-garam* and I craved pink candy-floss, neither of us could restrain ourselves when we spotted the yellow ice cream cart. As the ice cream began to melt, we ate quickly, ensuring not even a drop was wasted. One after another, *Haridaser bulbul bhaja* cart and another selling ice lollies steeped in green and red syrup went past us. As we carefully finished our ice creams, we cast greedy glances at those treats, making mental notes to try them the next time we went to the cinema.

Di-bhai, I must confess, life brought our family a rare spell of peace, success, and happiness after Titai was born. Parag's promotion added the much-needed financial stability, making things a little easier for us. But towards the end of that year, major political upheavals began to unfold.

By then, you had already returned to East Pakistan, and it became impossible for me to send you any news. The postal services were severely disrupted, and unlike today, there were no telephones in every household—let alone mobile phones tucked away in pockets and handbags as people have now. Staying in touch across the border became almost impossible.

Do you remember the terrifying Chinese attack on Tibet in 1959, Di-bhai? Thousands of Tibetans fled with the Dalai Lama, seeking refuge in India.

Since then, China had been provoking Indian soldiers along the Indo-Chinese border, launching attacks on the slightest of pretexts. Many brave soldiers from the Gorkha Rifles lost their lives during these confrontations. The Chinese menace spread across multiple fronts—from the Nathula Pass in Sikkim to Bomdila in the east and even reaching Tezpur in Assam.

The situation became so dire that the entire population of Tezpur had to be evacuated and relocated to the southern banks of the Brahmaputra River.

By late 1962, the scale of the attacks grew, striking a devastating blow to Nehru's dream of 'Hindi-Chini Bhai Bhai'.

Eventually, the Chinese Prime Minister declared that China would agree to a ceasefire—but only if Aksai Chin was ceded to them. Faced with no better option, Nehru had to concede. From that moment onwards, India never again regarded this neighbour as entirely trustworthy.

Meanwhile, when Titai was around two years old, she did not like the idea of me leaving for work. She would cry whenever she saw me getting ready for school. At our house at 41A Linton Street, the landlord and his wife would invite her and our maid into their room. The elderly gentleman would recite rhymes to Titai: 'Say *ek'e chandro, dui'e pakkho, teen'e netro, char' e ved*, one moon, two fortnights, three eyes of Shiva, four Vedas.'

Fully dressed and ready, I would quietly tiptoe towards the main door. Upon seeing me, the landlady would signal with her hand for me to leave quickly while she kept Titai engaged, kissing her and encouraging her to continue reciting.

In her sweet baby voice, Titai would chant: '*panch'e panchoban, chhay'e ritu*...five arrows, six seasons.'

Of course, I felt distressed leaving my little one behind. But I would look at the watch, wipe away my tears and depart for work.

Within a few years, we needed more space and had to move out of the house we were living in. We rented a slightly bigger flat in the Moulali area. It was heartbreaking to bid farewell to our kind landlord and his wife. They are no more, but we remain forever indebted to them for their support during those years. The location of the Moulali flat was ideal as it was easy to get buses and trams from the nearby main road. The daily hassle of getting to my school and Parag's office was greatly reduced.

I have never spoken of something that happened during that time. I feel like doing so today.

After independence, the Congress government under the leadership of Jawaharlal Nehru developed strategic relations with Russia. The Soviet government hoped that the Indian communists would adopt a middle path in criticizing the Indian state and be supportive towards the Congress government. But a large section of the Communist Party of India (CPI) claimed that India remained a semi-feudal country, and argued that class struggle could not be compromised for the sake of Soviet commerce and diplomacy. Additionally, the CPI still maintained a hostile attitude towards the political ideology of the Congress. In 1959, the central government dismissed the only non-Congress state government in the country—the Namboodiripad cabinet in Kerala—and imposed President's rule.

Around the same time, relations soured between the Communist Party of the Soviet Union (CPSU) and the Chinese Communist Party (CPC). By the early 1960s, the CPC was openly accusing the CPSU of deviating from the ideals of Marxism-Leninism. Meanwhile, relations between India and China deteriorated as well in 1962.

During and after the Second World War, the CPI led several mass movements, including armed uprisings in Telangana, Tripura, and political movements in Kerala. Many of these struggles laid the ideological groundwork for the eventual formation of the Communist Party of India (Marxist), or CPI(M) in 1964.

I vaguely recall that in November 1964–65, when Titai was around two years old, Asim came to stay with us. Asim was distantly related to us through our judge-uncle's son, who had moved to Switzerland. We were puzzled by this sudden rekindling of a long-lost connection, but we welcomed him into our modest Moulali flat.

Asim was a cheerful young man in his late 20s. His only vice was smoking cigarettes, which he bought from a nearby shop. My admonishments in this regard did not have much effect. He told us he would stay for about a month before returning to his ancestral home in Tripura.

Around the same time, a significant political upheaval unfolded. Hundreds of CPI leaders and workers were arrested on charges of being Chinese sympathizers. Titai's father read in the newspapers that the internal strife within the CPI showed no signs of resolution.

One evening, Asim went out and did not return.

I spent the entire night unable to sleep. Parag remained at the entrance gate, keeping a restless vigil. Little Titai stirred often, woke repeatedly, gazed at my face—perhaps wondering what her mother was up to. Di-bhai, I was both frightened by the tense, determined look on Parag's face and deeply embarrassed by the humiliation this harassment had caused us.

Asim finally returned the next morning. It was winter. Wrapped in a brown shawl that covered his head and face, he had brought along a friend in tow. At first glance, the friend's religion or background was not discernible—he could have been Hindu, Muslim or Christian. The bearded young man wearing thick glasses carefully avoided making all eye contact. It appeared as though he was intentionally trying to hide his identity.

'You'll hear a whistle at night. You should be ready then!' he whispered to Asim before taking his leave.

As soon as the friend left, Asim went for a bath. I entered his room and noticed his clothes heaped on the bed. I picked those up to give them for a wash when I noticed a large blood stain on his shirt. I screamed, shocked. Was Asim injured? But his gait had seemed quite normal and casual when he left the room!

Titai was down with a fever, so Parag had taken leave from his office that day. Hearing my scream, he entered the room silently and came to stand behind me. In a state of urgency, he pulled out Asim's bag from under the bed. On emptying it on to the bed, clothes and a bunch of papers tumbled out. Among them was a sheet of instructions, partly coded, but it was evident that Asim was a part of an operation linked to a homicide.

At lunch, I noticed Asim struggling to eat properly. Later, I heard him vomiting in the bathroom. Parag was visibly tense. I realized he was contemplating his next steps. Later in the evening, when we heard strange whistling sounds from outside, I finally told Parag what Asim's friend had whispered before leaving. For the first time, I saw Parag truly get angry. He chided Asim sternly. Asim, it seemed, had expected such a reaction. He said, 'Uncle, my job here is done. Last night I received some money with which I can manage to buy a ticket to Agartala at Dum Dum airport. Thank you for everything.'

As a central government employee, Parag was deeply disturbed to witness illegal activities unfolding right under his own roof. How could Asim be so recklessly indifferent, putting everyone who trusted him in such grave danger?

Parag knew full well that Asim's actions could destroy his career for good. So, when the young man made a casual, dismissive remark, Parag's restraint finally snapped—a sharp, resounding slap landed across Asim's face.

I had never seen Parag resort to violence before.

Without another word, he packed all of Asim's belongings into a bag, thrust it into his hands, and said in a cold, unwavering voice, 'Get out. And do not bother sending word when you reach wherever you are going.'

I do not know if Asim made it to his destination or not, but today, in my old age, that incident came back to me with vivid intensity.

After everything the people of this country endured—the suffering, the humiliation, the pain—in their fight against the British to turn India into an independent country, how did we forget the price of that freedom, Di-bhai? How could we, citizens of the same nation, take up arms against our fellow countrymen?

Sometimes I feel I have become quite outdated. But if honesty and humanity are now considered old-fashioned, I still believe I'll find happiness in holding on to these values.

Twenty-three

Days of hardship revisit periodically.

In 1966, just as we had enrolled Titai in a reputed English-medium school, food prices skyrocketed. During that time, a maid from north 24 Parganas used to come to our house for household chores. She was sharp, articulate and efficient in her tasks, which included cleaning the house, washing utensils and doing the laundry. I would prepare Titai for school, finish cooking and pack Parag's lunch before he left for work.

On one such day, I had finished all my work and was grabbing a bite before heading to my school when I was startled by some sort of disturbance near the entrance. Someone was opening and closing the door repeatedly. At the same time, I heard a commotion. Stepping out, I found the maid doing her best to push a dishevelled man out of the house and forcibly close the door on him.

Oh my God! Who is this? was my initial thought. But before I could shout or call for help, both of them became aware of my presence. Suddenly, the maid's sari came loose, and a large quantity of rice grains spilled out. This explained why, for the past two weeks, I had found the rice-measuring ladle in odd places—and why our monthly rice stock was always running short! It became clear that the man was not her husband but a rice smuggler.

We all called her Poppy's mother. Every day, she travelled by train from the suburbs, arriving in Calcutta early in the morning. After completing her chores in six different houses—including ours—she would rush back to Sealdah station in the evening to catch the train home.

That particular day, there had been a bit of extra work at our place, making her run behind schedule. The delay in smuggling out the rice must have left her accomplice—the rice smuggler—growing anxious. Unable to wait any longer outside, he resorted to that reckless act of intrusion.

Needless to say, I did not have to dismiss her; both she and her partner disappeared of their own accord.

That year, the price of rice shot up to five rupees per kilogram, which was exorbitant for the times. Cooking then was primarily done on kerosene stoves, and even the price of kerosene had risen. Prafulla Sen, who succeeded Dr Bidhan Roy as the chief minister of West Bengal, declared in his speech, 'Eating rotis than rice is healthier. As for vegetables, eating only raw bananas can provide a lot of strength to the body.'

People, especially those in the suburbs and the villages, could no longer endure this situation. Since independence, millions had poured into free India from East Pakistan, formerly East Bengal. The government had imposed taxes on inter-state trade, particularly on food grains. As the crisis deepened, smuggling thrived.

Di-bhai, in 1966, Bihar was struck by a devastating famine. The Bihar famine became yet another grim reminder of how the lack of timely food grain conservation could spiral into catastrophe, claiming countless human lives. That same year, around mid-March, tensions over rice distribution flared up in Swarupnagar.

The police opened fire during a protest, and news quickly spread that two young boys had lost their lives in the firing. The entire state erupted. People poured in from suburbs and nearby towns into Calcutta, blocking roads, pulling down electric lines, disrupting railway tracks, and continuing their protests even on empty stomachs.

The Congress government struggled to contain the unrest. By then, the CPI had already split into two factions.

In 1967, one faction of the CPI, along with a group of disillusioned Congress members, came together to form the United Front and assumed power in West Bengal. However, the embers of yet another rebellion were already smouldering in the shadows.

But I will come to that later.

During that time, one of Parag's cousins came to Calcutta to pursue engineering; additionally, his nephew enrolled at St Paul's School as well. We offered to support them in their studies by accommodating them to stay in our house. Thus, our extended family lived comfortably in the two large and one small room of our flat on Creek Row near Moulali.

Cricket fever was in the air, and both Parag's cousin and nephew were avid enthusiasts. That winter, they managed to secure two low-priced season tickets for the second match of India–England Test series being played at the Eden Gardens. While I had seen images of Gavaskar's attractive face, the turbaned Bishan Singh Bedi and Farokh Engineer, I lacked the patience to sit through a match that lasted five days. Still, I gladly packed food for them on match days—boiled eggs, bananas and bread—and sent them off cheerfully.

Yet I couldn't help remembering the tragic stampede during the India–Australia match at Eden Gardens a few years earlier. Young boys had lost their lives, crushed in the crowd. Mindful of that episode, I repeatedly warned the youngsters to remain careful. I only breathed easy when they returned from the stadium. Then, listening to their excited retelling of square-cuts and googlies, Parag would glance at me, and we would both smile affectionately.

One day, an unfortunate incident shook our lives. Kaki, upon returning from her school, collapsed unconscious in the bathroom. The doctor diagnosed it as a cerebral stroke due to aging. I was overwhelmed with anxiety, unable to sit still. Kaki became paralyzed and remained bedridden for six long months. Parag's patience and calmness during that time were truly commendable. Even in the midst of such a crisis, he gently reminded me of all that I owed to Kaki and stood by me as a constant source of strength. With mounting responsibilities and growing medical expenses, I began to feel the urgent need to increase our household income.

Twenty-four

Di-bhai, as you are aware, immediately after passing my BSc Honours examinations, I appeared for interviews at several renowned schools in the city to teach life sciences in the higher secondary curriculum. One of these was Brahmo Balika Sikshalaya, near Rajabazar. The headmistress of the school sent word for me to meet her. In 1964, I was appointed as a biology teacher there. It was a reputed school in the city at the time.

At this juncture, it is necessary to discuss the advent of Brahmo Samaj and their contributions to upliftment of the women in the society and education of the girl child.

When Ram Mohan Roy dedicated himself to the study of the scriptures of all major religions in his quest for spiritual truth, he did not confine himself to Hindu texts like the Vedas and the Puranas only. He also studied the Quran in Arabic and the Bible in Hebrew and Greek. After carefully examining the different faiths, he became convinced that the fundamental purpose of every religion was the same—the ethical upliftment of humanity.

However, he believed that each faith needed to be re-explained and re-evaluated in light of changing times. Rather than renouncing Hinduism or converting to another religion, he resolved to embrace universal moral values while discarding the prejudices, rituals and superstitions embedded within each faith.

By 1828, his religious vision had taken a clearer shape. In August of that year, he founded the Brahmo Sabha—later known as the Brahmo Samaj—meaning 'The Society of God'.

After Ram Mohan Roy's death in England in 1833, the

religious reform movement faced setbacks. His close friend Dwarakanath's son, Debendranath assumed the responsibility and continued his work. Under his leadership, the movement reached new levels of significance and importance. In 1839, he formed a committee called Tattwabodhini Sabha, which worked to promote this new religious idea. He also started publishing a newspaper, *Tattwabodhini Patrika*, which built public support for the reform movement and helped spread the principles of the new faith. During this time, Christian missionaries were actively launching aggressive propaganda against Hinduism.

Meanwhile, within the Brahmo Samaj, a more radical faction began to question the infallibility of the Vedas—a belief that had until then been an inseparable part of Brahmo ideology. Among these reformers, the most notable was Akshay Kumar Dutta. By 1847, after careful survey, the Brahmo leadership concluded that the Vedas could no longer be considered infallible. Therefore, efforts were made to realign their religious beliefs based on selected teachings from the *Upanishads*, which supported the idea of one true God. These amended ideas of the Brahmo Samaj were published in 1850 as a book titled as *Brahmo Dharma* or 'the religion of the worshippers of the one true God'.

Maharshi Debendranath Tagore gave a new lease of life to the Brahmo Samaj at a time when the movement was floundering after the death of Raja Ram Mohan Roy. Under his leadership, the Samaj gradually regained direction and purpose.

The movement gained further momentum and wider acceptance with the entry of Keshab Chandra Sen, who joined the Brahmo Samaj in 1857. Within a short span, Keshab won the trust and admiration of Debendranath. However, ideological differences gradually emerged between the two, particularly regarding the caste system and the extent of social reforms.

While Debendranath's methods leaned towards caution

and conservatism, Keshab Chandra Sen advocated bold social reforms. He called for the complete eradication of the Hindu Varna system and worked actively towards women's education, widow remarriage, and female emancipation. His progressive stand helped elevate the status and reach of the Brahmo Samaj significantly by 1858.

Keshab Chandra became a dynamic force within the Bengal Renaissance. Conferred the title of 'Brahmananda,' he emerged not only as a religious reformer but also as a symbol of the growing national consciousness of India. During his extensive travels across Bombay, Madras, and other parts of India, he propagated the core ideals of the Brahmo Samaj—monotheism, rationality, and social justice. His public debates with European Christian missionaries became widely known, where he countered their criticisms of Indian religions, civilization, and culture with sharp reasoning and powerful oratory. One of his most notable public engagements was his debate with Christian missionaries in 1861 at the Town Hall in Calcutta, where he forcefully defended Hindu spiritual philosophy and exposed the shortcomings of missionary approaches.

Keshab Chandra Sen's political philosophy was nuanced. Though he did not advocate violent resistance against the British Raj, his passionate speeches on individual freedom, human dignity, and social equality played a significant role in awakening nationalist sentiment in pre-independence India.

Favoured and respected by Sri Ramakrishna Paramahamsa, Keshab Chandra often promoted spiritual teachings at public gatherings, both in India and during his visit to England in 1870, where he addressed British audiences about Indian spirituality and social reform. His campaign for social legislation culminated in the passing of the Civil Marriage Act of 1872 (originally called the Native Marriage Act), designed to provide legal recognition to inter-caste and inter-religious marriages, largely owing to his efforts.

Though Keshab's attention remained primarily focused on the autonomy and progressive growth of the Brahmo Samaj rather than on mainstream Hindu society, the mutual respect between him and Maharshi Debendranath Tagore remained intact despite their philosophical disagreements.

The formal Brahmos generally belonged to the Brahmin community. They denounced idol worship and believed in a supreme, formless and absolute divinity. Informal Brahmos, who belonged to Kayastha, Baidya or other castes also followed the principles of the Samaj but continued to believe in reincarnation and karma. In contrast, the formal Brahmos believed that after death, the soul is simply assimilated into the supreme formless being. Eventually, due to these internal divisions, a new chapter began in the history of the Brahmo movement.

In May 1878, the Sadharan Brahmo Samaj was established at a meeting held at the Town Hall in Calcutta. Ananda Mohan Bose, Shivnath Shastri, and Umesh Chandra Dutta took charge of leading this new organization. In a gesture reflecting his enduring goodwill, Maharshi Debendranath Tagore sent a letter conveying his blessings and best wishes to the newly formed Samaj.

Twenty-five

At Brahmo Balika Shikshalaya, the day commenced with a prayer session in a large hall. There were discussions on the *Upanishads*, recitations of *shlokas* and renditions of *Rabindrasangeet*—a beautiful daily ritual. Teachers and students would sing hymns from the *Rig Veda*, along with Bengali translations that had been popularized by Srimati Indira Devi Choudhurani.

The Sadharan Brahma Samaj had established the school on 16 May 1890, a date that coincided with the foundation day of the Samaj. On that specific day, 15 young boys and girls began their education, seated on rugs on the floor of a rented house on Cornwallis Street. That same year, a girls' boarding facility was initiated. Within a year, the number of students rose to sixty-three. By its third year, the school had progressed to the entrance level and relocated to Mirzapur Street. Eventually, a large plot of land was purchased at 294, Upper Circular Road, where a permanent school building was constructed.

In the 19th century, when girls were not permitted to step out of their homes alone and speaking to anyone outside the immediate family was considered taboo, the very notion of educating daughters was rarely entertained. Girls were expected to accept their roles in silence, without questioning or aspiring for knowledge.

It was during such a restrictive era that the establishment of this school became a beacon of hope—illuminating a new path towards learning, self-respect, and personal achievement.

Though it initially catered to girls from Brahmo families, over time, many Hindu families also began sending their daughters here for education.

The name of the school, Brahmo Balika Shikshalaya, holds significance. Perhaps it was chosen as a lasting reminder that true education goes beyond conventional academic learning. It must also nurture values, compassion, and a strong moral character.

Over the years, the school's management and executive committees were graced by several eminent personalities who contributed immensely to its growth. Among them were Babu Madhusudan Sen, Babu Upendra Kishore Raychaudhuri, Adinath Chatterjee, Umesh Chandra Dutta, Labanyaprabha Bose, Pandit Shibnath Shastri, and Umapada Ray.

This institution was a pioneer in establishing a Montessori school in West Bengal. In January 1930, under the supervision of Lady Abala Basu, the wife of Acharya Jagadish Chandra Bose, the Montessori section embarked on its journey, becoming the first of its kind. Nalini Raha and Mayalata Shome were sent to Rome to study directly under Madame Montessori and learn her unique process of hands-on teaching. These included using the abacus for mathematics, incorporating origami, celebrating 'doll festivals' and organizing joint picnics for students and teachers—approaches that were considered highly progressive at the time.

After Bethune School, Brahmo Balika Shikshalaya became the second girls' school to be established in Kolkata. Its guiding motto—*'Sraddhaya, Tapasa, Sebaya'* (With Faith, Perseverance, and Service)—became a lifelong mantra for every student who passed through its doors. Each girl was nurtured to believe in this noble approach to learning and life.

Among its distinguished alumni were Labanya Prabha Bose, sister of Acharya Jagadish Chandra Bose, and Kadambini Ganguly, one of the first female graduates of India and among the earliest women doctors in South Asia. Another notable student was Nalini Das, the granddaughter of Upendra Kishore Raychaudhuri—an iconic figure in Bengali children's literature. Nalini Das completed her matriculation from Brahmo Balika Shikshalaya in 1932.

Her uncle was none other than Sukumar Ray, and she was closely associated with *Sandesh*, the famous children's magazine edited by her cousin, Satyajit Ray. Nalini's elder aunt, Sukhalata Rao, also a noted children's writer, had studied in the same school.

Punctuality was a strict norm at my workplace. Dressed in clean and crisp, though not necessarily expensive saris, I tried to reach on time every day. At the entrance of the school stood a large brass plate and an iron hammer that served as a bell. The elderly, burly *darwanji* would strike it 16 times each hour, its deep resonance echoing throughout the school. Adjacent the expansive playground was a grand auditorium, Mary Carpenter Hall, where bold letters above the stage declared the school's motto: Sraddhaya, Tapasa, Sevaya.

With a significantly higher salary, I endeavoured to work to the best of my abilities. Gradually, my botany classes began receiving appreciation. It was I who first established the Life Sciences laboratory at the school, which the senior students enthusiastically supported.

However, I remained anxious about little Titai—just three years old then—and constantly wondered what she might be doing at home while I was away at my school. The thought of leaving her behind unsettled me deeply. Finally, I gathered the courage to confide in the headmistress about my concerns. At the time, Montessori classes for three-year-olds were being conducted in the school. Acting on her kind suggestion, I began bringing Titai with me each day, carrying along her feeding bottle and a packed lunch.

Cheerful and extrovert—she adjusted quite well to the

Montessori classes, often displaying her dancing and singing skills. After the classes, the teachers would lull the children to sleep. By three o'clock, Titai would make her way to the senior teachers' common room with all her belongings, eager to present her own versions of the day's songs and dances. Her teacher-aunts, my colleagues, found great joy in her antics. She could recite the verses of entire *Abol Tabol* by Sukumar Ray. During their free periods, my colleagues would invite her to sit on their laps and treat her to cakes and biscuits. Meanwhile, I would finish my classes and finally descend from the second-floor laboratory to the staff room. Not once did I find Titai neglected or in tears.

Di-bhai, honestly, I can never forget how unrelated people have helped me in so many ways throughout my life.

At the time, Brahmo Balika Shikshalaya was considered the best in terms of discipline and academics. The Rajabazar Science College stood directly opposite the school. Our teachers often interacted with professors from the Science College and scientists and research scholars from the Basu Vigyan Mandir during seminars.

Once, Professor Jayanta Bose of the Science College and a few other professors came to our school to meet the headmistress, Sufala-di. I, the teacher in-charge of Life Sciences was summoned, along with my colleague, Totini, from the Physics department. It was 1965. They wanted to organize an exhibition at the Federation Hall to mark the birth anniversary of renowned scientist Sri Satyendra Nath Bose. The plan was to have science projects on display, with the students from our Class XI science section explaining them to the visitors. It was a highly prestigious opportunity! A group of smart, meritorious students were selected. For almost two weeks, we took the chosen students to the Science College after our tiffin break for training.

Di-bhai, it feels strange even now to recall how effortlessly the great scientist Dr Satyen Bose mingled with us! Every day after the sessions, he would order *muri* and *beguni*—simple snacks of puffed rice and batter-fried brinjal. Seated around him, we would listen with rapt attention as he spoke about various scientific topics or shared stories about the lives of world-renowned scientists with whom he had worked. Between bites and discussions, we absorbed knowledge and laughter alike. To have seen such a great man from such close quarters and and to have had privilege of working with him remains one of the biggest blessings of my life.

Just two days before Dr Bose's birthday celebrations, the programme-in-charge from the Science College surprised me with a suggestion—that little Titai should be the one to felicitate the great scientist by garlanding him on stage.

'It will look very nice,' he said.

I had explained everything to Titai beforehand. Though she was only about three years old, she had met 'Satyen Dadu' several times, often sitting on his lap and enjoying many a candy. During the function, without showing even a hint of hesitation or fear, Titai walked confidently on to the stage and garlanded the world-renowned scientist. Dr Bose affectionately patted her cheeks. I still vividly remember that moment. Titai still has a carefully preserved science magazine signed by Professor Bose on that memorable occasion.

Di-bhai, I would like to share a few things about Satyendra Nath Bose. He was a pioneering physicist whose research primarily focused on mathematical physics. Alongside Albert Einstein, he developed the Bose–Einstein statistics—one of the most significant discoveries in the field of physics.

Brilliant from his student days, Satyendra Nath was mentored by some of the greatest minds of his time, including

Rabindranath Tagore, Prafulla Chandra Ray, and even Madame Curie. Yet, alongside his academic brilliance, there existed a fervent patriot. He maintained secret ties with members of the revolutionary Anushilan Samiti and remained in contact with armed revolutionaries involved in India's freedom struggle.

Born in Calcutta, Satyendra Nath Bose was a passionate advocate for using Bengali as a language of scientific discourse. Throughout his life, he championed the idea that science should not remain confined to English alone. His famous statement on this remains widely quoted: 'Those who say there is no scientific discussion in Bengali either do not know Bengali or do not understand science.'

To further this belief, he founded and published a Bengali science magazine called *Vigyan Parichay*, encouraging scientific dialogue in the mother tongue and making science accessible to Bengali readers.

A student of the Hindu School, at 15 years, he secured fifth position in the school-leaving examination. After passing ISc from Presidency College and securing first position, he gained the mentorship of renowned professors like Acharya Jagadish Chandra Bose and Acharya Prafulla Chandra Roy. He graduated in 1913, again standing first, and completed his post-graduate degree in mixed mathematics with the same outstanding result.

During that period, Sir Ashutosh Mukhopadhyay established the Calcutta Science College, where Satyendra Nath joined as a lecturer in 1915. There, he started research in mixed mathematics and physics along with another great Bengali scientist, Meghnad Saha. When Dhaka University was established in 1921, he joined the Physics department as a reader.

In 1924, while teaching at Dhaka University, Bose wrote an article explaining Planck's principle of quantum radiation without using classical physics. This original approach laid the foundation for quantum statistics. When he failed to get it published, Bose sent it directly to Albert Einstein, who understood its importance, translated it into German and made efforts to publish it in the journal *Zeitschrift Für Physik*. Following this, Bose earned the opportunity to conduct research abroad, working with Luis de Broglie, Marie Curie and Einstein himself during a two-year stay in Europe.

Upon returning to India in 1927, Satyendra Nath Bose was appointed Professor and made Head of the Physics Department at Dhaka University. As the Partition of India drew near, he left Dhaka and returned to Calcutta, joining the University of Calcutta as Professor of Physics. After his retirement in 1956, the university honoured him with the title of Professor Emeritus. Around the same time, at the invitation of the Government of India, he took on the role of Vice-Chancellor of Visva-Bharati University, where he served until 1958.

While teaching quantum mechanics in 1924, Bose realized that photons—the particles of light—could not be treated as distinct, separable entities like classical particles. This insight led him to propose a new kind of statistical distribution for particles that are indistinguishable and can occupy the same energy state. His work laid the foundation for the theoretical classification of two kinds of particles: photons (as massless bosons) and, by extension, other particles with similar statistical behaviour, now known collectively as bosons.

Albert Einstein recognized the significance of Bose's work and extended it to atoms, predicting a new state of matter known today as the Bose–Einstein Condensate (BEC)—a phenomenon where particles occupy the same quantum state at very low temperatures. Though the theory was proposed in the 1920s, the first experimental proof of Bose–Einstein Condensate was achieved much later, in 1995.

In recognition of Bose's groundbreaking contributions, Paul Dirac later named this class of particles 'bosons'—referring to all particles with whole-number spin that obey Bose–Einstein statistics. These particles, which include photons, gluons, and the Higgs boson, are essential to our understanding of the universe today.

In his personal life, Dr Satyen Bose was active, hardworking and sympathetic. I can never forget the numerous things I learnt through my acquaintance with him.

Twenty-six

Di-bhai, I am sure you remember the Brahmo Balika Shikshalaya's annual reunion on 31 January every year? You even accompanied me to the grand occasion a few times. The Acharyas from the Brahmo Samaj used to attend the function. Brahmo songs were sung during prayer. Distinguished personalities like Dr Rama Chowdhury and Srimati Nalini Das attended as well. Once, the legendary Rabindrasangeet singer Suchitra Mitra graced the occasion and sang twenty-two Tagore songs! We were all mesmerized!

Lady Abala Bose had a special association with our school, serving as the secretary of the managing committee from 1910 till 1936. She was the daughter of the renowned Brahmo Samaj reformer Durgamohan Das and was among the earliest students of Mahila Vidyalaya and Bethune School in Calcutta. Denied admission to Calcutta Medical College due to her gender, she pursued medical studies in Madras. Unfortunately, health issues forced her to return without completing her degree. In 1887, she married the eminent scientist Jagadish Chandra Bose.

Abala Bose went on to establish an organization called Nari Shiksha Samiti, aimed at promoting women's education and providing financial assistance to widows. Through this organization, she established Murlidhar Mahavidyalaya and about two hundred schools in rural areas, where widows received training to become educated and self-reliant. After her husband's death, Abala Bose donated one lakh rupees to Sister Nivedita's women's education project. She was not only a pioneer in women's education, but she also showed great enthusiasm for training in home sciences, sewing, hygiene, physical education, jujutsu, tennis and basketball.

Preparations for the Brahmo Girls' School grand reunion would begin well in advance. Duties would be assigned. Welcoming and seating the guests, arrangements for their refreshments after the function and managing the collective lunch of 150–200 girls in the dining hall—everything was handled with remarkable efficiency. We, the teachers, would have our meal at the end, lovingly served by the senior students with utmost care and respect.

I recall an incident from that time. I had just returned to school after my maternity leave following the birth of my younger daughter, Vibhabari—or Bukai, as we fondly call her. That year, I was entrusted with the responsibility of organizing the school's annual sports meet. Given my lifelong love for sports, I gladly accepted the role. However, perhaps my body had not yet fully regained its strength.

During the final leg of the relay race, a Class X student lost her balance and stumbled straight into me. I instinctively caught her to prevent her from falling and injuring herself, but in doing so, I tumbled down and felt a sudden, sharp pain shoot through my left hand. The poor girl was so frightened by the incident that she burst into tears, especially after seeing me wince in pain.

I comforted her as best as I could and, after taking some pain medication, managed to oversee the rest of the event. For me, ensuring that the day's programme went on smoothly was far more important than tending to my own discomfort.

After the prize distribution ceremony, I was taken for an X-ray by the school authorities. The result showed a fracture in the radius bone of my left arm. I remember later, when Titai had become a doctor, she told me that it was a Colles fracture. My arm was put in a cast immediately, and thanks to adequate rest, it healed completely. The student later scored very well in her Higher Secondary examinations and kept in regular touch with me.

The boundless enthusiasm and insatiable curiosity of my students were always my greatest inspiration. At the end of each class, I conducted a question-and-answer session, a sort of rapid-fire discussion about what had been covered in the period. These helped identify the weaknesses of the students and gave me peace of mind knowing I had resolved their doubts.

Di-bhai, I worked in Brahmo Balika Shikshalaya for thirty-four years. My dedication was greatly appreciated, and the school committee displayed their faith in me by appointing me as the headmistress in 1992. I can never forget the day I retired—how the girls and the new teachers, many of whom had once been my students, wept and hugged me as they bid goodbye with heavy hearts. Most of them maintained loving contact with me even years after my retirement.

Even now, I sometimes find myself hurrying after breakfast and my bath, feeling as though it is time to head for school. My class notes ready, and I tell myself that my laboratory assistants, Nimai and Tarak, must have already made all the arrangements for the practical class. I love to imagine that the girls would be waiting inside their classroom for their favourite teacher. Brahmo Balika Shikshalaya will forever occupy a special place in my heart. Even today, the school song sung by students echo in my ears:

Jibone marone shoyone swapone jopibo mantro, rakhibo smoron,
Sraddhaya, Tapasa, Sevaya, Sraddhaya, Tapasa, Sevaya.

In life's journey, 'midst life, death, even in dreams, while asleep,
I'll chant these sacred words, their memories to keep.
Sraddhaya, Tapasa, Sevaya, Sraddhaya, Tapasa, Sevaya.

Those were my golden days, Di-bhai. How can I ever forget them!

I wish to return to an earlier topic now.

About a year after my wedding, a neighbour from our ancestral maternal home at Park Circus came to visit us. He brought with him news of a prospective match for you. We all liked the proposal, and the groom seemed like a fine young man. How we enjoyed your wedding! Your son was born about six months after Titai, and the two of them have always been fond of each other. It was I who named your son Dhruva. He is a grown man now—how swiftly time flies!

After your wedding, Chhoto Mama arranged the marriages of two of our younger sisters as well. By the grace of God and the blessings of our ancestors, all of us sisters, though orphaned at a young age, were married to good men and went on to lead peaceful lives.

Of course, there was a bit of last-minute drama at our youngest sister's wedding. The groom's family suddenly demanded a Singer sewing machine, causing quite a commotion. Chhoto Mama was furious and nearly called off the wedding then and there!

Parag somehow sensed his youngest sister-in-law wished to get married to that particular, handsome groom and declared, 'I'll buy the sewing machine, Mama Babu. Consider it a wedding gift from me.'

In those days, sons-in-law were treated as sons of the family. Though Parag never had the chance to receive the love of a father- or mother-in-law, you and everyone else in our family embraced him wholeheartedly from the very beginning. I still remember how affectionately Bordi would welcome him to her quarters at our Park Circus home during occasions like Bijoya Dashami or Jamai Shashti. Though unmarried, she was particular about hosting guests with care and attention. Serving food from outside eateries was out of the question—certainly not for her brother-in-law. Everything had to be prepared at home, so we always had to give her advance notice before visiting. As soon as we arrived, she would light the stove, knead fresh dough with care, and fry fluffy, golden luchis, served piping hot with her signature potato curry.

Di-bhai, I no longer find our charismatic and affectionate elder sister around me. She passed away too soon.

Later, unfortunately, Bordi started to have conflicts with Chhoto Mama and Mami. By then, our brother was frequently changing jobs and constantly travelling to either Manipur or Nagaland. No one had ever taught him to bear responsibilities. He relished living life as a wanderer. Eventually, Bordi left the Park Circus house and headed to Bosepukur with her belongings. She worked in a school, so nobody had to bear her expenses. To overcome her loneliness, she often visited her sisters' homes.

Mejdi used to sing very well in those days. She had received training under an *ustad* in Barisal. Recognizing her talent, even the renowned classical singer Sukhendu Goswami agreed to train her in Calcutta. Mejdi, too, got a job as a schoolteacher.

As I have already mentioned Kaki was bedridden after her stroke. However, within five or six months of paralysis, she made considerable progress. Although her right hand and foot never fully recovered, she managed to chop vegetables and help me with the household work using her left hand. When Titai returned from school, Kaki would feed her and then make her complete her homework.

We were living in a modest two-and-a-half-room flat—Parag, his nephew and cousin, Kaki, Titai and I—all under one roof. But the lack of space never bothered us! Nor did we feel the need for a larger flat.

Twenty-seven

Di-bhai, I cannot resist sharing a few incidents with you.

In those days, when we lived on the first floor of a two-storeyed building near Moulali. The flat opposite ours, on the same landing, was where the Datta's lived. Their rent was less than ours as their apartment was smaller. Mr De, who owned the apartments, lived with his wife and son on the ground floor, occupying the entire area.

The Dattas were not very well-off. Dalim was their only child. He was a brilliant boy and had scored distinctions in four subjects in his Higher Secondary Examination. He studied engineering, and since his college was located in Shibpur, a place just outside Calcutta, he stayed in the college hostel.

Our families had grown quite close over time. I had developed a warm friendship with Dalim's mother, Kusum-di. Both of us shared a fondness for chewing betel leaves, and she would often come over to sit and chat with me over paan. During those relaxed moments, while applying lime paste on the leaves, Kusum-di would talk about her son—how intelligent Dalim had been since childhood, how his school report cards were good enough to be framed. She spoke with pride about how those results had earned him admission to the prestigious Bengal Engineering College, now known as the Indian Institute of Engineering Science and Technology (IIEST) at Shibpur.

Dalim himself was not much of a talker. A well-behaved and serious young man, he would visit our flat every year on Bijoya Dashami to offer his pronam. With his sharp features and intelligent eyes, there was always an air of quiet dignity about him. He seemed to live by a simple principle: empathy for the poor and the hungry.

In those days, vaccine injections against Typhoid, Paratyphoid A and B and Cholera infections (TABC injection) had to be administered as a preventive measure. Both our families planned this together. I am sure you remember the pain and fever that followed each shot. One large vial contained ten individual doses. The neighbourhood doctor would procure the vial and visit our homes, administering the injection into the upper arm of each family member.

If any medicine remained in the vial, the leftover doses were given to the maids, the milkman's son, or even the Kashmiri shawl-seller who happened to be in the vicinity during such times. They accepted the injections quietly, with a touch of fear but immense gratitude, knowing it would boost their immunity. Yes, Di-bhai, such was that age—marked by trust, community spirit, and a sense of shared well-being. Those who arranged for the vials and called the doctor never thought of it as doing anyone a favour either.

Once everyone had been injected, Dalim's mother would prepare a large pot of tea. The first steaming cup, accompanied by a couple of thin arrowroot biscuits placed carefully on a porcelain plate with floral patterns, was served to the doctor. As we sat around, worrying about possible fevers, the doctor—an ex-military man—would sip his tea and if any of us complained about the pain, he would say with a smile, 'Think of the pain our martyrs endured before we won our freedom. Then this little discomfort will not trouble you.'

During one such episode, Dalim gently wiped Titai's tears and said, 'Ask the doctor, Titai, if that is the case, then why so many people are still dying of famine and hunger in a country that has achieved freedom?'

I don't know why, Di-bhai, but my heart started beating faster when I heard those words. Something stirred in me—an uncanny feeling.

One year, post-vaccination, everyone's fever subsided but Dalim did not recover soon. Still, he never complained. Kusum-di and I started to worry. When his fever persisted even after a week, Kusum-di urged Bibhuti Datta, Dalim's father, to bring in a healer from the *dargah* at Moula Ali.

Winter had set in. The healer arrived—a dark-complexioned old man with a *jhola* or a cloth-bag slung over his shoulder. He had long hair tied in a bun on his head and an unkempt beard that tumbled over his chest. He carried a short cane with long feathers tied to its end. This is what he used to chase away diseases!

He caressed Dalim from head to toe with those feathers, muttering mysterious chants under his breath. Through the several holes in his black cloak, one could see a dirty, ragged tunic. The torn ends of his pyjamas were visible around his cracked ankles. After he finished his process of healing activity, Kusum-di filled his jhola with rice, lentils and vegetables. These healers never asked for money.

As the man was about to leave, Dalim called out, 'Wait, uncle!'

He got up from his chair and walked slowly over to the healer, surprising us all.

'I do not know if my disease will get cured or not, but the winter chill will definitely get worse, which might make you fall ill. Please take this.'

He took off the brown woollen shawl wrapped around his shoulders and put it on the healer. The old man, feeling embarrassed, tried to return it immediately.

Dalim's father held the man's hands and said, 'If my son has given it to you, then it is yours; please keep it.'

Three days later, Dalim's fever finally went away. But he had to bear his mother's rebuke for a week. 'Do you know that shawl belonged to my Mama-babu! My uncles were landowners in Comilla? The old shawl may have been slightly damaged by bugs, but it was such a nice and warm one—and you gave it away!' she would taunt him.

'They may have been landowners, Mother, but I gave it to someone who has nothing! He is the one who needs it.'

There was nothing more to say!

After his initial years in Shibpur, whenever Dalim came home during holidays, I began noticing subtle changes in the bright young man. On one such visit, I had gone to their apartment to say hello. After handing some prasad to Kusum-di, I was coming out of their kitchen when I absent-mindedly glanced into Dalim's room. He was not there, but my eyes caught some paper rolls jutting out from beneath his bed. Unable to contain my curiosity, I entered his room, looked beneath the bed and found a tin of red paint and brushes! One of the posters unfurled screamed in ominous red letters: 'We want to fight back, blow by blow, The gun's nozzle will equalize the high and low.'

Though surprised, I did not mention this to anyone. However, a few days later, a complaint letter arrived from the college in Dalim's name. Bibhuti-babu told Parag that the college authorities were unhappy with his semester results. Apparently, they had already warned him several times that his grades were deteriorating. But on the day of the supplementary examinations, Dalim was missing from the campus altogether!

The authorities soon discovered that Dalim had forged his father's signature on a leave application, falsely citing his mother's illness, and had left for Darjeeling. During that time, a group of agitating farmers had launched a protest in the Naxalbari region, which escalated into violence. News of a police team being attacked made headlines in the newspapers. It was revealed that Dalim had run away to join the agitation.

The tribals of Naxalbari had launched an attack on the police with bows and arrows, resulting in the death of a police sub-inspector and creating a widespread uproar. Within days, the deeply angered the Principal of Bengal Engineering College signed Dalim's rustication order.

This, in fact, was the real reason Dalim spent nearly an entire year at home after the incident.

His father, a bank clerk, no longer held any hope or had faith in his only child; nor did he receive any financial help from his son. The gentleman turned grey almost overnight. Kusum-di was also distraught. She would light incense sticks in front of the idols of various gods and goddesses, praying and offering sweets every day. Seeing all this, I felt very sad. It was clear that the parents were extremely worried about their son. The young boy had been a brilliant student and Titai had regarded him as her elder brother since childhood. None of us could believe that he would be forced to stay at home, without studies or work.

To ensure he had something to do and earned a bit of pocket money, I asked him to help with Titai's studies. Dalim agreed happily. In fact, he turned out to be a very good teacher. Titai's academic scores improved soon after.

One day, he asked to use our telephone. He said he wanted to speak to a friend. I had just served him a cup of tea and was leaving the study when I overheard a strange conversation.

'Do not try to patronize me, Soumya! Let me remain as I am,' Dalim snapped, his voice shook with anger. 'How would a rich man's son, a bourgeois like you, ever understand what it feels like to be deceived? A farmer endures unbearable hunger, works in the fields under the scorching sun and pouring rain, with an empty stomach, day after day. And for what? Just to fill the granaries of the landowners? Do you even know how shamelessly a handful of powerful men have been exploiting them for years? Have you ever walked the dusty village roads of Kharibari or Phansidewa? Have you tried to understand how, in times of hunger, the entrails inside the bellies of the poor start to knot and twist?

'If you really want to realize, go learn about Jungle Sardar. Read Comrade Lenin's writings. Listen to Charu Majumdar's speeches. I cannot make you comprehend the way I have come to appreciate it.'

Dalim's appearance matched the intensity of his words—his unshaven beard, his unkempt hair, and the fiery conviction in his eyes—all left me shaken.

Everyone could sense that the times were shifting in strange and unsettling ways. Some people had already broken away from the existing Communist Party. The CPI (Marxist-Leninist), or CPI-ML, was born. News spread that farmers in Siliguri, North Bengal, were enduring unspeakable torture at the hands of their landlords. Despite working hard all year round, they went hungry, wore torn clothes, and watched their children die young. Organizing themselves, they seized their employers' lands in certain areas and began tilling them by force.

Di-bhai, reading about all this had become a daily habit for me through the newspapers. I admit that, by then, I had become somewhat selfish. Life at that time was dominated by grim realities—Partition, war, and famine had left scars everywhere. Amidst all this, ordinary people like us could hardly focus on issues of social justice or injustice. Whether in villages or cities, people were busy collecting whatever little they needed just to survive. More than anything else, we all longed for a sense of safety and security.

I read in the dailies that Jangal Santhal, the son of tribal leader Kanna Kisku, who played a pivotal role in igniting the farmers' rebellion in North Bengal during the years following the 1967 elections. For the landowners, he was nothing short of a nightmare—spoken of as the devil himself. But for the poor, oppressed, and landless peasants, Jangal Santhal became a symbol of courage and resistance. A penniless and barely educated man, he had risen to become a messiah for the downtrodden, fearlessly leading them against their exploiters.

The political environment after the 1967 West Bengal Assembly elections provided fertile ground for this unrest. The Indian National Congress, for the first time since independence, had lost power in the state. The United Front government—a coalition of the Communist Party of India (Marxist), Bangla Congress, and other leftist parties—came to power. The peasant movements intensified in the wake of this political shift. Jangal Santhal and other local leaders mobilized tribal and marginal farmers in places like Naxalbari and Kharibari, near the Indo-Nepal border in the Terai region. It was widely rumoured that under Santhal's leadership, the farmers began clandestine preparations for guerrilla warfare. Charu Majumdar's fiery ideology—documented in his *Historic Eight Documents*—was already becoming gospel for the youth inclined towards revolution.

In our own home in Calcutta, I noticed the change too. On Dalim's study table, I saw copies of *The Communist Manifesto* by Karl Marx, Mr Green's book on the Vietnam War, Charu Majumdar's *Historic Eight Documents*, and volumes on Mao Zedong and Che Guevara. These books, once foreign to our middle-class world, now lay scattered among Dalim's engineering textbooks.

One evening, I asked Dalim to come over to our house. Parag was still at office and Titai was at her music class. I wanted to speak to him—perhaps to understand the storm that seemed to be brewing inside this once-quiet boy.

'What are you doing, Dalim? You are destroying a potentially great career! Why are you keeping such incriminating books in your home? You are a brilliant student, and such a good teacher to Titai. Will you not consider your father's post-retirement days? How could you lie about your mother's illness to your college? What is wrong with you? You do not have to teach Titai anymore, Dalim!'

I was getting agitated as I spoke. Perhaps I felt I had the right to chide him as I had seen him grow up from a child.

Dalim stood silent for some time. Then he spoke, his tone impassioned, 'Yes, indeed I lied about my mother's illness to go to Naxalbari, but it was necessary then, Kakima. Are you aware that in the remote villages of West Bengal, Bihar and Madhya Pradesh starving people survive by eating field-rats? Thousands of poor, helpless people die during disease outbreaks for lack of proper treatment.

'My professor asked me with contempt, 'Are you not ashamed, Dalim? You lied about the illness of your mother—the woman who gave birth to you!'

'Kakima, I wanted to tell him, 'My lies will not make my mother ill, sir. She will remain healthy. But in our country, thousands of mothers go to bed hungry after giving away their portion of food to their husbands and children. In our homeland, hundreds of women give birth in fields, even in bamboo groves, utterly alone, without any medical help. When they lose their lives due to bleeding, sepsis, tetanus—do we even hear about them? So, tell me, what is the purpose of lecturing me about the virtues of truthfulness? Can you explain to me, sir?'

'Kakima, even if I stop tutoring your daughter, she will still do well in her exams. But as for me—I cannot live a life confined to a routine job and a steady income. I see that as a selfish existence. I refuse to spend my life endlessly chasing promotions, calculating salaries and increments, jockeying for positions, or even resorting to bribery just to climb the ladder. That is not what I call progress. No, I cannot turn my back on reality, focus only on my own comfort, and say, "Let the hungry and helpless people of this country suffer—it is not my concern."

'At this moment, the only right path to fight this totalitarian, exploitive system is the Naxal movement. Everywhere, embers are catching the fire of revolution—silently, slowly but surely. It will not be long before these sparks turn into an inferno. If a few lives need to be sacrificed for this, then so be it. The fires will only burn brighter!'

'But…Dalim…what about your parents?' I asked.

Dalim raised a hand to stop me and said, 'The college authorities would have sent me back sooner or later. They suspected that I was spreading Naxal ideology among the juniors. My father was devastated by this turn of events, but he has since gathered himself—he had to. He must have understood by now that even if he had not fathered me, somewhere in this godforsaken country, I would have appeared like an unexpected comet. Wherever I would be born inside the 'red corridor', I would have felt the same duty to repay the debts of my motherland. Kakima, if needed, thousands of comrades will rise from the soil drenched in my blood, much like the offsprings of the demon Raktabeej, who is unperishable.'

I shuddered as I listened to him.

Strange incidents were being reported in Calcutta with increasing frequency. Just days earlier, Parag had told me a horrifying story about his colleague's nephew.

'The boy, Papai, was the younger of two brothers. Friendly by nature and a voracious reader, so his friends said. The police picked him up from the footpath opposite Presidency College on College Street—right when he was browsing through second-hand books. They gave him no time, no explanation. He was arrested on the spot and taken to the lock-up. His distraught parents ran from pillar to post, trying desperately to arrange bail. But before they could do anything, one dawn, the police bundled him into a van and drove him to the Calcutta Maidan. Later that day, his body was found lying in a corner of the field, the grass around him stiff with dried blood.'

The usually calm Parag was trembling as he finished speaking.

Di-bhai, it was during this time that you sent your son away to the Ramakrishna Mission Boys' Home at Rahara. I remember your husband refused to let Dhruva come home, even during holidays. He had spoken to the Maharaj and arranged for Dhruva to remain at the hostel. You were not at all happy and often argued with your husband about it. Parag and I had to intervene a couple of times to end your arguments.

By 1971, the city's jails were bursting with thousands of young men, who had been picked up from workplaces, colleges, universities and even from their homes or their friends' homes. It was said that during interrogation about their and their friends' activities, molten wax was poured into their ears or iron rods were inserted into their anus.

Weapons were discovered at Uluberia High School—barrel guns and crude, amateur-made bombs. Ten boys were dragged away in a police jeep. Neither teachers nor guardians—not even the headmaster—could stop the uniformed men. In those days, lifeless bodies turned up with chilling regularity: near the Tollygunge film studios, along the edges of the Calcutta Racecourse, and in the open drains of North Calcutta. Some were identified; many remained nameless and unclaimed.

Unidentified miscreants also vandalized the statues of

Rabindranath Tagore and Raja Ram Mohan Roy. Meanwhile, under Chief Minister Siddhartha Sankar Ray, violence swept across college campuses, coffee houses, suburban towns, and distant villages. News of arrests flooded the papers daily, and almost every morning, another body was found—lifeless, discarded, and silent.

Titai's final exams had just ended. I was busy correcting examination papers of my school students, working late into the nights. I will never forget that night, Di-bhai; it will remain etched in my memory forever.

It was past midnight when we heard loud banging on banging our neighbour's front door.

'Who could be visiting the Dattas so late?' Parag muttered as he quickly dressed to go out and check.

We found Dalim's mother standing outside their door, her eyes wide with shock. Policemen entered the house, their heavy boots thudding loudly against the floor. Bibhuti-babu stood silently, his hands folded together as he looked on helplessly. I felt distraught.

When they woke Dalim and brought him out, I noticed a brown paper bag held by one of the police officers. As they turned his hands behind his back to put on handcuffs, he did not flinch or make a single sound. *Didn't it hurt him at all?* I wondered.

'Mr Datta, do we need to remind you that keeping an unlicensed gun at home is a criminal offence? We've been keeping an eye on your son for quite some time. But he's very clever, it seems. I have been ordered to put an end to his mischief. I am bound by my duty.'

With that, he gestured for Dalim to move forward.

'Long live Mao Zedong! Long live the revolution!' Dalim shouted suddenly, just before being taken away.

Something fell with a loud thud, jolting me back to my senses. Kusum-di had collapsed. I rushed to pick her up while trying desperately to suppress my urge to cry. Titai followed the column of marching men down a few steps before stopping suddenly and returning.

Days passed.

Bibhuti-babu had always been a quiet man, but he became even quieter, withdrawing himself. He kept his head down on the streets, avoiding eye contact with anyone. Yet he had to carry on, to earn a living, and continued commuting to his workplace.

Our landlord, Bijoy De, stopped talking to both our families for a few days. Then, one evening, Bhajahari, his servant, knocked on our door. As I stepped outside, I saw that the Dattas had also been summoned.

'Sir has asked for you; please come downstairs.'

Fearing the worst, we went down and entered the drawing room of our landlord. We never visited the place except to pay the rent every month.

To our utter surprise, the landlord's wife entered the room, followed by her maid who carried a large tray. It was laden with plates of *patishaptas*—sweet rice crepes, a seasonal delicacy. Under the stress of the recent events, we had lost all sense of time and had completely forgotten that it was Poush Sankranti, an auspicious day on the Bengali calendar.

For the first time, the landlord and his wife invited us to sit with them on their sofa. Mrs De spoke to us warmly as she served the sweets. I overheard Mr De speaking quietly to Dalim's father. 'We will have to let him serve a few months in prison, Bibhuti-babu,' he said gravely. 'In fact, his life will be safer inside. If he is released too soon, his so-called friends will drag him back into dangerous activities. The next time, we may not be able to protect him from the police's bullets. I know someone at Police

Headquarters in Lalbazar. I will do everything I can to ensure that Dalim returns home alive after sometime. After all, he is the son of this house.'

Kusum-di broke down, weeping so hard that her sari was soaked in tears. However, they were not tears of grief but of some fragile consolation. Mr and Mrs De made sure we finished all the sweets before we left. That night, neither the Dattas nor we needed to cook dinner.

Di-bhai, after five long and difficult years, Dalim was finally released from prison. By then, the political landscape had shifted dramatically. Factions within the Left movement were breaking apart. I remember reading in the newspapers that the Naxals were being blamed for the targeted killings of several CPI(M) cadres. Even *Deshbrati*, the CPI-ML's mouthpiece, which many once read with curiosity, had now earned the grim nickname 'murder mania' among ordinary readers.

Amidst this chaos, the Vice-Chancellor of Calcutta University imposed a strict ban on harbouring active Naxalites within the university hostels. The climate was tense and fearful. Justice Roy of the Calcutta High Court was assassinated, and soon after, the Vice-Chancellor of Jadavpur University was killed too. The violence seemed to have seeped into every institution, every corner of the city.

In this charged atmosphere, Dalim's family quietly sent him away to Bangalore to live with his aunt, hoping distance would give him a new start and keep him safe. Much later, I heard he had taken up work as an audio engineer in a recording studio. He never married.

Meanwhile, Naxals in Andhra Pradesh and Uttar Pradesh became increasingly vocal in their opposition to Charu Majumdar's ideals and methods. Kanu Sanyal was in prison during this period.

Moreover, the statue-breaking acts faced severe criticism, leading to the complete withdrawal of support from the common man.

Di-bhai, no matter how humane the fire that fuels a movement, its longevity depends on its alignment with the masses. Particularly in the villages, forcibly seizing food and shelter from the poor was a strategy that could not sustain the movement in the long run. We can have a better understanding of this if we analyse some more incidents.

Jangal Santal was the member of the Krishak Parishad in parts of the Darjeeling district with a majority Santal population. At the time, the Krishak Parishad was planning to redistribute land among the farmers through armed struggle.

In May 1967, a farmer tried to work in a field that had been allotted to him by the rebels. The landowner's musclemen attacked him. The next day, when a police team led by Inspector Sonam Wangdi, arrived there to arrest the leaders, Jangal Santal's troupe attacked them with bows and arrows. Wangdi died in this attack, marking the birth of the violent Naxal movement.

Jangal Santal subsequently joined the CPI-ML, which was formed in 1969, and operated under the pseudonym Biren Kisku while working among the farmers of West Dinajpur district. He was also active in the tea plantation workers' movement. Eventually, the police were able to identify him and sentenced him to seven years in prison.

Inspired by communist ideology, Charu Majumdar abandoned his academic pursuits and became actively involved in the Tebhaga movement in North Bengal, particularly in Jalpaiguri district, during the mid-1930s. By 1936, he was already a key organizer in the region, mobilizing sharecroppers and peasants against oppressive landlords. While living underground for nearly six years during the British colonial period, Charu Majumdar established his political network and formally became a member of the CPI.

In the post-Independence era, as ideological differences between the Communist parties of China and the Soviet Union deepened, the Communist Party of India had split in 1964. Charu Majumdar joined the newly formed CPI(M), which had a pro-China leaning. However, when the CPI(M)-led United Front coalition government came to power in West Bengal following the 1967 Assembly elections, Charu Majumdar grew increasingly disillusioned. He vehemently opposed the party's decision to participate in electoral politics and governance, arguing that it had betrayed the revolutionary path. His dissent soon led him to sever ties with the CPI(M).

Kanu Sanyal, another pivotal figure in the movement, was born in Kurseong, in the Darjeeling district. Financial hardship had forced him to discontinue formal education, and he took up a clerical job in the State Land Department in Jalpaiguri subdivision. It was during one of his imprisonments for political activism that Sanyal met Charu Majumdar, who had by then emerged as the ideological spearhead of the Tebhaga movement. This encounter marked a turning point in Sanyal's life. He embraced communist ideology and became deeply involved in grassroots mobilizations. After the CPI split, Kanu Sanyal too aligned himself with the CPI(M).

However, like Charu Majumdar, Kanu Sanyal soon became disillusioned with the CPI(M)'s parliamentary approach. He emerged as one of the most vocal supporters of an armed peasant uprising modelled on Mao Zedong's revolutionary tactics. Labelling the United Front government as 'reactionary', both Sanyal and Majumdar prepared to launch an armed struggle.

Immediately after the United Front government was sworn in, the duo led the infamous Naxalbari uprising in May 1967, in Darjeeling district. The revolt, aimed at redistributing land to landless farmers, soon escalated into violent clashes. Police

Sub-Inspector Sonam Wangdi was killed during one such confrontation. The Naxalbari uprising ignited a chain reaction of armed movements across parts of West Bengal, Andhra Pradesh, Kerala and Odisha.

To consolidate these scattered rebellions, the Communist Consolidation was formed in 1968. On 1 May 1969, at a massive rally in Kolkata's Maidan on May Day, Kanu Sanyal formally announced the formation of the CPI(ML), with Charu Majumdar elected as its first Chairman.

The CPI(ML) rapidly attracted thousands of idealistic youth, students, and intellectuals from across India. For many, it became a symbol of resistance against feudal oppression and state injustice. However, internal fissures soon began to appear. By the middle of 1970, growing state repression and differing ideological strategies caused severe splits within the CPI(ML). Leaders like Asim Chattopadhyay and Santosh Rana broke away, criticizing Charu Majumdar's approach as increasingly dogmatic and violent.

Amid escalating crackdowns, Kanu Sanyal, who was then operating underground, was arrested in August 1969 and imprisoned in Visakhapatnam jail.

Meanwhile, Charu Majumdar became the most wanted revolutionary leader in India. Branded by the state as the mastermind behind a 'conspiracy of murders and armed insurrection', he remained in hiding for several years. On 16 July 1972, Charu Majumdar was finally captured from a safehouse on Entally Road in Kolkata. His arrest was widely publicized. Just twelve days later, on 28 July 1972, the Government of India announced that he had died of a heart attack while in police custody. His death, under suspicious circumstances, continues to evoke debate and controversy.

Kanu Sanyal, released from prison in 1979, later openly criticized Charu Majumdar's line of annihilation and rejected violent extremism. Until his death in 2010, Sanyal remained active in politics, though committed to a democratic and non-violent path.

The common people of West Bengal began to believe that seasoned criminals and professional shooters had infiltrated and taken to violent operations. Gradually, the Naxals started losing their connection with the masses. Within the party itself, bitter clashes erupted over confusion and disagreement about who their true enemy really was.

By then, the political landscape of West Bengal had undergone a drastic transformation, and the Naxal movement had lost much of its momentum. Years later, in 2010, unable to bear the burden of age and prolonged illness, Kanu Sanyal took his own life at the age of 78 in his home at Hatighisa village, under the Naxalbari police station.

Amidst the growing internal mistrust, factional feuds, and manipulation by hidden enemies, the party leadership failed to recognize the shifting needs of the nation and neglected the very people they once sought to emancipate. Yet, amidst all this, Di-bhai, the dreams and futures of many brilliant students like Dalim were destroyed—lost to a movement that had begun with hope but ended in ruin.

Twenty-eight

Discontent was also brewing in our neighbouring country, Pakistan, Di-bhai. Back in August 1947, the Indian subcontinent, then under British rule, was divided into two nations: Pakistan was formed with the Muslim-majority provinces, and the Hindu-majority and other areas went to India.

The new dominion of Pakistan consisted of two landmasses separated by almost 2,000 miles—East Pakistan (now Bangladesh) and West Pakistan. These two regions, vastly different in geography and culture, had only one thing in common—the religion of the majority of their populations.

From the very inception of Pakistan, the eastern part started to face systemic neglect. The eventual birth of Bangladesh was preceded by a history of twenty-three long years of sustained oppression and marginalization of the East by the authorities in West Pakistan.

I would like to mention here that following the Partition of India in 1947, Sheikh Mujibur Rahman—then a young student leader—gradually rose to become a pivotal figure in the politics of East Pakistan. He assumed leadership of the Awami League, a political party originally founded by Maulana Abdul Hamid Khan Bhashani. Advocating socialism and committed to the cause of social justice, Sheikh Mujib became the voice of the oppressed people of East Pakistan, challenging the authoritarian control exercised by West Pakistan.

In 1966, with the aim of securing greater autonomy for the eastern province, Sheikh Mujib introduced his famous Six-

Point Programme. The demands included control over taxation, trade, and monetary policy by East Pakistan—effectively seeking self-governance within a federal structure. However, the military regime in West Pakistan, under the dictatorship of General Ayub Khan, viewed these demands as a serious threat to national unity. In 1968, Sheikh Mujib was arrested and implicated in the so-called Agartala Conspiracy Case, accused of colluding with India to destabilize Pakistan. Yet, amid growing public protests and mounting political pressure, he was acquitted the following year. This marked a turning point, further strengthening his position as the undisputed leader of East Pakistan's autonomy movement.

The situation in Pakistan reached a turning point in 1970. The Awami League, the largest political party in East Pakistan, achieved absolute majority in the National Assembly of Pakistan during the country's first general elections. Despite this, Awami League was not allowed to form the government.

Zulfiqar Ali Bhutto, the leader of Pakistan People's Party, which came second in the elections, opposed Sheikh Mujib's claim to prime ministership. He also refused to accept Mujib's six-point proposal of self-governance of the East. Although the session of the National Assembly was scheduled to be held in Dhaka, Pakistan's president Yahya Khan, in collusion with Bhutto and some army officers, hatched a secret conspiracy.

On 1 March 1971, just two days before the scheduled session of the National Assembly, the meeting was abruptly cancelled without any explanation. This decision triggered widespread anger and resentment across East Pakistan. The people's patience had worn thin. Dhaka transformed overnight into a city of unending processions, slogans, and protest marches. Bangabandhu Sheikh Mujibur Rahman, as he was affectionately known by his followers, called for strikes and mass non-cooperation. Within days, East

Pakistan came to a grinding halt, its administrative machinery paralyzed at his command.

The central government responded with repression, imposing curfews in an attempt to crush the agitation. However, the movement remained resolute and defiant. On 7 March 1971, following a five-day strike, Sheikh Mujib addressed a sea of people at the Racecourse Ground in Dhaka. It was here that he delivered his historic speech, where he declared, 'The struggle this time is the struggle for our emancipation! The struggle this time is the struggle for our independence!' His words stirred the hearts of millions and became a rallying cry for freedom from West Pakistan's oppressive rule.

Meanwhile, the military build-up continued. Between 10 and 13 March, all flights to East Pakistan were suspended under the pretext of accommodating 'government travellers'—many of whom were army personnel travelling in civilian clothes. At Chittagong port, when a ship loaded with arms and ammunition arrived from West Pakistan, the Bengali dock workers refused to unload the cargo. Their protest was met with orders to open fire, but in a remarkable act of solidarity, some soldiers from the East Pakistan Rifles defied their superiors and refused to shoot at the port workers. This marked the beginning of a widespread rebellion among Bengali soldiers—a pivotal moment in the struggle for liberation.

Though Dhaka remained the epicentre of the uprising, violence and state repression soon spread across the entire region. Both Hindus and Muslims became targets of the brutality. One of the most horrifying episodes unfolded at Jagannath Hall—the only Hindu residential hall at Dhaka University—where the Pakistani army massacred around 700 students. While the military officially denied any organized mass killing, the later findings of the Hamoodur Rahman Commission confirmed that extreme and disproportionate force had indeed been used within the university campus. Hindu-majority areas across East Pakistan were systematically attacked, looted and burned, with widespread destruction and loss of life.

On the night of 25 March 1971, under the codename 'Operation Searchlight', the Pakistani military launched a full-scale campaign of terror. Bengali soldiers were disarmed and summarily executed. Students, professors, writers and intellectuals were hunted down and killed. The streets of Dhaka and other cities turned red with blood as indiscriminate firing and house-to-house raids became the norm. That same night, while the city burned and its people cried out in fear, an underground guerrilla resistance began to develop. The mass uprising for independence had begun.

Bangabandhu Sheikh Mujibur Rahman was arrested and flown to West Pakistan. Meanwhile, from the end of March onwards, the Pakistani army began sweeping through the villages and suburbs of East Pakistan. Supporters and members of the Awami League were specifically targeted. Hindus, in particular, suffered relentless persecution, with many of their homes and temples reduced to rubble. In a desperate bid to survive, tens of thousands fled towards the Indian border. What began as a trickle in early April soon turned into a humanitarian catastrophe. By November 1971, nearly one crore refugees—mostly Hindus but also many Bengali Muslims—had crossed into India, seeking shelter from the unfolding genocide.

After unleashing the massacre in Dhaka, the Pakistani army turned its focus towards subjugating the entire region of East Bengal. Their mission was clear—crush all resistance and bring every inch of the land under military control. But what they had not anticipated was the sheer scale of defiance that awaited them.

Bengali officers and soldiers within the army, along with students and ordinary citizens, rose up with remarkable courage.

In Chittagong, Bengali soldiers and members of the paramilitary forces openly rebelled. For days, they managed to seize and hold large parts of the city. The Pakistani army, humiliated and enraged, retaliated with ruthless force—coordinating air raids with shelling from naval warships to flatten neighbourhoods and regain control.

Across the districts of Kushtia, Pabna, Bogura and Dinajpur, Bengali soldiers and freedom fighters carved out temporary pockets of liberation, fighting with whatever weapons they could find. For a brief, glorious moment, these areas stood as free territory—symbols of hope in the midst of despair.

But by late May, the Pakistani army regrouped. With overwhelming numbers, superior firepower, and endless convoys of ammunition, they launched a brutal counteroffensive. One by one, the free zones fell, drowned in gunfire and blood.

Di-bhai, I remember how, in those terrible days, Sheikh Mujib's defiant speeches crackled through loudspeakers in our neighbourhood. His baritone voice rang with unshaken resolve: '*Amra bhate marbo, amra panite marbo, tomra amago dabaiya rakhte parba na!*—We shall starve you, we shall leave you parched, but you will never be able to silence us!'

Those words became a lifeline of hope for the oppressed millions.

The freedom-loving citizens of East Pakistan wanted to see their land free from West Pakistani occupation. Within months, the Mukti Bahini was formed. Using guerrilla tactics, this force waged war throughout the country, making life difficult for the Pakistani army.

After August 1971, large numbers of Mukti-joddhas began targeting the Pakistani army by attacking their military bases, installations, roads, bridges and culverts to disrupt lines of communication. The fighters, though poorly trained, successfully destroyed the Pakistani war ships anchored at the Chittagong port using mines.

On 14 December 1971, just on the brink of East Pakistan's liberation, a chilling act of brutality unfolded. Acting under orders from the Pakistani Army, their local collaborators—the Razakars, along with the Al-Badr and Al-Shams militias—carried out a systematic massacre of nearly 300 of the nation's brightest minds. Professors, doctors, engineers, artists, poets, writers, and scientists were abducted from their homes and brutally killed. These pro-Pakistan Bengali collaborators had long sensed the inevitable outcome of the war. In the early days of December, as the Pakistani forces began to lose ground, the traitorous Razakars meticulously planned this slaughter, ensuring that, even in defeat, they would leave behind an irreparable wound in the heart of the emerging nation.

During the conflict, countless Bengali women lost their dignity. Though the exact numbers are not known, it is estimated that nearly two lakh women were raped during the war, many of whom later gave birth to 'children of war'. The Pakistani soldiers abducted many young women—most of them university students and girls from ordinary families—and held them inside military compounds in Dhaka.

Gradually, under relentless attacks and counter-attacks by the Mukti-joddhas, the Pakistani army began to lose its grip over East Pakistan. Facing mounting losses and seeing no other alternative, they attempted a desperate escalation. On 3 December 1971, the Pakistani Air Force launched a sudden air strike on Indian airfields in the western sector, hoping to internationalize the conflict and draw global attention.

At precisely 5 p.m. that day, Radio Pakistan interrupted its regular programmes with a special bulletin: 'India has initiated an attack along the Western border of Pakistan. We await further details.' The announcement aimed to paint India as the aggressor, even though the Pakistani army's atrocities in East Pakistan had been unfolding for months, forcing India's eventual intervention.

At 5.09 p.m., twelve Pakistani fighter jets took off from Peshawar airbase targeting Srinagar and Anantapur, while eight Mirage jets headed towards Pathankot and Amritsar. Two fighter planes flew deeper into Indian territory to attack Agra. In total, thirty-two fighter planes participated in this attack.

On the evening of 3 December 1971, as Prime Minister Indira Gandhi stood before a massive gathering at the Brigade Parade Ground in Calcutta, addressing thousands with calm resolve. The Pakistani Air Force unleashed coordinated air strikes on multiple Indian air bases. The timing could not have been more ominous. Even as her voice echoed across the ground, news of the attacks began to trickle in. Without wasting a moment, Indira Gandhi rushed back to Delhi.

That night, the atmosphere in the capital grew tense. An emergency cabinet meeting was convened at once. In the early hours, just after midnight, her voice reached the nation through All India Radio. Calm yet steely, she declared, 'The war that was going on in Bangladesh has now turned into a war against India.' The gravity of her words left no room for doubt—India had been drawn formally into battle, however, swiftly repelled the attacks along its western frontier.

Di-bhai, surely you remember that at the time, anticipating aerial attacks from Pakistan, we would shut all the windows of the house as soon as evening set in. The top halves of the streetlights were painted black, and the lights inside buses and trains were similarly dimmed with black paint, for fear that Pakistani fighter planes might detect any illumination anywhere on Indian soil and drop bombs.

After this, the Indian Army, in coordination with the Mukti

Bahini, formed an allied force and entered Bangladesh. Faced with the relentless and coordinated assaults of the allied troops, the Pakistani forces began to lose ground at almost every border front. Though the Pakistanis had concentrated their troops at key strategic locations, the allied forces skilfully bypassed these strongholds and advanced rapidly towards Dhaka. Ordinary Bangladeshi citizens, driven by the hope of freedom, voluntarily supported the Mukti Bahini at every step.

Within just thirteen days of the formal declaration of war, the allied army reached the outskirts of Dhaka. Before this ground advance, Indian air strikes had effectively crippled the Pakistani Air Force and destroyed the runways of all airports in of the war-torn country, cutting off any possibility of aerial reinforcements. Senior Pakistani officials stationed in Dhaka had been given repeated assurances from West Pakistan that support would arrive—from China in the north and from the United States via the south. But, in reality, no help reached.

East Pakistan, on the other hand, received economic, military and political support from India throughout the war. One by one, areas were liberated from the enemy. Overwhelmed by the joint assaults of the Mukti Bahini and the Indian army, the beleaguered and hopeless Pakistani army decided to accept a ceasefire.

On 16 December 1971, at the Racecourse ground in Dhaka, the Pakistani army signed the instrument of surrender—not a ceasefire—with 93,000 troops laying down their arms. On behalf of the Pakistani army, Lieutenant General Amir Abdullah Khan Niazi signed the document. Thus ended the nine-month-long bloodshed, and East Pakistan emerged as the independent Bangladesh.

Varying estimates continue to circulate in the mass media regarding the number of lives lost during the Bangladesh War of Independence. Globally, in various encyclopaedias and books, the figure is cited as being between 2,00,000 and 30,00,000. During the war, nearly one crore refugees took shelter in India, who in all probability, would have faced genocide had they not left their country when they did.

On 10 January 1972, Sheikh Mujib returned to Bangladesh after being released from imprisonment in Pakistan and assumed office as the nation's first president. Two days later, on 12 January 1972, he initiated a parliamentary system of governance and took on the role of prime minister.

Ideologically, Sheikh Mujibur Rahman stood for Bengali nationalism, socialism, democracy and secularism—principles that later came to be collectively known as 'Mujibism'. After independence, a constitution was framed based on these ideals, and he made sincere efforts to govern the newly formed Bangladesh along these lines. However, the challenges were immense. Severe poverty, widespread unemployment, administrative chaos and rampant corruption plagued the nation. Struggling to contain the political instability that followed, in 1975, Sheikh Mujib introduced one-party rule under the banner of BAKSAL (Bangladesh Krishak Sramik Awami League). Yet, barely seven months later, on 15 August 1975, he was assassinated, along with most members of his family, by a group of military officers.

Twenty-nine

I found myself ruminating on the history and politics surrounding the formation of Bangladesh. After the Indo-Pak war of 1971, yet another border came into existence. Waves of people poured across the newly drawn Bangladesh border, seeking refuge in makeshift camps. The compassionate people of West Bengal did their utmost to provide food and shelter, but the sheer scale of the crisis made it impossible to meet the basic needs of everyone, everywhere, all the time. Tragically, many never made it to the camps at all—succumbing to hunger, exhaustion, or illness along the way.

Between March and December 1971, Bangladesh witnessed a wave of atrocities—murders, rapes and looting—orchestrated by the Pakistani army and the Razakars. Our neighbour Dinu-da's elder brother Binoy-da had, after great difficulty, managed to reach the Indian side of the border along with his wife and daughter. They had boarded the last train to India, clutching whatever little food they could carry in a small bag. Not only was that snatched away from them at a check-post midway, but someone in the crowd also tore away his daughter's nose ring. Binoy-da could not utter a word. He had wet his undergarments in fear.

Once bitten, twice shy, we visited Dinu-da in his tiny room to meet his brother and family who had travelled across the border. The godforsaken migrant family sat before us with vacant stares.

'We were sitting in a coach of the last train leaving East Pakistan for India,' Binoy-da recounted, his eyes like those of a madman! 'Suddenly we heard that only the coaches that had already crossed into India would be allowed to proceed. Apparently, Mr Bhutto had instructed that, after those four cars, the coupler would be removed and the remaining coaches set on fire.' His voice still trembled with terror as he spoke. He seemed to be still living in those formidable circumstances.

'Looking out of the window, I saw people jumping out in hordes, desperately trying to push their way to get into the coaches in the front. But not all could make it. Only the first four compartments moved along with the engine. The screaming from the rear coaches was heart-rending. I can still hear those voices in my mind; I feel like pulling out my hair whenever I think of those people.'

He started taking deep breaths. His wife, long accustomed to wearing a veil, pulled it lower. Their daughter, trying to hide her torn nose, sat behind her mother with her gaze fixed on the floor.

Di-bhai, in those days, hundreds of thousands of terror-struck Hindus were pouring into West Bengal from every district of East Pakistan; the tide was impossible to contain. Binoy-da and his family somehow managed to survive on the platforms of Sealdah station for a couple of days. Later, in a government camp, after surrendering the only asset—a gold chain—his wife had smuggled into India hidden in her sari, they finally received a certificate identifying them as a 'refugee family'.

They were given half of a tiny tent in the most congested corner of the camp. The wind would rush in relentlessly through the gaps in the frail tarpaulin walls. Some distance away, the men relieved themselves in the open. The women bathed in makeshift bathrooms made of jute curtains, shielding their modesty as best they could. Twice a day, they were handed a small helping of rice and a ladle of watery lentils—just enough to keep their frail bodies alive. Gradually, they were dispersed to other camps. Somehow, through scattered contacts and desperate efforts, they managed to reach out to Dinu-da. By then, his wife and daughter had already taken up the back-breaking, humiliating job of washing dishes in strangers' homes—hands roughened from constant exposure to soap and cold water. As for Binoy-da, he had suffered permanent nerve damage around his groin in a brutal stampede—trampled by panicked feet as people ran for their lives. Even so, I later heard he had managed to find work as a cashier in a local garment shop.

Yet, amid this sea of suffering, the birth of Bangladesh stood as a glorious chapter. A nation had been carved out—freedom was snatched at a terrible cost. But, Di-bhai, not all stories from that time glowed with triumph. Equally heart-wrenching were the tales of how the homes of the most vulnerable were forcibly seized during the war. Within the newly drawn borders, some with a lingering 'Paki' mindset masqueraded as 'Bangladeshi' patriots. They spoke the same language, but they did not understand the true meaning of the word 'ours'.

The real sufferers were those who had left everything behind—who had crossed rivers of blood and walked endless miles to safety, accepting the branding of 'refugee' as their new identity. Some of them returned later to look at the houses they had left, but the agony only increased. They would stand beside the pond they had fished in as children, now forbidden to cast even a single net. The mango tree, once a giver of countless summer delights, now belonged to strangers. Across the clothesline on the old porch, there were unfamiliar faces who occupied familiar spaces.

Most never returned again to their old homes. Even when the ache of longing pulled at them, they stayed away, choosing instead to begin life anew on unfamiliar soil. Rootless, displaced again and again, they accepted the brutal reality of survival and set out, once more, in search of firmer ground beneath their feet.

What is a border, Di-bhai? A line drawn on a map? A political convenience? Or a permanent scar on human history? Have we not witnessed enough cruelty enacted at these border fences across the world? Syrian refugees still run from country to country, carrying their children, their fear, their loss. Little Aylan, once from a relatively stable home, lay lifeless in his red shirt and blue jeans on a foreign Mediterranean shore—snatched from his mother's arms forever. Is this the price of civilization?

When the displaced Rohingyas, manipulated and betrayed by cunning geopolitical games, dream helplessly of Arakan, longing for the land that disowned them, one wonders—when even their own homeland becomes unreachable, foreign lands deny entry—where, then, can the homeless go?

Di-bhai, independence cost us millions of lives. Yet, we must not forget the brave souls who toiled for it. Once upon a time, the frontiers of India were vast. Surya Sen, popularly known as Master-da in Chittagong, and Bhagat Singh in Punjab's Lyallpur district, were duty-bound to fulfil the dream of freedom. They did not hesitate to sacrifice their lives.

During the British Raj, a sign outside the Pahartali European Club read: 'Dogs and Indians not allowed'. Protesting against this insulting message, Chittagong's Preetilata Waddedar—a student of Bethune College in Calcutta—and her aides set fire to the club. When, as a last resort, she bit into a cyanide capsule to avoid British capture, could she have imagined that her hard-won motherland would one day be fractured, torn apart into pieces?

Dinesh Chandra Gupta had joined the freedom movement from Jasholang village in Munshiganj district. From Rohitbhog, in the same district, Binoy Krishna Basu gave up a promising future at what was then Mitford Medical School and took up arms. Badal Gupta, from Shimulia village in Dhaka's Bikrampur, joined them to complete the legendary trio of Binoy-Badal-Dinesh. Together, they fired bullets at the brutal Colonel Simpson. They dreamt of a free and joyful nation. Had they foreseen so many strange new fences cropping up within?

We redraw the maps ourselves, again and again. Perhaps, as free land becomes smaller, people's mindset and outlook shrink as well.

Di-bhai, our children will never know the simple, forgotten joys we once took for granted. They will never taste that bowl of puffed rice soaked in fresh, amber-hued date-palm juice, lovingly served by our mothers and aunts on crisp winter mornings. They will never sit gazing out at mist-laden paddy fields, heavy and golden with harvest, swaying gently in the winter breeze.

I did not have sweaters then. My nanny would take an old shawl, fold it twice over, and wrap me in it from head to toe, tying a knot at the back like some makeshift armour against the cold. It sounds almost like a folklore now—those moments, those scenes—fragile, golden slivers of a world that no longer exists.

It was during those childhood mornings that I first heard our grandfather chant Sanskrit verses from the Upanishads. The phrase *'Vasudhaiva Kutumbakam'* stayed with me, lingering in my mind long after the sound of his voice faded. As I grew older, I read and re-read that line—'The whole world is one family'—a beautiful dream written into ancient scripture.

Yet, Di-bhai, looking at the world today, I cannot help but wonder—was it only a dream after all? That promise of universal kinship…has it ever truly been kept?

My grandson plays the guitar well. Whenever he is in high spirits, he sings to me. One day, he told me he wanted me to listen to a song by Bob Dylan:

> How many times can a man look up
> Before he sees the sky?

How many years must one person have
Before he can hear people cry?
How many deaths will it take till he knows
That too many people have died?
The answer, my friend, is blowing in the wind.
The answer is blowing in the wind.

These words touched my heart deeply, and I noted them down in this diary. Even a teenager in this century can grasp the cruelty of mankind and the tragic loss of faith in humanity.

After the Bangladesh war, a distant cousin of Parag migrated from Faridpur to Calcutta. A bright student, he hoped to study at Calcutta University. When he visited our home, he said, 'Boudi, as soon as I reached the frontier, I saw health workers waiting with injections in hand. They would not stamp my papers unless I agreed to be vaccinated. When I did, one of them showed me five fingers thrice—asking for fifteen rupees as a bribe. If you didn't, they'd harass you by touching you inappropriately. I endured it. But then someone said, 'Brother, we've got to send something to the other side too. If you have Bangladeshi money, leave it here. What use will it be in India?"

That day, I bowed my head in anger and shame. Is smuggling inevitable wherever there's a border? Is humiliating poor, innocent people part of every diplomatic policy? Isn't it the same group of *bauls* who wear saffron in India and white in Bangladesh, singing with the same fervour about their *moner manush*—their beloved? Do Bijay Sarkar's songs from Narail change their tunes when sung in Nadia?

No matter how often we call the world a global village, why is the spirit of that idea never truly respected?

Mankind builds civilizations, yet with each stride forward, we draw more partitions, more frontiers—walls both visible and invisible. Birds do not pause at borders; clouds drift across them freely; rain falls where it wills. The sea creatures that do not care about dividing lines, move freely as they please.

And yet, we humans—who call ourselves the most evolved, the most 'civilized' of all living beings—what are we really doing? We threaten and kill each other over lines on a map. We drop bombs on lands we have never walked, tear apart mountains, dam rivers that once flowed freely, and strip forests bare with a ruthless hand.

Sometimes, I wonder, Di-bhai…perhaps we were safer, wiser even, when we were a little more 'uncivilized'.

Poet Taslima Nasreen once wrote with poignant nostalgia:

Amar jonye opekkha karo Madhupur, Netrakona
Opekkha koro Jaydebpurer chourasta
Ami phirbo. Phirbo bhire, hattogole, khoray, bonyay
Opekkha karo chouchalaghar, uthon, lebutala, gollachuter math
Ami phirbo.

Wait for me, Madhupur, Netrakona,
Wait for me, crossroads of Joydebpur.
I shall return amidst crowds, in commotion, in drought and flood.
Wait for me, four-roofed huts, porches, lemon trees, and the football ground
For I shall return.

I once heard that Shri. Jyoti Basu, former Chief Minister of West Bengal, visited his ancestral home in Barudi, Narayanganj. When he reached the spot, he sat hours altogether in complete silence. The wife of Pranab Mukherjee, former President of India, wept inconsolably when she visited her ancestral home in Narail. They had done nothing to deserve such separation from their roots.

Do you remember my dear friend Basona from the village in East Bengal? Even after Bangladesh's independence, her family remained there—they did not cross over to India. I wanted to invite her to visit me after the war. She never came. Tuberculosis claimed her life.

She had a younger sister, Sadhana, who looked just like her. About a decade ago, Sadhana's son arranged a trunk call between us. I was in my 60s then, still relatively healthy.

'Apu re,' she said, her voice trembling. 'Basona sister is no more, but I haven't forgotten you. I have pain in my knees. I take so many medicines; my blood pressure stays high. Still, I wish I could see you just once. I truly want to.'

One fine morning, she started from her home in Khulna, Bangladesh, along with her nephew, to meet me at the border. They took a bus from Khulna to Benapole in Jessore, where the border crossing lies. I, on my part, boarded a train to Bongaon with Parag. Once we arrived, I hired an auto-rickshaw from the station. I urged the driver to take us to the border quickly—I could hardly wait to see Sadhana.

The driver joked, 'Didima, who are you going to meet so urgently? An old boyfriend?'

Parag Babu laughed on hearing this.

I patted the boy gently on the back and replied, 'Whatever it is, dear guy, just take me there quickly.'

Two massive iron gates stood on either side of the border, dividing the two countries like silent sentinels. The national flags of Bangladesh and India fluttered in the breeze—each a symbol of pride, and of parting. Between them lay a narrow strip of no man's land, a space belonging to neither, yet witness to so many divided hearts.

On the other side, I spotted a woman seated in a wheelchair. Her face—worn, lined with years, yet unmistakably familiar—startled me. For a moment, it felt like looking at my friend Basona. Her white hair danced in the wind, framing a face that still carried echoes of the small, dark-skinned girl I remembered —almost my age—who once used to run about in a frock.

In a voice almost identical to Basona's, she spoke, 'I cannot walk properly now. I could come only because this boy helped bring me here.'

The land where my parents had been born and had spent their childhood lay barely five or six yards away. Yet for me, it remained unreachable. I did not have a passport.

Did Sadhana carry hers? Could she, perhaps, cross over to this side?

I held a small box of sweets, soaked in sugary syrup—prepared specially for her with my own hands. I had hoped to serve them to her myself.

But now, with two countries and a scrap of no-man's land between us, even that simple gesture seemed like a distant dream.

'Come over to this side, Sadhana! What are you waiting for?' I cried out, full of hope, praying she could hear me.

Her young companion responded, 'Aunty, she doesn't have a digital passport. We couldn't get a visa for her. Taking an old woman in a wheelchair from one office to another is so difficult these days. How could I manage to get a visa done?'

It slowly sank in—those few feet between us would remain forever unbridgeable.

Sadhana smiled and waved. 'Stay well, sister. At least I could see you in person.'

I waved back—whether I smiled or cried, I do not know. I could not speak. I simply kept watching the wheelchair as it rolled away, farther and farther, its wheels leaving faint marks on the earth. The wind swept over and covered those tracks with dust almost instantly.

I opened the box with the sweets I had carried and dropped them one by one onto the ground. The sticky syrup meandered its way towards the direction in which Sadhana had left.

A border security man shouted, 'Move away! Go on now! Time's up!'

Parag took my hand gently and led me back to the auto-rickshaw.

Di-bhai, I could never bring myself to visit the border again.

Thirty

I had arranged for Titai's dance and singing lessons alongside her academics when she was young. She had always been sincere in her efforts to fulfil her parents' wishes. Geetabitan Music School awarded her a medal for securing the first position in their final examination. She also topped the Manipuri dance examination and earned the degree of *Nritya Visharad*. Kaki was her biggest fan. She was very fond of dance. After Titai's performances, we would bring her home in her costume and make-up. Kaki would gaze at her from every angle, eyes brimming with tears. She would say to me, 'Titai looks even prettier than you!'

Watching them together, I felt that by doing this much for Kaki, I had perhaps begun to repay a small fraction of the immense debt I owed her in my life. Titai, in turn, was devoted to her grandmother. When Kaki taught at the primary school, there was a tradition of teaching 'Bratachari' to students. Mr Gurusaday Dutta had initiated the practice when he was the District Magistrate of Birbhum during pre-independence times. He had also coined the term. The core of Mr Dutta's innovative movement was to ignite patriotism and a spirit of *swadeshi* through physical activities, practice of songs and dances.

It was 1932. The thumping of British boots echoed across imperial India. Amidst it all, *Bratachari* rituals were taught to children to build physical strength, self-respect, and nationalism. Songs were composed in a unique style for this. Mr Dutta was a visionary—he knew that brotherhood must be cultivated from childhood. Titai had learnt one such song and its accompanying dance from her grandmother:

Chol kodal chalai, bhule maner balai
Jhere olosh mejaj, hobe shorir jhalai
Joto byadhir balai, bolbe palai palai
PeTe khider jwalay, khabo kheer ar malai.

Let's work the plough, ego put aside,
Banish laziness, with strength abide.
Diseases depart, as bodies tone,
Savour pudding and butter, hunger overthrown.*

Kaki would beam with joy whenever she saw Titai sing and dance. I still remember those days with much fondness.

In our locality, the *Baar-Thakurer Puja* was held regularly under a huge banyan tree on Saturday evenings, followed by prasad distribution. Parag and I would take Titai with us to pray for health, peace, and a little prosperity, just as many Bengali middle-class families did. During the prasad distribution, Titai would gather as many batasha sweets as she could in the fold of her frock—but she would not eat a single one on the way back. Once home, she would pull her grandmother to the balcony and share them with her. Both would wash their hands together afterwards. Kaki was her confidante, playmate, and companion in joy and sorrow.

I understand, Di-bhai, that although Parag and I deeply desired another child, we simply could not consider expanding our family at that time. Kaki's health had become increasingly fragile, and she frequently fell ill. Once, she suffered a serious head injury after slipping in the bathroom late at night, prompting us to arrange around-the-clock nursing care at home. Despite

---

*Song by Gurusaday Dutta

her deteriorating condition, Kaki remained adamantly opposed to hospitalization, repeatedly urging me never to admit her to a medical centre. Respecting her wishes, we arranged daily home visits from a doctor. As she gradually began to recover, we faced mounting expenses from necessary physiotherapy, pushing us into considerable financial strain.

Sometimes I wonder if it was the resilience inherited from the Pal family and the unwavering strength passed down by the Bose family that enabled me to face life's hardships. Even during the most testing times, I never allowed myself to surrender. However, I must also acknowledge that my greatest source of strength during those difficult days was Parag—my life partner and constant companion. He firmly held my hand throughout our struggles, offering steadfast support and infusing me with courage and hope, much like a seasoned sailor calmly steering his ship through a turbulent storm.

Kaki wavered between periods of recovery and worsening. However, she soon had another vascular stroke that pushed her into unconsciousness this time. After a brief period of less than a week of coma, she passed away. In 1973, one rainy morning, I lost my mother-figure, who was more than a biological mother to me.

I have always felt that the void left by Kaki's passing could never be filled. It seemed to me that not only had she gone, but my childhood, adolescence, and youth had also ended with her. In the days that followed, time stretched out endlessly before me. My eyes would fill with tears now and then. Fortunately, early the next year, I became pregnant again. Our second daughter, Vibhabari—whom we affectionately called Bukai—was born in 1974. It felt as though God had returned Kaki to us. Titai's happiness knew no bounds. Her sister was twelve years her junior, and she eagerly took on the responsibilities of an elder sibling. Parag, too, was rejuvenated by this newfound joy. Our little family resumed its journey with Titai and Bukai, finding a new path together.

In those days, on the dawn of Mahalaya, even if the others slept, Parag would rise early and switch on our large radio. Inside the mosquito net, our daughters lay curled up together, half asleep, listening to the voice of Birendra Krishna Bhadra chanting, '*Ya Devi Sarvabhuteshu Shakti Rupena Samsthita.*'

Di-bhai, I hope you remember how it used to be a little chilly in the mornings and evenings during those autumn months—our Durga Puja season.

After Bukai's birth, my days became a whirlwind of school duties, household chores, and caring for the children. Around this time, Parag was transferred from the Pay and Accounts Office to the Income Tax Department in Calcutta. Managing everything single-handedly was not easy. Often, I had to leave little Bukai at a crèche for the day or request our kind neighbour, Kusum-di, to look after her.

Titai, after returning from school, would feed her younger sister and keep an eye on her while completing her own homework. She would also entertain Bukai with stories, keeping her engaged and cheerful. In this way, both our daughters began learning independence and taking responsibility from a very young age.

Parag always made it a point to buy at least one pair of new clothes for the girls on the day of Bengali New Year. He would visit familiar shops after receiving friendly invitations from them on that auspicious day, accompanied by both his daughters. It was considered best for businesses to begin a new ledger on that day. Titai and Bukai especially enjoyed visiting Rakshit Jewellers in Bowbazar. Titai was fascinated by the complimentary diary they offered each year, while Bukai liked sitting in the air-conditioned shop, sipping Coca-Cola. Mr Rakshit never forgot to send me a Bengali calendar either.

I recall another moment from Bukai's childhood. At the time, it was fashionable to tie rakhi wristbands on brothers' wrists during Rakhi Purnima. Even in our home, Parag would buy rakhis and made sure that Titai tied one on Bukai's wrist. The absence of a son never bothered him. He loved his daughters as he would have loved a son, gave them educational opportunities, and encouraged them to be independent. They were the apples of his eyes, and they, in turn, respected and adored him deeply.

Our brother Parijat had finally settled into a modest job in Calcutta. At Bordi's request, we began planning his marriage. He eventually married a colleague from his office. You must remember how much we all enjoyed the wedding ceremonies, Di-bhai! Sadly, Kaki did not live to witness that happy occasion.

During this period, we also attended the weddings of Chhoto Mama's five daughters and two sons, one after the other. We helped with preparations and celebrated joyously with our siblings and cousins. We consciously decided not to let any resentment over our mother being denied a share in the ancestral property affect our relationships. I don't quite know how all of us siblings managed to carve out decent lives for ourselves, Di-bhai, but I'm certain the blessings of our departed parents have always been with us. Except for Bordi, who never married, each of us had well-behaved children who excelled in their studies. Bordi, in particular, hoped that Titai would become a doctor, as I couldn't pursue medicine after our father's passing.

Titai studied at Calcutta Girls' High School after completing her Montessori schooling at Brahmo Balika Shikshalaya. She scored very well in her Class XII exams and qualified for medical studies through the Joint Entrance Examination. We were all overjoyed. When Titai began her classes, Bordi visited us, a smile of deep satisfaction on her face, and said, 'Apu, our father's soul will finally find peace.'

Titai's first stethoscope and blood-pressure measuring instrument were gifts from Bordi, bought with her modest salary. Di-bhai, Titai still keeps them carefully to this day.

When Bukai was born, West Bengal was under the rule of the Congress Party, led by Mr. Siddhartha Shankar Ray. The government had draped the city with posters declaring, 'Work more, Talk less.' I still remember the full-page advertisement in the *Amrita Bazar Patrika*, urging citizens with the slogan, 'Punctuality is not just for the Railways, it is for you too.'

Within a few months, the central government imposed the Emergency. The majority of opposition leaders were arrested, and democratic rights were suspended. Then, in 1977, when the Emergency was lifted and general elections were held, the Janata Party came to power at the Centre, ousting the previous Congress Prime Minister, Indira Gandhi.

In West Bengal, the political landscape shifted dramatically. The Left Front government came to power, making the iconic Writers' Building in Calcutta its seat of governance. Led by the CPI-M and supported by other leftist allies, they won decisively in the state elections.

However, the Janata Party's hold at the Centre was short-lived. Internal conflicts and power struggles weakened the coalition. In the 1980 general elections, Indira Gandhi's faction—Congress (I)—returned to power, marking yet another turn in the nation's political journey.

In West Bengal, the Left Front government came to power in 1977, with the CPI(M) and its allies winning the state elections and occupying the Writers Building in Calcutta.

The new chief minister, Shri Jyoti Basu, and Left Front chairman, Pramod Dasgupta, led a government largely made up of leaders who had migrated from East Pakistan during Partition. Committed to Marxist and socialist ideals, they focused on improving the lives of ordinary people from the middle and lower classes. It appeared that the hapless Bengalis would finally be getting some relief. Everyone remembers Operation Barga. The government began registering sharecroppers' names on an unprecedented scale. By amending land reform laws and banning the eviction of sharecroppers, they granted peasants traditional rights to the land. Additionally, surplus land above ceiling limits was redistributed.

Teachers' salaries in private and government-aided schools were finally brought on par with those in government schools, and the state began providing pensions upon retirement. A quiet sense of stability and comfort slowly began to settle into our lives.

For the first time, Parag, Titai, six-year-old Bukai, and I ventured out of Calcutta on a guided tour organized by Tirupati Travels. We journeyed across southern India, soaking in the sights and sounds of places we had only read about. At the end of our trip, we arrived at Kanyakumari—the southernmost tip of our motherland—where the Indian Ocean embraced us from all sides.

Standing atop Vivekananda Rock, I was overcome with a surge of emotion. Parag held little Bukai in his arms, while I stood holding Titai's hand. Facing north, I told my daughters:

'Look closely, my dears—this is your motherland stretching out before you. No matter how much success, fame or wealth you achieve in life, never forget that you are Indian. This is the land where we were born, and we owe an unpayable debt to its soil.'

Di-bhai, Titai's eyes were brimming with patriotic tears that day. However, according to our tour itinerary, we couldn't continue on to Madurai from Kanyakumari, as her medical classes had already commenced. So, we returned to Calcutta.

Thirty-one

Like her older sister, Bukai too started attending Calcutta Girls' High School after spending a few years in the Montessori section of Brahmo Balika Shikshalaya. In 1984, we embarked on a trip to Himachal, Delhi, Punjab and Kashmir in North India. Unfortunately, we found ourselves severely affected by the situation prevailing in the aftermath of Operation Blue Star on our return journey.

During the tour, we visited Jallianwala Bagh in Amritsar. We were all overcome with emotion, recalling the horrific massacre and brutality of British colonial rule. In April 1919, about four hundred lives were lost on the orders of General Dyer.

The bullet-riddled walls and the old well—into which countless innocent people had flung themselves in a frantic bid to escape the hail of bullets—stood as grim, silent witnesses to that unspeakable tragedy. As we stood there, a wave of emotion swept over us. The sheer horror of what had unfolded in that place felt almost unbearable. And yet, amidst the sorrow, witnessing all this, we felt blessed that our motherland had already gained its freedom.

When we reached the Golden Temple, we were captivated by its beauty—the intricate carvings, the golden artistry on the marble, the crystal-clear water in the pool, and the delicious prasad prepared in ghee. Titai and Bukai were delighted. In accordance with Sikh customs, we all covered our heads with large handkerchiefs. After leaving the temple, we were praising the city and trying to do some shopping, when a group of Sikh mounted policemen rode past us, whispering, 'You should not loiter around any more; go home now, go to your homes.'

Why would anyone say that to tourists? Taken aback, we quickly rejoined our travel group. We wanted to have our lunch and rest in the train compartment reserved for us. Oh! I forgot to mention, Di-bhai—fourteen families from Calcutta had booked an entire compartment for the long journey under the arrangement of a reputed travel and tour company.

That evening, the train left Amritsar and reached Jammu the following day, only to halt unexpectedly. We learnt that major unrest had erupted at the Golden Temple—the very place we had visited just 24 hours earlier.

For the previous two to three years, the militant Sikh leader Jarnail Singh Bhindranwale and his followers had turned the Golden Temple complex into a fortified base. His goal was to establish Khalistan—a separate Sikh nation breaking away from India. Since 1982, with support from Pakistan, he had stockpiled weapons, including guns, machine guns, and bombs, in the basement chambers of the temple.

Indira Gandhi was the Prime Minister of India at the time. As you know, the Nehru family had long been deeply involved in the country's political landscape. From her childhood, Indira Gandhi had shown a natural inclination towards the political ideology of both her father, Jawaharlal Nehru, and her grandfather, Motilal Nehru. It must also be acknowledged that Mahatma Gandhi had a profound influence on her political outlook and leadership style.

After India gained independence, Indira Gandhi remained by her father's side, observing and participating in the workings of the new nation. Following the untimely death of Prime Minister Lal Bahadur Shastri in 1966, she rose to become India's first female Prime Minister. Winning successive electoral mandates, she continued to lead the country as Prime Minister until 1977.

The astute leader was fully aware of the Khalistan conspiracy. She discovered that the president of the Sikh political party Akali Dal, Harchand Singh Longowal, had helped Bhindranwale seek refuge in the Golden Temple. She also received reports that some Khalistani leaders had been regularly travelling to Pakistan. Intelligence agencies—both India's CBI and the Soviet KGB—reported that weapons were being smuggled into the temple through Jammu and Kashmir and Himachal Pradesh.

In June 1984, Indira Gandhi decided it was time to reclaim the Golden Temple—the sacred seat of Sikhism—from the militants. The then Army Chief, Lieutenant General S.K. Sinha, opposed any military action inside the temple premises, and was unceremoniously removed. He was replaced by the daring General Arun Shridhar Vaidya.

On the night of 2 June 1984, Indian soldiers surrounded the Golden Temple. From 3 June, curfew was imposed across Punjab, and all transport and communication services were suspended. The military operation was codenamed Operation Blue Star.

Due to this, our train remained stationary at Jammu station from 3 June 1984 onwards.

We read in the newspapers how the Indian Army had surrounded the Golden Temple and, using loudspeakers, repeatedly appealed to the militants to release the trapped devotees and tourists. In response, gunfire erupted from within the temple complex. The Khalistani extremists, heavily armed with Chinese rocket-propelled grenade launchers and machine guns, retaliated fiercely.

When the deadlock dragged on until 5 June, the Indian Army was left with no choice but to deploy tanks and artillery to break the siege. The gunfire raged until 8 June. Many Indian soldiers were wounded, and eighty-seven lost their lives. Around two thousand Khalistani militants were arrested. Only then was the temple complex finally cleared, bringing an end to the Khalistani stronghold within its sacred walls.

Our tour group operators were efficient in planning our next steps. They arranged for our security. We spent a total of eleven days at Jammu station, eating food provided by the Shiv Sena and kept ourselves occupied playing board games and singing. Our stay in the reserved train compartment continued smoothly, with no problems regarding sleeping arrangements. Thankfully, there were no incidents of harassment towards women during the entire period.

The group included elderly individuals, honeymooning couples, and families with children, just like ours. The tour conductor stayed with us throughout, ensuring a safe environment. The first-class waiting room at the station was well-maintained, allowing us to go about our daily washing and cleaning without disturbance.

Little Bukai didn't give us much trouble. At ten, she adored her older sister and listened to her devotedly—we had raised her that way. Titai was almost like a second mother to her. She took responsibility for her meals, sang with her, told her stories, and put her to sleep during this time.

Later, of course, Parag and I were rebuked by all of you for not sending any news via letters about our well-being. But there was no way to do so—no one knew when we would be able to return to Howrah. Despite our concerns, we relied on one another and on the basic humanity of those around us. Naturally, little Bukai was the only one without a care in the world.

After eleven days, on 14 June, our compartments were detached from the parked train and attached to a different engine bound for Kolkata. We began our journey home late that night, travelling in complete silence with all the lights switched off. The train moved at a snail's pace. Despite our fear, we eventually fell asleep. Two days later, we finally arrived at Howrah station—

surviving the ordeal. On arrival, passengers celebrated, sharing sweets with the relatives who had come to receive them—a simple yet heartfelt expression of relief.

However, opposition to Indira Gandhi was intensifying across the country. Many Sikhs resigned from the army, and others left civil services. Four months later, on 31 October, Indira Gandhi was assassinated when fired at point-blank range by two of her Sikh bodyguards—Satwant Singh and Beant Singh. Yet, the country and its people had to carry on.

Following her assassination in 1984, as part of the aftermath of Operation Blue Star, the Congress leadership elected her son, Rajiv Gandhi, as the next Prime Minister. At 40, he became the youngest Prime Minister in Indian history.

Before entering politics, Rajiv had been a professional pilot with Indian Airlines. Though his mother was the Prime Minister, Rajiv had remained outside the political sphere until the death of his younger brother, Sanjay, in 1980.

Earlier, when Sanjay Gandhi had entered politics, he seemed poised to serve the country for a long time as a successful politician. Like Rajiv, Sanjay had studied at the prestigious Doon School in Dehradun before travelling to England to study automotive engineering. He had a deep interest in sports cars and also held a pilot's license.

In 1971, the Indira Gandhi cabinet proposed developing a people's car for India's middle class. Sanjay Gandhi, then the director of Maruti Motors, took charge. Though the early test models drew criticism, with support from the German company Volkswagen, and later the Japanese company Suzuki, the car eventually appeared on Indian roads.

The year 1974 witnessed widespread political unrest across India, coupled with a sharp economic downturn. Then, on 25 June 1975, Indira Gandhi declared a state of Emergency, plunging the nation into a period of fear and uncertainty. Prominent freedom fighters like Jayaprakash Narayan and Jivatram Kripalani were arrested for raising their voices in protest. What disturbed many even more was the growing influence of Sanjay Gandhi during this time. Alongside his close associate Bansi Lal, Sanjay tried to build his own power base by bringing in young politicians and introducing his own five-point programme alongside Indira's twenty-point agenda for governance.

While people welcomed some reforms—like steps towards promoting education, encouraging tree planting and efforts to reduce caste discrimination and dowry practices—they were appalled by Sanjay Gandhi's aggressive population control drive, which included forced sterilization. The looming spectre of dictatorship within a democratic framework made many uneasy.

Di-bhai, for families like ours, those were days of turmoil and fear. The lives of ordinary citizens, already difficult, were thrown further into chaos.

In March 1977, Sanjay Gandhi was shot at by unknown assailants at a place about 300 miles from New Delhi. Though he survived the attempt, he later died in a plane crash in June 1980. Sanjay, his mother's favourite, had been her political heir. After his death, and at her urging, Rajiv stepped into public life.

Rajiv Gandhi went on to reorganize the license system, revise tax policies, and liberalize regulations governing economic activity. He championed the modernization of telecommunications, supported science and technology, and sought to improve relations with the United States.

He served as Prime Minister until 2 December 1989, when his party lost the general election. Tragically, he too lost his life in a terrorist attack. I shall come to that later.

Thirty-two

Di-bhai, your beloved Titai captivated everyone with her singing at the freshers' welcome festivities after her admission to Calcutta Medical College. Throughout her five years there, she was often invited to sing at various inter-college events. She was the lead-singer of a music group comprising of students from her class—there were accompaniments too. One of the students would play the harmonium, another played the tabla, while others sang along with her.

After their medicine classes, the gang would often come to our home to rehearse. Sometimes, they would request me to make their favourite snacks and tea. Titai would occasionally walk back home with her friends via College Street and Bowbazar, using the money saved from her bus fare to buy fish cutlets or other treats from the reputed Kalika and Banik's takeaway for us.

Her friends created a delightful ruckus, insisting, 'Aunty, you and uncle must sit with us and enjoy the snacks too! Tell us, is Dipali singing in tempo? Isn't Apurba playing the tabla off-beat? Is Himadri out of tune?'

Parag and I would burst into laughter. Those evenings were truly beautiful. Our children had no demands. We noticed that the boy, Himadri, spoke very little. Yet, whenever Titai sang, he would gaze at her with such expressive eyes. It was clear from Titai's demeanour that she also appreciated his quiet attention. Indeed, Di-bhai, we were joyfully aware of the imminent arrival of spring.

While a medical student, Titai back home from college, was

never tired of recounting the funny rhymes crafted by seniors to memorize complicated medical terms, mimicking the teaching styles of her various professors, or sharing amusing stories from class—thanks to the naughtier students. She also wanted us to listen to every detail of the tales of the patients in the hospital wards. During internship too, even after being on duty for twenty-four, sometimes even thirty-six hours at a stretch, she would come home and still find the energy to talk about the small, everyday moments from her clinical experiences. Likewise, we were never tired of hearing them.

She passed medical school with excellent marks. I had seen first-hand how hard she worked during her tenure as a house-surgeon. Di-bhai, by that time, your son and Mejdi's daughter had both finished their studies and become graduates too.

Even after completing her MBBS, we advised Titai not to begin practising medicine immediately. We didn't want her to be a general physician for the sake of earning a livelihood. Instead, we encouraged her to pursue further studies and specialize in a field of her choice.

I always remembered Bordi's words: 'Titai will become a great medical practitioner like her grandfather, Apu. You'll see—she will be such a compassionate doctor that no amount of money will ever cloud her spirit. Our Titai will be honest like Parag, and resilient and hardworking like you. Our blessings will be with her always.'

So, Titai resumed her studies, preparing for the postgraduate entrance examinations. During those months of her preparation, Parag, an early riser, would return from the washroom in the morning and whisper to me, 'What do we do with this girl? She studies even after we go to bed. And no matter how early I wake up, I still find her surrounded by and busy with her thick books. Does she never sleep?'

I could sense his concern—it was his love for his firstborn speaking. But I knew my Titai. She had stood by us through difficult times. As the elder child, she had been a young fighter during our most challenging days. She inherited the same never-give-up spirit that runs in my veins.

Eventually, Titai secured admission to the prestigious Post Graduate Institute of Medical Education and Research in Chandigarh to pursue an MD in Gynaecology and Obstetrics. She earned one of just two seats in the general category—out of thousands of applicants. Our dreams had come true.

Alongside Titai, we had watched 18-year-old Himu grow into a determined and focused young man, completely immersed in his studies. He matured before our eyes and, with dedication and perseverance, successfully cleared his final MBBS examinations.

After graduation, Himu too secured admission to the Post Graduate Institute in Chandigarh. Though both studied at the same institute, they lived in separate hostels. The course spanned for three demanding years. Naturally, questions began to surface in our minds—would the typical distractions and restlessness of youth distract them from their goals? Would emotional entanglements or the pressures of early adulthood interfere with their academic progress? These silent concerns lingered at the back of our minds.

Around that time, Parag's elder brother, who had been practising medicine in Arunachal Pradesh, returned to West Bengal and settled with his family in Basunagar, Madhyamgram, on the outskirts of Calcutta. He set up a pharmacy-cum-multi-speciality clinic on the ground floor of his house. His reassuring words gave us confidence regarding Titai and Himu.

'Don't worry,' he said. 'Titai is a very sensible girl. She will choose her life partner with care. Besides, both of them are extremely intelligent and deeply focused on their studies. They understand life's challenges. Their priority is academic success. They will not stray from the path—you'll see.'

Indeed, they decided to marry only after successfully completing their post-graduation and receiving their MD degrees from PGIMER.

Di-bhai, do you remember the weeks when we were arranging Titai's wedding in Calcutta? At that time, we were still living in our modest two-and-a-half-room flat in Moulali. You had voiced another concern—the groom being a doctor, what if they demanded a handsome dowry? We still had another daughter pursuing her education. At the end of each month, Parag returned home with a regular but modest salary paid by the government, which was not unlimited. His true wealth, however, lay in his deep sense of self-respect.

Let me share an incident that reflects this quality. Despite having reached a senior position in the Income Tax Department after passing several departmental examinations, Parag held firmly to the honesty and integrity inherited from his father and grandfather. On one occasion, he even threw a visiting officer out of his office who had attempted to bribe him. That evening, when he returned home, he recounted the incident to me, his whole-body trembling with emotion. I turned pale with fear as I listened. To see Parag—usually calm, composed, humorous, and jovial—in such a state of anger was unprecedented. Yet, when I reflect on that day, I cannot help but salute his unwavering commitment to what is right.

He was a man of simple needs. His friends and colleagues were fond of him. When Titai was about seven, some of his office colleagues including Suranjan-babu would occasionally accompany him to our house in the evenings. We never had much to offer, yet they would cheerfully request, 'Just serve us some puffed rice! And if there are a few green chillies and onions, it will feel like a grand feast.'

As soon as I arranged the snacks, one of them would drag out the old harmonium that had belonged to Titai's aunt, from beneath the bed, and start singing:

John Henry was his good name.
He worked as a full-fledged engine,
He struck a hammer here and struck a hammer there
And smiled and made a merry din!*

It was an impassioned song recounting the plight of Black labourers who laid railway tracks in 19th-century America. Their spirits were high, and they all sang along, despite a long day of work at the office.

From the kitchen, while preparing tea, I would hear Suranjan's booming voice singing Tagore's famous creation:

Bipode more rokkha koro e nohe mor prarthona
Bipode ami na jeno kori bhoy.

My prayer is not that you protect me from danger,
but that I may not be afraid when danger comes.

Titai would join in, responding in her sweet, childish voice:

Dukkho, tape, byathito chite, naai ba dile shantona
Dukkhe jeno korite pari joy.

In sorrow or agony, may you not offer me
consolation—pray that I may overcome all the misery.

Di-bhai, Titai was not even in her teens then, and perhaps she couldn't fully grasp the meaning of the words of Tagore. But once

---

*American folklore, translated to Bengali by Hemanga Biswas

everyone had left, she would ask me, 'Ma, why did I feel the same way listening to Henry's story as I did when watching *Uncle Tom's Cabin*? Why did Black people have to suffer so much?'

Her eyes welled up. Parag swiftly wiped away her tears and spoke gently, 'Titai, my dear, this world is a mixture of joy and sorrow, of suffering and hardship. When these reach a tipping point, revolutions do happen. At times, extraordinary souls like Ramakrishna and Vivekananda appear—incarnations of the Divine. Just as a fierce storm clears the earth of dry leaves and debris, even if many lives are lost in the fight against injustice, it is through such struggles that tyranny and oppression have been overcome throughout history. That is the natural order of this world.'

That was her first lesson from her father about justice, truth, humanity, and compassion.

Let me return to Titai's days in Medical College. We had realized that Himu was clearly enamoured by our beloved daughter. We were naturally curious about his family. As it happened, Parag and Himu's father had chatted casually while waiting during their children's admission to Calcutta Medical College. During their conversation, Himadri's father told Parag that he too hailed from Tangail in Mymensingh district of East Bengal—just like Parag. They discovered that both had once attended Bindu Basini Boys' School and fondly reminisced about the famed sweets from a nearby shop.

Di-bhai, those were peculiar times. People displaced from East Bengal—who had left behind lands adorned with rivers and lush greenery—whenever they met each other often recalled these memories with warmth and nostalgia. In those moments of shared history, it felt as if they had known each other for years.

That same sense of connection was felt during Titai's wedding. Like me, Himadri's mother—Dipesh Babu's wife—was also from Bikrampur, with family roots in Barisal.

The bride and groom could only take leave from their institute in Chandigarh a few days before the wedding. We had everything prepared in advance. Poor Titai didn't even have the time to go shopping or choose her wedding trousseau.

When we asked the groom what he wanted as a wedding gift, it felt as if history were repeating itself. Sitting beside Titai, Himadri smiled radiantly and said, 'What do you mean? You're giving me your precious daughter—isn't that more than enough?'

All of you were surprised to hear the young man speak with such simplicity and quiet resolve. We were left speechless. The neighbours, who had gathered were surprised as well, while Himadri's principled parents looked visibly pleased. Parag wore a broad smile—only I knew the reason behind his happiness. Had we not wished for just such a partner for Titai? After the wedding, Titai and Himu returned to Chandigarh. Once they completed their assignments at PGIMER and after a brief period of working as faculties in a medical college in Bombay, called Mumbai now, they finally travelled to and settled down in Delhi.

Meanwhile, the internal situation of the country was steadily changing. Under Prime Minister Rajiv Gandhi's leadership, India found itself increasingly entangled in several regional controversies across South Asia. Our school's art teacher, Maitrayee-di, was married to an officer in the Indian army. During tiffin breaks, she would often share updates about the activities of the Indian Peace Keeping Force (IPKF).

In 1988, Rajiv Gandhi took a firm stand against militant groups like the People's Liberation Organization of Tamil Eelam (PLOTE), and India played a decisive role in thwarting a coup attempt in the Maldives. At the same time, Rajiv Gandhi authorized the deployment of the IPKF in Sri Lanka to intervene in the island nation's escalating ethnic conflict. Intended as a peacekeeping mission, the IPKF soon found itself in direct combat with the Liberation Tigers of Tamil Eelam (LTTE), the dominant Tamil separatist group fighting for an independent Tamil homeland in Sri Lanka's northeast.

This intervention triggered widespread resentment in Tamil Nadu, as many sympathized with the LTTE on ethnic and emotional grounds. Despite growing public anger and political pressure from within India, Rajiv Gandhi refused to withdraw the troops prematurely. Instead, he sought to contain the LTTE through diplomatic means and military pressure. Yet, the violence dragged on relentlessly. The IPKF suffered heavy casualties—more than 2,400 Indian soldiers lost their lives before the mission finally ended.

Around this period, in mid-1984, the Bofors scandal erupted, severely damaging Rajiv Gandhi's carefully built image as an honest and youthful leader. Allegations of kickbacks in an arms deal with a Swedish firm shook public confidence and became a major point of criticism for the opposition. This scandal played a significant role in the Congress Party's defeat in the 1989 general elections.

Following that electoral loss, Vishwanath Pratap Singh became Prime Minister and oversaw the eventual withdrawal of Indian troops from Sri Lanka. However, his government proved unstable, leading to the announcement of fresh elections in 1991. Until that point, Rajiv Gandhi remained the president of the Indian National Congress, continuing to play an active role in national politics despite the setbacks.

That same year, during the election campaign, Rajiv Gandhi travelled to Sriperumbudur, a small town near Chennai, to address a rally. His convoy of white Ambassador cars moved steadily from one public meeting to another, with crowds gathering at each stop to catch a glimpse of the former Prime Minister. Accompanying him that day was a foreign journalist, who interviewed him along the journey, capturing the mood of the campaign.

When they finally reached Sriperumbudur, Rajiv Gandhi stepped out of his car and began walking towards the open-air podium from where he was scheduled to address the people. Local Congress workers, supporters, and schoolchildren lined the pathway, greeting him with garlands and cheers.

Amidst this warm and chaotic reception, a young woman emerged from the crowd. Appearing to bow down to touch his feet in traditional gesture, she moved closer. Her name was later revealed as Dhanu, an LTTE operative. Concealed beneath her clothing was a belt packed with RDX explosives. In one horrifying instant, she detonated the bomb at point-blank range.

The blast was devastating. Rajiv Gandhi was killed instantly, along with several others standing nearby, including police officers, party workers and onlookers. Among the dead was a local journalist who had been covering the rally. His camera, found later at the site, still contained the undeveloped film capturing the exact, fatal moment of the explosion.

And thus, Di-bhai, came the harrowing end of Rajiv Gandhi—a brutal and tragic continuation of the fate that had already claimed both his mother, Indira Gandhi, and his younger brother Sanjay.

Thirty-three

As Himadri and Titai settled down in Delhi, Himu did well in his job at Ranbaxy Laboratories, which was at its peak at the time, and Titai's medical practice gradually flourished as well. Meanwhile, Bukai was studying English Literature at Jadavpur University in Calcutta. Our younger daughter graduated with first-class first honours and received a gold medal in her BA. She aspired to study abroad, but we lacked the financial means to support her dream. Parag's retirement was also approaching.

However, God had other plans for her.

Our little princess applied for both the Inlaks and Rhodes scholarships. As she did well and qualified in the written tests, for the final selection interviews she had to travel to the capital. She was nervous and anxious in the days leading up to the interaction session. However, once in Delhi, her elder sister and brother-in-law supported her wholeheartedly. On the day of the interview, they accompanied her, carrying her books along with food and water. Back in Calcutta, we could only pray and wait.

Two days later, the phone rang. Titai's voice was brimming with excitement.

'Ma! The interview results are out! My sister is going to England on a scholarship—she'll study at Oxford and Cambridge Universities!'

Di-bhai, that day, as we embraced each other, we were trembling with emotion. It felt almost unreal—we could hardly believe our ears when the announcement came. With hearts full of pride and eyes brimming with tears, we finally saw off our younger daughter at the airport, her two large suitcases trailing behind her. That flight, which carried her away from us that day, has since taken her to great heights—lifting her towards success, with the blessings and good wishes of everyone who loves her.

Thirty-four

Titai used to tidy up both her father's and my almirahs in turn from time to time. It was a task she loved doing spontaneously. During one of her visits to Calcutta, she decided to undertake her favourite chore. While sorting through her father's wardrobe, she came across a government letter. Surprised, she dragged me out of the kitchen and insisted I read it.

We discovered that a few years ago, the government had allotted a small plot in the new Salt Lake Residential Scheme in Calcutta in the name of Mr Parag Kumar Das. To our astonishment, all these years he had neither informed us about it nor communicated any decision to the government regarding it.

Di-bhai, I was frustrated and angry. That day, I bombarded him with countless questions and even accused him of being selfish. By then, most of you—my siblings—had already built your own homes. Mejdi had her husband's ancestral abode in north Calcutta, and Parag's brothers had constructed their houses in Madhyamgram. On learning about the Salt Lake plot, I felt as if we had been oblivious to even the most basic material aspirations all these years. How had we endured life in the cramped two-and-a-half-room flat in Moulali for so long? We'd even had to rent a house temporarily for Titai's wedding!

In those few moments, years of hardship came flooding back: the smoke-filled kitchen, water seeping through the balcony roof, broken tiles in the bathroom, and the landlord's monthly reminders for rent. The weight of it all overwhelmed me. Titai had to try hard to calm me down.

Parag remained silent for a long time, listening with composure and patience as I poured out my frustrations. When at last I fell quiet—exhausted by my own outburst of complaints—he gently took my hands in his and spoke in a soft, steady voice.

'Apu,' he said, 'did we not dream together that one day, when our daughters—the true jewels of our lives—would stand on their own feet and make a name for themselves, our struggles would finally find meaning and peace?'

He paused for a moment before continuing, his tone deep with quiet conviction. 'Do you not remember how, back in 1947, we left behind the comfort of our ancestral home and migrated to an unfamiliar land? With whatever little education we had, we built a life here—holding on to our dignity every step of the way. Later, I gave up my rightful share of my ancestral property without hesitation, just to avoid conflict and bitterness. At that time more than in wealth or land, I believed in the promise of their education and their future.'

Parag was holding my hand by then. His grip tightened slightly, as if willing me to understand every word. 'Houses of brick and mortar will not last forever. Nor will we. But our daughters must always know that for us, they came first. Their father never stood in the way of their dreams—even when it meant sacrificing his own. That has been my purpose all these years. Did you not understand that, Aparajita?'

Di-bhai, I had no words. I was crushed by an overwhelming sense of guilt. My moment of selfishness and my misplaced frustration shattered my self-respect. Titai embraced us both, and we remained in silence for nearly an hour. It rained heavily that evening. As the pitter-patter continued outside, the four of us sat cross-legged on the floor, holding hands, and sang old IPTA songs that we had always loved:

Dheu uthchhe, kara tutchhe, alo futchhe, pran jagchhe.

The waves are surging,
prisons are crumbling,
as the light breaks through,
life is stirring within the darkness around.

As we sang, our eyes welled up and our hearts swelled with love. A new light of hope flickered within us.

That night, I quickly prepared some khichuri for dinner. Titai and her father began mapping out their plans to follow up on taking possession of the land that had been allotted by the government years earlier. The plan was set in motion. Although we had to pay a fine for the delay, the plot was eventually granted to us. After his retirement, Parag began travelling regularly from Moulali to Salt Lake. It was quite a distance to cover. Though he would return home exhausted, he never once voiced his fatigue. It became clear that he was determined to fulfil this next responsibility with equal dedication.

At last, our single-storey house in Salt Lake, Bidhannagar, was ready. It stood there—a beautiful, gleaming white building. We had poured all our savings into it, and by then, Titai had begun supporting us financially on a regular basis. My teaching job still contributed, and Parag's pension had also started coming in. On the day of the house-warming ceremony, my face must have lit up like a thousand-watt bulb as I welcomed the guests. They showered our new home with praise. I noticed Parag's gaze lingering on me again and again. How deeply he loved me! How happy he was to see me content.

Di-bhai, it was very hard to leave behind the Moulali flat, where we had spent more than 30 years of our lives. The neighbours—especially the Dattas, who had helped us raise Bukai—almost wept as they bid us farewell. I shall never forget their brilliant son, who suffered lifelong trauma after becoming involved in the Naxalite movement.

How could we forget the school days of our daughters near Wellington Square? Parag remembered his daily walk from Moulali to Dharmatala to reach his work. We recalled visiting the holy Moula Ali Dargah when the children fell ill, and Titai's joyful face when she bought little birds from the fair at Entally during *Rath Yatra*. Di-bhai, building a home is difficult—but leaving one is no easier.

We couldn't take along the old bed that had once belonged to Titai's grandmother. We donated it to a poor elderly man in the neighbourhood. Titai was sad and had whispered softly, 'Dear Grandpa, please take good care of my dear lady's old bed.'

Around this time, Parag's sister suffered a cerebral stroke. Though her children were grown up by then, it was heartbreaking to see someone who had always seemed healthy and active, lying paralysed in bed. Their elder sister had died at a young age back in East Bengal before independence, so Parag and his brothers had grown deeply attached to their only surviving younger sister. After my marriage, I witnessed how, during bhai phonta ceremonies, Parag would lovingly share sweets offered to him and feed them to his darling sister.

My sister-in-law remained bedridden for a long time. All attempts at treatment proved futile. The youngest of the siblings was the first to leave this world. Within a few years, we also lost her husband, our dear brother-in-law. I still remember the spirited IPTA songs he used to sing with such zest and flair. Titai had learnt those songs from him, and now she sometimes sings them to her children. Whenever she does, I think of him and those cherished days.

We, the displaced people from East Bengal, were poor, but we took pride in our poverty. We were emotional, but the light of education had truly illuminated our lives. Above all, our indomitable will to survive helped us endure and overcome hardship.

The series of unforeseen deaths did not end there. On a Vijayadashami day, my other sister-in-law—Parag's younger brother's wife—suffered a massive cardiac arrest and had to be hospitalized. Her son was about Bukai's age, while her daughter, who was married by then, was working at Basunagar School. Perhaps no one can hold on to anyone when the time to let go arrives. She was the youngest among the daughters-in-law who had been married into this family, yet she was the first to leave this world. Parag's elder brother and his wife were heartbroken too.

However, time is a powerful healer. With its passage, we slowly learnt to accept reality and move forward. Parag's brothers lived in Madhyamgram, now much closer to our new home in Salt Lake. We could meet them more often, and gradually we grew fond of our new surroundings.

As a botany teacher, I had always a deep affinity for plants and trees. To deepen that connection, I slowly built a garden with the help of a gardener, filling it with many flowering plants. Before visiting Titai in Delhi, I would often pack pomegranates from my garden to take to my beloved daughter.

Meanwhile, Titai was expecting her first child. Parag was eager to ensure she received the best possible care. At the same time, my retirement was fast approaching. Eventually, we all agreed that I would go and stay with Titai as the delivery date drew near.

It is so difficult to put into words the joy I felt on seeing my first grandchild! I checked her little hands and feet again and again. I named her 'Papri'. Her fingers were long and slender like Parag's, her face resembled Titai's, her large eyes were like her father's, and her chin and lips were just like mine! As I sewed little bedclothes and garments by hand for her, I often thought of Kaki. How overjoyed she would have been to bless the little one! While massaging Papri with baby-oil and bathing her, I recalled Kaki's words: 'This precious one is the best of the best, so lovely, so beautiful!'

The leave I had taken from school soon came to an end. We were worried about leaving Titai and Himu with the added responsibilities of caring for a newborn. Once back in Calcutta, we arranged for a reliable nanny to travel all the way to Delhi with the promise of a tempting salary in order to help them. Parag accompanied the nanny and also stayed with them for a few weeks. Still, raising little Papri was not easy. Due to my job, I could not travel again to Delhi for several months.

At times, the child had to be left at a crèche. Parag, always full of enthusiasm, would take her there with a bag packed with food, toys, and spare clothes. Her mother would collect her on her way home from work. Himadri's parents also did visit them and stayed with them for a while.

Little Papri turned out to be as independent as her mother and grew up quickly. By the time I retired from Brahmo Balika Shikshalaya, dear Papri was already attending nursery school in Delhi.

Their lives continued to be eventful. Himadri often had to travel overseas for work. By then, Titai had worked with several well-known hospitals. Yet, after four years, she found herself increasingly disheartened by the way medical practice was conducted there. The hospitals would often charge patients exorbitantly, at times inflating bills without real justification. Almost half the medicines prescribed and sold through the hospital pharmacies were, in truth, unnecessary. There were other troubling practices too, which Titai could never bring herself to accept. Her conscience simply would not allow her to follow some of the unjust directives handed down by the hospital administration.

At times, I felt that her upbringing had made her so upright and shaped this resistance. I remembered that during her childhood summer holidays, the librarian at Brahmo Girls' School would send her a carefully selected collection of books. These included not only Jules Verne, Alexandre Dumas, Conan Doyle, and the works of Sarat Chandra, Bankim Chandra and Rabindranath, but also those of Maxim Gorky, Nikolai Gogol, and Dostoevsky. Their words must have made a deep impression on her. Titai could not tolerate injustice or oppression. She resigned from her job and began practising medicine and gynaecology independently.

The story of how she established her own nursing home with very limited funds is one of grit and determination. Her second child, Viswayan—a baby boy—was born when Papri was five years old. After the birth of our dear grandson, whom we fondly called Vishu, Himadri's parents stayed with them for many months. Their presence provided the much-needed support that helped a very busy Titai raise both her children.

To this day, Titai recalls the first day of her practice. 'I was a fresh gynaecologist starting out in Delhi, the capital of India. On the first day at the clinic, not a single patient turned up. Disheartened, I was about to call it a day and head home when from my consultation room, I faintly heard someone speaking to the nurse at the reception. Then the nurse seemed to be checking someone's blood pressure. Then the door opened, and in walked a tall, pleasant-looking lady, dignified in a starched cotton sari. Her hair had turned grey long ago, but her sweet familiar face carried a warm smile.

'I wanted to be your first patient. So I hired a rickshaw to come here. Is my blood pressure high? I've had a mild headache since evening. Please examine me properly and prescribe a few medicines, dear.' That's how Titai recounts the day. How can we ever forget the affection shown to my daughter by her in-laws?

Titai still speaks of those times fondly with her children.

This makes me remind, how much we, the parents of both Himu and Titai, had been fond of each other too. Himu's parents lived in a joint family, and his grandmother was still alive—she was very fond of me too. His parents could not leave Calcutta for long as they were the primary caregivers of the family matriarch. However, when Titai and Himu lived in PGIMER campus in Chandigarh, her in-laws would often visit. During those times, Titai and Himu would invite us to Chandigarh as well. Di-bhai, we truly enjoyed staying with them in that beautiful city. We visited the nearby hill stations as a big group and shared many happy moments.

Titai and Himu's fathers were never tired of reminiscing about their younger days in East Bengal. The two of them often went out together, returning home with ice-creams in hand like excited schoolboys. Neither spoke fluent Hindi, yet once in the market they managed to converse in a charming, improvised mix of colloquial Hindi and Bengali. Once back, they would regale us with tales of how cleverly they had navigated the city's shopkeepers, prompting peals of laughter from Himu's mother and me. Little Bukai loved playing with Himu's younger sister, and the house often rang with the sound of their giggles. Though those days have grown a little blurry with time, the memories remain close to my heart.

Just as memories of sunny days visit my mind, I suddenly tend to remember cloudy ones too. Some of our sisters were not as fortunate and died very young, Di-bhai. Do you recall, we lost our youngest sister first—taken far too soon. The small hole in her heart, undiagnosed in her childhood, became her undoing. During Titai's final year of study, she had strongly advised that her dear 'Kutti Mashi' be brought to Calcutta from her in-laws' home in Tribeni, some 60 kilometres north of the city, for better treatment. Sadly, her in-laws delayed. By the time she was finally brought to us, it was too late. Despite all our efforts, we could not save her.

A few months later, Mejdi collapsed suddenly and died of a cardiac arrest. The following year, Bordi, unable to bear the string of losses, also passed away. She had long suffered from high blood pressure. Titai and her seniors at the hospitals in Calcutta treated her with utmost care, but once it is time to leave, who can prevent death?

After Bordi, our beloved elder brother left us too. Among the sisters, only you, one of our younger sisters, and I remained.

Thirty-five

Meanwhile, our younger daughter Bukai earned her master's degree from Oxford University and enrolled for her doctorate, which she completed in due course at Trinity College, Cambridge. Parag brought up the subject of her marriage a few times, but she showed little interest.

On one occasion, Titai and Himu travelled to England with their children on holiday. At Cambridge, Bukai lived in a small, one-room studio apartment, so she arranged for her sister and family to stay at a friend's two-storeyed house. Being twelve years older than Bukai, Titai quickly realized that this friend—an Englishman—was fond of a certain young Indian princess. The man had studied engineering at Oxford with Bukai and had recently started on a new job.

Bukai found herself standing at a crossroads: should she return home to be with her family, or stay on in England and marry Oliver? Titai and Himu approached the situation with remarkable calm and maturity. They sought to understand Oliver's intentions with care and sensitivity. Gently, they asked him if he truly wished to settle down with the Indian girl he had fallen in love with. They also took the time to visit his family in Cambridge—his parents, brother and sister-in-law—hoping to understand the environment in which he had been raised. What they found reassured them. The family was well-educated, the members gainfully employed in respectable professions, open-minded and unfailingly courteous.

When Titai returned to Calcutta and told me about the situation, I must confess, I felt deeply disappointed. True, I had sent my daughter abroad for higher education, but in my heart, I had always nurtured the hope that she would return, marry an Indian man—someone who spoke our language, or at least a language we could comfortably understand. He need not have been Bengali, but perhaps, he would have shared with us the familiar rhythms of our culture and tradition.

I had imagined that, he would smile when I said something affectionate in my mother tongue, even if he did not fully grasp the words. I had hoped that probably, like my Himu, he too would sometimes request steamed hilsa on a rainy day or look forward to a feast of khichuri and fried aubergines on a winter afternoon. Maybe, off-tune but with great feeling, just like Parag did, he might also sing a Tagore song on a lazy Sunday morning. All of a sudden, it felt as though that quiet dream I had woven for years had been shattered.

Parag said little, but I could sense the storm of emotions brewing within him too.

Titai tried to help us see reason. 'If you oppose her, Bukai may return home, leaving her heart behind. But what if the man you later choose for her doesn't turn out to be her soulmate? Would you be able to bear her sorrow then?'

Interestingly, Titai's father-in-law—an English professor who also dabbled in astrology and palmistry—spoke favourably about the prospects of Bukai marrying a foreigner. Slowly, we began to warm to the idea.

Soon after, Titai invited Oliver to visit Calcutta for a week. Bukai came along with him. When he arrived at our Salt Lake home, we were amused to hear him speak fragments of Bengali! He would walk into the kitchen and begin chopping potatoes and tomatoes to help me cook, leaving me quite embarrassed. The boy surprised me by saying, 'When I'm home, I always help my mum in the kitchen!'

Titai would stroll past the kitchen door, smiling and enjoying the spectacle. Bukai would take out bowls of payesh from the refrigerator for all of us to enjoy. Funnily enough, Oliver would heat his portion in the microwave before eating it with great relish! At lunch, he was perfectly content with simple rice and lentils. 'Wonderful soup, so tasty, can I have some more?' he said, clearly delighted. Bukai laughed to see me constantly fretting over what more to cook for him.

Di-bhai, it didn't take us long to get acquainted. Do you remember how surprised everyone was to meet the prospective English son-in-law? Oliver quickly made a good impression on Parag. However, I wanted to speak to his parents personally. They told me over the phone that they would be delighted to have a well-educated and well-mannered girl like Bukai as their daughter-in-law.

One more thing helped put my mind at ease. Neither Oliver nor his family held any religious prejudices. They were free of fanaticism and did not follow rigid conservatism. In fact, they did not even attend church regularly on Sundays. They believed in humanity as the only true religion—a sentiment that deeply resonated with us. With that understanding, Parag and I felt no further hesitation in giving our consent to the marriage.

The wedding was registered in England. On the invitation of Oliver's parents, we flew there to attend the ceremony. Later, we hosted a reception in Salt Lake, which Oliver's parents happily attended. They were genuinely delighted to witness the Bengali traditions—*gaye holud*, *mala bodol*, and other customs we hold dear. Their son looked striking in a silk angrakha, and to our surprise and joy, he willingly wore a *topor*, the traditional Bengali groom's headgear.

You will surely remember, Di-bhai, how we visited Bukai and Oliver in England several times after the wedding. They took us sightseeing—to Buckingham Palace, Blenheim Palace, Oxford University, Cambridge University, and even punting on the River Cam. Oliver's parents welcomed us warmly into their home, inviting us for an intimate lunch. Their house had a sprawling lawn with apple trees blessed with fruit-laden branches. Just beside the garden stood a lovely glass-walled studio where Oliver's mother spent her time painting. She was a gifted artist, and many of her beautiful works adorned the walls of their home, each one reflecting her keen eye and gentle spirit.

We were also pleasantly surprised to hear Oliver play the piano. We hadn't known that the English engineer was a musician too—it turned out his grandmother had been a celebrated pianist.

We noticed that Oliver's parents were exceptionally affectionate. How touching it was to see people from a different country, speaking a different language, welcome a homesick girl into their family with such warmth and love! The hearts of doting parents are the same everywhere. From that point on, we no longer had any concerns about Bukai's marriage—whether it was the geographical distance, religious differences, or social customs, none of it seemed to matter. We also met Oliver's elder brother, his wife, and their two delightful young daughters. Surprisingly, despite having met only recently, we grew very close to them all.

However, life is never without its ups and downs. Amidst all this, we received distressing news. Himu's mother was diagnosed with breast cancer—a heartbreaking revelation for Himu, who was devoted to her. He and Titai promptly began her treatment. After surgery, she underwent radiotherapy and showed some improvement. She returned to Calcutta from Delhi; chemotherapy was a necessity, but it was still pending.

Adding to their challenges, Himu's father, now retired, began experiencing serious health issues caused by respiratory discomfort. During his years at Lumding College in Assam, the professor had been a heavy smoker. Although he gave up the poison-stick later in life, the damage had already been done. After several episodes of worsening health, his condition deteriorated into a critical state that required ICU care. Leaving their children in the care of nannies, Titai and Himu rushed to Calcutta—only to be confronted with the devastating reality of his father's passing away.

His sudden demise left us all in shock. Within a year, Himu's mother's cancer metastasized. Despite completing chemotherapy, she too departed this life, joining her beloved companion on the other side.

The four of us, more or less the same age, shared a history shaped by the Partition of India, carrying within our hearts the common pain of leaving our ancestral homes in East Bengal. We had faced equal struggles and held on to memories of similar golden days. These shared life experiences formed the foundation of our bond, making conversations about our joys and sorrows flow naturally. After the passing of Himu's parents, it felt as though we had lost two dear old friends. The quiet sadness of their absence lingered with us for many years.

Thirty-six

Though Bukai and Oliver were happy, they were not eager to have children. Bukai had just become a faculty and Oliver was working as an engineer in a reputed company. In their world, the prevailing belief was that parenthood should come only after establishing absolutely stable careers.

Bukai had entered our lives when we were relatively older. In fact, I attained menopause within almost a year after her birth. Parag, though content and carefree, harboured a quiet longing to see Bukai with children of her own. Amidst Oliver's light-hearted phone conversations and the playful banter between the couple during their visits, Parag often forgot to express this wish aloud. A cheerful and easy-going man, he expected very little from life.

But happy days, Di-bhai, have a habit of slipping away far too quickly.

One winter night, Parag was engrossed in watching a film on television. I sat beside him, knitting a sweater, breaking into laughter now and then at Rabi Ghosh's witty lines. After the film ended, we closed the windows and went to bed—marking the end of a peaceful evening and the beginning of well-earned rest. Unbeknownst to me, the Almighty had decided not to halt time, not even for a moment.

Around three in the morning, Parag returned from the toilet and sat on the bed, looking at me strangely.

'What's the matter? What are you thinking?' I kept asking, but he simply lay down with his head on my lap. I gently caressed his hair, unaware that the moment of parting had arrived—that my companion of so many years had crossed silently into the land of no return.

It was only after some time, when he no longer responded, that I realized his hands and feet had grown cold. Neighbours rushed in as soon as I screamed for help. The ambulance arrived, but the attendants hesitated to take him away. Eventually, our family physician came and signed the death certificate.

Titai guessed the situation the moment I called her on telephone. She, Himu and their children immediately left for the Delhi airport and arrived in the morning on the first flight.

Parag's body was preserved at Peace Heaven mortuary. We informed Bukai too, and she arrived with Oliver the following evening. Titai's children were deeply attached to their grandfather. The girl wept uncontrollably, and the little boy kept coming up to me, asking after his grandpa, hugging me now and then. The loss affected Titai profoundly—she withdrew from everything around her and did not speak for hours altogether.

She accompanied the relatives to the cremation ground, stoically holding her younger sister's hand throughout the rituals. But as they began to immerse Parag's ashes in the Ganges, her composure finally gave way. Tears she had held back for days spilled over in a flood of grief. It took great effort to console her and bring her back from the riverbank. It would be a long time before she could come to terms with the loss.

Do you remember, Di-bhai, how you used to visit and stay with us for a week or two when Parag was alive? Those days were like a brief return to our second childhood—so full of laughter and warmth. On summer evenings, after dinner, Parag would step out and buy ice creams from the street vendor. The simple joy we found in those moments remains unforgettable.

When Parag turned eighty, his blood pressure had started to rise slightly. Titai took over his health care with quiet determination. She made sure all his check-ups and medical tests were done on time. She even arranged for the local pharmacy to deliver his monthly stock of medicines at one go. Parag followed her instructions dutifully. Yet, he could not resist the occasional craving for tasty food—like a child stealing a treat. With all the burdens of responsibility finally behind him, he found immense joy in sharing stories from his life with neighbours and friends. They were very fond of him too. It became his favourite pastime in his twilight years.

Only a few weeks before, one night, he woke me up from sleep.

'You know, Apu, my last moments will be peaceful. I dreamt of my mother tonight. She came to reassure me of that.'

I knew how deeply he missed his mother, having spent only a short part of his childhood with her. Yet, that night, I was offended by his words.

'If I had known you were this selfish, I would never have married you. You only think of yourself. Have you thought about how lonely I'd be without you?'

He smiled and went back to sleep.

Little did I know that he truly would leave us—without suffering, and in complete peace—on 9 November 2011.

I, too, felt as though I had turned to stone in grief. That dreadful morning after his demise, as realization fully dawned, I went into the bathroom to have a bath. I tidied Parag's towel, arranged his safety razor and shaving brush, as though he might come to use them again. However, you had dutifully whispered some instructions in my ear—I knew I had to remember them. About a year before Parag's passing, you too had lost your husband. He had suffered a stroke that left him paralysed, and for a year, we had looked after him in our home. Despite your unwavering devotion, his death left behind a strange emptiness.

After my bath, I wiped the vermilion from my forehead. When I glanced at the mirror, the face staring back at me felt unfamiliar, almost like that of a stranger. As I removed the red and ivory wedding bangles from my wrists, my appearance seemed even more alien. Traditionally, a widow wears white, but at Titai's gentle insistence, I dressed myself in a light green sari she had bought for me. As I stepped out of the bathroom, it felt as though the entire universe was watching—silent, solemn, weighed down by disbelief and sorrow, whispering about my misfortune.

Parag's elder brother, three years his senior, came to visit us soon after. The veteran doctor sat quietly before Parag's photograph, struggling to hold back his tears. His wife and Parag's younger brother embraced me tightly. In that shared grief, we found a kind of fragile solidarity—no words were needed then as we silently tried to console each other.

Neighbours came too. The fish vendor from the market, the hairdresser from the nearby salon, the boys from the medicine shop—all stood by us in those dark hours. Each person had a story to tell about Parag—how he spoke to strangers with warmth, how he comforted the anxious, how he made people feel heard and cared for. Many wept openly. The residents' association of our block organized a memorial service, where friends and acquaintances said the same thing: Parag and the warmth he spread around to the known as well as unknown, would be impossible to forget.

Dear Di-bhai, every life must come to its inevitable end. Grief is unavoidable, but slowly, with time, recovery follows—that is how the world finds its rhythm again.

'Time is the best healer,' Parag himself used to say. How true those words have turned out to be.

How long could my children remain in Kolkata, away from their responsibilities? Bukai and Oliver returned to England. Titai and Himu stayed on for a few more days, taking care of important matters, but soon they too left for Delhi. Their children had already missed school for quite some time. Though they insisted I accompany them, I did not agree to leave right away.

You had promised to stay with me for a while, and you did. But your son, daughter-in-law and granddaughter needed you too, so before long, you had to return home.

Thankfully, Naren, who sat near the garage during the day, was a great help to me. Years ago, seventeen-year-old Naren, an orphan, had been working as an assistant at an electrical shop in the local block market with a small salary. Parag had been especially fond of him. Without the shelter of parental care, a child faces the world alone, exposed to all its cruelties.

One day, the shop owner threw Naren out after he accidentally broke some electric bulbs. He had been living in a nearby slum and was three months behind on rent. After losing his job, the landlord evicted him. One morning, he rang our doorbell in desperation. Parag and I took him in, allowing the helpless boy to stay in our garage, which had been lying vacant.

Naren was intelligent, hardworking and determined to stand on his own feet. He nurtured the dream of starting a small electrical shop of his own. With whatever modest means we could manage, we helped him get started. From that day on, he arrived around ten in the morning to open his shop and worked without any break. After a quick lunch at Dadur Bhater Hotel in the local bazaar, he would return to work, continuing late into the evening. At night, he slept on one of the benches at the same eatery. Slowly but surely, he managed to hire a few workers and expand his business.

Eventually, his younger brother Biren arrived from their village. With little scope for work back home, Biren joined Naren in running the shop. Together, the brothers began taking on small repair jobs and local contracts, gradually building a more stable and secure livelihood.

After Parag's passing, Naren took it upon himself to look after me in his own quiet way. Around that time, my elder brother-in-law and his wife also had kindly invited me to come and stay with them. But I asked for time—to adjust to my new and unfamiliar life.

While trying to come to terms with my loss, I noticed something small yet deeply moving. Parag's favourite plant, the Madhabilata, had climbed over the bower near our main gate. The marble bench where he once sat on quiet afternoons, exchanging words with neighbours, was now almost covered by cascade of pink blossoms. And yet, even in the midst of such beauty, I found myself struggling—struggling to cope with his absence, struggling to accept this new life without him.

Thirty-seven

The days began getting longer, the nights were filled with loneliness. It was difficult to pass the time after losing a partner at this age. With whom could I now argue about market expenses? Whom would I scold for not folding the newspaper properly after reading it? Who was there to wake up in the middle of the night ready with the pain-killer ointment at hand without a second thought, when my frozen shoulder ached?

My long-time companion—my partner in listening to our favourite radio programmes, the man whose cigarette packets I once tried to hide in all sorts of places, the one who always wanted mouth fresheners after dinner—there was now no way left to communicate with him. An eventful married life of 50 years had come to an end. Those were dark days and darker nights, Di-bhai. My entire being refused to acknowledge anything beyond the pain of Parag's absence. Life flowed on all around me, but I remained fixed, anchored to his memory, lingering always in my heart.

At night, just as I was about to drift off to sleep, I would feel as though I heard a rustling in the tree outside our bedroom window—or perhaps the sound of heavy footsteps on the terrace. Uneasy and alone, I could almost hear my own breathing then. I would instinctively reach out and gently caress Parag's pillow, kept next to mine, to comfort myself. The night watchman of our locality would strike his baton against the iron railings of the neighbouring houses and blow his whistle sharply from time to time, making his presence known to all. These sounds disturbed my slumber too, and once awake, it became difficult to fall asleep again.

In those restless nights, Di-bhai, my thoughts wandered endlessly. I would think of my childhood, of joining Parag's family after marriage, of our children's early years, their weddings, our joyful moments, interspersed with a few disappointments—and the passing away of the one who was closest to me, so unexpectedly. When I closed my eyes, these images played over and over, out like the ever-shifting pictures in a kaleidoscope—a thing we used to marvel at in our childhood.

I rose at dawn, never inclined to remain in bed after waking. After a quick bath, I would wander through the bedroom, the verandah and the prayer room. The girls' rooms remained closed. Some days, a sudden urge would rise within me to enter those rooms and glimpse into their world once more. Pushing open the doors, I would check out Bukai's bed, her bookcase, and her study table—all covered with large plastic sheets to keep away dust. In Titai's room, the walls bore her childhood photos, and the showcase proudly displayed the medals she had earned through her achievements.

Titai and Himu, both doctors, led busy lives, scarcely having time for themselves. My younger daughter, Bukai, immersed in her demanding job, called me now and then. They spoke so fast that I struggled to follow. After a call ended, I would sit with the receiver still in my hand, drifting into absent-minded contemplation, trying to recall every word of the conversation, again and again.

Titai had bought me a mobile phone as a solution to the landline that so often stopped working. She taught me how to make a call—by finding a specific name on the screen and tapping on it. She had saved her number in my phone in just that way. Yet, I would often find myself reaching for the phone diary to look up their numbers and attempt calls from the landline instead. Both my daughters would laugh at my discomfort with modern gadgets. Even so, I never let go of the mobile phone. It was a gift from my elder daughter, and I made sure it stayed fully charged at all times, just in case there was ever a disruption in communication.

As familiar faces faded into the mist of forgetfulness, the house and I became each other's companions. My eyes often rested on the seven-year-old Chinese rose plant—a living reminder of Parag's care. Sometimes, I would reach my hands out of the bedroom window and gently touch the bowed leaves of the papaya tree. Each friend with foliage held a special place in my heart.

The Kanthali Champa tree had grown so tall that its branches now crossed the cornice and reached the terrace. A pair of birds built their nest there. Whenever I climbed the stairs to the terrace, I would pause at a corner and watch them. After some weeks, they laid eggs, and soon tiny nestlings emerged. Both the mother bird and the father bird remained busy all day, caring for their young. When the fledglings found strength in their wings, they flew away. For several days, the empty nest stayed behind, swaying gently in the breeze—holding within it the memory of the chirping birds who had once called it home.

As I roamed around in the terrace once in a while, I kept remembering the exact spot where a pandal had been erected to commemorate the first anniversary of Parag's passing. Friends and relatives had been invited. It is customary to offer morsels of food to birds in the days following the death of a loved one. They say such gestures of kindness bring peace to departed souls. As I did the same, Di-bhai, a fleeting hope lingered in my heart—that if I turned back, I might somehow catch one last glimpse of the person I had lost forever.

A few months later, you came to stay with me again. Your companionship brought comfort once more. But shortly after your arrival, you fell ill with a fever. I thought placing cold packs on your forehead might help bring the temperature down. I tried everything I could to comfort you—you were my only companion at the time. The doctor came, examined you and prescribed medicines. You seemed to drift in and out of a febrile trance.

I tried to remind you of our childhood games, the silly squabbles we had when we were young. But you did not respond to anything I said, Di-bhai. One day, they took you to the hospital. They didn't take me along, perhaps because I was too distressed. You never told me when you'd return. Why, Di-bhai? Why did we never meet again?

Loneliness tightened its grip on me once again, and forgetfulness began creeping further into my daily life. A middle-aged lady—an extra pair of helping hands—stayed with me throughout the day but left in the evenings. Something stranger happened during those peculiar times. On one particular occasion, I was under the impression that I had already given Naren the money needed for two weeks' groceries. Yet, within four days, he gently informed me that it had actually been quite some time since I had last handed him any cash at all! He added that he had been using his own money to buy things for me in the meantime. Embarrassed by my oversight, I promptly gave him a thousand rupees to set things right.

Parag's pension continued to be withdrawn regularly from the bank, and my own pension arrived on time. Naren's brother, Biren, helped me each month with the process—all I had to do was sign the cheque. One day, he proudly showed me how perfectly he had learnt to copy my signature. He said that if I ever faced difficulty, he could sign on my behalf!

Meanwhile, the steel almirah—a relic from my wedding—had started to malfunction. With age, the handle became stiff, and I found it hard to open. Thankfully, Naren was always there to help retrieve money from it. I had become somewhat dependent on him.

When Parag was alive, I would always ignore his requests to familiarize myself with our valuables and finances. I never knew the location of the bank locker where we stored our jewellery, nor did I understand how the electricity and telephone bills were paid each month. Naren and his team took over these responsibilities. Checking bills or counting money felt like too much of a bother. The boys, happy with a glass or two of cold drinking water in summer and the chance to watch cricket on the television, were always eager to help.

Occasionally, Naren would suggest, 'Perhaps I should move in here with my wife and children now. You live alone—anything could happen at night. The rooms would be looked after, and we could all live a better life. You wouldn't need to depend on anyone else for care.'

But I couldn't accept his offer. I don't know why. Each time I declined, Naren would grow more taciturn.

Thirty-eight

Di-bhai, you know that the habit of staying awake till late at night—marking examination papers of the school and the board for decades—had made me somewhat an insomniac. I always had very light sleep. The nights were tiresome. Without you beside me, there was no opportunity to converse while staying awake either.

Every dawn, the morning newspaper would arrive, signalling the start of my day. Then the maid would come, soon serving me a morning cuppa. After that, I would bathe and offer prayers at the altar, with flowers and Tulsi leaves. I had stopped reciting the prayers aloud, as I often forgot the chants midway. The maid did the cooking; by sundown, I could barely recall what I had eaten for lunch.

As evening approached, the large windowpanes sighed in symphony, swaying to and fro as the wind picked up. To silence this unsettling noise, I would ask the maid to shut them. I always tried to remember that it was my duty to protect the house from potential thieves or dacoits. Naren would leave by five in the evening, and his manner had grown noticeably indifferent. Sometimes, if I asked him for a favour, he would casually dismiss me, saying he didn't have the time.

On one occasion, Titai visited from Delhi. She was shocked when she went to the bank and checked my account. 'Why are you withdrawing so much money, Mother? What do you do with these large amounts?' she asked, bewildered.

But the amounts withdrawn using cheques were beyond my

comprehension! I had no use for such large sums. I managed to deflect Titai's suspicions about Biren that day, but I could not forget how effortlessly he had replicated my signature in front of me. Di-bhai, it is said that losing faith in fellow humans is a sin, yet one must be wary of the growing greed and covetousness within those around us.

I was beginning to realize the difficulties of living alone at this age, without my near and dear ones. Still, I resisted leaving the house and everything tied to it. My attachment to the property and possessions acted like shackles, binding me to that house in Salt Lake.

At this point, I must tell you about the political scenario of that time, otherwise it will be impossible to understand the cause of my later helplessness.

Di-bhai, the Left Front, led by the CPI(M), governed West Bengal for 34 years, winning seven consecutive elections. But it seemed ruling parties found it difficult to sustain welfare schemes for the people. The public's initial support gave way to disillusionment. The Left appeared to have become too comfortable in power.

In 2006, a powerful farmers' movement began in Nandigram, a village in East Midnapore district, against the proposed land acquisition for a mega chemical hub. This was supported by the Trinamool Congress and the Maoists. Police firing led to the tragic deaths of fourteen villagers, and many others were injured. Under growing pressure, the government decided to relocate the project.

No one seemed to advise our respected Chief Minister, Buddhadeb Bhattacharjee, that a foundation for chaos was being laid in the state. No one urged the morally upright, free-minded poet to view things with greater practicality and let go of old-school Stalinism. His well-wishers began distancing themselves from him due to his stubbornness. The CPI(M)'s policies and their practice of democracy were no longer aligned, and the party's thirty-year-old perspective failed to evolve. People could not accept the mass killings in Nandigram.

The 2008 Panchayat elections brought a humiliating defeat for the Left Front. The Maoists had effectively 'liberated' Lalgarh in West Midnapore, as well as large areas of the 'Jungle Mahal' region. Di-bhai, I'm sure you remember the farmers' protests in Singur, Hooghly district, against land acquisition for Tata Motors' Nano project. The Left Front once again responded wrongly. In October that year, Tata Motors withdrew and relocated the factory to Gujarat.

The Trinamool Congress had been formed in 1998 as a breakaway faction from the Indian National Congress, with Mamata Banerjee as its leader. In the 2011 Vidhan Sabha elections, the Trinamool Congress, supported by the Congress, came to power, ending 34 years of Left rule in West Bengal. At the time, the Trinamool was the second largest party in the United Progressive Alliance, which governed at the Centre. The slogan 'Ma, Mati, Manush' (mother, land, people) gained immense popularity in West Bengal during the elections.

Parag had always idolized Jyoti Basu, the CPI-M leader, while support for the Congress was more common within my own family. However, like many ordinary people, we were slow to grasp the true significance of the 'Ma, Mati, Manush' slogan. There seemed to be a general sense of uncertainty; people appeared caught in a dilemma, and trust in the new leadership was taking time to take root. I often felt confused, unable to make sense of the changing political landscape. Meanwhile, conversations with neighbours brought me little joy now—perhaps because I was frequently distracted, lost in my own thoughts.

One night, I was in deep sleep—a rare occurrence for me. In

a distant dream, I felt Parag was trying to convey something. It seemed he was urging me to call Titai. Why did he insist? Why was it so crucial to connect with my girl urgently?

Amidst these strange thoughts, I became aware of the doorbell ringing persistently. I woke up with a start.

It was already dawn, and the maid was waiting at the gate. I wanted to hurry and open the front door.

However, in my haste, my foot became entangled in my sari, and I ended up falling heavily. The pain was too intense for me to stand up. Nevertheless, I somehow managed to drag myself and crawl to the door.

Outside, the morning was still foggy. The excruciating ache in my left hip joint scared me.

Learning of my condition, the neighbours rushed to help. Sons of Parag's elder brother, Borda, arrived and admitted me to a hospital. Our younger sister, who lived nearby, and her husband also came to support me. Even Naren and Biren ran around to arrange assistance. I had broken my left femur—the longest and strongest bone in the body. I felt awful for not listening to Titai. I had stubbornly insisted on staying alone. Her requests that I wear nightgowns instead of saris to bed had also fallen on deaf ears. I felt sorry—for myself and for my daughter.

Fortunately, Bukai was scheduled to visit Kolkata that same week for some work at Jadavpur University. Just to mention, the anglicized name of Calcutta had been changed to Kolkata by then. Bukai arrived as planned and immediately took charge of caring for me. Titai, who had urgent work in Delhi and couldn't leave station, sought help from an old classmate of hers. Her doctor friend—a renowned orthopaedic surgeon in Kolkata took charge and also spoke to me the same day. Over the phone, my elder daughter reassured me that everything would be taken care of, and that things would be fine. The operation was a success.

My younger one showed remarkable courage too. Bukai stayed with me in the hospital for three days after the surgery. She wouldn't let me out of her sight for a moment. A day before my discharge, Titai joined us. By then, it was time for Bukai to return to England.

Gradually, I was able to walk a little using a walker, with help from the nurses. However, Titai and Himadri would not hear of my staying alone in Salt Lake. Placed in a wheelchair, I travelled once again by flight to Delhi.

What a troublesome time it was! Being bathed by the ayah was uncomfortable, as I could not move on my own. A physiotherapist began visiting every evening before Titai left for her clinic. He guided me through exercises and helped me walk, initially by holding his hands. About a week later, a sturdy, three-legged walking stick arrived, improving my mobility further. I began walking by myself. I even started accompanying Titai and her family to watch films at the cinema. My daughter also suggested that I join the senior citizens' 'Laughing Club' in the society to enhance my social life. But I didn't feel inclined to converse in Hindi.

On Sundays, Himu would take me to the Chittaranjan Park market for grocery shopping. 'Shall I get some *saag*, Mamoni? It's been ages since you've prepared that delicacy for me,' he would say.

Himu bought the saag, looked for hilsa fish to enhance its flavour, and searched for a smile on my old face at the same time. He also suggested getting *daler bori*. I recalled a time in Salt Lake when I would grind lentils into a fine powder, make a paste, and prepare nuggets with my own hands. I'd lay them out to dry on a mat spread on the terrace. Parag's meals wouldn't be complete without those delicacies.

I stayed in Delhi for a few months. As my movements

improved, the unseen wings on my back began to flutter, making their presence felt. Di-bhai, how could I stay there and leave the house unattended—the house Parag had built with so much struggle, love and dedication? Even though the servants were on leave, we had appointed a night guard. Naren, busy with his business in the garage, would report to me about the house over the telephone. Yet I couldn't help fretting over the AC not being serviced in summer, the inverter-power-backup's battery water not being replenished, or pomegranates being stolen from my favourite tree. Eventually, I insisted on returning home.

Titai did not speak to me for two days, though she still helped me pack. I returned to Kolkata with Himadri. As I tried to re-acclimatize to daily life, I sensed a disrupted rhythm. However, amidst the persistent realization of emptiness, I learnt that my younger daughter was pregnant.

Oh, what wonderful news! I so wished Parag had been there! After nine years of marriage, there would finally be a birth in their family. They preferred the delivery to take place in England. Throughout the nine months, Titai kept track of her sister's health, relaying updates to me over the phone. The long wait came to an end in June.

It was a sleepless night for Titai and Himadri when Bukai went into labour. They stayed awake and remained in constant touch with Oliver, Bukai's husband, over the phone. Later, Oliver told me everything. A little princess had arrived—Bukai's daughter. I had to content myself with looking at her photos. What could I do? I couldn't hold her in my arms or even send her any gifts. I kept thinking about what Parag would have done or said if he had been here. Perhaps I often muttered things to him whenever I was alone.

The following year, around spring, Bukai came to Delhi for a week to attend a conference, accompanied by Oliver and her seven-month-old daughter. Titai's son, my grandson, suggested celebrating his birthday and his little sister's *annaprashan*—her rice-eating ceremony—together, insisting that I should be there to bless them both. Himu arranged my tickets, and once again, I headed to Delhi.

The little one had a peach-and-cream complexion like the Sahebs, and her cheeks were rosy red. Her hair, though, was a beautiful shade of brownish black. Titai's children—her Dadabhai and Didibhai—cuddled her endlessly until she cried out in protest.

In a small ceremony at home, I first blessed my grandson for his birthday and gave him a present. I performed a puja, blessed my baby granddaughter, and fed her payesh with a tiny silver spoon I had brought as a gift. That was how Anandi Gloria's rice ceremony was held. While placing a dainty gold necklace around her neck, I tried to find a glimpse of little Bukai in her face. Indeed, she looked very much like baby Bukai! Would you believe it, Di-bhai, her eyes were deep and beautiful—just like her Dadu's, whom she had never met. I whispered silently to Parag in my heart, 'What was your hurry? You missed everything. Anyway, just look at this beautiful little princess. Hold my hand—let's bless her together.'

By then, I could walk comfortably with my three-legged walking stick. After they returned to England, I too was relieved to board my flight back to Kolkata. I was tired of all that discipline—living in Titai's house under the strict supervision of two doctors had worn me out.

From the moment I boarded the flight, it felt wonderful. No more taking medicines by the clock. No more reminders to eat eggs, fruit or protein-drink at fixed times. From now on, I could watch TV as long as I pleased. If I didn't feel like eating rice for dinner, I could simply have a snack and go to sleep. I loved having betel leaves with flavoured tobacco, but even that had been banned by my elder daughter! I might have been the esteemed mother of a lady doctor, but there was no respite for me!

As per Titai's wishes, a 24-hour caretaker-cum-cook was arranged in Kolkata to look after me. Although I never liked her cooking, I had no choice but to eat whatever she prepared. Still, I never allowed her to cook the dishes Parag had loved. Why? Because deep in my heart, I felt he hadn't gone too far. I remembered how, during his years of service, he had once gone on election duty to Diamond Harbour for two nights, only to return the very next morning by the earliest train. Perhaps one day he would return to me like that again.

I imagined him sitting down for his lunch after his daily bath. I would first serve him *shukto*—that light, slightly bitter Bengali starter he loved. Then would come dal, garnished with a dash of freshly sliced lemon. On one side of his plate, there'd be his favourite crispy fried potato strips, followed by a bowl of delicious green jackfruit curry. And I'd say, 'I've made your favourite dish too—spicy fish flavoured with sour curd. But don't have more than two pieces. You should leave some space in your tummy for the nice dessert I've kept ready.'

Thirty-nine

Di-bhai, indeed, those were the times I had really not taken care of my body—partly out of laziness, and partly out of lingering resentment towards Parag. Why did he have to leave so soon? Did he not realize that no matter how strong I might have seemed—despite retiring as the formidable school headmistress, despite managing every little detail of the household—I had never once imagined living alone all these years? I had not even learnt how to operate the DVD player to play my favourite movies with Uttam Kumar on screen! I remained completely unaware of daily market prices, so I could never calculate how much refund to expect from Naren and Biren when they gave me the household grocery accounts.

Yes, Di-bhai, while I brooded over my situation and loneliness, I often skipped dinner. On some nights, I insisted upon the maid that I would make do with puffed rice or a bowl of instant noodles instead of a full meal. I knew I was growing weaker.

At night, lying in bed, I would stare at the ceiling where the shadows of tree branches outside danced in the dim light. I felt restless, trying to sleep alone on that huge teakwood bed. Dogs would suddenly begin barking, someone on the street would shout an expletive, and then burst into laughter. I decided the guard needed to be replaced—probably he wasn't alert enough.

Let me confess something, Di-bhai. In those days, I resented you too. You, too, departed—leaving your sister to navigate life alone! I even found myself feeling irritated with Kaki and our mother, whom I missed terribly.

My health worsened over the months, but I still kept a hawk's eye on the house. However, when I finally fell ill, the neighbours weren't much help. Even our younger sister, who lived nearby, couldn't visit easily due to her knee pain. One night, I struggled to breathe, and when I mentioned it to Titai over the phone, she grew anxious.

'Mother, please call the pharmacy nearby and ask them to check your blood pressure,' she said. 'Keep in touch and update me. Your sister stays close—I'll inform her too.'

Titai wanted to rush to Kolkata immediately, leaving behind her packed schedule of surgeries and deliveries.

In those difficult days, many familiar faces became strangers. Those I considered my near and dear ones behaved with indifference, and those who were already distant became invisible. Titai eventually had to fly down to Kolkata, leaving her family and work behind. She packed my belongings, settled the wages of the servants, locked up the house, and took me to Delhi the very next day.

Di-bhai, that was when a new chapter in my life began.

Forty

Delhi, the capital of India, is a sprawling city with large houses and colossal hospitals. Even the people are well-built and burly. Their fluent Hindi was difficult for me to understand. Still, I could sense that Titai and Himu were genuinely worried about my health. They took me to various places for chest X-rays and blood tests. Despite my repeated requests for them not to fuss, they would not listen. Yet I thought to myself: *I raised my daughter to become a doctor, and she married another one—how can I ignore their concern?*

The breathing trouble wouldn't subside. One night it became absolutely unbearable. The blood reports hadn't yet arrived, but they wanted to rush me to the emergency department of a reputed hospital immediately.

'What are you doing? Dinner is ready, at least have a few bites!' I implored as I panted for breath. But Titai was unwilling to wait even a minute longer. Their children stayed back with the nanny, unfed. Titai and Himu hadn't had their meal either.

It was discovered that I had a severe blood deficiency, leading to anaemic heart failure. I underwent a blood transfusion, and after a few days of hospital stay, I felt better. A good diet chart was made for me by the nutritionist. Vitamins and iron were added to the daily medicines to be consumed. Other than the arrival of a few pending reports, there was not much to wait for. I was on the verge of being discharged; I was in a fine mood.

The weather was changing, and people all around were down with viral fever. Sitting in the hospital reception, I felt a chill too.

Wrapped in Parag's Kashmiri shawl, I stared out of the large glass windows, watching autumn leaves fall, one by one. The hospital had a beautiful lawn. Children played in the soft sunlight; little birds fluttered across the garden. My mind drifted back to my daughters' childhood.

With the pending report finally at hand, the doctor called Titai in privately, beckoning her into his room with a grave expression. After a final word with my physician-in-charge, when Titai emerged from the doctor's room, her eyes were red and her lips trembling. That was the unmistakable sign of my daughter in distress. She spoke to someone over the phone, and we were once again in her car, the driver speeding us to another hospital.

Himadri was waiting for us there. *What was all this about?* I was exasperated. I had hoped Himu would now plan and book my return tickets to Kolkata. Instead, he stood there holding a thick bunch of hospital papers.

'What's all this, Himu? Have you two decided to make me ill by constantly rushing me around, shifting me from one hospital to another? I've been given blood, and I feel much better now. I must return home. I've been staying far from my house—you must think about my state of mind too, mustn't you?'

The words came out a bit harsh, but even as I spoke, I realized I still felt faint. They looked at each other. What Himu said next made my limbs go numb.

'Mamoni, we can't let you go. I mean, we won't. The X-ray doesn't look good. Bukai stays too far away—it wouldn't be right to call her just yet. But if Baba were here, he would agree with our decision. You used to be a science teacher yourself and you must listen to us. A small suspicious shadow that was seen on your chest X-ray, as per the Radio-diagnosis Board of Consultants', it does not look totally harmless. Yes, the shadow in your left lung—needs to be investigated with a PET scan. Then we'll need to carefully avoid the heart and insert a needle into your lung for a biopsy. The sooner, the better.'

He said it all in one breath. Perhaps it took him effort to say those words.

I was disheartened too. I am the daughter of Dr Angshu Mohan Bose, and a science teacher myself. My students once revered me, even feared me. How could someone like me be reduced to this? Do I now have to lie in bed like a weakling, relying on others for everything? Must I now endure life supported by others?

'But Himu, it's just a slight deficiency of blood, nothing more! Besides, after your Baba's passing, there isn't much money left. Can't all this wait?' I tried again. The treatment costs in Delhi hospitals were shockingly high—I'd checked some of the bills in secret.

'Mamoni, both my parents are no more. I'll never get another chance to do anything for them. Only you remain—to remind Titai and me of our childhood. I've already added you to my employer's medical insurance. Even Baba knew that before he left us. So please, from now on, don't worry about the cost of treatment.'

Himu's voice faltered despite his resolve. I was touched that he had thought of all this. Still, I felt sad that I wouldn't be able to return home soon.

They informed Bukai but requested that she should not fly to Delhi immediately. She was busy with her little one, though her in-laws supported her well. Bukai spoke to her sister every day, and sometimes to me too.

Di-bhai, what a procedure it was! They made me lie down, changing my position and posture repeatedly while performing different scans. Afterwards, a senior doctor—someone known to Titai and Himu—came to check on me.

'Mother, my name is Anup. I've known your daughter and son-in-law since their postgraduation days in Chandigarh. Brilliant students, both of them. I will conduct your biopsy myself while your scan is running. It may cause some discomfort, as I can't use anaesthesia. But believe me, I'll carry it out as gently as I would for my own mom.'

My heart began to race as I heard Doctor Anup speak. In this vast, air-conditioned hospital—where people sit together for hours without exchanging a word, where the busy nurses never pause long enough to chat about their families, and where the middle-aged woman in the bed next to mine shows no interest in hearing about my gardening—this towering, six-foot giant of a man suddenly became almost like a family member! He took my frail hands in his own and, with such ease and affection, became a son to me, overwhelming me with his love.

I was terrified. At least I can admit this to you in confidence, Di-bhai. I hadn't been this frightened even during the Caesarean when I gave birth to Titai, nor when Parag passed away so suddenly. But in that large, dimly lit room, when they changed my clothes and laid me down, I was overwhelmed by fear. In those moments, the senior schoolteacher of Brahmo Girls' School, the brave daughter of Dr Angshu Mohan Bose, who had not shed a tear during life's greatest struggles, could not even recall the names of the gods she prayed to daily.

Had you been there, you would have scolded me. 'Chant the name of Goddess Adya Kali! Or say the *Maha Mrityunjay* mantra our elder sister Bordi, had taught us. Have you gone dumb? Have you forgotten everything? You can even pray to Baba Lokenath, an incarnation of God on this earth!'

Yes, Di-bhai, lying alone in that large room, I had gone dumb. I could just make out the vague outlines of doctors behind a glass window far away, sitting under a bright light. I tried to believe that my Titai must be among them, watching everything, ensuring nothing bad happened to me.

I don't remember exactly when they gave me the injection that put me to sleep after the test. I only recall waking to a child's voice.

'Didan, see? I brought you a chocolate. Will you not have it?'

Titai's son was holding a Five Star chocolate bar near my face, his voice anxious and eager.

'Hey, brother, wait a bit; Didan will wake up properly soon. Then we can chat with her,' said my granddaughter, her voice sweet and caring.

Hearing Papri, her brother calmed down, though I had already stirred.

I tried to say, 'I wish they'd let me go home. I'm so fed up here, dear,' but my voice was too faint, even for me to hear. Titai broke off a small piece of the chocolate and fed it to me while the children clapped in delight.

Children? Papri was nearly done with her masters, and the boy was about to take his school leaving exams. Still, they were simple-hearted and endowed with childlike innocence. In my drowsy state, I vaguely remembered how I used to love dressing up little Papri. She still remembered some of the lullabies I used to sing to her.

And the boy—what a brat he was! He loved climbing up and down the iron grills of the Salt Lake house windows, creating chaos. Sometimes he would hide my pickle jar in his mother's suitcase. Only I could save him from Himadri's wrath in those moments.

'Didan, quickly hide me! I have not done much. There was no one at electric-uncle's shop in the garage, so I picked up a few screwdrivers and opened up the TV that was not working. Grandfather likes to sit there watching games, secretly smoking a cigarette. That is why I was trying to fix it. But now my father has found out and is looking for me!'

Having said this, the little boy would stand quietly behind me in the corner of the kitchen, hiding himself within the folds of my sari. The food would begin to burn on the stove; the electric kettle would whistle as the water came to a boil. What a predicament it was for me! I would stand hiding the mischievous boy for a full fifteen minutes until Himu finally gave up searching for him.

Though the little ones have grown in age, for me, Di-bhai, they will always remain the same cuddly darlings for me.

After my discharge, it was they who wheeled me into the lift and brought me down to the hospital foyer. Titai and Himadri had settled the bills and waited at the parking lot with my bags. The reports would be ready in seven days.

During the day, Titai managed the household and her work, while a day-shift nurse took care of me. But at night, she insisted on sleeping in my room on a sofa-cum-bed. The poor girl hardly slept! I couldn't lie on my left side because of the painful biopsy site. Even if I groaned a little in my sleep, Titai would leap to her feet, sit beside me and gently place her hand on the bandaged spot. If I woke up with an urge to visit the washroom, as soon as I stirred, I'd find her already at my side, ready to help.

'Won't you sleep at all, dear? You have patients to attend to throughout the day!' I'd say.

'Yes, I have many patients—but I have only one mother, my most precious asset. Come, let me help you, Ma,' Titai would say, holding my hands gently.

Di-bhai, I recovered. The biopsy report for the lung tissue came back negative for malignancy. Strangely, it was tuberculosis that had affected my lungs. Titai and Himu were actually a little relieved. With proper treatment, they said, it could be cured. But

I sat sulking, wondering how on earth I, of all people, could catch an infection that usually affects the poor.

'I won't stay with you, Titai. TB treatment takes time, and I don't want the children to be at risk,' I told her. She looked at me for a long moment, then calmly walked to her bedroom, fetched the key, and locked the main door of their spacious flat.

'You are a doctor's mother—but I'm a doctor myself, and so is Himu. Why do you keep forgetting that? Not all types of tuberculosis are infectious,' she said firmly.

And here, Di-bhai, I must tell you about Sukhalata—someone who became very important to me at this stage of life.

Forty-one

'Sukhalata, you can start from today. You look strong enough to handle the work. Let me show you where Ma's toiletries and towels are kept in the bathroom. Her lunch is kept in the kitchen. She naps a little after eating—you can rest then too. But do open the main door as soon as you hear the bell in the evening when I return. The telephone's in the drawing room. My number is written in a small notebook just below it. Call me if needed. Don't keep the TV on all the time, let Ma rest when she wants. I have your address, and I'm taking a photo as well.'

My daughter quickly clicked Sukhalata's picture on her mobile. She was being appointed as my new caregiver.

Titai had patients to attend to that morning. She rattled off her instructions to the new attendant hurriedly.

'I'm leaving. Don't take leave except on Sundays. I'll pay you Rs 12,000 at the end of the month. You won't face any issues about that.'

Sukhalata's face lit up when she heard her Boudimoni mention the handsome salary. Before she could mumble a word, Titai had waved me goodbye and left for work.

I'd had a surgery, but did that make me an invalid? I was an active person. I could walk around easily with my stick. Every morning, Titai herself handed me my medication. The day's food was kept ready in the kitchen. So why did they need to appoint this woman and pay her such a large sum? What exactly was she meant to do? I couldn't fathom it!

But the girl was affectionate. She had common sense too.

When she saw me slowly trying to get down from the bed to go to the washroom, she rushed forward.

'Here, here, Auntie, let me give you some "sapot". Get up now, let me put on your slippers,' she said, using her own version of English to pad her vocabulary.

Yes, Sukhalata had already begun her duties without even realizing it. I had no trouble understanding her curious English—but truth be told, Di-bhai, I laughed my heart out once I was inside the bathroom. Clearly, she was trying to impress me with the few bits of English she had picked up somewhere. She had no formal education, as is often the case with girls from the villages.

'Doctor Madam told me, "Look, I've selected you from the others because you're Bengali and can speak Bangla. My mother doesn't understand Hindi."' Sukhalata told me with a smile as she brought my breakfast from the kitchen and served it.

When I had finished, she wiped my face with a napkin and brought me my tea. There was more in the flask, so I asked her to help herself to the rest, along with a couple of biscuits.

How she relished sipping that hot tea! You wouldn't believe anyone could derive such joy from tea and biscuits alone. I spread the newspaper on the table and began reading, though I kept one eye on her. One must remain alert when there's a new maid in the house.

There were four rooms in Titai's spacious flat—simply decorated, but neat and well-maintained. Sukhalata seemed captivated by the curtained glass windows and framed pictures on the walls. She wandered to the balcony off the drawing room. There, struck by the potted marigolds, lilies, roses and bright petunias and pansies, she stood wide-eyed.

Like me, my daughter loved gardening, though she rarely found the time to care for her plants. They were healthy but covered in dust. Then Sukhalata did something unexpected. She filled the watering can and began spraying the plants, washing the dust off the leaves and flowers. I found myself enjoying the sight.

She didn't realize I'd followed her to the balcony and was standing just behind her. She was startled when I gently touched her shoulder; the bucket and mug nearly fell from her hands.

'You're a very good girl! You love plants too? You must be from the villages. Still, you've done your hair neatly and are wearing a clean sari!' I said.

By then, I had noticed that she had also cut her fingernails short. Though there was a slight excess of oil in her hair, she had tied it neatly in a bun. With a small red bindi on her forehead and a few glass bangles on her wrists, she looked simple yet smart. She listened to me and smiled faintly. Di-bhai, I sensed that she could not quite remember the last time someone had complimented her on her appearance.

Absent-mindedly, Sukhalata began to tell me about her life—her childhood, adolescence, motherhood and the constant poverty that had shadowed her.

She said she had walked with the slight limp since she was a little girl, yet she excelled in housework. Her two elder sisters were married into respectable families in the village and led comfortable lives. Her two older brothers also lived well with their wives. Sukhalata could not be married off.

Sukhalata's mother had a younger brother who used to roam the cities in search of work. At some point, he had asked her for a photograph of Sukhalata. One day, he arrived at their home and whispered something to her mother and brothers. Apparently, he had found a groom for Sukhalata—someone who lived far beyond Midnapore, beyond even the borders of West Bengal, in a remote village in Uttar Pradesh. According to the uncle, the groom owned houses, land and farms in his village. The family just wanted a young bride for him. His mother, suffering from gout, needed a hardworking girl to run the household.

The groom's side had raised no objection, even after her uncle had told them about her weak leg. They must be kind people. The family included the groom's parents and the groom. Surely, she would be looked after. There would be no lack of food or clothing. Yet, at night, Sukhalata would lie awake, her mind churning with apprehension and before falling in deep slumber, she would try to reason with herself. While living in Uttar Pradesh—she could learn the 'Hindustani' language in a few days; there was no reason she could not.

After her marriage, she tried to adjust to the dry climate, the absence of greenery and rain. She was initially happy in her new home, slowly forgetting the lush farms, fishponds and earthy fragrance of Bengal. But though she toiled with household chores all day, she gradually realized that the property and possessions her uncle had spoken of were nowhere to be found.

She couldn't understand why, in her case alone, her mother had married her off and had sent her far away from home, that too, to a man who was also found to be an alcoholic. Was she to blame for being the last of the three girl-children born from her mother's womb? Hadn't she grown up to be a hard-working girl—threshing paddy, milking cows, caring for vegetables and flowers she herself planted around their small hut in the village? Was that not enough reason for her to deserve better in life?

Life was hard. Amidst these struggles, she became pregnant. Still, the idea of sending her back to her parental home for rest, never came up. It was wheat harvest season—there was work to be done in the fields. Early in the morning, she had to prepare meals for the entire family and then head to the fields to toil in the sun.

Sukhalata went into premature labour in the eighth month of pregnancy. While relieving herself in a bamboo grove nearby, her water broke. She cried out for her mother, but the fields and the wild shrubs were her only audience. She severed the umbilical cord with a sharp piece of bamboo, picked up her dust-covered baby and held him close. In that instant, she had crossed the threshold from girlhood to womanhood.

Fortunately, a village lass working nearby noticed her.

No one could say if the child would survive. Only her mother-in-law knew what had to be done. Whenever the baby cried, she would bring him to Sukhalata and say, 'Feed him, Bahu, feed him more milk.'

Ignoring the pain of her own gout in the biting cold, she would sit with the baby in her lap, warming him with cloth-towels heated over a fire. She would murmur, 'It's a boy; he must be kept alive.'

No one from Sukhalata's own family came to visit. They seemed almost relieved that she had not been sent to them for childbirth. A month later, her uncle came with a red cotton sari and a tiny outfit for the baby. Handing them over to Sukhalata, he said, 'They've sent these for you and your son.'

Within a year, she felt faint movement in her belly again. In that household, it was not customary to send women to the hospital for childbirth. Still, this time they called a nurse from the village dispensary.

Sujan and Suman, her two sons, had just started school when her father-in-law passed away. Later, when her elderly mother-in-law developed breathing difficulties, Sukhalata repeatedly told her husband to get tests and a check-up done. But Prahlad, who once earned well as a carpenter, had fallen into bad company. Most of his earnings were then being squandered on alcohol.

Her mother-in-law probably died from lack of treatment. Prahlad showed no remorse. He would often stagger in drunk at night and drag Sukhalata to bed. Seeing no other option,

Sukhalata one day left her two sons with her neighbour and walked four kilometres to the government hospital to get her tubectomy done by laparoscopy.

From that point on, she worked hard to raise her children, doing odd jobs to keep them fed, all while enduring regular beatings from her husband. The house was falling apart. When money ran short, Prahlad sold household items to buy alcohol. The boys refused to work in the fields and food was scarce—hunger loomed constantly.

Then one day, Sukhalata locked the door of their crumbling house, packed their meagre belongings and left the village with her family. Surprisingly, Prahlad followed her obediently, abandoning his ancestral home. They eventually crossed the Ramganga River and reached the town of Bareilly.

Di-bhai, I hadn't noticed when my eyes had welled up, listening to the poor woman's harrowing story. It reminded me of the difficult days I faced after losing both Baba and Kaka. But this was a different kind of nightmare altogether. To send a daughter far away from home because of poverty! Must village girls always live lives like this? Illiteracy, dependence, hunger—she had endured it all and somehow found her way to my doorstep.

Should I not do something for her? Isn't this a sign from the Almighty, pointing me towards some unknown duty? Sukhalata washed the crockery and sat on the low stool beside my chair. It seemed she wanted to tell me more. Di-bhai, I recognized her terrible struggle to suppress the urge to cry. I wondered how many unnamed girls like her continued to battle on, alone, in cities and villages alike.

She drank a little water and continued. 'Mashima, Bareilly felt like a crowded jungle. The city seemed to swallow up anyone who came. The man we had relied on to help us find work had already taken a large sum of money. Much of our savings had been spent, yet he kept stalling, never arranging any job for us.

'Luckily, my sons had studied up to Standard VII and VIII in the free school in our village. I didn't need to teach them about the struggle of life—they already knew. There was a truck depot beside the slum where we stayed. Suman slowly got to know the truck drivers and began helping them with small tasks. In the beginning, when the boy stayed out with them overnight, I was terrified. Each time he returned, I would sniff his mouth for alcohol.

'"What do you think I will smell of, every day, Ma? I haven't had drinks. Believe me, I'll never make the same mistakes as Baba," my son would assure me. I would feel relieved and serve him food.

'It was then when one of the truck drivers took pity on us. He wanted to take both my sons to Delhi for work. He said Prahlad could also find work there as a carpenter. So once again, we packed our meagre belongings and set off for a new place. We reached Delhi. Many new buildings were being constructed nearby. My husband found work as a carpenter, but it didn't take him long to find the shops that sold cheap liquor. His liver is damaged now and gathering funds for his treatment has not been easy.

'It was Moni Bhabhi, the wife of Prahlad's boss, who told me that you needed an attendant to help you around the house. "I don't know anything about medicines, nor do I know how to care for patients. Will they really hire me?" I had asked her.

'"If your husband dies, you'll be a widow. Who's going to look after you then?"' she had replied. I didn't think too much after that—I needed this job badly.'

Sukhalata finally stopped to catch her breath.

After my bath, the girl warmed my lunch and served it to me. She would eat only after I had finished. I noticed that she had brought just two rotis wrapped in a plastic packet. Di-bhai, despite my repeated requests, she agreed only to eat two bananas from the fruit basket kept on the dining table. It's not easy to hold on to dignity and self-respect in the face of such poverty. I felt both surprised and moved—and, quietly, a small dream was awakening deep within me.

I kept remembering the vibrant days of my past. It had been such a long time since I had taught in school, surrounded by my beloved students. I kept yearning for the academic responsibilities, the classes, the active life I had once lived. My grandson had brought my microscope from our Kolkata house and carefully placed it in my room here in Delhi. Sometimes I used to caress it and felt a rush of emotion. Titai's children scored very well reading from the notes I had prepared for their lessons in life sciences. Titai had proudly shared her happiness with Himu. That also had been a deeply satisfying moment for me.

But this girl—this girl who had been driven by hunger and poverty away from her village to a strange, faraway city—could I not do something for her? I knew my daughter would pay her full salary at the end of the month, but I needed to help her in another way, using my own knowledge?

I kept asking myself this question over and over during those days.

You weren't there beside me, Di-bhai, but if you had been, I know I would have pestered you with this question too.

Forty-two

'Great! It looks as if you've settled into your job, Sukhalata. But did you bring any food for lunch?'

Titai had returned home early one of the days. Noticing the woman's haggard, tired face, she suspected something was wrong.

Sukhalata had indeed come without lunch that day. I then took time to inform my daughter of everything. She insisted that Sukhalata eat something, and we decided that from the next day, her lunch would be provided at our house. That evening after her duty, Sukhalata walked home to her nearby slum looking happier.

Within a month, her husband had found a small job. Yet, he would often return home drunk. Noticing bruises on her forehead or cheeks, I could tell that she was being beaten once or twice every week by the rogue. He would snatch away money from her salary. Her sons had grown up, so he no longer dared to torment her every single day. Yet, knowing the situation at her home, I could picture her lying on a mat at night after yet another ordeal, wiping away her tears, cursing her fate, and waiting for dawn to break. As soon as it was day, she would quickly finish her household chores and rush over to our house. She could not wait to leave for work.

I found the girl extremely sensitive and observant, Di-bhai. As I struggled to bend down these days, she would shampoo my hair with great care and even trimmed my toenails. My tea and snacks given in time, meals warm and ready, I hardly found any reason to complain. Sometimes, she would glance at Titai's mobile number kept written on a writing pad beneath the telephone, running her fingers over the number pad as if contemplating something. I noticed this and often tried to read her thoughts.

The plants on the balcony garden also displayed the effects of good care taken by Sukhalata's adept hands. While strolling in the balcony, I would admire the Calendulas gleaming with joy in the early winter sunlight. Walking beside me, Sukhalata asked, 'Mashima, what are the names of these pretty flowers?'

'Those over there are Phlox. They bloom in this season. Look how many colours—blue, violet, pink! They belong to the *Polemoniaceae* family,' I replied absent-mindedly, slipping into my teacher's voice.

'Poly Mashi? Is she one of your sisters?'

Listening to Sukhalata's innocent question, I burst out laughing with amusement.

In response to Sukhalata's attentive care, Titai's beloved Adeniums had bloomed profusely that year, and soon fruits began to appear on the plant as well. I knew these elongated fruits would ripen after basking in the sunlight for a few weeks. Gradually, fissures would form on their thick outer coats, revealing seeds nestled within a cotton-like substance. I believed, I had told Sukhalata that once the seed-pods burst, the seeds, attached to their cottony threads, tend to drift away—nature's own way of propagation. Sukhalata asked me for some old handkerchiefs, and to my surprise, she ingeniously wrapped the fruits with them—loosely enough to let in sunlight and allow the fruits to ripen properly, but carefully enough to prevent the seeds from scattering when the pods burst. It was such an innovative approach! With a bit of luck, planting those seeds in the coming season should give rise to new Adenium plants. It was a remarkably clever idea!

Sukhalata was ever curious about plants and her questions were endless. 'Mashima, should I put more used tea-leaves as fertilizer into the pot with the red flowers? I remember you asked me to put some in the pot with the white ones.'

'Oh no, don't be hasty. That's *Ranunculus bulbosus*. They just need plenty of sunlight. They'll bloom even without fertilizers—and with very little water,' I instructed her, before glancing back to the magazine I had been reading.

Behind me, the girl whispered, 'Baal-bo-zus.'

I suppressed a laugh. Her curiosity simply could not be ignored.

Each morning, Titai would hurry to my room to give me my medications, reminding me of their timings, before heading off to work. One day, Sukhalata expressed a keen interest in learning about the medicines. She brought three saucers from the kitchen, each a different colour, and carefully sorted the tablets according to their scheduled times—morning, noon and evening. Titai and I laughed heartily at her playful organization. And yet, amidst the laughter, my suppressed desire hidden in my heart, flared anew.

One morning, after finishing my tea, I said to her, 'Could you fetch a few things from the drawing room? There are some scrap papers on the work desk, along with a pencil and eraser. There's also a very old Bengali book tucked into the corner of the desk—bring that too.'

I had discovered some chalks in my room. I had made up my mind then—we would use the lovely dark red floor of Titai's house as our blackboard. That old alphabet book, once bought for Vishu, Titai's son, would finally find purpose again.

Di-bhai, that afternoon, I held Sukhalata's hand in mine and guided her to write the first letter of the Bengali alphabet.

I had mostly taught the senior students at school and had little experience of teaching young learners. Yet she eagerly filled sheets of paper with her handwriting at remarkable speed, and soon moved on to writing on the floor with chalk. I felt that this effort by a poor, rural, and illiterate woman had truly received the blessings of the Goddess of Learning.

Titai was astonished when she returned in the evening. Sheets of paper and floor tiles across the house were covered with letters in plenty, written by an unpractised, yet zealous hand.

Titai did not allow us to clear any of it until Himu came home. He, too, was as surprised as he was delighted.

'Mamoni, I'll go to Chittaranjan Park on Sunday for groceries and fish. I remember Bablu, the owner of the stationery shop there—he keeps basic Bengali readers. I'll get them this time. You'll have to work with this girl,' Himadri said, smiling with quiet satisfaction.

Sukhalata started learning to write more confidently. Each day, she practised signing her name ten times—once in the morning, again in the evening. She also learnt to write numbers in Bengali. Still, she occasionally gazed at the telephone, lost in thought.

Then, something strange began to happen. One morning, while I sat reading the morning newspaper with my back to the sun, she stood quietly behind me, trying to peer over my shoulder. Her shadow falling on the paper gave away her presence. One day, I realized that while standing behind me, she was actually attempting to copy things with a pencil on a sheet of paper she held in the other hand. I told her to walk around and face me then. It became clear that she had been studying the page numbers in English, following how they changed as I turned each sheet.

'I used to be a teacher, you know—I have eyes at the back of my head too!' I tried to sound stern. At my tone, she lowered her head, lips trembling in nervousness.

I had to smile. I gestured for her to sit beside me. By then I already knew my workload would increase with her growing enthusiasm.

Sukhalata struggled with English numbers. She would often sigh, 'If only I had gone to primary school with my sons and learnt all this earlier! On my very first day here, your daughter told me to call her if I ever needed help. But how could I? I didn't know the numbers at all!'

I understood her intentions now and encouraged her. The girl had come to realize that dwelling on the past or dreaming endlessly about the future served little purpose. It was only the present in which we truly lived, and that mattered most. One simply had to keep striving, step by step, to move forward and sustain oneself, while seeking to improve along the way.

At the end of each month, my medicines needed replenishing. The first time Sukhalata rang Titai and reminded her about that, Titai did not recognize the voice. She hung up, only to call back immediately, just to confirm. That night, she told me jubilantly, 'You did it, Ma! Sukhalata called me on the landline herself, dialling all the numbers! This will help her immensely.'

Di-bhai, I knew I would not live long enough to witness Sukhalata's full journey. Yet that day, I silently thanked God for granting me a sense of fulfilment. With Himu's help, we opened a savings account for her at the bank in our neighbourhood. She celebrated the occasion by bringing sweets for us. After depositing half her salary in her bank account, that day she touched my feet in gratitude and respect. I forgot our formal roles as the employee and the employer, and I simply embraced her.

Sukhalata no longer had to hide money inside pillow covers. Prahlad's greedy hands could no longer steal her hard-earned wages to be spent on liquor. She had even sent money home to her village upon learning of her mother's illness. Later, her brother requested Rs 4,000 for his daughter's wedding. How strange is the world, Di-bhai. As if touched by magic, the same family who long stopped enquiring about her, had now started asking after her again. She sent the money, though she could not attend the ceremony due to her husband's condition. Yet it seemed no one in her village was particularly upset by her absence.

Sukhalata was pleased, but she had learnt caution. Her older son married and moved out. She then married off her younger son too.

Subsequently, when I read the English newspaper, I'd also be teaching her the meanings of select words. She began noting them down in a small notebook she found somewhere—writing the English words alongside their Bengali meanings.

Due to my physical weakness, the doctors had advised against surgery for my eye cataracts. I found it increasingly difficult to read small print, especially in English newspapers. Aside from Bengali, Sukhalata could read the English paper aloud to me now.

One day, I told her about a verse penned by her namesake—Madam Sukhalata Rao, sister of Sukumar Ray, the master of Bengali nonsense verse, and daughter of the writer Upendra Kishore Ray:

Dik-nogorer buri elo, teenti meye muthoy dhoreekti sheke,
ekti bare, ekti bhalo ranna kore.

The old lady from Dik-nogor came,
Holding three girls in her grasp just the same.
One roasted, one served,
One she cooked well and praise she deserved.

Wide-eyed in wonder, Sukhalata exclaimed, 'How beautifully written! How does someone write with such skill! The person must have been born and brought up in a very rich and educated family?'

I found myself murmuring aloud, 'Not all beautiful lotuses grow in the comfort of clear lakes; some bloom in muddy waters, without care. And yet, the flowers are the same, their grace undiminished. You are one of them, dear girl. Your success is your own, born of enthusiasm and effort. I have merely played a small part.'

She touched my feet with such gratitude that my heart melted with joy of being of some help to the poor helpless village girl, when life was throwing only challenges and defeat at her sorry existence.

Sukhalata remained forever as a memory in my heart, as an acceptance of a challenge, resulting in triumph over despair, conquest over dejection, victory over despondency.

Forty-three

Despite being occupied with teaching Sukhalata how to read and write, I often thought about the house I had left behind in Salt Lake. I insisted on visiting it occasionally. However, Titai disagreed, and even Bukai tended to side with her sister.

'Why do you want to go back, Ma? What's left there? And who will take care of you? I can't come from so far to help you. At least Didi is taking good care of you in Delhi and arranging your treatment—just go with it. Let Naren and Biren manage the house,' my younger daughter advised.

She was right. Naren was quite dependable. Thanks to the quality of his work, he had secured contracts with several housing societies in Rajarhat, a growing suburb.

When Naren had grown into a mature man, he had married a girl of his own choice, Moyna, a kind and homely lass. Although they had been married for some years, yet Moyna was unable to conceive. I however constantly encouraged them not to lose hope.

Parag was fond of the young couple too and actually appreciated the constant support that presence of the young man provided in the household. Any difficulty with the water-pump, the TV, or a repair urgently required at the main gate of the house, Naren was handy and always beside him. 'Why trouble the sisters repeatedly? I am here to look after you. Am I not like their younger brother? From now on, I will handle not just the electrical work but all the repairs, painting, everything needed to maintain this house. Just bless Moyna that she may soon carry a child. I'll even pay half the expenses for the Lokenath Baba festival, where you distribute prasad to hundreds of neighbours,' he promised.

About five years after their marriage, Moyna gave birth to twins. Naren came to me with a red-bordered silk sari and handed Parag a maroon kurta, offering his respects. 'What would have become of us if this boy had not been there? Thankfully, we gave him shelter that day!' The words had slipped out of my mouth almost involuntarily.

Di-bhai, did the Almighty wish to prove me wrong?

While I stayed in Delhi, Naren's son and daughter had grown up to be clever and smart children and I felt happy for them. However, I kept thinking of the house, Parag and my prized possession, and pined to be there, almost all the time.

A few neighbours from Kolkata still enquired after my health, though over time their phone calls grew somewhat infrequent. One day, I called Mrs Mitra, our next-door neighbour of the Salt Lake house. She asked a strange question, 'Have you permitted someone to stay in your house at night? Sometimes it seems the lights are on, and we hear unknown voices.'

Shocked, we contacted the security agency in Salt Lake responsible for assigning the guard in our locality. Himu also spoke to Naren and Biren. They dismissed the concerns, calling them rumours, and assured us the house was secure. For a while, this brought me peace.

Then, a few days later, the guard informed me that Naren had chopped down the tree at the main gate. This tree had been Parag's favourite. Furious, I waited for Titai to return and then called Naren from her mobile.

'What's the matter, Mashima? Caterpillars were infesting the tree. My workers sit and chat there in the evenings. Would they continue working if the place is full of insects? Please understand, I run a business here. I can't afford losses.'

There was something strange in Naren's voice this time. Titai, listening on speakerphone, raised her eyebrows. I ended the call without another word.

I vividly remembered the flowering creeper over the gate; it had been quite young when a storm had battered it severely. With the gardener's help, I had wrapped an old cloth around its broken stem, anxiously hoping it would recover. Remarkably, the plant survived and flourished, its flowers brightening the space even now. How surprising! Even a plant, when cared for with love, seems to show its gratitude in its own way.

Autumn was approaching. Durga Puja was a month away. The sunlight had begun to take on a softer hue. Watching it, I realized my homesickness would not pass so easily. I called Mrs Mitra again.

'What have you done to this neighbourhood, Mrs Das? Whom have you allowed into your garage,' she said, sounding irritated.

I was apprehensive. Seeing my face, Himadri came and stood beside me and put the phone on speaker mode.

Mrs Mitra continued, 'Naren and his men have pitched a tent in front of your main gate for the Vishwakarma Puja, blocking half the road. The way they blast music on loudspeakers, you'd think they own the entire house—and the area! Recently, one evening, my daughter Montuli was returning from tuition, and Biren, probably drunk, also made a vulgar remark at her.'

My heart skipped a beat. I was so distressed that my feet felt almost frozen.

'Don't worry, Auntie. I'll do something about this,' Himu assured Mrs Mitra on the phone. Then he looked at me and Titai. There was deep concern in his eyes.

Thereafter one night, the security guard on the phone informed us that a windowpane in the drawing room of our house had been lying broken for some time. It was visible from outside how rain lashed at the curtains within, in absence of the glass pane. He had, as instructed by me on a previous such occasion, asked Naren to have it fixed. To our shock, we heard that he had flatly refused, saying he didn't have the time for such trifles.

Although we were surprised by Naren's audacity, we still did not know that our ordeal had just started. We learnt that in order to gain political support in the area that Naren and Biren had begun to donate funds to the local ruling party.

I realized he was no longer the 17-year-old who once stood before us with tears in his eyes—homeless, desperate for survival.

'We can't keep the house any longer, Ma. Leaving you alone there would put your life at risk. The relatives are too busy with their lives to help. On the other hand, if someone were to break in through the terrace door and enter the premises at night, would you confront them like Rani Lakshmibai, steel plates in your hip and all?'

I was worried and anxious, troubled by Titai's words.

From then on, sleep deserted me. My blood pressure rose. So did the number of medicines I had to take. Despite the care Titai and Himu gave me, the dread did not ease.

Meanwhile, there was trouble brewing up elsewhere too. The meagre pension I received from the central and state governments stopped due to some issues with the paperwork. Himu had to take leave from work and travel to Kolkata to sort it out. During his stay, he had to work from his sister's home and could not even step inside the Salt Lake house as the attitude of Naren and Biren had become increasingly aggressive.

When they sensed the possibility of our selling the house, they were even more furious. They flatly opposed the idea. With the garage already in their use and a spare key to the house in their possession, it seemed they would have little difficulty in forcibly occupying the entire property.

I spent restless days. I spent sleepless nights.

We had left our home in East Bengal and started a life from a scratch in Kolkata. While focusing on the children's education primarily, with great difficulty, we could build a home of our own, much later in life. And now, greedy hands were reaching even for that asset—not a stranger's but those of someone close, someone we had helped in his darkest days.

Himu returned from Kolkata with his head bowed, feeling defeated and humiliated. When contacted on the phone, Naren had showered a great deal of insult on him, paying no heed to any reasoning; greed had taken over his better instincts and values completely. Seeing the helpless expression on Himu's face—for the first time—I wept hopelessly.

Forty-four

Truth be told, I do not remember how long it has been since I last wrote to you, Di-bhai. I am told that I fainted one day, from constant anxiety. It happened while I was in the bathroom. When I did not respond to Sukhalata's calls, she forced the door open and saved me. I was lying unconscious inside.

On hearing this, Titai left her work and rushed home. Then she took me to the hospital. I believe I lay unconscious in the ICU for two days. I had heard that many elderly people suffer cerebral strokes in winter. Himadri was abroad at the time—office work, tours—these cannot always be avoided when one has a family to support.

That winter night, it rained heavily. After being turned away from two hospitals due to lack of vacant beds, Titai finally managed to secure an ICU bed at the third. Later, I learnt that while I lay unconscious, tubes in my nose and mouth, my daughter ran from department to department inside the hospital, desperately trying to arrange an MRI at midnight—by any means.

Failing to reach her husband abroad did not stop Titai. With presence of mind and immense courage, she got the necessary tests done so that treatment could begin without delay, reducing the risk of internal damage.

Her children wanted to accompany her. Thus, Papri and Vishu, sat huddled in the reception area of the hospital that night, hungry and in wet clothes.

Bukai could not come. She was in a foreign country, busy with her job, child and other concerns. Even if she had come, what could she have done? I was with my elder daughter, a doctor, who knew what needed to be done. None of us realized that, apart from being a doctor, she was also a human being—tired, anxious and lonely.

I recovered, once again. Himu returned from South Africa on a Sunday. I was discharged from the hospital and we all came home. The physiotherapist resumed his visits. He made me walk again, like a child taking her first steps. During one session, he said, 'Why do you insist on going home to Kolkata, madam? Why worry about the house all the time? Have you ever thought about your daughter? She, too, is ageing. Her work is demanding. At the very least, you should stay peacefully here—and let her live in peace too.'

Di-bhai, I would be lying if I said his words did not make me angry. But later that night, Parag came to me in my sleep. I do not know if it was a dream, but he said that if Titai were to fall ill, the clot in my brain that had unfortunately appeared would be untreatable.

My face still twisted slightly when I tried to speak. Either Titai or Sukhalata fed me with a spoon. A metal railing surrounded my bed, adjustable so that I wouldn't fall from the bed while turning over in sleep. An expert caregiver was appointed for the night.

Yet one night, I woke up feeling discomfort between my legs. What did they think of me? That I would wet the bed and not even notice? Was my body growing numb? Making a strange noise, I called the new nurse and asked her to remove the diaper. She was kind and acted on my request. She supported me and took me to the bathroom.

I did not speak to Titai for three days after that. My own daughter had not consulted me before making such a decision about my body and care. When had my little girl become so knowledgeable?

Titai bore all my tantrums with patience. She doubled the nurse's salary for the night shift. Still, she managed everything with a smile—inspite of presence of a night caregiver, she herself started visiting me several times during the night with silent diligence, providing me the bedpan at fixed intervals, ensuring I didn't soil the bed, leaving me to sleep clean and comfortable.

Meanwhile, Titai's son excelled in his studies and left for Rajasthan to pursue engineering. Her daughter had completed her MA and now hoped to embark on her MPhil curriculum. Watching their dedication, I couldn't help but imagine how pleased Parag would have been to witness their academic achievements.

As I slowly recovered and regained my speech, I could manage to eat lunch on my own, with minimal help from Sukhalata. But forgetfulness still clung to me. Just before my evening tea, I would often ask, 'Sukhalata, didn't I just have breakfast?'

Yet, old memories continue to resurface with quiet insistence.

One dawn, I was unexpectedly enveloped by the sweet fragrance of Shiuli flowers—the night-flowering jasmine. Puzzled, I could not discern where the aroma was coming from. I could not recall having seen Shiuli blossoms anywhere in my present place of stay.

Di-bhai, that morning, in the depth of my sleep, I saw Parag and Kaki approaching me. They seemed to emerge from a distant, glowing light, walking slowly towards me before sitting down on my bed. I instinctively shifted to one side to make space for them. The faint fragrance of Shiuli flowers seemed to emanate from Parag's body, while a few delicate blossoms were visible, scattered through Kaki's white hair.

Although she had never seen our Salt Lake house, was Kaki trying to convey something about it? I was not feeling particularly well that day. But one thing I realized— the longing for that house was ailing my aging heart.

I had owned the place. I was the rightful owner. All our furniture lay within that space.

'Absolutely not! I shall never allow Naren to take over my house and possessions. All our efforts will be wasted if that happens!'

My cries greatly frightened the nurse. That dawn, her startled screams woke everyone. It was a Sunday morning. Though Himadri managed to calm the hysterical nurse, she was reluctant to continue working.

'I kept telling her to sleep properly, sir, but she insisted that her dead husband and her aunt had come to visit her—she said they were sitting on the bed beside her. But I couldn't see anyone! Please settle my dues and let me go.'

Saying this, the night nurse, Shakila, resigned. Daughter of a poor Muslim man, she worked as a tailor in a factory during the day and stayed with me at night.

It was futile to reason with her. Titai had to arrange a new night nurse from the placement agency. During the day, there was no worry—Sukhalata remained devoted to my care. Still, both Titai and Himu sensed that unless something was done about the house, my mental condition would remain severely disturbed. Putting aside their many responsibilities, they resolved to take action—for my sake at least.

Despite the strain it placed on their professional lives, they committed to visiting Kolkata once every two months. On one such visit, they managed to pack up all my furniture from the Salt Lake house and shift them safely to a rented flat within a nearby housing estate. As it was a weekend, they could avoid a confrontation with Naren. His shop was closed. Himu and Titai worked tirelessly to set up the flat—often skipping meals or grabbing rushed ones at nearby eateries. Throughout they kept in touch with me over the phone from the hotel room they had rented for those few days.

They unpacked the transported furniture, installed geysers in the bathrooms, fitted air-conditioners in the three newly done bedrooms, hung fresh curtains at the windows and mounted the TV on our lovely wooden wall-cabinet. Himadri even arranged for an induction cooker to replace the gas stove. The kitchen was modernized with a new microwave, electric kettle and rice cooker. The flat's area was almost equal to the covered area of the ground floor of our Salt Lake house.

Later, Di-bhai, I did visit the new flat. Bukai came with her husband Oliver and their child, and we took Sukhalata along. We flew to Kolkata and stayed in the newly furnished flat for a few days. Three airy bedrooms on the sixth floor, with large balconies overlooking the children's swimming pool below. It was winter, and I greatly appreciated the morning sunlight streaming into my bedroom. How I enjoyed the stay!

Bukai invited some of our relatives in Kolkata for high tea, and we enjoyed a few pleasant days together. One morning, I discovered Kaki's old hand-knitted tea cozy in my almirah. I arranged to get tea made. In the vintage porcelain teapot I had bought long ago, there lay a warm pot of beverage covered by the precious pretty tea cozy, on my beautiful dining table. In the drawer of my dressing table, I came across Parag's comb. I brought it back with me to Delhi.

On returning to the capital, I asked Himu and Bukai to look for potential buyers for our Salt Lake house. I had made up my mind—I would not allow that house to fall into Naren's greedy hands. I would rather sell it and use the proceeds for the benefit of my daughters.

We repeatedly requested Naren to vacate the garage on phone—our pleas went on for nearly a year with no avail. Bukai called him from England several times. Titai and Himu called him almost daily. Yet, nothing changed. Eventually, we learnt that whenever a potential buyer visited, Naren would scare them off, claiming ownership of the house.

Di-bhai, I fell ill again. Once more, I found myself in the ICU due to another brain haemorrhage. But as before, with two doctors in the family, I received timely treatment. Death, like a vulture, circled over me but could not carry me away.

Meanwhile, Titai kept pushing relentlessly for a resolution regarding the Salt Lake property. On her frantic requests, old neighbours spoke to Himu over the phone.

'Times have changed, dear. We can't interfere anymore. We've seen these boys grow rich using your garage without paying a rupee in rent. Parag Babu was a gentleman. He never realized he was feeding a snake. Now, that same guy speaks so high-handedly that we all feel insulted and avoid him.'

I hadn't kept up with local politics, but now I had to. The younger neighbours told Titai, 'The party office might pressure Naren to vacate. But you'll likely need to pay him hefty compensation. The local club will also expect a good donation of a few lakhs. Still, nothing is guaranteed. Try writing to your block councillor—some say she's a former student of Brahmo Balika Shikshalaya. Perhaps she'll help.'

Himu and Titai were exhausted. Yet, there was a trace of a freedom fighter's spirit in Titai. She had been raised never to compromise with injustice. Taking the unlawful route was something she could not agree to.

However, the block councillor did offer us some reassurance. She advised us to keep looking for potential buyers.

Amidst the turmoil, Parag's words echoed in my mind. At that time, the two of us had been living in our Salt Lake home while our daughters were away. One evening, Parag shared his thoughts with me: 'Apu, our girls will not be bound to this house forever. We didn't raise them for that. We raised them to spread their wings and soar. May their efforts be blessed by us and our ancestors. But I believe something extraordinary will happen in this house—perhaps Titai will set up a nursing home here, or maybe something completely unexpected. One day, many people will visit and benefit from this very place. Even in the evenings, the house will be aglow with light. From afar, we'll look on and say, "How wonderful! We never imagined this could really happen."'

Eventually, word spread among Titai and Himu's medical circle that the house was up for sale. A gentleman showed interest—Dr Debnath, an ENT specialist and alumnus of Kolkata Medical College, a few years senior to Titai and Himu. He was particularly drawn to the property because it was a corner plot facing a park. He had once lived just a few blocks from us in Salt Lake.

At the time, I could not travel to Kolkata. Though I could walk with the help of a walker after my leg fracture, I no longer dared to fly after suffering two strokes. As it happened, Dr Debnath's daughter, who lived in Delhi, was expecting a child. The doctor came to Delhi and met us at Titai's apartment. His warm, affable manner made it feel as though we'd known him forever.

In the drawing room, Titai had placed a large photograph of her father. Dr Debnath caught sight of it and stood up in surprise.

'Is this gentleman your father? Of course, you do resemble him a lot! Parag Babu was such a cheerful person! He used to be my patient!'

Dr Debnath's voice rang with emotion.

We were astonished. Could it be true? Could Parag, long gone from this world, be witnessing our struggle? Was he guiding us through some divine force, now that he had become one with the divine?

So many memories, so many emotions—tears of joy. It felt as if a long-lost relative had appeared to help us just when we were ready to give up, defeated by fear and despair. Finally, a kind soul had stepped forward to hold our hand.

We later learnt that Parag had visited Dr Debnath a few times for his hearing difficulties—quietly, without telling any of us. Toward the end of his life, his listening had worsened, and I would often scold him. 'Hey! The overhead tank is overflowing. The alarm is ringing—can't you hear it? Why haven't you shut off the motor?'

He would smile sheepishly, get up and do as I asked. But he never told me he had gone to see an ENT—he disliked the idea of using hearing aids.

We also came to know that Dr Debnath's son-in-law was a successful legal practitioner in Delhi, having connections with many lawyers in Kolkata. He could help us if we faced legal hurdles while selling the Salt Lake house. From then on, we faced no further trouble.

Naren finally vacated the garage and shifted his shop to the local market. Dr Debnath built an additional floor on top of the house and started a well-appointed nursing home called Sraban Seva Nursing Home—a facility for the hearing impaired. We received a fair price for the house and, with that, were finally able to purchase the flat we had previously rented.

Sometime later, Titai visited the Salt Lake house, now transformed into a beautiful nursing home, and met Dr Debnath and his wife. She was deeply moved.

'Ma, they've expanded the Lokenath temple near the gate. The neighbours still offer flowers there, just like before. Dr Debnath now sees his patients on the very spot where our puja room used to be—right at the place where I used to draw *alpona* patterns for Lakshmi and Saraswati Puja. The reception is in what used to be our dining area. Many people wait there while their documents are being prepared. I felt I could see Baba clearly—sitting at his favourite place, on the stone slab near the gate, smiling. It was as though he looked at me and waved. Ma, his soul must be very happy.'

Dr Debnath came to Delhi a few more times after that and always made it a point to visit me. It never felt like we were connected only through a property transaction. He stayed in touch with Titai and Himu for professional reasons too—more as a mentor than anything else.

Isn't it strange, Di-bhai? Who says dreams don't come true?

Dr Debnath sent some photos to Titai. I tried to match them with my memories—some did, others didn't. Some things looked new, but I could still sense what they had replaced. Nothing escaped my eyes. I kept thinking—when the Almighty had decided that the house should shelter us, it did. Subsequently, if it could serve the sick and the helpless, that too must be an angelic sign. It's beyond my will to object. Neither I nor Parag could have tolerated unknown and unworthy people demolishing the house or see it standing in a dilapidated condition, neglected and lacking maintenance. This was the best outcome possible.

Forty-five

Di-bhai, Titai's son was in his hostel, and he still had a couple of years left before completing his engineering degree while, her daughter Papri, had finished her MPhil and gone abroad with a scholarship for doctoral studies. Before leaving, she had come into my room to seek my blessings.

'I still do not have a steady boyfriend, but when I do, you will be the first to know. Only then will I marry him. Promise me you will stay fit till then, Didan.' I blessed her with all my heart and wished her well.

Thereafter, there was a phone call from Kolkata informing that my husband's elder brother had passed away a few days earlier. He had a pacemaker fitted in his heart, but the dutiful doctor continued to see patients twice a week in his chamber on the ground floor of his house. I couldn't go to bid him a final farewell, but Titai and Himu did. On their return, they said his face bore no sign of suffering; it seemed he had left this world in complete peace. His wife, though afflicted with arthritis, was still living with their sons.

My other brother-in-law, Pramatha, was still alive. He used to teach economics at a school, and he and I had always shared a friendly bond. His eyesight had weakened due to glaucoma, but he was receiving treatment. Titai called him regularly, and on such occasions we used to speak over the phone. He used to recognize my voice immediately and exclaim, 'Hey, Boudi! Where have you been? It's been ages since we spoke!'

I could hear the faint note of complaint in his voice. Though

Titai explained my present circumstances to him several times, and I myself did so during our last call, time seemed to be blurring his memory.

'Do you remember our fights while playing Ludo? You always cheated to win,' I kept teasing him time to time.

'And do you recall your betel-leaf habit? You once didn't speak to me for two days because I hid your box of paan!' he fired back.

We laughed together, pausing now and then, comforted by reminiscences of old memories. For a little while, we lived fully in the present—by reliving the past.

In the meantime, Sukhalata's daughter-in-law had a baby, so she took a few days' leave. Himadri and Titai were continuously worried—the night-shift caregiver was doing double duty. If she also went on leave, my support system would crash. Watching them struggle, I felt guilty.

After a while, one day, I told Titai, 'Am I not being too much of a burden? I think I'd be more comfortable in Kolkata.'

She looked at me helplessly and asked, 'What will you do there, Ma?'

'Why, I've got my school! I haven't seen your father in so long. I need to check if the house is being cleaned properly. The property is all for your sake, isn't it?' I said these things and instantly realized I had made a mistake.

Sukhalata had joined her duties by then and tried to soothe Titai. 'Mashima gets mixed up with past and present, but that doesn't mean she's uncomfortable here.'

'Please, Sukhalata, don't interfere. Ma, there's no need for you to worry about leaving me the house or anything else. I just want to see you healthy. Don't you understand how these small remarks and your distress affect my work? When I return after delivering babies late at night, I enter quietly so as not to disturb your sleep. Yet, every day I operate, trying to save lives—and during it all, my constant focus is your well-being.

'I became a doctor to fulfill your dream. I may be older now, but I'm still your little girl. If I don't share my difficulties with you, would you also stop anticipating them or bothering about my comfort and mental peace altogether?'

That day, Titai looked exhausted—probably worn down by the demands of her work. Her face showed signs of fatigue. It was evident that my daughter had been neglecting her own well-being while working tirelessly at her job. How old was she? She seemed older than her actual age.

'Bukai is far away—busy with her baby and her new university job. We can't send you there. Even if Oliver offers to help, in India he'll have to immensely struggle to communicate with the officials in Kolkata. Even in Delhi, how can he handle your check-ups, MRIs, medications? Himadri and I have to manage everything—your pension, life certificate, health checks, tax, banking.

'For the past eight or nine years, our children have grown up while we have been busy managing all these responsibilities. Can you not see that I, too, get tired? There are moments when I feel unbearably lonely. After spending the whole day with patients and being preoccupied with countless worries, whenever I hear you voicing your grievances like this, my patience wears thin. I end up venting my frustration on Himadri. It strains our relationship, Ma. In such moments, we really struggle to remain tolerant towards each other.'

Titai was gasping for breath as she spoke. I had begun to feel guilty. But that did not help.

Before she could finish her sentence, she suddenly slumped forward onto a chair. Sukhalata sprang up from her seat and caught her just in time.

I was terrified—was Titai seriously unwell?

It was a Saturday. Fortunately, Himu would be home earlier than usual. But could we really wait that long with Titai in this state?

Helplessly, I watched as Sukhalata called Himu on the phone and urged him to rush home. With great effort, Titai lifted an arm and gestured towards the windows, suggesting they be opened.

Parag's portrait on the wall stared down at me, his face marked with an anxious expression.

Later, I learnt that Titai's heart rate had increased so much that she was struggling to breathe. One of Himadri's friends also arrived shortly after Himu, and together they took my daughter—my pillar of support—to a hospital in a wheelchair, right before my eyes.

Even while leaving, Titai reminded Sukhalata of my medicines, speaking with difficulty. She tried to bend and touch my feet but couldn't. What greater punishment could there be than the thought of losing my child before my own passing away? Di-bhai, when I saw her lips turning blue, I remembered the time she was a tiny baby and I breastfed her. She had been a bonny child. As her mother, how had I failed to realize that she was growing weaker from constant stress and anxiety? That day, I felt I had been extremely selfish. I was completely consumed by guilt.

It was soon discovered that Titai had an irregular ectopic focus affecting her otherwise regular heartbeat. Due to stress, her blood pressure had risen sharply, causing her already fatigued heart to beat at an alarmingly fast rate—something extremely dangerous for any person.

Thankfully, the situation was brought under control with an injection administered inside the cardiac ambulance itself. Even so, a surgery was necessary. The operation was carried out at a renowned hospital in Delhi by a senior cardiac surgeon—someone who had been a senior to them at PGIMER.

Suddenly the person who had always been tirelessly occupied with the well-being of everyone in the family, especially me, was absent from home. Her absence left the house with a palpable void.

I could not go to see her. They could not take me there. But Di-bhai, I spent the entire time lost in memories of little Titai. I recalled bathing her as a baby, feeding her rice while telling her fairy tales when she was a child and playing the old harmonium while teaching her a popular Rabindrasangeet:

Bhubaneshwara hey, mochano karo shwartho pasho,
mochano karo hey.

O Lord, free me of my selfish intents, may the
ungenerous me receive salvation.

I sang those melodies within myself, transforming them into silent prayers. It felt like a turning point—a moment to loosen my grip on my self-centred pursuits, to relinquish my material possessions, properties, and all the attachments tied to my ego.

Ironically, those who had worked tirelessly to protect my well-being and health were now burdened with immeasurable anxiety—an unintended consequence of my actions—amid their already demanding lives. My daughter, stepping into a maternal role, cared for me with quiet devotion. And my son-in-law, who would so tenderly embrace me and say, "Mamoni, you are precious to us; both my parents are gone—only you remain now,"—how could I bring such distress upon them?

A prayer began to take shape within me. In the quiet recesses of my mind, I whispered to Parag, 'Please forgive me. I know that if you were here, my behaviour would have vexed and hurt you.'

After the operation, Titai was confined to the hospital for some time. Di-bhai, she came home after five days. The moment she entered, she walked slowly but steadily, to my room. She took my hands in hers. 'Hope you won't talk about going away from me again, Ma!'

Her words struck deep, and we melted into each other's arms, tears rolling down our cheeks.

Sukhalata brought over a chair for Titai and dashed off to prepare tea. Himadri arrived soon after and sat near my feet with Vishu who had come over from his hostel, learning about his mother's illness. Despite growing up outside Bengal, the boy was well-versed in Bengali culture. He began to sing a song that his mother had taught him and his sister once:

Prabhu mochano karo bhoy, shobo doinyo karoho loy
Nityo chakito chanchalo chito, karo nishshongshoy
Timiro ratri, andho jatri, somukhe tabo deepto dwipo
Tuliya dharo hey.

O Lord, quell my fears, remove my penury
Sweep away doubts, I am restless and I am weary
In this dark night, a blind traveller's quest,
Hold a bright lamp, guide me on my request.*

Di-bhai, Titai made a gradual recovery, yet I continued to carry the weight of my guilt for many days afterwards.

Bukai had not been able to come immediately during her sister's illness. Himu did not want to trouble Papri and did not inform her about what had happened. He did not want Bukai to fly down either, knowing how difficult it was to arrange a ticket and travel from such a distant place at short notice. Still, Bukai was deeply affected on hearing the news of her sister's condition—a sister who had raised her from childhood with love and care.

She understood well the challenges Titai had been facing: looking after me, managing issues related to the Kolkata property,

---

*Song from *Geetabitan* by Rabindranath Tagore

and dealing with the complications surrounding my pension. Despite this understanding, Bukai felt helpless, unable to do anything from afar.

Adding to her distress was the painful awareness of her sister's declining health and the visible aging of Himadri, whom she still remembered as a bright and youthful college student.

Amid all this, Oliver too was preoccupied—caught up in his own work and responsibilities.

Bukai eventually came for a few days with her husband and young daughter. In the room next to mine, someone began speaking loudly. Oliver was a clever man, and I soon realized he was trying to persuade others that I—who needed round-the-clock care, would do better if moved to a modern senior citizen's home with all amenities. This was in keeping with the norms of his country.

In their world, most couples worked, and hiring help to care for both children and ageing parents was prohibitively expensive. He suggested that if the newly bought apartment were sold, the proceeds could ensure my comfort in an excellent old age home. This would also ease the burden on Titai and allow Himadri to focus on his own work. If the arrangement could be made in the same city, they could visit me whenever they wished too.

The costs for treatment and care are exorbitant overseas—a fact my faculties could still comprehend. Hence, despite having once spent time abroad at Oxford with Parag, I had never ever entertained the idea of staying there for prolonged period.

As such, it had taken me quite a while to establish a sense of belonging after relocating to Delhi from my own home in Salt Lake, Kolkata.

Now, as my body and mind approached the concluding chapter of life, I found myself unexpectedly entwined with these roots I had finally grown amidst my beloved ones. The prospect of adapting to a new existence in unfamiliar surroundings, amongst unknown faces and a different kind of loneliness, unsettled me. I knew I would be left grappling with the uncertainty of it all.

When Titai came into our lives, Parag and I were not financially stable. Yet, we gave her whatever we could. In the winters, Parag would take his little girl for day trips, heading to Shahid Minar, Eden Gardens and the Maidan. By the end of the day, Titai would return home brimming with joy and countless stories.

We experienced similar happiness when we were blessed with Bukai. Despite some relatives offering sympathetic glances at the arrival of a second daughter, Parag and I reassured each other that she would one day achieve a lot of success and do us proud. We were determined to turn that dream into reality. Though haunted by the middle-class fear of inadequate funds—especially as no one in our families had ever travelled overseas—we managed to arrange expenses for her travel boosted by the fact that she had earned a scholarship.

Di-bhai, however I realized that I was unnecessarily burdening myself with self-pity. As if to dispel my doubts, Titai spoke firmly.

Being emotional by nature, even if it meant facing numerous monetary challenges related to my care, Titai vehemently refused to sell the spacious flat filled with my old furniture. Having reached the maturity of middle age, they understood that the magic of their youth was preserved in those memories—priceless treasures! She also refused to part with me or send me away elsewhere no matter what happened.

Caught in the middle of this peculiar disagreement, poor Bukai tried to pacify both sides. But Himadri remained firm, saying, 'Mamoni is the only elder member of the previous generation still living with us. I intend to care for her for the rest of her life. My decision will not change.'

I listened and realized that none of them were at fault. Oliver, coming from a foreign culture, had likely made his suggestion to ease the burden on ageing Titai and Himu. Yet, the very people he wished to protect and help were not ready to accept his suggestions.

I did not notice how long the argument lasted. It was already late; I had my dinner and the night nurse helped me to bed.

Bukai and her family travelled to Kolkata after a few days. Not only did they arrange for the flat's regular maintenance, but they also had it thoroughly cleaned. They even submitted my pension documents. This time, Bukai didn't let Himadri take leave and run around as he had to do everytime. Titai was surprised—but pleased. As she told me all this, I noticed a few lines on her forehead disappear, replaced by a calm glow. I, too, felt a sense of relief.

Then, Di-bhai, something strange happened. A newly married couple from Kerala called Titai from Kolkata. They had heard about our apartment from their friends and were eager to rent it. The couple had come to Kolkata to pursue their postgraduate studies in a medical college and had no furniture of their own. A furnished place would be ideal for them.

Although Titai had by that time brought many of my personal belongings to Delhi, the almirah, showcase, bed and dining table were left behind in that apartment. The thought of selling them was painful for everyone. They were remnants of our happiest days.

It never ceases to amaze me how the Almighty often provides solutions to man-made problems—as though the pieces of a jigsaw puzzle quietly fall into place.

At first, I did feel a little sad when I heard about the prospect of renting out the apartment. After all, everything there—the few furniture—had once belonged to me, had they not?

But soon, a deeper sense of reality settled in my mind. The place lay unused, gathering dust. This young couple, from a faraway land, was in need of a place to live in. And above all, the values Titai had nurtured—the very values that made her so fiercely opposed to the idea of sharing her mother with anyone else in this world, be it the best old-age home or any senior citizen's facility in the city—these were, I realized, my true and priceless treasures.

The furniture, after all, is just lifeless wood. No matter how many memories they hold, one day we must leave them all behind when the final call from beyond arrives. That night in my sleep, I saw Parag's smiling face after such a long time.

The young couple from Kerala sent us photographs of the apartment. There was the photograph of the celebration of our fiftieth wedding anniversary, a trip to Darjeeling arranged by Titai, Himu and their children, displayed in the drawing room. They also made a video call on Titai's phone and showed me around. A new lace curtain hung over the mirror adorning my dressing table, fresh flowers sat in the pretty vase in the dining and they had planted a small bougainvillaea in a pot on the sunny balcony. I blessed the young man and his wife. My heart was content.

I have carried the weight of countless things through life, deeming them assets. Now, as I try to untangle myself from these attachments, it sometimes feels impossible. Yet, when I contemplate what is truly precious—something I can carry with me beyond these walls, and something I can leave behind in abundance—it is love. I am certain that my beloved Parag, now united with the infinite, would find peace in that thought and nod in agreement.

Forty-six

Nowadays, whenever I see Titai's face up close, I notice a few silver strands of hair on either side of her forehead. Much of Himu's hair has turned grey too.

Bukai's daughter has started school in England. Sometimes, the little one speaks to me over video call and asks in her accented Bengali, 'How are you, Didan?' I find it amusing.

Oliver also inquires in his staccato Bangla, 'Hey Mamoni, how are you doing?'

He is a foreigner, yet Bukai has taught him to lovingly call me 'Mamoni' too. It is a wonderful gift. I laugh as I listen, and I think as I laugh. Nowadays, I cannot talk much—the words get entangled in my mouth.

Sukhalata conveys to them on the phone, 'Ma laughing… blessing.'

I like the situation. The whole world is now within reach. I can see it in its entirety. Nobody is a stranger anymore. I see my near and dear ones around—and I see you too, Di-bhai! I see Bordi, sometimes Dada and Professor Sukhen Roy, my dear Dadu too.

Di-bhai, my mind travels without restrictions. I like glancing at the newspaper every morning after breakfast. It is not that I read it fully. However, the bald-headed old man who smiles at me from the front page looks like Lalit Bose, and a little below him, the burly gentleman in a suit reminds me of Angshu Mohan Bose. Sometimes, on the inside page, I see someone who resembles you—a slim model posing with beautiful long hair. My morning passes thinking of the lovely times I have shared with you all.

I have heard the doctors talk about how dementia is gradually encroaching on my memory bank after the two vascular accidents in my brain. They have prescribed intake of virgin coconut oil and walnuts, solving crossword puzzles and using colouring books—as if attempting to reignite the dormant sparks within my brain cells.

Yet, when I take a leisurely stroll on the balcony in the evening or indulge in some TV time, memories from my childhood surface with such ease. It is comforting.

I cannot help but think how long it has been since we played together, you and I. Would you still have the stamina to play our old games of *Ekka-dokka* and *Chu-kit-kit*? Perhaps I could give it a shot; after all, I am a bit younger than you! What do you say?

In truth, now that I have traversed all the milestones of life, I find myself embarking on a reverse odyssey. I have skimmed through adulthood and adolescence, and now I am slowly retracing my steps towards the innocence of childhood—a time of unburdened bliss.

Look, there they are! That couple on the next page of the newspaper, with a little girl in a frilly white frock. They are my Kaka and Kaki. And that adorable child nestled in their lap—well, that is unmistakably me! I used to perch on Kaka's lap with that same cute expression when he cuddled me.

Look at that young girl there, engrossed in dressing her doll, it feels like she is extending an invitation to me, whispering, 'Hey, will you play dollhouse with me?' She is none other than Basona, my delightful playmate!

Whether it is day or night—or the liminal moments in between—Titai unfailingly keeps making her way to my room to ensure I am all right. She instructs the maid to bring me tea, and before the tea arrives, my girl never misses planting a gentle kiss on my forehead. With a tender smile, she places a candy in my mouth, as if I am her little doll, and for a brief moment I hold her hand, wrapped in the warmth of her care.

In those precious seconds, I catch a glimpse of my mother's visage reflected in her eyes. As Birajbala gazes at me with affection, I discern a reassuring certainty that she would not slip away, leave or forget me. Not now, not ever.

Glossary

Adya Kali	:	Primordial form of Goddess Kali
Alpona	:	Floor art made with rice paste
Anchal	:	Loose end of a sari
Annaprashan	:	Rice-eating ceremony for a child's first solid meal
Arakkhanya	:	A grown-up daughter in a family without living parents and with few guardians, whose marriage is seen as a liability due to strained family circumstances
Bahu	:	Daughter-in-law
Bangabandhu	:	Title of Sheikh Mujibur Rahman, leader of Bangladesh's independence (literally 'Bengal's Friend)
Baul	:	Mystic minstrels of Bengal, known for spiritual folk songs
Beguni	:	Batter-fried slices of aubergine
Bhaiphonta	:	Festival where sisters pray for their brothers' long life
Bhepu	:	Toy horn or whistle, popular in fairs
Bhistiwallah	:	Traditional water carrier, often with leather water bags
Bhog	:	Food offering made to a deity

Borda	:	Eldest brother
Bordi	:	Eldest sister
Boro Bou	:	Eldest daughter-in-law
Boro Dida	:	Eldest paternal grandmother figure
Boro Mama-Boro Mami	:	Eldest maternal uncle and his wife
Boro Mashi	:	Eldest maternal aunt
Boudi	:	Elder brother's wife; sister-in-law
Boudimoni	:	Respectful address for elder brother's wife
Boumoni	:	Affectionate form of address for a new bride
Bratachari	:	Socio-cultural movement promoting folk traditions and values
Broto	:	Religious vow or fast, often observed by women
Chaitra Sankranti	:	Last day of the Bengali year, observed with festivities
Checha paan	:	Betel leaves ground smooth in a mortar and pestle
Chhoto	:	Youngest; here, the youngest son
Chorda	:	Youngest brother-in-law
Dada	:	Elder brother
Dadabhai and Didibhai	:	Affectionate terms for elder brother and elder sister
Dadu	:	Grandfather (usually, maternal)
Daler bori	:	Sun-dried lentil dumplings

Dargah	:	A shrine built over the grave of a revered Sufi saint
Darwanji	:	Gatekeeper or caretaker
Devipaksha	:	Fortnight dedicated to Goddess Durga, culminating in Durga Puja
Dhai-ma	:	Traditional midwife; nanny
Dholak	:	Traditional two-sided hand drum
Di-bhai	:	Affectionate term for an elder sister
Ekka-dokka; Chu-kit-kit	:	Traditional hopscotch-style children's games
Firni	:	Creamy dessert made with ground rice and milk
Gamchha	:	A thin cotton towel
Gaye holud	:	Pre-wedding turmeric ceremony
Ghomta	:	Veil drawn over the head, part of traditional modesty
Ghoti garam	:	Spiced mixture, often street food-style snack
Haat	:	Weekly rural market
Harir loot	:	Distribution of sacred food during religious ceremonies
Jhola	:	Shoulder-bag made of cloth
Jyatha	:	Father's elder brother; paternal uncle
Kaka and Kaki	:	Paternal uncle and aunt
Kanthali Champa	:	A fragrant variety of champa flower; also known as Plumeria or frangipani

Khartal	:	Pair of wooden or metal clappers used to keep beats during performance of devotional songs
Khayal	:	Classical Hindustani vocal form
Khichuri	:	Rice and lentil dish, often eaten with fried vegetables
Khuro	:	Younger paternal uncle
Kul	:	Indian jujube, also called *ber* or *boroi*. A small seasonal fruit, tart when unripe and sweet when ripe. In Bengal it has ritualistic importance during Saraswati Puja, when it is first offered to the goddess before being eaten as prasad.
Luchi	:	Deep-fried puffed bread made from refined flour
Maha Mrityunjay Mantra	:	Vedic chant for longevity and overcoming death
Mahalaya	:	Auspicious occasion marking the beginning of Devipaksha
Mala bodol	:	Exchange of garlands during a Bengali wedding
Mama	:	Maternal uncle
Mamabari	:	Mother's ancestral home
Maran	:	Death
Mashi	:	Maternal aunt
Mashima	:	Aunt (formal)
Mejdi	:	Second eldest sister

Mejo Bhai : Middle brother

Mejo Jamaibabu : Middle sister's husband

Meshomoshai : Husband of one's maternal aunt

Mukti Bahini : Liberation Army of Bangladesh during 1971 war

Mukti-joddhas : Freedom fighters of Bangladesh

Mullah : Islamic religious leader or teacher

Muri : Puffed rice, a staple Bengali snack

Neelkanth : The Indian roller (Coracias benghalensis), a bird with brilliant blue throat and wings. Associated with Lord Shiva, who is also called *Neelkanth* ('blue-throated'). Considered auspicious when sighted during Dussehra.

Opar Bangla : Refers to Bangladesh (literally 'the other Bengal')

Panjabi : Traditional knee-length tunic for men

Patishapta : Bengali sweet crêpes stuffed with coconut and jaggery

Payesh : Sweet rice pudding, flavoured with milk, sugar and cardamom

Piri : Large wooden planks, often used as low platforms for sitting or rituals

Pishima : Paternal aunt

Poush Sankranti : Winter harvest festival, marking the end of the Bengali month of Poush

Prasad	:	Food sanctified after being offered to a deity
Pronam	:	A respectful salutation or bow, usually made by touching the feet of elders
Rabindrasangeet	:	Songs by Rabindranath Tagore
Rath/Rath Yatra/Rath er Mela	:	Festival of Lord Jagannath's chariot procession, when the deity is taken out of the temple on a grand chariot, accompanied by a fair (Rath er Mela)
Rosogollas	:	Famous Bengali sweets made of chhena (cottage cheese) balls in sugar syrup
Saag	:	Leafy greens cooked as a vegetable dish
Sewai payesh	:	Sweet pudding made with vermicelli and milk
Shakha	:	Conch-shell bangles worn by married Bengali women
Shakosh machher lej	:	Tail piece of a carp fish
Shashthi	:	Sixth day of *Devi Paksha*, marking the formal beginning of Durga Puja. On this day rituals are performed to welcome Goddess Durga to earth, initiating the main festivities.
Shejo Dadu	:	Third eldest grandfather figure
Shejo Didi	:	Third eldest sister
Shlokas	:	Verses from Sanskrit scriptures, often chanted in rituals

Shona mama	:	Literally, 'golden uncle'; here, the second-eldest maternal uncle
Shona moong	:	Golden yellow split lentils
Shraddho	:	Ritual performed after a person's death in memory of the departed, symbolizing the release of the mortal soul from worldly bindings
Shukto	:	Bitter vegetable curry, often eaten at the start of a Bengali meal
Sindoor	:	Vermilion powder traditionally worn by married Hindu women in the parting of their hair
Swadeshi	:	Self-reliance movement during India's independence struggle
Tal-pata	:	Palm leaf, used for fans, plates or rituals
Thakurda	:	Paternal grandfather
Thumri	:	Semi-classical Hindustani vocal style, often romantic or devotional
Topor	:	Traditional conical headgear worn by Bengali grooms
Ustad	:	Master musician or respected teacher in Hindustani music
Wuju	:	Ritual ablution before Islamic prayers

In Gratitude

I acknowledge the significant contributions and encouragements received from:

Dr Bina Biswas, Translator

Prof. Sukanta Chowdhury, Fellow of the British Academy; Emeritus Professor, Jadavpur University

Dr Nandini Das Barnes, Professor of English Literature, University of Oxford; Fellow of the Higher Education Academy

Dr Nilanjan Saha, Professor & Head, Department of Translational & Clinical Research, Jamia Hamdard, New Delhi

Brahmo Balika Shikshalaya, a heritage institution

This Book A Life Remembered

Gayatri Das, born in pre-independence Bengal, lost her father—a reputed doctor—in her childhood. She was brought up by her father's brother, a World War I veteran, and his wife, who doted on her, yet remained strict disciplinarians.

As a young girl, Gayatri witnessed the socio-political afflictions and changes during and after World War II. Although she dreamt of pursuing a career in medicine, she had to start earning at the age of 17 after the untimely demise of her uncle.

In independent India, she completed her education while teaching in primary schools to make ends meet, simultaneously looking after her widowed aunt with devoted gratitude. She later joined the prestigious Brahmo Balika Shikshalaya as a Life Science teacher for senior classes and eventually retired as the principal of the institution.

After the sudden demise of her husband, advancing age, illnesses and successive cerebral strokes took a toll on her health. Still, she loved to share her life experiences—often travelling back to her childhood memories before returning to the present, reflecting on her journey as a whole. The shadow of vascular dementia loomed over her once brilliant mind, yet the knowledge she had gained, the values she held and her inner explorations remained deeply inspirational.

In the final months before her demise, Gayatri often remained in a state of semi-consciousness. Sensing the unspoken expressions of her mind, her elder daughter, Indira Das felt compelled to resurrect her mother's fading memories. The result is the unforgettable journey of 'Aparajita', a woman of great wisdom, substance, whose priceless life experiences, is portrayed in these pages.